MW01196655

YOUR LITTLE LIES

SUE FORTIN

Storm
PUBLISHING

Ebook ISBN: 978-1-80508-201-9
Paperback ISBN: 978-1-80508-203-3

Cover design: Dissect Designs
Cover images: Depositphotos, Adobe, Shutterstock

Published by Storm Publishing.
For further information, visit:
www.stormpublishing.co

ALSO BY SUE FORTIN

The Missing Wife

The Dead Wife

Schoolgirl Missing

The Birthday Girl

Sister Sister

The Girl Who Lied

The Dead Husband's Secret

The Nanny's Lie

To Val and our many years of friendship. Wish there could have been more. x

ONE

Hannah

They say you should never meet your hero in real life, that you'll be disappointed should everything you thought about them turn out to be an illusion. A facade. A deception. Perhaps that should be the same for your dreams and ambitions, because once you've achieved them, the grass isn't always greener on the other side. When you scratch below that polished and pristine surface, you find those hopes and aspirations aren't quite so sparkly. In fact, they're tarnished and fake. Jasper always said I was his dream come true. At that time, he hadn't found out that all my sparkle was just a disguise. An elaborate deception.

I exchanged a smile with Jasper as he pulled up outside the estate agent's office. We were about to pick up the keys to our new house – a new start for us, our seven-year-old daughter, Pia, and obligatory crazy cockapoo, named Luna. A new start away from London, traffic, pollution, packed-in living and the proverbial rat race. A new start on the south coast of England on Silverbanks – a sandbank peninsular reserved for the rich and sometimes famous. A new home where we could wake up to the sound of the waves breaking, seagulls crying and fresh air in our lungs was something we had dreamed of for a long time.

We got out of the car and Jasper took my hand. 'Excited?' His grin was wide, and his blue eyes sparkled.

I forced myself to return the smile as a ripple of nerves turned my stomach and I tried to kid myself it was indeed excitement. 'Of course,' I replied. Who wouldn't be? Only me it seemed.

'Ah, here's the lucky couple. Jasper, Hannah, do come in,' said Hugo, the estate agent, with the exaggerated excitement of a first-year drama student audition. He stood and shook our hands, offering more congratulatory comments. 'Please take a seat.' Hugo sat down and from the drawer produced a set of keys which he dangled between his finger and thumb. 'Ta-da!'

'Ta-da, indeed,' said Jasper, and accepted the bunch of keys Hugo passed over.

Hugo then leaned down and picked up something from behind his desk. It was a wicker hamper with a bottle of champagne, chocolates and a fancy box of teabags which were no doubt labelled as 'luxury', 'handpicked', probably organic and grown in the hills of Burma. That's the sort of tea people who moved to the Silverbanks drank, I decided. 'A little housewarming present,' said Hugo.

'That's lovely, thank you,' I said.

'And I hope you will be very happy at 9 First Avenue,' continued Hugo. 'I expect your daughter can't wait to explore her new home.'

'Pia will have to wait a few more days,' said Jasper. 'She's staying with my parents to give us a chance to unpack.'

'Wise decision,' said Hugo. 'You'll be able to meet the neighbours without worrying about her running around.'

I was sure 'running around', for Hugo, was shorthand for causing havoc, screaming, and screeching.

'Can't beat the sound of children playing and laughing,' I

found myself saying. I looked Hugo directly in the eye, daring him to contradict me or challenge me on this point. 'And then, of course, there's Luna, our dog.'

Hugo fussed with the knot of his tie and cleared his throat. 'No, of course not. Anyway, the Residents' Association are looking forward to welcoming you onto Silverbanks.'

'Ah, yes, the Residents' Association,' replied Jasper. 'Hannah has already had an email from them about the fees.'

'That will be Elizabeth Rooke. She's, how shall we say it, very proficient.' Hugo gave an apologetic smile. 'Used to be a children's governess back in the day. Treats everything as a military operation. Heart of gold really. Surprisingly, she's very popular at the school where she goes in to help listen to the kids read. Her bark is worse than her bite. You know the sort.'

I wasn't particularly convinced by the stream of idioms and wondered, in a nod to Hugo, whether we should pop on our rose-tinted glasses and overlook the red flags. After eleven years, I still second-guessed everyone. Trust didn't come easy. I would go home later and think back to the conversation, analyse every word and nuance. Replay body language in my mind and read between the lines, searching for a hidden agenda. I had to. It was the only way I could survive.

Twenty minutes later, we drove onto Silverbanks. We were no longer just tourists driving around ogling the gated driveways and high-walled boundaries, trying to catch a glimpse of how the other half lived. We were no longer day visitors strolling along the beach looking up at the million-pound properties, so much so, we would crick our necks from the effort. We weren't gawping at the glass-fronted balconies, the colonial-style cladding, art deco windows, sneaking a look through fencing at the swimming pools and manicured lawns, or simply staring wide-eyed at those who like to flaunt their wealth where there is only a low wall to mark the boundary of garden and beach. No, we weren't observers anymore, we were participants.

That's what selling up our two-bed terrace house in Twickenham, plus a sizeable inheritance from Jasper's grandmother had done for us – it literally opened doors that would have once been closed.

A few short minutes later, we were standing in front of our new home. The sun was a golden globe against a sapphire-blue sky and the keys glistened like jewels in Jasper's hand.

Jasper put his arm around my shoulders and kissed the top of my head. 'Happy new home, darling.' He passed the key to me. As I turned the key and pushed open the door, he scooped me up into his arms and, ignoring my squeals of delighted protest, he carried me across the threshold, before twirling around several times in the oversized entrance hallway and putting me down. He then popped back to retrieve Luna from the car.

The house was a 1930s art deco property with black-and-white tiled flooring and a sweeping staircase with black wrought-iron spindles shaped in arches to imitate the waves outside.

Two reception rooms flanked the hallway, overlooking the front of the property, but the design of the house provided an overwhelming pull to the back. The 1930s was left behind at this point. The original kitchen and dining room had been replaced with an all-mod-cons, open-plan kitchen/family room with bifold doors out onto a terrace with the garden stretching out and beyond the steps that went over the sea wall and onto the sandy beach.

I opened the bifold doors fully and breathed in the salty sea air. To the east was the nearby town of Seabury, which had almost an idyllic village feel to it. There was a small parade of shops, including a fashion boutique, a hairdressers, a florists, a deli, a mini-supermarket, and, of course, a café. The latter had somehow managed to avoid the hipster makeover of smashed avocado on soda bread and coffee beans from Ethiopia with notes of bergamot and lavender served in hand-crafted ceramic mugs. Instead, its coffee and tea experience were far more traditional, as was its menu of sandwiches and baps, with paninis being the most cosmopolitan option, clearly catering for the older demographic of the town.

To the south was the rest of Silverbanks and beyond that the lighthouse denoting the rocky end of the peninsular. The further into the estate the houses were, the more expensive and luxurious they became. The sand was a mix of sparkly gold and silver colours, with breakwaters jutting out into the sea every so often. A lifeguard tower was roughly halfway along to the tip of the bank. It was about fifteen feet in height, with a small, shaded platform and a chair at the top, reached by a metal ladder. Manned in the school holidays, according to the estate agents when we'd come to view the property. For a moment I forgot my past and imagined a golden future here, without any fear or sorrow. Maybe this time I would really feel the happiness and contentment that had been missing from my life.

Jasper came to stand behind me, wrapping his arms around my waist and resting his chin on my shoulder.

'What are you thinking?' he asked.

'Just how beautiful everything is.'

'I really want us to be happy here,' said Jasper, kissing my neck and turning me around to face him. 'I want you to be happy.'

Jasper had always had an uncanny ability to tune into my thoughts. I would worry that he could see the dark memories lurking behind my eyes, refusing to stay completely locked away. His gaze was intense as he tried to unravel my fiercely guarded secret – one we both knew I held but in an unspoken mutual agreement, we never talked about it. Jasper had tried in the past, but I had always managed to brush away his questions. I wondered how long I'd be able to do that now. If I could convince him I was finally happy, then maybe he wouldn't ask or worry again. Maybe I would even stop worrying. Maybe.

'I am happy,' I replied, going on tiptoes to kiss him. 'Thank you for making this move happen.' I buried my face against his chest, so he couldn't see my eyes.

He kissed the top of my head and I felt he was about to say something, when the sound of the doorbell rang out, making us both jump.

'Who on earth is that?' I asked, pulling away and looking down the hallway. Through the obscured glass panel, I could see the figure of a woman.

Jasper followed my gaze. 'I expect that will be Elizabeth Rooke. She did say in her welcome letter that she'd pop by. I just didn't imagine it would be within minutes of us arriving.'

'Ugh.'

'Wait there. I'll deal with it.'

I hooked Luna's collar with my fingers to stop her running down the hall to greet the visitor and I listened from around the corner of the doorway where I was out of sight.

'Oh, hello. Mr Gunderson,' came the woman's voice as Jasper opened the door. 'Elizabeth Rooke. Chair of Silverbanks Residents' Association. Lovely to meet you. I do hope I've pronounced your name correctly?'

'Yes, you have and, please, call me Jasper.'

I imagined Jasper throwing one of his charming smiles at our visitor. When she gave a giggle, I knew for sure he had.

'Jasper, it is then,' she tittered. 'Gunderson. It's Scandinavian, isn't it?'

'Yes. Danish to be precise.'

'Wonderful. I think you're the first Scandinavian couple on Silverbanks.'

'Actually, we're British. My parents are Danish. Anyway, how can I help you?'

'I wanted to welcome you personally to Silverbanks and to

give you all the necessary information about our wonderful community.'

'Thank you,' replied Jasper. 'I did get a letter.'

'Yes, that's right. That's part one and this pack is part two. Too costly to post. And I don't want the information falling into the wrong hands.' She gave a laugh. 'There's everything you need to know in there: Association Members, Silverbanks Residents' Directory – we like to exchange phone numbers, in case of emergencies. There's a form in there for you to add your contact details. Also, there's things like bin collection day, recycling day, garden waste day. The contract for the gardener who tends to the grass verges, trees and bushes on the estate, the window cleaner, the house cleaners, maintenance man, parking permits and...'

'Thank you very much,' said Jasper, cutting the woman off. 'I'll look through this later and, if I've got any questions, I'll get back to you.'

'Is Mrs Gunderson in? I was hoping to catch her. I wondered if she'd like to join the committee. We're always on the lookout for new members.'

'Hannah – she's probably unpacking boxes somewhere in the house,' said Jasper. 'She'll catch you next time, no doubt. And it's Miss Towers. We're not married.'

'Oh, sorry. I didn't realise.'

I withheld a chuckle at the rather affronted reply from Elizabeth Rooke.

She carried on. 'Well, we do have some residents who aren't married. On First Avenue there's Henry Tilford, you know, the footballer. Don't ask me who he plays for, but he's not married. Lives with his girlfriend and their daughter.'

'Chelsea. Left-back,' said Jasper.

'I've no idea. Anyway, like I said, they're not married, so you're not our only couple to be living in sin.' Elizabeth gave yet another laugh.

'I'm glad to hear it,' said Jasper. 'Wouldn't want to cause a scandal.'

'No. No. Of course not,' gabbled Elizabeth. 'We're very broad-minded and welcoming on Silverbanks. We're actually a very diverse bunch. Footballers, bankers, entrepreneurs, TV celebrities, mixed-race like Darren Jenners, then there are the Lings, they're Asian. You know, we even have a lesbian couple. Julie and Sharon. They live on Second Avenue and next door...'

I couldn't hear what she said as she lowered her voice to impart the last piece of information, but I heard Jasper reply.

'Very avant garde Silverbanks is.'

I could hear the irritation in his voice now. Jasper was clearly getting frustrated with our visitor. If she didn't go soon, I would have to rescue him, I decided.

'You'll get to meet most of them at the upcoming residents' barbecue tomorrow. All the details are in the booklet,' said Elizabeth, clearly not taking the hint. 'Also, before I forget, as Silverbanks is a private estate, we have to pay for the upkeep of the road and verges. As such, we discourage parking on the grass outside. I noticed your vehicle out there.'

'I didn't want to block the removal men,' said Jasper. 'I'll move it once they've gone.'

The roads on Silverbanks were just wide enough for two cars to pass. There were no pavements, only grass verges to mark the boundary between road and properties.

'Oh good. Don't want to churn up the grass,' replied Elizabeth. 'That would look awful. We're very mindful of keeping Silverbanks looking pristine. That's why I mentioned the vehicle, we don't want it to end up looking like a car park.'

'Yes. Sure. Look, I'd better get back to the unpacking and, of course, moving the car.'

'Wonderful. I'm sorry I didn't get to speak to your... erm... partner,' said Elizabeth. 'Hopefully, I'll catch her tomorrow.'

'I'm sure she'll look forward to that,' said Jasper, managing to keep the sarcasm from his tone. 'Thanks again for the info. Bye.'

Elizabeth Rooke had barely uttered goodbye when I heard the door close. Jasper walked back into the kitchen.

'You can stop hiding now,' he said. 'That was our friendly neighbourhood Chair of the Residents' Association. Elizabeth Rooke. I managed to fend her off from coming in and bending your ear about parking faux pas, joining the committee and whatever's in this folder.' He dumped it on the countertop. 'Only managed to escape by pretending we had unpacking to do.'

'I heard. Fancy lowering the tone of the neighbourhood on your first day! You make sure you move that car. You'll have the Rooke swooping down on you again.' I laughed at Jasper's God-give-me-strength expression.

'You know rooks are part of the crow family,' he said. 'They're bad luck.'

'Things are only bad luck if you're superstitious.'

'Let's hope she doesn't fulfil her legacy.'

'What did she say about next door?' I asked.

'Oh, something about him being an ex-policeman. CID apparently,' said Jasper, moving away and filling the sink with cold water to chill the bottle of champagne Hugo had given us.

'Ex-policeman?' I asked, trying to sound casual.

'Bryan someone,' said Jasper, switching on the built-in fridge and fiddling with the temperature dial.

If he'd given me the champagne to hold, he wouldn't have needed to put it anywhere to chill – I felt my whole body freeze, goose bumps pricked my skin and the hairs on my arms stood to attention. I couldn't withhold the physical shiver that shot through me. 'Bryan? Bryan who?' I needed to know his surname. This was ridiculous. It couldn't be who I thought it was, could it?

'I'm not sure. Chambers. Chamberlain. I wasn't really paying attention.'

'Chamberton,' I whispered.

'Not sure. Might have been. Chamberton.' Jasper turned to look at me. 'You all right, Hannah?'

I couldn't look at him. My stomach churned. I was going to throw up. I rushed past him, diving into the downstairs loo and locking the door behind me.

TWO

Hannah

Jasper made me sit down outside with a cup of tea, putting my sudden rush to the toilet down to tiredness and excitement. I didn't try to correct him. Instead, I accepted the hot drink, grateful we had packed the kettle, coffee machine and necessary provisions in the car with us so we could at least have a drink before the removal men arrived. And to make them one too.

Their timing was immaculate. Before Jasper could even join me, we heard the sound of the lorry engine grumbling and revving away as the driver navigated the two brick piers on either side of the driveway.

'Wait there. No need to get up,' said Jasper, resting his hand on my shoulder.

'I can't sit here,' I protested.

Jasper grinned. 'At least wait until they've started unloading. Have your tea. I don't want you overdoing it.'

I gave a small smile in agreement. I didn't know what I had done to meet such a wonderful man as Jasper. For once in my life, luck had been on my side. I hadn't planned on falling in love, but it had been impossible not to. We'd met in London on the South Bank outside a bar where he had been stood up and I was contemplating a future alone. Loneliness is so underrated. It's real. It's visceral. It's painful.

We'd chatted idly, and in a candid moment, I had revealed more about myself than I had to anyone for several years. We had ended up going for something to eat and, after a lovely evening, we'd gone our separate ways. Jasper had insisted I take a cab home, at his expense, but didn't accompany me. As he later told me, he didn't want to freak me out by appearing like a stalker.

It was another three weeks before we bumped into each other again. I had gone back to the bar that overlooked the Thames and had been thinking of Jasper and how nice it had been to connect with someone. And then he'd appeared at my side with a sparkling white wine – the same drink I'd opted for when we'd dined together.

'I've been here every Friday night for the past three weeks,' he confessed. 'I was beginning to give up hope.'

And that was that. I hadn't been able to help myself. And I didn't see why I shouldn't look for a new life, a new love and happiness. I was at the angry stage of grief for my former life.

Jasper saved me that first night. I had never told him, but as I had gazed out across the expanse of the Thames, intrusive thoughts had been lurking.

He had continued to save my life every day since then and he never knew.

As soon as I'd finished my tea, I got up and began to start unpacking. I'd diligently packed away every room, labelled every box and in big red letters, written which room in the new house the box was destined for. Fortunately, neither Jasper nor I were hoarders. Jasper because it wasn't in his Danish psyche to hold on to things or clutter as he referred to it, and me because, well, I just didn't have anything from the past. Not even a photograph.

It didn't take us that long to get the basics in place with only a handful of boxes, mostly to do with Jasper's work as an architect, that needed unpacking later.

Jasper came into the living room, where I was fluffing cushions and making sure the few photographs I had of Jasper, Pia, Jasper's family and I were all looking good in their new places.

'It looks lovely in here,' said Jasper, gazing around the room.

Our London palette of creams and beige, highlighted with slender Scandinavian styled furniture, really lent itself to the coastal position of the property. Like most things in life, I didn't go for big and bold – it was always soft, inoffensive, and quite frankly not very memorable. Exactly as I liked it.

The doorbell sounded out. 'God, I hope it's not Elizabeth again,' I said.

'No. Not unless she's got a part-time job at Store to Door,' said Jasper with a wink.

'Store to Door?'

'Local delivery service. It was in the Silverbanks Bible Elizabeth gave me,' confessed Jasper as he went out of the room. 'I've ordered us tea to save either of us cooking.'

Honestly, that man was a godsend.

And so was the food. We sat on the terrace, at the garden table and chairs, eating our salmon salad, accompanied by a glass of champagne, feeling very satisfied with ourselves. Luna seemed to be happy in her new home too. She sat in the shade at our feet and every now and then got up and trotted to the end of the garden, climbing the stone steps to look through the gate at the beach beyond.

'The beach isn't as busy as I thought it would be,' I commented.

'No. I remember Hugo saying that, although it's not private, the only access to it is through the estate, which is private to a certain point. People can still come here, but they tend not to. The gates at the front of the estate give them the impression it's for residents only.'

'That's what appealed to me, the privacy here,' I replied, lifting my head up towards the warmth of the sun.

'You'd be happy on a desert island with no one around at all,' said Jasper, and I could hear the amusement in his voice.

'Apart from you and Pia,' I said. 'And your parents.' I looked at him and smiled. His parents were the most wonderful people I'd ever met. So kind, warm and welcoming. They had made me feel at home right from the word go and had never pried or pressed for too many details about my own family. Being an adult orphan with no siblings didn't lend itself to long conversations.

'I think I could cope with that,' replied Jasper. 'Although, like you say, it's more peaceful here than I imagined.'

As if to prove us wrong, it was at that moment that Luna jumped up and ran down the end of the garden, up the stone steps and gave a bark.

I heard a female voice and looked down the garden to see a young woman ruffling Luna's ears. She looked up after a moment and waved. 'Hi!' she called out. 'Sorry, couldn't resist making a fuss of your dog.'

'Hi!' I called back and smiled to show I didn't mind.

Jasper raised a hand in acknowledgement.

I thought the woman was going to head off, but she continued to stroke and ruffle Luna's ears, bending down at one point and almost kissing the hound. Luna was delighted with this affection and licked the woman's face enthusiastically, before jumping up and putting her paws on the woman's shoulders.

'Shall I go and rescue her?' asked Jasper.

I was about to say yes when his phone began to ring. 'I'll go,'

I said, getting to my feet and heading down the garden. 'Luna! Luna! Here.'

Luna's recall was usually very good but she, of course, chose this time to totally ignore me and show herself to be the rebel she occasionally was.

'She's fine,' said the woman, as I neared. 'What a lovely dog. What breed is she?'

The woman was younger than I had thought from my position on the terrace. Now I was closer, she was maybe in her very early thirties. She had long rich brown hair, tied up in a ponytail with a few wispy strands lifting on the clement sea breeze. She looked like someone who spent a lot of time outdoors, probably sporty. I glanced at her hand as she continued to fuss Luna – no wedding ring and no sign of one ever having been worn on her ring finger, although a silver Pandora heart ring was on her other hand, together with a charm bracelet around her wrist.

I assessed the woman in a couple of seconds, a skill I was well versed in and one I did automatically. My threat radar wasn't even registering. I relaxed and smiled at her.

'Looks like you've a new best friend there,' I said. 'She's a cockapoo – don't judge me, I caved under pressure from my daughter.'

'Oh, I totally would too. I always wanted a dog when I was a kid, but my mum was allergic to them. Apparently.' She gave a laugh. 'I still suspect to this day that was merely an excuse.' She stood up, one hand stroking Luna under the chin. 'Have you just moved in?' She nodded towards the house.

'Yes. Today, actually.'

'You'll be Hannah, then, and that's your husband, Jasper.'

'Err, yes. Partner. We're not married,' I said, smiling politely but at the same time wondering how the hell this woman knew. A little flutter of nerves rattled in my chest.

'I live on Silverbanks too. Down on The Loop. It's the road

that horseshoes around at the end, joining all the avenues together.'

'Oh, I see,' I said.

'I'm sure you'll guess how I know.' There was a mischievous sparkle in the woman's eye.

Realisation dawned on me. 'Ah, Elizabeth Rooke.'

She grinned. 'Couldn't be anyone else, really.' The woman held out her hand. 'Annabelle Burton.'

I shook hands, feeling rather formal, and as I caught Annabelle's eye, we both laughed. 'Nice to meet you,' I said, feeling an unusual instant liking to this woman. I wasn't one for forming friendships easily.

'I'm glad I got to speak to you,' said Annabelle. 'I must thank you for taking up the baton of being the new girl. I only moved here myself a couple of weeks ago.'

'Oh, really? Tell me, does Elizabeth back off after a while?'

Annabelle sighed. 'Think of it as an initiation ceremony. A rite of passage. A watershed. Something every new resident has to go through for a few weeks.'

'Shit. As bad as that?'

Annabelle laughed. 'Sorry. I'm doing her a disservice. She's not that bad. She means well but she has clearly never lost that air of governess.'

I glanced back to where Jasper was still on the phone. 'I was going to say come and meet my partner,' I said in an unusual gesture of openness. 'But he's on a work call.'

'Oh, that's OK. I should get on really. Are you going to the barbecue tomorrow? I'm sure Elizabeth would have mentioned it.'

'Yes. She did. We've had rather an overload of information already,' I said. 'I think our parking was her utmost concern.'

Annabelle rolled her eyes. 'Parking. Ugh. You didn't park in the road by any chance. You know, a road that's designed for cars but seemingly here on Silverbanks only moving cars.'

I laughed again. 'Sounds about right.'

'You can redeem yourself by coming to the barbecue,' said Annabelle. 'In fact, if you don't, I'm sure Elizabeth will make it her mission to come and seek you out.'

I pulled an eek kind of face. 'I'll warn Jasper.'

'Yes. Good idea.' She gave Luna another hug. 'Lovely to meet you and your owner.' She looked up at me. 'See you at the barbecue, Hannah.'

Then she was off, jogging along the beach, her long, tanned legs covering the sand with ease.

I went back to the house where Jasper was just ending his call. 'All good?' he enquired. 'Looked like you were having a good old chat there.'

'Yeah. I think I've made a friend,' I said, laughing at myself for sounding like Pia rather than the grown woman I was.

Jasper gave a raise of his eyebrows. 'Things are looking up already,' he said, catching my hand and pulling me onto his lap, before kissing me. 'Have you made the bed up yet?' he murmured into my hair.

'Yes. But it can be made again,' I replied.

As we hotfooted it upstairs, I felt a lightness in my heart I didn't often feel. This move was a good idea. Already it was having a positive impact on us.

THREE

Hannah

By the following morning, my earlier enthusiasm at attending the barbecue that afternoon had deserted me. I was missing Pia and had suggested to Jasper that we collect her early from his parents – in my mind, preferably when the barbecue was taking place.

'Mum and Dad are loving having her there,' countered Jasper, not getting on board with my suggestion at all. He was, of course, right. Pia thoroughly enjoyed spending time with her grandparents, and I did feel guilty taking that away from her. She didn't get to see them too often. They had moved back to Denmark when Jasper went to university but every year came to the UK for an extended visit to catch up with old friends and, of course, us. This year they had taken an apartment about half an hour away from Seabury.

'I know. I just miss her and I'm excited for her to see her new home,' I replied, looking out from the kitchen bifold doors. I wasn't sure I'd ever grow tired of that view. Despite that, I had woken that morning with a sense of unease which was growing with every passing hour.

'It will be fine,' said Jasper, joining me to admire the view. 'The thought is always worse than the act. I'll be right by your side all the time.'

I appreciated his reassurance more than he would ever know. But today, my nerves were hitting high anxiety levels and I wondered if I should take one of my beta-blockers. I had been prescribed them before I'd met Jasper, but I had tried to avoid taking them unless absolutely necessary. Since I'd been with Jasper the need for them had diminished and it was alarming that I was even thinking about them now. I didn't want to need them but at the same time, I knew there were times when I depended on them. I longed for that woman I had been once, who didn't need them, but I knew she was gone. This was me now. I had to deal with it.

'I'll be OK,' I said. 'Just don't leave me with Elizabeth.'

'I promise.' He dropped a kiss on my shoulder. 'Anyway, you can find your new friend and introduce me to her.'

The barbecue was being held further down the beach at the end by The Loop, and Jasper and I took the opportunity to walk barefoot along the water's edge to get there.

A gazebo had been erected where a bar had been set up. It was giving Caribbean vibes, with some grasses and bamboo canes attached to the front of the bar. Two men in brightly coloured shirts, one depicting palm trees and the other toucans, looked to be in charge of making sure everyone was lubricated. Next to that was the barbecue, a stainless-steel gas-fuelled affair. Again, two men were on burger flipping duties and had obviously got the memo about garish shirts.

'Jesus, is this for real?' said Jasper under his breath as we made our way up to the bar, where there must have been twenty to thirty people gathered. It seemed the bar and catering crew weren't the only ones adopting the brightly coloured shirt theme.

'I'm going to have to get you one of those shirts,' I said.

'You most certainly are not,' muttered Jasper. 'It could be grounds for a separation.'

'Hannah! Hi there!' It was Annabelle. She emerged from the gazebo with three bottles of beer in her hands and headed over to us. 'So glad you came,' she said. 'Beer?'

'Lifesaver,' I said. 'Annabelle this is Jasper. Jasper, Annabelle.'

'Hi, there,' said Jasper, taking a beer she held out to him. 'Nice to meet you. Sorry I couldn't say hello yesterday.'

'Oh, no problem,' said Annabelle, giving a smile and flicking her hair back over her shoulder. She was wearing a crop top and probably the smallest pair of cut-off denim shorts I'd ever seen in my life, and I suddenly felt frumpy and old in my linen trousers and T-shirt. I swiftly corrected any thought I had of wearing anything that brought attention to myself. I was not here to stand out, far from it.

'Ah, Jasper. Hannah!' It was the unmistakable voice, or rather squawk, of Elizabeth. I idly wondered if she turned into a rook at night and roosted somewhere up in the rafters of her house. 'Glad to see you made it. And I see you've met our most recent addition to Silverbanks. I'm sure Annabelle will help you settle in and, if she can't, you know where to come.' She smiled proudly at her own recommendation.

'We met yesterday, actually,' said Annabelle. 'Had a very nice chat.'

I smiled at the two women, not quite able to make out if there was some sort of tension between them or whether I was being too analytical.

'Well done,' said Elizabeth to Annabelle, rather like she was addressing a child. She turned to Jasper and me. 'How about you let me introduce you to some of the other residents? This way.' If she had a flag on a pole, I swear she would have driven it into the ground and claimed the territory as her own. Woe betide anyone, especially the most recent new girl, to cross that line.

Nevertheless, the three of us duly followed Elizabeth across the sand. I had been distracted, seduced by the beauty of Silverbanks, and then the little power battle Elizabeth had embarked on, to forget about meeting any of the other residents.

I wondered if Bryan Chamberton was here this afternoon. I had convinced myself last night that it was a coincidence that there was a Bryan Chamberton on the estate. What were the chances of it being the Bryan I knew? Pretty slim, I had determined. Jasper had said he wasn't sure if he'd got the name right anyway. Still, it would be good to meet him, and put any lingering worries aside.

We approached a group of three couples, standing around talking, obviously very comfortable in each other's company. They parted to make way for Elizabeth and as she greeted them, they turned towards us. I immediately sought out the faces of the men.

And there he was. Bryan Chamberton. Standing right in front of me.

I gripped Jasper's arm, fearing my knees were going to give way. I couldn't take my eyes off the man.

He was smiling, looking at Jasper and then at me. There was no flicker of recognition on his face whatsoever. Absolutely none. I looked harder as he stepped forward and shook Jasper's hand.

'Hello,' he said. 'Bryan Chamberton. I believe we're next-door neighbours.'

'Pleased to meet you,' said Jasper.

Bryan was then looking at me. The smile still on his face.

I couldn't hear anything properly. It was like I was

submerged under water. I couldn't move. I knew I was simply staring at him.

I felt Jasper nudge me. 'Hannah,' he said. 'Hannah.'

Something made me snap out of the frozen state I was in. 'Sorry,' I muttered. I automatically shook the extended hand. 'Hi. How are you?' I could hear myself speaking but it didn't feel real. None of this was real. I was convinced of it.

'This is my wife, Sandra.' He put a hand on his wife's back, drawing her into the conversation.

Sandra looked to be around Bryan's age. She was a slim and petite blonde with bobbed hair touching her shoulders. A fringe grazed the arch of her thinly pencilled-in eyebrows. Her shorts were rather more modest than Annabelle's, coming slightly above her knee and the fabric matched the blue of her stripy T-shirt perfectly. She had the golden glow to her skin of someone who wasn't afraid to sit out in the sun.

'Hi,' said Sandra, and again shook hands. 'I thought about popping around to see you yesterday,' she was saying, 'but I didn't want to bother you on your first day. "Let them get settled in," Bryan said. "We're bound to see them at the barbecue." And here you are. You really must come around for drinks one evening though.'

I knew my face was smiling and my head nodded while my voice was saying things like 'how lovely' and 'of course that would be wonderful' but all I could think was that Bryan Chamberton had not even shown the tiniest fraction of recognition.

I spent the rest of the afternoon only superficially joining in with conversations, asking questions, fending off questions, always trying to turn the conversation away from me. I stayed practically glued to Jasper's side for the most part, letting him do the talking. At one point, I couldn't help thinking I was behaving like some sort of Stepford wife. This was confirmed when Annabelle had managed to prise me away and asked me if I was all right.

'I'm fine,' I said. 'I just... you know... it's a lot to take in. Lots of names and faces.'

'A bit overwhelming,' she suggested.

'Yes, it is rather.'

'Look, I'm a trained counsellor,' she said. 'If you ever need to talk about anything, I'm more than happy to listen. Free, of course.' She slipped her arm through mine. 'I mean, we're friends, aren't we?'

I smiled at her. 'Thanks. I appreciate the offer.' Not that I was ever going to take her up on it. I'd had counselling before, and I had no intention of ever revisiting anything that had been discussed then.

I somehow made it through the next couple of hours and when Jasper said we really needed to get back, I was relieved.

'You look exhausted,' he said as we made our way back to our house. 'Was it all a bit too much?' He knew what I was like in social situations, and I appreciated his understanding.

'It was OK,' I said. 'Annabelle's nice. In fact, they all seem nice.'

'Yeah, they do. Bryan and Sandra from next door seem like good neighbours too.'

I didn't comment for fear of giving anything away but changed the subject and was relieved when we got back home.

I'd only had the one beer, but Jasper had drunk two or three bottles, and it wasn't long before he was snoozing on the sofa. His blond hair had fallen over his forehead and there was a look of contentment on his face.

Luna was whining at the back door to the garden. She had been locked in all afternoon while we were at the barbecue and although I didn't particularly want to venture out on my own, I knew it wasn't fair to make her wait or to wake up Jasper.

'Come on, then, Luna,' I said quietly, opening the door and stepping out onto the terrace. 'Just stay in the garden.'

I might as well have saved my breath. Luna immediately bolted down the garden and up the steps, disappearing over the wall, through the gate I had inadvertently left open and out onto the beach.

'Shit,' I muttered and ran after her. Just what I needed, to be chasing the dog along the beach. I sprinted up the steps, expecting to see her disappearing into the distance but came to an abrupt halt.

Bryan Chamberton was standing there, holding on to Luna's collar.

I stood there in silence again. Not knowing what to say or do.

'Aren't you going to put that lead on her?' he said, nodding towards my hand.

'Oh. Yes.' I stepped forward and quickly hooked up the lead and collar. 'Thank you.' I looked at him again. Waiting for him to say something. I couldn't believe he didn't know who I was.

'Did you enjoy the barbecue?' he asked.

'Yes. I did.' My reply was stilted. Was that really all he was going to say to me?

'That's good.' He gave a nod of his head.

He was about to turn away. 'Bryan,' I said. He stopped mid-turn and faced me again. I swallowed hard. 'You do know who I am, don't you?' I said at last.

He looked at me for a long moment and drew in a deep breath, exhaling slowly, controlled. 'Yes, of course I do.' He gave a nod of his head. 'Hello, Laurel.'

FOUR

Laurel

My heels clipped fast on the Kensington pavement as I hurried to my car. The appointment with my latest client had overrun. They had recently moved to their Georgian terrace house and wanted the living room and dining room refurbished and I'd come recommended by a previous client – Laurel Jordan was apparently the go-to interior designer. I was flattered by the compliment and grateful for the recommendation. Interior design was a tough market to break into, and the couple of years away to have my son, Declan, hadn't helped. That said, I did feel I was making headway and gradually building up my portfolio.

I used the remote to unlock my Mercedes and as I hopped into the driver's seat, I unceremoniously dumped my bag in the passenger footwell. I turned the key in the ignition and glanced at the clock in the car. Damn it. I was going to be late getting home. I was accompanying my husband, Matt, on a networking evening and there was no way I could be late for that. It would mean precious little time with our son Declan. I would literally have to dive in the shower and get ready straight away. If I was lucky, I'd have five minutes with him.

Amy, our nanny, was babysitting tonight. She was an absolute angel, and I would have been lost without her. I certainly wouldn't have been able to return to work, albeit three days a week. To be honest, I hadn't even wanted to go back to work, but Matt's construction company was struggling after losing a major backer and we needed the money. By the time I'd covered Amy's wages, there wasn't a great deal left to put in the pot, but we were at the stage where every penny counted. It was a bit of a moot point between Matt and I. While it hurt his misplaced Alpha Aussie pride that I needed to shore up our income, he was realistic enough to know that, without it, we'd be up the proverbial swanny.

The event this evening was like speed-dating for businesses but en masse. Twenty small businesses had pitched for backers and interested investors would be at the event tonight, to chat with the companies they might be interested in offering financial backing to. I didn't particularly like the idea of sucking up to some businessman, but Matt was keen to go and, quite frankly, if this didn't yield an investment in a new property development Matt was desperate to fulfil, then we were likely to be looking to sell up and downsize, and Matt would be looking for paid employment. I knew that would hurt his pride even more than me working did. Matt had come over to England three years ago and, despite all the advice that the opportunities were in his homeland, he'd stayed. For me, apparently.

We'd met through mutual friends at a party one night and we'd hit it off straight away. I loved his dark hair and equally dark eyes that simultaneously sparkled when he laughed, the crinkles around his eyes and his honey-coloured skin. When he asked me out for a drink, I was delighted. Six months into our relationship I'd unexpectedly found myself pregnant and Matt had immediately asked me to marry him. I hadn't hesitated in saying yes. At thirty, Matt was five years older than me, and we both felt we had life cracked. We were madly in love, and no one could tell us otherwise. In fact, the nay-sayers only strengthened our resolve to do things our way. And the rest is history, as they say.

My handsfree began to ring. It was Matt. I pressed the accept button.

'Hiya,' I said trying to sound casual, like there was no drama about my timekeeping.

'Laurel, where the hell are you?' he asked. I could hear Amy in the background shushing Declan.

'I won't be long. Twenty minutes,' I said. 'And, yes, I'm OK, thanks for asking.'

'Sorry, babe. You OK?'

'I'm fine. Got held up with the new client, that's all.'

'We have to leave in an hour.'

'And we will. Don't panic.'

'It's important we're not late,' he reminded me for the umpteenth time.

'I know. Honestly, Matt, I'll be ready in time. See you soon.'

Twenty minutes later, I was bundling in through the front door, calling out to Matt from the foot of the stairs, before hurrying down the hallway of our Victorian mid-terrace in Fulham to where Amy and Declan were.

'Here's Mummy,' said Amy, passing Declan over to me.

'Hello, my darling,' I said, kissing his face and snuggling into him, devouring his smell, the softness of his skin and the feathery tickle of his dark hair. I smiled at him, and I was rewarded with a squeal of excitement and a big slobbery smile. 'Everything all right today?' I asked Amy.

'All fine. He's just had his tea, which he ate all up. I'll give him a bath soon.' She began to clear the highchair which, covered in macaroni cheese, carrots, and peas, looked like it should be an art installation at the Tate Modern.

I spent five minutes making a fuss of Declan, before Matt came into the family room. 'Hadn't you better start getting ready?'

I sighed. 'I suppose I should.' I kissed Declan several more times, before leaving him with Amy. I hated having to juggle my time and Declan coming lower down my priority list right now didn't sit comfortably with me.

Twenty minutes later, I was trotting down the stairs, showered, hair done, make-up applied and wearing a black evening dress.

Matt gave a low whistle. 'You look gorgeous,' he said, kissing me as I reached the front door where he was waiting. 'And you're wearing my favourite perfume.'

'You don't look bad yourself,' I joked, giving his backside a playful smack. And he did look handsome in his suit and tie, his dark hair with a hint of curl, pushed back from his forehead. I could see the anticipation on his face of the evening ahead. 'Don't be nervous,' I said. 'You'll be fine. You've several companies already showing an interest in backing the new development. Just be natural and believe in yourself.'

He smiled back at me. 'Thanks, babe.'

Underneath the tough, rugby-playing Aussie exterior, there was a gentle guy who sometimes didn't have the confidence in his own ability. He just needed reminding of it sometimes.

Amy came into the hall with Declan, and I gave him a kiss goodnight, trying to ignore the envious feeling that she would be bathing my baby and putting him to bed. I was practical-minded enough to know that Declan would never remember this evening and I was still the person who his life revolved around, but even so, mum-guilt was real.

'Don't be worrying about him,' said Matt as we got into the waiting taxi. 'He'll be fine.'

'I know,' I said, not wanting to get into the whole it's not whether he'll be fine but whether I'll be able to wrestle the guilt into submission issue. I needed to think about Matt. This was his night, and it was important that it went well for him. Ultimately, it was important for us as a family.

The networking dinner was being held at a hotel near Tower Hill and the taxi successfully navigated the Friday-evening traffic, delivering us to the door of the venue with a few minutes to spare.

Drinks were being served in a reception area and we were encouraged to take our seats at the tables as per the seating plan on display.

Matt quickly scanned the board, and I could see by the smile on his face that he was pleased with the table we'd been allocated.

'We've only been seated with Daniel Sully,' he whispered in my ear as we shuffled along with the other guests as we bottle-necked through the doors into the dining hall. 'He was top of my list.'

'Oh, that's brilliant,' I replied. I remembered him telling me about Sully who was a self-made millionaire, the epitome of entrepreneurship so much so that *The Sunday Times* listed him as the next Alan Sugar. Sully's main business came from a chain of hotels and a nightclub he owned called The Enclave Club, but he had a keen eye for the market and had successfully invested in several businesses over the past ten years or so.

'Now, you know what Sully's like. Apparently, he has an eye for beautiful women,' said Matt. 'Make sure you get on his good side.'

I wasn't entirely enamoured with being offered up like a prize or being a carrot dangling on the end of a string, but it wasn't the time to pull Matt up on it. 'Are we sitting next to him on the table?' I asked.

'I am, but you're next to me. I'll make sure you're brought in on the conversation.' Matt frowned. 'Maybe we should swap seats?'

'No. I don't think so,' I replied. 'It's you he's interested in. Your business.'

'Yeah. You're right. Not sure what I was thinking of.' Matt put an arm around my shoulder and gave me a squeeze. 'Let's do this.'

Daniel Sully turned out to be very charming and I could see how he might have gained his reputation for having an eye for the ladies, although I wondered whether it was more the ladies that had an eye for him. He was without doubt an extremely handsome man, with his dark brooding looks, apparently of Italian descent according to the Google search I'd done when Matt was preparing his pitch earlier in the year. He was divorced and had one child who lived with his ex-wife. Information on his personal life was scant, as it should be, with most of it focusing on his business achievements.

'And this is my wife, Laurel,' Matt was saying.

I smiled at the businessman and held out my hand. 'Hello,' I said.

'Pleased to meet you, Laurel,' he replied, taking my hand, and shaking it but, at the same time, managing to graze his thumb across my knuckles. He let go and gave a thoughtful look. 'The application only mentioned yourself,' he said to Matt. 'Are you here as business partners?'

'Oh, no. The business is mine,' said Matt, rather like a proud father. 'Laurel helps with the admin side of things from time to time. My secretary, if you like.'

I wasn't sure I'd ever been described as Matt's secretary and wondered if that was usual for him when I wasn't about.

'Secretary, eh?' said Daniel. He looked at me and there was a note of amusement to his voice. Daniel Sully didn't miss my small raise of the eyebrows.

'Yes, something like that,' I replied, smiling as best I could manage. I wasn't sure who I wanted to throttle first as we took our seats at the table.

'Is that all you do?' asked Daniel.

'Well, apart from being a mum and domestic goddess, I have my own business,' I replied, keeping straight-faced and daring Daniel to laugh at me.

'Your own business. What do you do?' asked Daniel.

Before I could even open my mouth to reply, Matt supplied the answer. 'She's an interior designer. Cushions. Curtains. And all that stuff.'

Daniel kept his gaze on me. 'An interior designer. I'm sure there's more to that than cushions and curtains.'

I felt embarrassed on Matt's behalf. He was like a puppy, eager to please his master and in doing so was making a bit of a tit of himself. 'Yes, that's right. Private homes mostly,' I replied.

'And does your portfolio include any of Matt's properties?'

Matt shifted in his seat. 'I sell as soon as they're ready.'

Daniel looked thoughtful for a moment. 'Cash flow?'

'Yes, hence the application for an investor,' said Matt.

'Yes, of course. I do remember reading that,' replied Daniel reassuringly. 'It can be hard work building enough funds to maintain a property and also buy another. You've raised some capital through your own home, is that right?'

'That was our Kickstarter, if you like,' explained Matt. 'It's in the business plan to pay it back.'

Under the table, I put my hand on Matt's knee to reassure him he was doing OK. He was tense and I could feel his leg jiggling a little. I squeezed gently and he stopped. This deal meant a lot to both of us, offering not just financial stability for our family but for Matt's pride too. He didn't have to prove anything to me but being successful in the UK was how he justified his absence to his family back in Australia. His mother had made her feelings known about Matt not bringing his family to Oz, where they could have a much better quality of life than in dreary wet London. Quote-unquote.

I could sense Matt relaxing and the conversation was amicable, with Daniel asking questions, offering advice, and even congratulating Matt on several things. I really had a good feeling about the night. Maybe it was the turning point we needed.

There was a woman sitting on the other side of me and she began to make small talk about the event and the food. She said she was here hoping to get backing from Daniel Sully too.

'I've a Christmas pyjama company,' she was saying. 'There's a big demand for matching family pyjamas on Christmas Eve and I want to expand this to other times of the year too. Have you got children?'

'A son, he's nearly two,' I said. I could see her sales pitch on the horizon heading straight for me. There was nothing I wanted less than to dress in matching pyjamas and have my picture plastered on social media, even if it was something the likes of the Beckhams did – although, admittedly, Victoria Beckham was rather more stylish than I could ever hope to be.

As the dessert course was served, I realised Daniel was now in conversation with the chap on the other side of him.

'All OK?' I asked Matt in a low voice.

He gave a grimace. 'Not sure. He's so hard to read,' he whispered back.

'Poker-faced businessman,' I replied. 'I'm just nipping to the ladies.' I got up from the table, relishing the opportunity to escape the other dinner guests.

There was no phone signal in the toilets, so I slipped out into the reception area and sat down in a seat tucked away in the corner. I messaged Amy to check on Declan and was pleased to get a very prompt reply telling me he was fast asleep in bed. She even sent through a photo of him. Bless her, she was so thoughtful like that. I never felt she was trying to take my place as Declan's mummy, something I'd heard other working mothers experienced with their nannies. I smiled at the image and a surge of love for my son swelled in my heart.

'Now there's a look of love,' came a voice. I looked up and saw Daniel Sully standing there, looking effortlessly sexy, one hand casually in his trouser pocket and the other holding his mobile. He had unfastened the top button on his shirt and loosened his tie a fraction.

I briefly flashed my phone screen at him. 'Very astute,' I replied. 'It is indeed the look of love.' I nodded at his phone and then looked up at him. 'Hmm, not sure if your phone is holding such a heartfelt moment.'

He laughed. 'Very astute,' he echoed. 'May I?' He indicated the wing-backed chair next to me.

'Sure.'

'I was just looking at your husband's pitch again,' he said.

'Oh, right.' I felt slightly uncomfortable with this knowledge. I wasn't sure if he was expecting me to ask about his feelings on it or not. I remained silent, waiting for him to speak again, but before he could, a waiter appeared at his side.

'Can I get you anything, Mr Sully?' he asked reverently.

I thought for a moment the waiter was going to bow.

'I'll have a Scotch.' He looked at me. 'Can I get you a drink?'

'A water would be good.'

There was that small look of amusement on his face again, before he turned back to the waiter. 'And a water for Mrs Jordan here.'

'Of course, Mr Sully.' The waiter disappeared.

'You can call me Laurel,' I said.

'Thank you. And you must do me the honour of calling me Daniel.' He put on an exaggerated upper-class accent reminiscent of a Jane Austen film.

I laughed. 'Thank you, kind sir.'

'It's a good pitch,' said Daniel, looking at the mobile cradled in his palm. 'I like Matt. He seems a decent person. I admire anyone who can move across the world and start a new life for themselves from scratch. He's a hard worker.'

I nodded. 'He is. He deserves this opportunity.'

'You're a loyal wife,' replied Daniel. 'I like that too.'

I wasn't quite sure where this conversation was going. 'So, you've come out for some fresh air?' I said. It sounded lame but I didn't want to talk about my personal life.

'Yeah. It's full-on in there. I mean, don't get me wrong, I like the hustle and bustle of business, but I also like a bit of head-space, especially when there are a lot of people eager to get me to invest. What's your excuse?'

'Checking in with home,' I said.

'Ah, yes. Of course.' He slipped his phone back into his pocket and thanked the waiter, who had appeared promptly with our drinks. 'You sure I can't get you a glass of wine?' asked Daniel.

'I need a clear head for the morning. My son has no consideration for hangovers.'

'Fair enough.'

'Plus, I have a client to visit in the afternoon. Can't be breathing leftover alcohol fumes over them. Doesn't go down too well.'

'Ah, then I won't insist.'

'No, best not to.' I got the feeling Daniel was used to getting his own way and I wasn't entirely convinced that didn't extend to all aspects of his life.

'So, tell me a bit more about your interior design business,' said Daniel, switching back to professional mode. 'Have you been trading for long?'

'I was lucky enough to get an apprenticeship when I was eighteen. Skipped the whole university thing. By the time I was twenty-one, I was taking on clients of my own,' I said. 'Took a break when I had Declan – that's my son – but now I'm my own boss. I was keen to get back to it. I missed the creative outlet. I love going into places and re-imagining the space for my clients. I get a real buzz from it. And at the end, when they are utterly delighted, I get a great sense of satisfaction. Although I am of course directed by the client, there is still a part of me left in the room.' I was suddenly aware that I was gushing about my work. 'Sorry, that all sounded pompous and egotistic.'

He laughed. 'Nothing wrong with being egotistical – it's just another word for passion. You clearly love what you're doing and get an immense sense of pride from your work. You shouldn't be embarrassed by that.'

'Granted, but still rather pompous.' I went for humour, and he laughed again.

'Do you advertise?' he asked, after taking a sip of his drink.

'Not yet. I'm mostly word-of-mouth, but it's something I need to look at when I get a moment.'

'So, you're looking to expand your portfolio?'

I hesitated. This was sounding more like a job interview than a chat over a drink. 'Always looking to improve but not overstretch. It's just me on my own at the moment,' I replied. I took a sip of the water and went to stand up. 'I should get back. Matt will think I've abandoned him.'

Daniel rose. 'Shame, but needs must. I should go back into the lion's den myself.'

'It's not that bad, is it?'

Daniel gave a shrug. 'I shouldn't really say this to you, what with your husband pitching and everything, but...'

'But you're going to,' I said.

'Yes. It's not really a lion's den in there, more like a play-ground, but I like the challenge of taking a fledgling business and transforming it into the real deal. That's my satisfaction point.' He downed his Scotch and placed the glass on the table.

He stepped to one side to allow me to move out from the corner I'd positioned myself in and as I did so, I felt his hand momentarily touch my bare back as he guided me around the chair.

'You do know we're going to set tongues wagging,' he said conspiratorially in my ear.

'Are we?'

'They might think you've been bribing me.' I felt my face flush with embarrassment, and he chuckled as he walked alongside me. 'It wouldn't be the first time,' he said.

'Don't worry, I'll soon put anyone straight who even suggests such an idea,' I said, sounding rather more prudish than I intended, which only added to my embarrassment and Daniel's laughter.

FIVE

Hannah

It had been a long time since anyone had called me Laurel. So long, I barely recognised it as belonging to me. Laurel didn't feel like me anymore. Not after eleven years. I wasn't Laurel. I was Hannah.

'You can't call me that,' I heard myself reply after several seconds of silence.

Bryan nodded. 'And I never would have done if you hadn't just asked me outright if I knew who you were. I did know Laurel.'

'But you don't know me. Hannah,' I said.

'No. I don't know you, Hannah.' Another long pause. He ran his hand around the back of his neck before finally speaking again. 'When did you know I was your next-door neighbour?'

'Yesterday. Elizabeth Rooke mentioned your name to Jasper,' I explained. 'I wasn't sure until I saw you at the barbecue though. When did you know about me moving in?'

'A couple of hours ago. At the barbecue. I thought I'd have been told if you were about to become my neighbour.'

'No one mentioned me to you before then? Not Elizabeth?'

'She might have mentioned it. I probably forgot. Your name isn't exactly unusual. It's supposed to blend in.'

Wasn't that the truth, and I had spent the past eleven years trying to do just that. Blend in. Not stand out. Not be seen. Or at least not be remembered. 'I think I've managed that well up until this point,' I replied. 'I wouldn't ever have moved here if I'd known.'

'No one told you?'

'I'm not in the system anymore,' I said, meeting his gaze. 'Or not deemed important enough to have tabs kept on me. It's been a long time since I had to report back to anyone. I'm no longer an asset.'

Bryan let out a sigh. 'You and me both.'

'I think at this point we're supposed to comment on what a small world it is.'

He gave a wry smile. 'Now that's the sort of thing Laurel would say.'

'Maybe I haven't left her as far behind as I thought.'

'Your husband seems like a nice fella.'

'We're not married. But, yes, he is. He's the best thing that's ever happened to me since...' I tailed off. My past wasn't something I verbalised to anyone. It was simply my internal thoughts and memories. I wouldn't allow myself to talk about it as it made what I'd lost so much more painful. A crippling and agonising grief for Laurel and everything she had once had.

'Does he know?' asked Bryan.

I shook my head. 'And he mustn't, ever.' I glanced over my shoulder towards the house, suddenly fearful that Jasper might have woken up and come out into the garden and heard what we were saying. The anxiety in my stomach made me want to throw up.

'Have you ever been compromised since then? Since Hannah?'

'No.'

'Good. We need to keep it that way.' He rubbed his neck once more. 'We are never going to have this conversation again. Never. No one can ever find out we know each other.'

'Fine by me.'

'I'm going back indoors now and from that moment, you are only ever Hannah and today is the first time we've ever met.'

'As I said, fine by me.'

'Good.'

We shared a long look. A morass of emotions pitched up. Fear and relief in direct opposition to each other, but also an unexpected yearning to have one more moment as Laurel. Saying goodbye to Bryan tonight would mean saying goodbye to Laurel again. I missed her. I hadn't realised quite how much. The grief was overwhelming, and I swallowed a lump in my throat.

'It will be all right,' said Bryan, in that fatherly way that reminded me so much of my past. He reached out a hand and rested it on my shoulder, giving a gentle squeeze. 'Goodbye, Laurel.'

I couldn't speak. I stood there, stock-still, watching him turn and walk back across the beach to his house. He paused at the gate and gave me one last look, before disappearing into his garden.

It was only then I allowed the tears to trickle from my eyes. I'd had one moment of my old self, my real self, and now it was gone again. Forever. The grief hit hard as it had done the first time I'd lost myself.

I sat down on the stone steps and looked out across the beach at the fading light. The warm amber glow of the sun was disappearing to the west, crowning the tops of the houses in gold. The tide was on its way in and soon the silvery sand would be swallowed up for another six hours.

I sensed, rather than saw, something or someone else on the

beach. I snapped my head around to the left, expecting to see someone there, but there wasn't. Luna gave a bark and her body tensed as, on high alert, she looked in the same direction as I was.

'Hello!' I called out, reminding myself of one of those annoying females in an underwhelming Hollywood movie where not only does she call out to danger, but she gets up and walks towards it. All the viewers would be shouting at her to turn around and run. Well, that's exactly what I was going to do.

I jumped to my feet. 'Come on, Luna,' I said, already on the first step. I gave the lead an encouraging tug. Luna didn't move. She gave another bark. I looked again into the fading light but could only make out the breakwaters extending out to sea. 'Luna,' I said more insistently, ascending another step. I gave the lead a harder tug this time and with one last bark, she turned and followed me up over the wall.

I almost broke into a run as I hurried down the lawn towards the house. As soon as I was inside, I yanked the door closed and locked it. The outside light was still on, and I scanned the garden and beyond. I half-expected to see someone appear on the top of the wall.

I wished we'd brought curtains or blinds for the bifolds. I suddenly felt exposed and vulnerable. The sensor light in the garden went off and I jumped at the sudden sight of my own reflection in the glass.

'Stupid,' I muttered to myself. I needed to get a grip. Despite the admonishment, I double-checked the door was locked.

When I woke the following morning, my overwhelming sensation was excitement. Jasper's parents were bringing Pia back today. I had missed her. Our family wasn't complete without her. Having Pia and Jasper around me, kept me grounded. It stopped me from falling over the edge into the black hole I had been teetering on when I'd first met Jasper. They both gave me something to live for when everything had seemed so lost.

Jasper was already downstairs, making coffee and pancakes.

'Oh, those look delicious,' I said, pecking him on the cheek. He caught me around the waist, stopping me from going.

'Just like you,' he said, with a grin.

'God, that's so cheesy.' I gave him a playful smack on the shoulder before wrapping my arms around his neck and kissing him properly.

'I can put the pancakes on hold,' muttered Jasper.

'We could always have our pancakes and eat them,' I replied.

'We've got time before my parents get here.'

'It's a deal.'

I held Jasper tightly, taking a deep breath, my face buried in his shoulder. 'Hold me,' I said.

He let go of the spatula and pulled me tighter into him. 'It's OK,' he said. 'Whatever it is, Hannah, it's OK.'

'I know.' I used to have moments of anxiety like this more often, but over the years those moments had become less and less. They hadn't disappeared, merely lessened. Despite that, I still needed that physical reassurance when the surge of vulnerability came – often when I least expected it.

By the time Jasper's parents arrived an hour later, I had regained my composure. I had focused on seeing Pia and giving my seven-year-old a massive hug.

'Oh, you wouldn't think it was only two days since you last saw her,' laughed Elina, Jasper's mother. 'She's been very good, and we've done lots of things. Pia has something for you.'

'You do, darling? What's that?' I asked.

Elina took out a Tupperware box from her bag and handed

it to Pia, who after a little effort, managed to open the lid and reveal to me the contents. The huge smile on her face told me how proud she was.

'It's Drømmekage,' said Pia. 'Dream Cake.'

'It looks delicious,' I said, eyeing the traditional Danish sponge cake topped with coconut caramel. It was one of Elina's specialities and was one of my first memories of meeting Jasper's parents. Elina had made the oh-so sweet cake for me.

'Try some,' said Pia.

'I certainly will, when we have a cup of tea,' I replied, giving my daughter another hug. 'Shall we show Nanny and Granddad around the house? You haven't seen your room yet.'

As we took Jasper's parents on a tour of the property and out into the garden and then down to the beach, the conversation with Bryan seemed unreal. I could almost convince myself that my two worlds had never overlapped. Almost.

'This is a fine home you have,' said Jasper's father, Christian. He patted his son on the back in a display of parental pride. He turned to me. 'You have done an amazing job of making it feel like home already.'

'Our forever home, as they say,' said Jasper.

I smiled broadly at father and son. I felt such a traitor. On the outside, it was a dream come true, but on the inside, I was sure I'd entered a nightmare.

We were just sitting down on the terrace with our cake and tea, looking out towards the beach, when Annabelle appeared on the other side of the wall.

'Hello!' she called out.

I waved back. 'Hi, you OK?' Thinking this was a casual acknowledgement of each other but was more than a little surprised when Annabelle climbed up the steps to our garden.

She waved a bouquet of flowers in the air.

I thought because she could see we had visitors that

Annabelle would just pass on by, but no, she was stepping into the garden as I reached her.

'I wanted to give you these as a housewarming present,' she said. 'I'm sure you've got everything you need, so I thought flowers, they always brighten up a place. That's what I think anyway.' She thrust the bouquet of sunflowers towards me.

'Thank you. That's really kind.' I admired the bright yellowy-orange petals with the black seeded centres.

'Oh, I didn't realise you had visitors,' said Annabelle, looking down the garden. 'Is that your daughter?'

'Pia, yes. Jasper's parents have just brought her back.'

Annabelle waved at them. 'Hello!' she called out. 'Beautiful house, isn't it?'

Elina and Christian politely waved and agreed it was indeed beautiful, while Jasper put up a hand in acknowledgement.

There was a small silence. 'Err, would you like to join us?' I felt obliged to ask.

'I don't want to intrude on your family,' said Annabelle. 'Maybe another time.' She looked almost wistfully back at everyone.

I couldn't help feeling a little guilty, not to mention rude for not being more insistent. 'You won't be intruding,' I said, before I could talk myself out of the invite. 'Jasper would love to meet you and his parents are lovely. They won't mind at all.'

'That's really kind, thank you,' replied Annabelle, her face lighting up.

As I made the introductions to the family and went inside to make Annabelle a fresh cup of tea, I couldn't help wondering if she was lonely. She hadn't mentioned a partner living here with her. She seemed to be enjoying chatting to everyone and was making a big fuss of Pia, having accepted a slice of cake.

'This is delicious,' she said, as I went back outside with her drink. 'I was just asking Pia if she'd make me a cake. It's my birthday soon.'

'I'm sure she would,' I said, smiling at the beaming look of happiness on Pia's face.

'When's your birthday?' asked Pia, her eyes bright with anticipation at making another cake.

'Actually, it's my birthday on Thursday,' said Annabelle.

My breath caught in my throat, and I thought for a moment I was going to drop the tray as my feet stumbled on the terrace.

'Whoa!' Jasper jumped up, putting a hand out to steady me. He caught my arm and then swiftly took the tray from me. 'You OK?'

'Sorry, yes. I'm fine. Tripped over my own feet,' I said quickly.

'Come and sit down,' said Annabelle. 'You're probably over-doing it with all the moving and everything.'

Jasper set the tray down on the table and then pulled out his chair for me. He moved over to the one on the other side of the table next to Annabelle. 'You're probably right,' he said to her.

'I'm fine. Honest,' I repeated. I picked up the cups and handed them out, while I silently composed myself. Thursday was Declan's birthday. It had been rattling around in the back of my mind for the past week or so and it was only the stress of the move that gave me some relief from it. Every year it was the same. I felt his absence fiercely. It was almost crippling at times, both physically and mentally. It made it hard that I had to pretend that nothing was wrong. I had no one I could talk to about my son. No one in the world. Internalising everything was bad enough, but the beginning of May was the absolute worst time, more so than Mother's Day and Christmas. I could just about cope with those, especially so since I'd had Pia. But Declan's birthday belonged to him and wasn't something I could share.

'So, you live here alone?' Elina asked Annabelle. I was grateful for the change in direction of the conversation.

Elina was one of those people who was genuinely interested in others. It did mean she asked a lot of questions, but she also didn't mind answering questions, so it always seemed a fair exchange. I, on the other hand, much preferred to keep things to myself. It was therefore ideal for my own curiosity to find out more about Annabelle.

'Yes, I'm single,' replied Annabelle. 'No children.' She glanced down at her hands, and I got the distinct impression there was more to that story than appeared on the surface. There was a slight pause as if we were collectively waiting for Annabelle to elaborate.

'It's not a prerequisite to have children, these days,' replied Christian kindly, breaking the silence.

'No, of course, not,' said Elina. 'And more people these days are choosing not to have any or just to have one. Take Jasper and Hannah, they've got Pia and are very happy at that.' She stopped talking abruptly. 'Oh, I'm sorry. I didn't mean to speak out of turn.'

'You'll have to excuse my mother,' said Jasper, patting Elina's hand in forgiveness. 'She gets carried away at times. Loves nothing more than to chat to everyone about everything. She doesn't mean any harm.'

Although Jasper spoke to Annabelle, I knew he was also directing the response my way. I struggled with the guilt at having another child in my new life but, at the same time, I somehow thought having a baby was my atonement. Not a day went by when I didn't think of Declan and, although time was supposed to heal, it never had. I didn't want it to. I wanted to feel that pain, it made losing him real, raw and it made his presence close. Without that pain, I was scared it meant I had stopped loving him so much.

'You didn't want another child, then?' said Annabelle. She looked at me as she spoke.

I ran my hand down the back of Pia's Viking blonde hair. 'We're very happy as we are.'

'Wouldn't you have liked a boy as well?' pressed Annabelle. She looked at Jasper. 'Isn't that what men want? A son of their own? Or is Pia a daddy's girl?'

It prickled me that she was digging for information that I didn't necessarily want to share. Even Elina had boundaries, despite what Jasper said. I looked at him for his response.

He put down his cup and gave a shrug. 'It's not about having a boy or a girl,' he replied. 'It's about having a child. And as Hannah says, we couldn't ask for more with Pia.'

I was grateful for his display of loyalty, even if it wasn't entirely the truth. Jasper had wanted another child, but I had always said no. I was too scared. I was frightened the universe would punish me for being greedy. I'd lost one and kept one. Asking for a third seemed too much of a gamble. I'd been terrified the whole time I was pregnant that something would go wrong, or something would be wrong with the baby. I'd been a complete bag of nerves. I knew I'd never be able to go through that again. Not even for Jasper. And in some perverse way my brain had of trying to accept that I had lost my son, I felt disloyal to Declan. What if I had another boy? I'd be forever comparing him to my firstborn, even if I tried not to, I knew I would. So, no, I wasn't having any more children.

'Do you have siblings?' asked Elina to Annabelle.

'No. I'm an only child. I would have loved a brother or a sister.' Again, there was that look on her face, one where she had let the barrier slip a little and was now shoring it up.

I didn't need to be an empath to unequivocally know that I wasn't the only one with a secret. Annabelle had one too.

SIX

Hannah

Over the next few days, my mind alternated between memories of the past and thoughts of the present. As Declan's actual birthday neared, the yearning for him increased and so did the dreams. In a strange way I looked forward to those dreams where I was with Declan again. It enabled me to relive those times, each one soothing the pain in my heart, but with that came the waking from those dreams and the slip into consciousness where I knew I would have to leave my son behind. I hated waking up.

During the day, I could keep myself busy with settling into the new rhythm of Silverbanks. Pia starting school was a great distraction, even though she took it in her stride and there was no need to worry on my part or Jasper's.

Pia was blessed with confidence and ability. She barely looked back over her shoulder at us as the school receptionist took her by the hand and led her away to her class to meet her new teacher and soon-to-be school friends.

I'd once overheard Jasper's mother say to Christian how

fortunate it was that Pia took after Jasper and not me when it came to confidence and making friends. I wasn't hurt by the observation, but I was saddened because I too had once been confident and sure of myself. Well, Laurel had at any rate. Laurel never worried about walking into a room full of strangers, meeting new people, going to parties on her own. Laurel chatted happily with people and found others fascinating.

It was comments like that from Elina that made me miss Laurel.

The eve of Declan's birthday, I barely slept. I hadn't expected to. I never did. My mind was too full of the day fourteen years ago when I had Declan. My contractions had woken me, and I knew by midday I was in labour. I'd phoned Matt and he had rushed home. We were a mix of excitement and nerves as it was going to be real now. That bump was cradling a soon-to-be-born baby who would be real and totally dependent on us.

It had been a long labour in the end and Declan was born in the early hours of 9 May.

In my life as Hannah, I had woken at two o'clock, the same time my son had been born to Laurel. I remembered those labour pains as if they were happening right at that very moment in time.

I made a vain attempt to go back to sleep, but I knew it would elude me, like it did every year. So, two hours later I slipped out of bed, careful not to wake Jasper, and pulling on my dressing gown I padded quietly downstairs.

Soon I was sipping tea in the fancy new kitchen of my fancy big house, looking out across the garden, where the tide was high and crashing gently on the shoreline. This time I was cradling a mug instead of my newborn – my first born.

I pictured Declan's little pink face and quiff of dark hair; it was almost ebony. Matt and I had been mesmerised by him. We had fallen in love with our son from the moment he took his first breath. We had loved the thought of him long before that, but holding him in our arms had been the single most amazing thing that had happened. To me, certainly.

My heart craved my son. If only I could reach out across the years and pull him back into my arms. To say I wished to relive that moment when I last held him would be an understatement. There really needed to be a word that described that utterly cavernous and deep yearning to cradle my child once again. Even just one more time. It would never be enough, but I would gladly settle for that.

I turned away from the window and curled up on the sofa, wrapping my arms around my body, bringing my knees up to my chest. If I held myself tight enough, I could control the pain – just about.

I must have drifted off into a dream-filled sleep of newborn babies, snuggles, talcum powder and white baby-grows; the next thing I was aware of was Jasper swearing.

'What the fuck?' His voice penetrated my sleep.

I sat up, pushing my hair from my face. 'What's wrong?'

Jasper was putting his cup down on the countertop and opening the bifold door. 'The garden furniture is all across the lawn,' he said.

I blinked and rubbed my face. 'What do you mean?' But he was already striding out onto the terrace in his jeans and T-shirt. I got up and went over to the door. Two sun loungers and a chair were strewn about the garden as if they had been picked up in a whirlwind and dropped haphazardly. 'What happened?'

'Fuck knows,' came Jasper's reply. Followed by some more swearing as he picked up the first sun lounger.

I followed him out and gasped as I saw a long slash down the centre of the fabric. 'It's ripped,' I said needlessly, which earned me a look from Jasper for stating the obvious.

'And this one too,' he said, righting the second sun lounger.

I looked at the chair and, as I picked it up from the ground, that too was sliced. 'This is the same.'

Jasper stood there and looked at the chairs for a moment. 'Someone's done that,' he said. 'No way is this an accident from some freak gust of wind.'

I stood there, frozen to the spot, staring at the chair before looking up at Jasper. 'Someone was in the garden last night,' I said. 'Someone came into the garden and did this on purpose. It's malicious.'

I got another *no shit Sherlock* look from Jasper but then his expression softened, and he came over to me, pulling me in for a brief hug. 'It's probably just kids or something,' he said. 'Don't worry. I'll speak to Bryan and see if this sort of thing has happened before.'

'Why would someone do this?' I asked as Jasper moved away to collect up the furniture.

'Who knows, but I'd love to catch them in the act.' He let out a long breath. 'Why don't you go back inside? Pia will be getting up in a minute. I'll get this tidied away before she sees it.'

I had momentarily been distracted from the day and its significance but as I went back into the house, the wave of grief and utter desolation hit me again, knocking the wind from my lungs. I put out a hand to steady myself, grabbing the worktop as I concentrated on breathing in and out.

All I had to do was get through the day, just like I did every year. Silently. Privately. Secretively.

We dropped Pia at school and, instead of going straight back home, Jasper suggested we grab a coffee first. I suspected it was because he could sense my tension and, no doubt, attributed it to the garden furniture being vandalised. It suited me to let him believe that was all that was wrong.

The café was busy. A group of mums from the school sat on the other side of the room on the soft sofas, laughing and chatting away to each other. I couldn't help thinking that Laurel would have been one of those mums. She'd no doubt be discussing birthday party arrangements for Declan and family get-togethers to mark the occasion.

'You OK, Hannah?'

It was Jasper. His gaze reassuring but not quite hiding the flicker of concern behind his eyes.

'Fine,' I replied, plastering on a smile. I took a final sip of my drink and pushed the cup away. 'Let's have a wander.' I got to my feet, gathering up my bag, readying to leave.

Jasper left his half-finished coffee and, as we stepped out onto the pavement, he took my hand and gave it a gentle squeeze, his way of reassuring me that everything was going to be OK.

We had a leisurely browse in a couple of shops. There was a lovely craft shop with all things seaside, and we bought a little seashell wind chime to hang in the garden.

From Dizzy's Boutique, I bought a lovely cream-coloured blouse with a rather large flamboyant black tie-up bow at the back of the neck.

Jasper had remarked it wasn't my usual style but that he loved it. And I guess it wasn't what Hannah would normally wear. Hannah liked to blend into the background. It was totally the type of thing Laurel would have worn though. I wasn't sure if that was a conscious decision or not, but it felt good. I also wasn't sure what a psychiatrist would have made of the purchase; probably they would say I was trying to cling to my old life in some way. Whatever the reason, I didn't care.

We arrived home and I was making us both a drink before attacking some more unpacking, when the doorbell rang.

As always, I waited while Jasper answered the door. It was a habit I'd adopted many years ago. I didn't like surprises and not knowing who was calling at the house was one of those things that, even after all this time, unsettled me. It was a reminder of my old life and stirred too many unpleasant emotions I'd rather not revisit in any depth.

'Hi,' came the voice. I leaned back a fraction to snatch a glimpse of who was there, but Jasper was blocking my view.

'Oh, hello, Annabelle,' Jasper said, louder than necessary. Again, a tactic I don't know whether Jasper purposefully used, but it was his way of letting me know who was there so I could prepare myself. He thought it was just one of my quirks – one of many he found endearing, he once said. Now they were part of everyday normal life for us.

'Hi, Jasper.' Annabelle had one of those singsong voices that came across as sweet and kind. 'Is Hannah there by any chance?'

'Hiya!' I got to my feet and went down the hall, remembering today was also her birthday. 'Many happy returns of the day,' I said.

'Oh, what? Yes. Thank you.' She looked down as if a little embarrassed. 'Thank you for remembering,' she said, this time looking up and smiling.

'Happy birthday,' said Jasper. 'Have you got anything nice lined up?'

She shook her head and shrugged. 'Not really,' she replied.

I realised it must be a difficult day for her. The first birthday as a single woman and seemingly no family or friends to celebrate the day with her. 'Err... do you want a coffee? There's some cake left that Pia made.'

'Actually, I was about to go for a swim,' said Annabelle. 'I thought I'd see if you fancied coming with me. It's always best to go in pairs. We could have a swim and then have cake afterwards.'

'Oh, right,' was all I could say, surprised at the invite, not to mention apprehensive at the thought of swimming in open water. I shifted uncomfortably from one foot to another.

Annabelle looked from me and then to Jasper. 'Have I called at a bad time?'

'No. Not really,' said Jasper. I shot him a warning look and quickly interjected before he mentioned the slashed furniture. I didn't want all the attention it would bring.

'We've not long got back from taking Pia to school,' I said.

'How's her first week been?' asked Annabelle.

'It's gone really well,' I replied.

Another awkward pause before Annabelle spoke again. 'So, about the swim – do you fancy a quick dip?'

'Now?'

'It's a good time to go,' said Annabelle. 'The tide is in and won't be turning for another hour or so. It's very flat out there today.'

'I don't know. I'm not even sure where my swimsuit is.'

'I have a spare one,' said Annabelle, looking very pleased with herself. She patted the straw beach bag slung over her shoulder. 'I thought a swimsuit would be the last thing you'd worry about when unpacking, so I came prepared.'

I looked at Jasper, silently pleading with him to think of an excuse, but for once he seemed oblivious. 'Don't mind me,' he said. 'I have a few work things I could get on with.'

'I'm still not sure,' I began.

Annabelle whipped out the swimsuit and thrust it into my hands. 'Here, go and get changed. I'll wait down here for you. It will be fun, honestly.' She was practically spinning me around on my own doorstep and herding me into the house to the foot of the stairs.

I glanced back at Jasper and could see the look of amusement on his face. He threw me a wink as I glared at him. 'You wait,' I mouthed at him, but this only succeeding in promoting the amused look to an outright grin.

'Can I get you a drink while Hannah gets changed?' he said

to Annabelle, who was already heading down the hall to the kitchen.

I went upstairs, wondering how the hell I had been coerced into sea swimming. Still, I couldn't exactly say no now. I, of course, knew exactly where my own swimsuit was, I'd unpacked it yesterday – an all-in-one black no-fuss suit. I held up the red number Annabelle had given me, which was basically a bikini, with the top and bottom joined together by a gold ring. The bottoms were little more than a T-bar to cover up only the essential part of my backside, leaving rather more flesh exposed than I was happy for. Definitely not my style. I wriggled into my own costume and grabbed a beach towel from the linen cupboard.

As I went downstairs, I could hear Annabelle laughing, or rather giggling. I nudged away the little feeling of irritation at the idea of her and Jasper sharing a joke together.

'Ah, there she is,' said Jasper, holding his arm out to pull me into an embrace. He gave my shoulder a gentle squeeze and I relished the reassurance this gesture always brought. Once again, he was telling me, without words, that I had nothing to worry about. God, that man could read me like a book. Mostly.

I passed the red swimsuit back to Annabelle. 'I found mine,' I said, needlessly pinging the shoulder strap of my costume as if she hadn't noticed.

'Excellent. Come on then,' said Annabelle. 'This will be good practice for the Summer Swimathon.'

'The what?' I asked.

'Tut-tut, you two,' said Annabelle. 'You clearly haven't read the Silverbanks handbook.'

'Guilty as charged,' said Jasper.

'Apparently, every year there is a Summer Swimathon to raise money for a local charity chosen by the Silverbanks Residents' Association.'

'How very noble of everyone,' said Jasper.

'Yes, isn't it,' said Annabelle. 'They all get to pat themselves on the back and tell each other how wonderful they are. Anyway, enough of that, we need to get training!'

'Don't you want to join us, darling?' I said, offering a sickly smile to Jasper.

'No. It's fine. You ladies enjoy yourselves. I'll get on with my work.'

'Spoilsport,' said Annabelle, already at the back door. 'You don't know what you're missing.'

'I probably do,' muttered Jasper as I gave him a quick goodbye kiss.

'Chicken,' I whispered, before catching up with Annabelle.

'Oh, what's happened to your chairs?' Annabelle was on the terrace looking at the furniture Jasper had stacked to one side.

'We're not sure,' I said, going out to join her. 'Found them like that this morning.'

'Wow. They look like they've been slashed. Cut with a blade.' Annabelle was examining the fabric closely. 'You found them like this?'

'Yeah. Must have happened overnight,' said Jasper, stepping out onto the patio. 'Have there been problems with vandalism around here?'

'I don't know, to be honest,' said Annabelle. 'Gosh, I'm so sorry. Maybe speak to our leader... Elizabeth. She'll know.'

'I thought that would be the case,' sighed Jasper. 'Look, I should get on. Catch you later.' He went back into the house.

'Try not to let it bother you,' said Annabelle as we made our way down the garden. 'I'm sure it's not personal. It'll be kids, most likely. Or teens. One too many drinks. You know what they're like.'

'Yeah. You're probably right.' I looked out at the sea. It was so beautiful and blue. I mentally shrugged off the incident of the chairs and smiled at Annabelle. 'Let's go swimming.'

'High five, sister!' said Annabelle, holding up her hand.

I wasn't one for high fives but found myself slapping hands with her all the same. It made me laugh. Who'd have thought Hannah Towers would ever high-five someone and secretly enjoy it?

I felt surprisingly light-hearted as we went down to the water. I usually took my time getting to know people, but Annabelle made it seem like we'd been friends for a long time. I scolded myself for feeling a little jealous that she was laughing with Jasper. I was over-analysing things – as was my habit. We'd come to Silverbanks for a fresh start, and I had promised myself I would try to relax and put the past firmly behind me. Surely, it was time to do that. Maybe I could really start to believe I was safe.

The sea was colder than I'd imagined, and I squealed several times, catching my breath as the waves hit my thighs. I tiptoed, trying to stay out of the water as much as possible.

'It's fine once you're in!' called Annabelle who had no such qualms. She ducked down in the sea, the water covering her shoulders. 'The more you think about it, the worse it is. Just do it.'

At that moment a big wave crashed right into me, smothering me. I spluttered and cried out, half in shock and half in laughter. It was good to laugh, and it had been far too long since I'd done anything frivolous.

We'd been in the water for about twenty minutes and, despite my enjoyment, I was thinking it might be time to get out. It was after all the south coast of England, not the Med. I had been floating on my back, looking up at the cloudless blue sky. I rolled onto my front. 'Shall we get out now?'

'I was about to suggest that myself,' called back Annabelle.

It was then I realised we were a long way from shore. 'Shit! We need to swim back!' I called over to Annabelle as I tried to swim towards the shore. We must have been a good two hundred metres out to sea. Thoughts raced through my mind.

Would Jasper look out and see us in trouble? Would someone walking along the beach see us? Why couldn't the lifeguard tower be manned every day of the year?

'Oh my God,' said Annabelle.

It was then I realised that the tide was too strong, and we had been oblivious to the danger we were in. The panic rose in me as my futile attempts to make headway against the tide became highly apparent.

'We're in a riptide!' shouted Annabelle.

The panic was real. I'd heard plenty of stories about people being carried out to sea and drowning after getting caught in the riptide. I looked at the shoreline. Was there anybody on the beach? I thought I could make out someone walking along and began to shout and try to wave my hand in the air, but the waves were hiding me from sight and as soon as I stopped swimming, I was being pulled further out to sea.

I looked around for Annabelle. She had disappeared. 'Annabelle!' I shouted. I spun around like a synchronised swimmer but all I could see was water.

'Hannah! Over here!'

Then I saw her head bobbing above the waves as she tried to make her way closer to me.

'What do we do?' I shouted, trying to keep calm. I briefly entertained the idea that this might after all be my destiny as thoughts of Declan pushed their way to the fore of my mind. But, just as quickly, images of Pia swamped my mind, and I knew I couldn't leave her. This wasn't how I was going to die. I wasn't going to be washed out to sea and never seen again. I refused to entertain the idea.

For a second time, I lost sight of Annabelle, but she reappeared a few moments later. This time close enough not to have to shout. 'There's no point trying to swim against it. We're too far out,' she said.

God, I wished I had never agreed to this. I wanted to cry. 'What do we do?' I asked for a second time.

'We have to swim out of it.' Annabelle was only a few feet away from me now. 'Let it take us out further to sea and then, once we're out of the rip, we swim to the left and try to make it to that buoy over there.'

'Go further out to sea?' It went against all my instincts but at the same time I knew I couldn't get back to shore from here.

'Trust me,' said Annabelle. She was next to me now.

I looked at the shoreline, which was even further away now, and then to the buoy. 'I don't know if I can make it.'

'You have to make it. We both do.' There was a sharpness to Annabelle's voice that I hadn't heard before. 'Just let the rip take you out. Don't panic. Save your energy. I'll tell you when we're clear.'

I looked at the young woman in the water next to me. Trust her. I didn't have any choice. She didn't seem to be panicking like I was. I nodded. My arms were aching from swimming and my shoulders were totally submerged. It was all I could do to keep my head out of the water.

'OK?' asked Annabelle.

'OK,' I replied.

I cast one more look at the beach and the row of houses on the bank, which now looked like monopoly pieces, so tiny were they. I could hear the hum of a motor engine, but I couldn't see any kind of boat nearby.

It took less than a minute for us be expelled from the riptide and the force of the current disappeared.

'Swim!' called Annabelle as she set off towards the buoy.

I considered myself reasonably fit, but it was clear Annabelle's stamina was far better than mine. She was leaving me behind with every stroke she took. My arms and legs were burning with pain as the effort to stay afloat began taking its toll. My head was dipping lower into the water with every stroke and I was having to constantly spit salt water from my mouth as the waves were now starting to lap over my head. I was sinking. I gulped for air, my lungs burning with exertion. I was finding it hard to breathe, not just from the effort of swimming but from the panic that was taking hold of me. I wasn't going to make it.

Another wave broke over me, pushing me down below the water. My whole body felt like it was being weighed down from above and pulled from below. Was this where I should relax and let myself go?

The pressure in my chest as my lungs begged for air shook me into action. I needed air. I fought the urge to gulp as I found some inner strength and forced my way to the surface, breaking through the water, gasping for oxygen.

I was again aware of the engine noise I'd heard before, but I was disorientated and still trying to catch my breath as I prepared myself for the next wave to engulf me. I frantically looked around for Annabelle. The engine noise was loud now and then I saw a jet ski bearing down, thankfully coming to a controlled stop alongside me. The man reached out a long, tanned arm.

'You look like you could do with a lift,' he said, hoisting me out of the water. I could have cried with relief. He unceremoniously grabbed my thigh and pulled my leg up over the back of the jet ski.

'My friend,' I gasped, limp and exhausted.

'She's OK. Just over there.' I looked across to the left and saw Annabelle sitting on the back of another jet ski as it zoomed towards the shore. 'Hold on tight,' said the man. With that he opened the throttle and raced back towards land.

The two young men were brilliant, and we couldn't thank them enough. They were very calm and made light of their heroic actions and were soon disappearing back out to sea.

'Thank God they saw us,' I said, as Annabelle and I sat down on the beach, collecting ourselves. My hands were beginning to shake from nerves, and I suspected my body was going into shock. 'Are you OK?'

'I'm fine, physically, but I feel awful. I'm so sorry,' said Annabelle, blinking back tears. 'I should have realised it was a riptide.'

'It's fine, honest,' I said, even though I wasn't quite sure how I felt about it. My overriding emotion was one of relief that it hadn't ended badly for either one of us, or both. Although, I rather suspected Annabelle would have been able to get herself out of danger, while I'd had no idea about swimming out of a riptide.

Annabelle blew out a long breath. 'I guess that goes to show how easy accidents happen. And no one would have known.'

SEVEN

Hannah

After the swimming, or near-drowning incident, Annabelle had come in for coffee and cake. Although it was more to ward off the effects of shock than to celebrate.

I showed her upstairs to the guest room where she could use the en suite to warm up under a hot shower.

While she did that, I took a shower myself, grateful of some warm clothes to put on afterwards. I hooked out some sweat pants and a shirt for Annabelle, remembering she'd only been wearing a flimsy overshirt when she'd turned up earlier.

She emerged from the guest room and I could see she was still shivering. I handed her the clothes. 'Put these on. You need to keep warm after that. I'll go and make us a hot drink.'

I left her upstairs while I went down to the kitchen. As I was filling the kettle, Jasper appeared, having just finished a call with a client in his office.

I relayed the whole event to Jasper, who was mortified he hadn't been there to help us.

'Thank goodness those two lads on their jet skis came along when they did,' he said.

'Sorry, it's my fault,' said Annabelle, coming into the kitchen. I was pleased to see the colour back in her face. 'I shouldn't have asked you to come out with me.'

'It wasn't anyone's fault,' I said.

'Not much of a birthday celebration either,' said Annabelle. She looked at me and grinned. We both broke out into laughter. Probably verging on the hysterical as the thought of how close we'd come to drowning hit us.

'Can I get you another drink?' asked Jasper, once we'd both calmed down.

'I really should get home,' she said, getting to her feet and picking up her bag. 'I'll wash your clothes and return them to you tomorrow.'

'Oh, no rush,' I said, walking with her to the door. I accompanied her down to the end of the garden where Annabelle unexpectedly hugged me.

'Thank you,' she said and then with a grin added, 'for making this birthday memorable.' We both laughed again and then she was off over the wall and heading back to her house.

I went back inside, suddenly feeling exhausted.

'Maybe you should have someone on the beach as lookout when you go again,' Jasper said, as I stepped into the kitchen.

'Oh, don't worry, I'm not going again.' I had flopped down on the sofa. I tried to laugh but couldn't manage it.

In fact, when I went to bed that night, I lay in the dark, reliving those few minutes a good ten times or more.

'Try not to think about it,' Jasper murmured, snuggling down under the duvet. 'Go to sleep now, sweetheart.'

I must have fallen asleep in the end. When I woke the next morning, to the sound of the sea gently lapping at the shore, it was hard to believe how misleading it had been yesterday. The memory of just how close I'd come to drowning made me shudder. Jasper was already up, and I forced myself to follow suit, leaving the comfort of our bed, pausing at the window to look at the sea. Beautiful though it was, it wasn't to be trusted.

'Are you nearly ready?' Jasper's voice came from the bottom of the stairs a few minutes later.

I was rummaging through my wardrobe for something to wear. We were taking Pia to school and then going for brunch at the café in town today.

'Won't be a minute!' I called back. I was looking for the blouse I'd bought in Dizzy's Boutique yesterday, but it was nowhere to be seen. I was sure I'd left it hanging on the front of the wardrobe door in the dressing room, but no, it wasn't there.

I jogged downstairs to where Jasper and Pia were waiting. 'Sorry about that,' I said, slipping my feet into my shoes. 'Couldn't find my new blouse. You haven't seen it, have you?'

Jasper shook his head in a vague way that translated into he didn't know and wouldn't trouble himself as I was bound to find it sooner or later. He was probably right.

'All set?' he asked, picking up his car keys.

We trundled out to the car and drove off the estate towards Pia's school.

Pia was just as excited about her second day at school as she had been her first. While we were in town, we grabbed a coffee at a little café and sat outside to drink it. It was nice that Jasper had been able to reduce his workload this week while we moved in. Even though he worked from home three days a week, going out for coffee was not a regular habit, not back in London anyway. Maybe here we could do it more often.

By the time we had finished, I felt much better than when I'd woken up thinking about what happened yesterday. I liked this new feeling of happiness. Even the thought of Bryan Chamberton living next door couldn't dampen my spirits. He might be a ghost from my past, but he wasn't here to destroy me. He had made that clear and I believed him. I had to, if I was going to preserve the happiness and love I'd found with Jasper and Pia.

I idly wondered if, here on the south coast, I could consider getting some sort of part-time job. I'd been lucky enough that Jasper had been able to support us both when Pia was born. When I'd met Jasper, I was working in a low-key admin job for a building suppliers. I had no desire to return to an office-based role, but maybe working somewhere like Dizzy's Boutique would be fine. I was hardly likely to run into my past in a place like that.

We finished our drinks and headed back home. I was smiling to myself as we turned onto Silverbanks.

'You look happy,' said Jasper.

'I am,' I replied. 'Very happy.'

'Good. You know that's all I've ever wanted.'

However, the feeling of contentment was short-lived. I shouldn't have jumped the gun, thinking everything was going to be all right. As we slowed down to turn into our drive, I noticed the flowerbeds at the edge of our garden wall. Or at least, what used to be flowerbeds. The pretty red and yellow tulips which had stood tall against the backdrop of the white wall were now beheaded. Their petals were strewn across the lawn and the stalks had been stamped on. Every single one of them.

Jasper stopped the car. 'What the actual fuck?' he muttered under his breath. 'Were they like that this morning when we left?'

'I don't know. I didn't pay any attention. I was too busy checking Pia had everything she needed for school.'

At that moment, Bryan and Sandra appeared from their driveway. They smiled and waved, and then, noticing the expression on our faces, came over. 'Is everything all right?'

asked Bryan across the hedge. He may have been retired from the force but his sense that something wasn't right hadn't gone on gardening leave. Jasper nodded at the flowerbed and both Bryan and Sandra followed his gaze, making appropriately shocked noises as they took in the devastation.

'Oh, my goodness,' exclaimed Sandra. 'What on earth happened?'

'I guess someone didn't like the tulips,' replied Jasper.

'When did this happen?' asked Bryan.

'I assume last night,' I said.

Bryan frowned. 'We haven't had anything like this happen before.' He stood up straight and looked up and down the road. 'Wonder if anyone else has suffered any damage.'

'Are you on the Silverbanks Facebook group?' asked Sandra.

We both shook our heads. 'Didn't know there was one,' I said.

'Oh, you'll probably get an invite. Elizabeth is one of the admins.'

'Of course she is,' said Jasper. He moved the car onto the driveway and we both got out, walking back to where Sandra was tapping away at her phone and Bryan was standing with his hands on his hips, surveying the crime scene. I thought for a moment he was going to tape the area off and don a white boilersuit. He crouched down and picked up a discarded flower head. The petals all dropped to the ground. Then he parted some of the stamped down stalks and leaves.

'Trying to look for a clear footprint,' he said. 'Might tell us what size or type of shoe, which would tell us if it's male or female.'

I knew later Jasper and I would probably laugh privately at the comment.

'Anything?' asked Jasper.

'Nothing of significance,' said Bryan, as he straightened

himself up into a standing position. He winced and rubbed his knee in the process.

'Oh, look,' said Sandra, giving her mobile a little wave in the air. 'Amanda Dixon has posted in the Facebook group. Her flowerpots have been broken.' Sandra looked up at me. 'Sounds like vandalism. We've never had this before on Silverbanks though.'

'Where does the lady live?' I asked. Hope hooked onto the fact that someone else had been a victim of vandalism and I wasn't being singled out.

'Amanda? Sea Crest.' Sandra pointed further down the road. 'There are a few replies already. I'm going to send you an invite to join the group.'

'I'm not on Facebook,' I said.

'Oh, really? That's unusual these days.'

I shrugged. 'Not my thing. Jasper is though, mainly for work. Can I take a look?'

'Of course.' Sandra handed over her phone and I scanned the post, looking at the replies.

Amanda Dixon: The flowerpots either side of my gate have been knocked over in the night. One's broken. So annoyed. Must have been done on purpose. They are too heavy to be blown over. Who would do that?

Karl Baxter: Delivery driver?

Amanda Dixon: In the middle of the night? I don't think so.

Karl Baxter: Foxes maybe?

Amanda Dixon: Hardly. Honestly, Karl, you're not helping.

Hazel Brampton: My KEEP OFF THE GRASS sign has been

pulled out the ground. No tyre marks so definitely not a delivery driver. That's been done on purpose.

Amanda Dixon: It's sabotage.

Karl Baxter: Feral kids.

I handed the phone back to Sandra, feeling relieved, although noting no one had had their furniture slashed like we'd had. That seemed quite an extreme act of vandalism.

'Not you as well,' came a voice I was beginning to know rather too well for my liking. It was Elizabeth. 'Your beautiful tulips. Amanda Dixon has just posted on Facebook about her flowerpots.'

'We've been reading it,' said Sandra. 'Hazel had her KEEP OFF THE GRASS sign pulled up, too.'

I couldn't have been certain, but for a fleeting moment I thought I saw a look of pleasure in Sandra's eyes.

Elizabeth sighed. 'This is terrible. What must you think of Silverbanks?'

I smiled. 'Don't worry. These things happen everywhere.'

'You need to note yours down too,' said Elizabeth. 'On Facebook. That way we can keep a log.'

'Hannah isn't on Facebook,' said Sandra.

'Really? Even I have social media,' said Elizabeth, standing a little straighter as if it was a badge of honour. 'I can show you how to set up a profile and then you can join the group.'

'No. It's OK. Jasper's on it. I can always look via his account.'

Jasper and Bryan, having finished their inspection of the flowerbed, joined us. 'Bloody mindless,' Bryan muttered. We stood there as Elizabeth went through the Facebook post again.

'I'll get this all cleared up,' said Jasper. 'Hopefully it's a one-off.'

'I'll call a neighbourhood watch meeting,' said Elizabeth. 'We can set up some patrols. Take it in turns to walk around the estate in the evenings. Maybe we should get CCTV installed. I'll ask if anyone has doorbell footage. We might be able to spot who did it.'

'I think you might be getting ahead of yourself there,' said Bryan. 'Even if we did get footage, we're not going to be able to recognise them. It's hardly likely to be anybody on the estate.'

'I know, but we should at least try to find out what we're up against,' countered Elizabeth.

I exchanged a glance with Jasper and was sure he was of the same mind as me – that Elizabeth was getting a bit carried away. 'It's just some flowers,' I said, trying to placate everyone.

'It may well be,' said Elizabeth. 'But if we are complacent about this, then we are opening the doors for all and sundry to come onto the estate and cause havoc. Next thing we'll be getting break-ins and thefts. No, we must stop it now. I'll put it to the vote and see what everyone else thinks.'

It was several more minutes before the gaggle broke up and Jasper and I were able to escape into our house. 'Gosh, Elizabeth is a bit full-on,' I said. 'Good thing you didn't mention the furniture.'

Jasper shrugged. 'There seemed to be enough drama as it was. Adding in slashed garden chairs might have been a bit too much for Elizabeth. And Bryan, for that matter. For a minute there, I thought he was going to seal off the area and call forensics in.'

We both chuckled at the thought. And then, more seriously, I asked Jasper, 'What do you think? Should we be worried? The flowers are one thing, but the slashing seems, I don't know, more nasty.'

'Yeah, I know what you mean but, honestly, Hannah, I don't think we have to worry. I'll get CCTV put up outside, if only for night-time and during the day when we're not here. How does that sound?'

I smiled, grateful he wasn't totally dismissing my worries. 'Thanks.'

The sound of the letter box flapping and an envelope dropping onto the mat had Luna jumping up. She gave a little bark. I went down the hallway and picked up the post. It was a handwritten envelope addressed to The New Family. 'Weird,' I said, walking back to the kitchen. 'The New Family.' I showed the envelope to Jasper.

'It's probably a new home card,' said Jasper. He checked his watch. 'I've got that conference call in ten minutes; I'd better get organised.'

'Yeah, sure.'

He gave me a kiss. 'Don't worry about the flowers and the chairs,' he said. 'They can all be replaced. We'll get some CCTV sorted. Promise.'

I smiled and watched him leave the room for his study.

I looked at the envelope again. Jasper was probably right about it being a good luck in your new home type of card.

Luna sat at my feet expectantly and I knew she was waiting for a walk. It was a clear bright day and perfect for getting out on the beach. I gave the dog a stroke. 'Give me two minutes,' I said, before opening the envelope.

I pulled out the card.

Congratulations on the Birth of Your Baby Boy!

I baulked at the blue-and-white embossed image of a traditional pram, knitted booties and a baby rattle. This was a coincidence, surely.

With a shaking hand, I opened the card and read the handwritten message inside.

Congratulations

So happy for you – a baby boy!

And Declan is such a lovely name.

Love from Laurel

I gasped and dropped the card as if it had burned my fingers and jumped back from it. Struggling to breathe, I stared at the card, now lying open on my kitchen floor, the words taunting me.

EIGHT

Hannah

I was too shocked to cry. I didn't know what to do. Panic was rising.

The door to the study opened and Jasper appeared in the hallway. 'Hannah? You OK?' I was only vaguely aware of his voice. And then he was beside me, his hand on my shoulder. 'Hannah?'

I screamed and jumped back again. 'Oh my God. You frightened the life out of me.'

'Hey, it's OK.' He gave me an uncertain smile. 'Sorry.'

We both stared down at the card. Jasper went to bend down to retrieve it but I practically body-checked him out of the way and snatched up the card.

'Not a new home card,' I said quickly.

'Can I see?' he asked. 'What was it?'

I realised I had stuffed my hand with the card behind my back. I must have looked absolutely ridiculous or guilty. Probably both. Judging by the quizzical and slightly concerned look on Jasper's face, there was no probable about it.

'Guess what it is?' I said instead, trying to recover some ground.

Jasper gave a small smile, still not sure what the hell was going on. 'I don't know. Birthday card?'

'Nearly.' I placed the card on the worktop. 'New baby. Must be the wrong address or the previous owners.'

Jasper picked the card up and looked at it. 'Strange the sender, Laurel, whoever she is, hasn't addressed it to anyone inside.'

'There's no return address or anything,' I said, taking the card from him. 'I'll put it in the recycling.'

'I can ask Hugo at the estate agents.'

'Don't bother him about it,' I said.

Jasper moved around the kitchen island and took a glass from the cupboard, filling it from the water jug in the fridge. 'Going to need this for the meeting. Apparently the big boss is joining us.'

'Oh, good luck, then,' I said, relieved that this would give me more time to myself. The big boss, as Jasper called him, could easily extend the call by another hour. 'I'm going to take Luna for a walk.'

'Good idea. Catch you later.'

My hand was still shaking as I took the dog lead from its hook by the door. I picked up the card, intending to throw it in the bin, but instead pushed it into my handbag. I wasn't sure why. Maybe I needed to have another look at it later when I wasn't in such a state of shock. Whoever had sent this had done so intentionally. This wasn't a mistake. 'Come on, Luna. Walkies.'

Luna's feet skidded and clattered on the tiled flooring as she excitedly bounded towards the back door.

The sky was a lovely clear blue and as I stepped onto the beach I breathed in the salty sea air. The waves were lapping gently on the shoreline and seagulls drifted up above. I closed my eyes for a moment, enjoying the warmth of the sun on my face as I strove to ground myself.

Luna whined and I unhooked her lead, letting her scamper on ahead, her paws making shallow imprints on the soft, wet sand.

Silverbanks was essentially a small spit of land with the most expensive houses on the perimeter, and three avenues running lengthways down the spit, unimaginatively named first, second and third avenue, all leading to The Loop.

Our house was at the beginning of the estate and, although it had beach access, it was one of the less expensive perimeter houses. The nearer The Loop, the higher the price.

As I walked along the beach towards The Loop, my thoughts oscillated from Declan to the card and back again. I didn't know what to make of it, but my underlying feeling was pure, rampant fear, even though I had no idea where the danger was coming from. Who knew about my past? Why send the card? What did they hope to gain from it?

I'd have to try to speak to Bryan when he was on his own. He might be able to shed some light on it or tell me what I should do. He might even have some contacts who could help me.

My stomach churned with the thought that my carefully concealed past as Laurel had clashed with my carefully constructed life as Hannah. This was never supposed to happen, and it terrified me.

As I rounded the end of the spit, the glare of the sun impaired my vision, and I didn't see the figure sitting on the beach until I was a short distance away and it was far too close to turn around or change track without it being obvious.

I held my hand up to shield my eyes from the sun and realised it was Annabelle. She turned her head in my direction. There was no doubt she'd seen me. She was sitting with her arms wrapped around her legs and her chin resting on her knees as she looked out across the water. She raised a hand and I felt obliged to wave back.

I couldn't help thinking she had an aura of sadness about her. I debated whether to carry on walking, trying to convince myself that maybe she wanted to be left alone, but also arguing that perhaps something was wrong, and I should at least offer her the chance to talk if she wanted to. Besides, after what happened in the riptide, it would seem odd to ignore her now.

'Hey,' I said as I trudged on the soft dry sand towards the dune she was sitting on.

'Hey,' she replied with a weak smile.

'How are you?' I asked.

'After yesterday? I'm OK. You?'

'Fine,' I replied, sensing she didn't want to talk about it.

'That's good.' She gave a small smile. 'Look, I'm really sorry about what happened.'

'It wasn't your fault,' I told her, echoing my reassurances of yesterday.

'Maybe not entirely, but I did kind of encourage you to come out with me.'

'I'm glad I did,' I replied. 'In fact, I'm glad I was with you. If I'd been on my own, I would never have known about swimming out with the riptide. I would have tried to swim against it.' I gave a shudder at how that might have ended.

'I don't mind telling you now,' replied Annabelle, 'I was actually quite frightened. At one point, I wasn't sure we'd make it, but I didn't want to worry you. I could see you were panicking. I just kept thinking I needed to stay calm and get us to safety.'

A small surge of warmth welled up inside me. I couldn't remember when I had last been the priority for someone other than Jasper. I didn't know what to say, without gushing how happy that made me. To anyone else that would have been a normal comment but, for me, it was definitely extraordinary.

'Thank you,' I managed to say after a moment.

'No big deal,' said Annabelle. She blew out a breath. 'There is something else, though.' She paused before continuing. 'I was just debating about whether to come and see you.'

'About what happened?'

'Not that particularly,' said Annabelle. 'When I came over yesterday, I was hoping to catch you on your own, but Jasper was there. I thought maybe after our swim, I'd be able to talk to you, but then of course...' Her voice trailed off.

'I haven't got to rush off anywhere now, if you still want to talk,' I said, bemused. She was, after all, the trained counsellor. I couldn't think how I'd be able to help her.

She twiddled the diamond ring on her finger. 'I wanted to apologise,' she said.

'Apologise?'

'Yeah. I didn't mean to gate-crash you with your in-laws last weekend, and I certainly didn't mean to appear rude or offended when Jasper's mum asked about children.'

Gosh, she looked like she was about to cry. I plonked myself down in the sand next to her and gave her arm a gentle squeeze. 'You didn't come across as rude or offended at all,' I said. 'I'm sorry if you were put on the spot about what I know can be a sensitive subject for a lot of women.'

'Jasper's parents are lovely. I shouldn't have got snippy.'

'Honestly, Annabelle, it's not a problem. I don't think they even noticed.'

She nodded and gave another diluted smile. 'It's just...' She stopped talking and looked away, wiping her face with her fingertips.

'You don't have to explain anything,' I said. 'Some things are too private or personal to share.'

'You're very understanding. But it's also good to talk. I should really practise what I preach to my clients.' Annabelle looked back towards the sea. 'I came out of a bad marriage; I left my husband because he was having an affair.'

'I'm sorry,' I said.

'Prior to the affair, I'd lost a baby. I'd had a miscarriage and he had somehow got it into his head it was my fault. We hadn't been getting on, but at the same time he wouldn't ever discuss a divorce. Said he'd never divorce me. That I was his forever.'

My eyes widened. 'His? Forever?'

'Mm. Yeah. He was a textbook narcissist. I was totally taken in by him and had basically given up everything to please him – my family, my friends, my job. I was left with nothing.' She dropped her head into her arms. 'He had total control over me. And it was all my fault. You'd think I'd have known better.'

'It's hard to see things, especially when you love someone. You don't necessarily want to see their bad points.'

'I blame my father,' said Annabelle.

'Your father?'

'Yes. He thought loving and supporting his daughter could be done with money and gifts.' She closed her eyes and swallowed before looking back at the sea. 'All I wanted was his time. His attention. It sounds such a cliché, but all I wanted was to be loved.'

'And you thought you had that with your ex-husband,' I said, unsure if I was saying the right things.

'Daddy issues, as they like to say these days. Although, technically, it's far more complex than that,' said Annabelle, dipping her head onto her knees.

I was taken aback by this sudden sharing of such personal details. Oversharing had never been an issue for me and I had to remind myself that some people felt better after talking about their problems. Just because I couldn't bring myself to do that, didn't mean I should stop someone else drawing comfort from it.

I put my arm around Annabelle's shoulders. 'I'm so sorry.'

She kept her head dipped and took some deep breaths as if steadying herself. Eventually, she lifted her head up. 'I'm sorry,' she said. 'I didn't mean to drop all that on you.'

'It's not a problem,' I replied. 'I'm glad you felt able to talk to me.'

She nodded. 'Yes. Bottling things up isn't something I do as a rule, although being with him, Scott, made me do exactly that. I didn't want to admit to anyone that I was in a bad relationship. So, I covered it up – both the emotional and physical side of things.'

'Physical?'

'It wasn't that bad,' she said. 'And I can be annoying at times.'

'Hey, no!' My words came out firmer than I'd intended, and I felt Annabelle shudder. 'Sorry. What I mean is, physical violence, domestic violence, is always bad. Always. Never play it down. It doesn't matter if it's a push, a shove, a slap, or a punch – it's all violence. And never, ever, take the blame for someone else's actions.' I could hear the wobble in my voice as a sudden image of Daniel and Beaumont House surfaced. 'You are not responsible for what they do. They have to deal with the consequences, whether they like it or not.'

Annabelle looked at me for a moment. 'You're right. I know that, of course, but old habits and all that.'

'Sure.'

'Keeping it a secret was the hardest,' she said. 'Have you ever had to keep a secret? I mean a serious one, not a birthday surprise or anything like that, but something important?'

I moved my hand from her shoulder as I felt myself bristle at the question. *How about my whole fucking life story?* I wanted to say, but of course, I didn't. I shook my head. 'No, but I can imagine how difficult it must be.'

'You've honestly never had to keep a secret from someone, a friend or your parents or Jasper?' She sounded surprised.

'Not that I can think of,' I said, wishing she would drop the subject. 'Hey, do you want to go for a walk or something? We could go into Seabury, if you like?' I suggested, thinking a change of scenery would do Annabelle good. I couldn't work out what was drawing me towards her – I usually kept people at a safe distance – but it felt like, after what we'd gone through yesterday in the riptide, we had formed some sort of bond.

It sounded like she'd had a really shit time with her husband and was still struggling with the aftermath. I knew how that felt – trying to move forward when the weight of the past wouldn't let you go.

Luna came bounding back up the beach, her long pink tongue lolling out one side of her mouth. She sniffed around and then sat down next to Annabelle.

'Tell you what,' said Annabelle, ruffling Luna's ear and running her hand along the ridge of the dog's back. 'Why don't you come to mine? I've got a bottle of wine in the fridge waiting to be opened.'

'Sounds good,' I replied, feeling buoyed by the invitation and the fact that I had accepted, even though it was so out of character for me. For Hannah, anyway. Laurel wouldn't have hesitated. Allowing new people into her life was a normal and regular thing for her to do.

As I followed Annabelle into her apartment, I had a real sense of being my old self and, for a moment, I yearned to be Laurel again.

NINE

Laurel

A week had gone by since the business event at the Tower Hill hotel and Matt had been almost unbearable the whole time, on tenterhooks as he waited to find out if he had been successful in making it through to the next round of interviews.

'If I don't hear by the end of the week, I guess that means I didn't make it,' said Matt down the phone to me. I was at my studio on Kensington High Street trying to get the CAD software to work properly. I really needed a new PC, but that would have to wait until I made some more money. Hence my working late.

'I honestly think you're in with a chance,' I said. 'Daniel Sully seemed really interested.'

'I wish you could have talked me up a bit more when you had that private tête-à-tête with him in the reception.'

'I did talk you up,' I said. 'Of course I did. Stop going on about me meeting with him; we literally sat down together for five minutes, that was all.' I was trying, but failing, to keep the impatient tone from my voice. We'd had this conversation several times over the past week. When I'd initially told Matt, he'd made me relay practically word for word my exchange with Sully. And then accused me of not talking him up, as he put it. Honestly, I wanted to throttle him. I'd got past being insulted and had now reached exasperation level. I was almost hoping he wouldn't get through to the next round, because I wasn't sure how much more of this I could take. I had to remind myself that it was all for a good cause; not only did we need it for the sake of our bank balance but Matt needed it for his self-belief.

'Do you think I should email them? No. That's not a good idea,' said Matt, answering his own question. I heard Declan in the background. 'I'd better go, Declan's having a squawk. Amy's just left. How long are you going to be?'

'About another hour,' I said, feeling my heartstrings pull at the sound of Declan crying. 'He probably wants his bottle. It is nearly his bedtime.'

'Yeah. I'll catch you later.'

'Give Declan a kiss and...' My words trailed away. Matt had already hung up. Charming.

I looked at my laptop and was about to give up when the screen blinked and the programme opened. I really needed to get this new design completed and sent over to the client as I had promised. It didn't do to let deadlines slip by, especially with this particular client who appeared to have an open chequebook when it came to budget.

A rap on the front door of the shop made me jump. I had a desk situated at the back, from where I had a clear view of the shop. I kept the door locked, whatever the time of day, only letting people in once I'd seen who they were. I tended to operate a by-appointment-only system, but I did occasionally get walk-ins from the street.

This was past business hours though and I recognised the walk-in immediately. It was Daniel Sully.

I got up from my seat and he smiled in that confident and

disarming way of his. I unlocked the door. 'Daniel, I wasn't expecting to see you,' I said.

'Hi, Laurel. I was passing and saw the light on. It's late, so I wanted to check everything was all right.'

'Everything is fine. I'm working late, that's all,' I replied, surprised by his explanation. 'You were passing? And you just happened to notice the light on?'

He grimaced. 'Kind of. OK, I admit, I was specifically looking. But I was honestly passing. On my way back from a property I've purchased.' He looked beyond me into the shop. 'Are you on your own?'

'Err, yes. I am.' I was still standing on the threshold with the door ajar.

'You're making yourself quite vulnerable. You can be seen from the street.'

'Oh, I'm OK. That's why I keep the door locked. So the bad guys can't get in.'

He gave that amused look of his, raising his eyebrows a fraction. 'Is that why you're not letting me in?'

'Are you a bad guy?'

'That's a matter of opinion,' he said, and then winked.

Jesus, he should not be allowed to wink at women. Honestly, that one cheeky gesture, which he clearly knew the impact of full well, sent all sorts of thoughts through my head. Thoughts that I should not be having.

There was an awkward silence. Well, awkward on my part as I tried to regain my composure. I couldn't think of a single thing to say back, witty, or otherwise.

I shifted on my feet and finally found my voice. 'Well, erm, thanks for stopping by. As you can see, I'm perfectly fine.'

Instead of moving away, he leaned a hand casually on the doorframe. 'Why are you working so late anyway?'

'Deadline.'

'You look tired.'

'You know how to flatter a woman,' I replied, very aware of how close he was to me. I could smell his aftershave – an earthy scent mixed with something zingy. It reminded me of Italy and lemon groves.

'I do actually, but you're not very good at taking compliments,' he said, his face serious as he held my gaze.

I wanted to look away, but it was impossible. How was this man doing this to me? 'I'm not easily won over,' I said, willing myself to get a grip.

'How long are you here for?' he asked.

'Not sure. I think Matt might be calling by. In fact, he is.' I stopped talking at my blatant lie and I could tell Daniel didn't believe a word of it.

'OK. I'd better go then,' he said, moving his hand away from the doorframe.

I wanted to call after him to try to make up for my obvious lie, but I didn't know what to say. Had I just blown Matt's chances of getting a contract by rebuffing Sully? Was he even trying anything on? My gut said yes, but as I locked the door and analysed our exchange, I began to doubt myself.

I spent another hour at work, but it was hard going. My mind wasn't fully on the job in hand, I kept replaying the interaction with Daniel. I hoped I hadn't offended him, not for my sake but Matt's. At one point, I considered phoning him to apologise, but something made me stop. I hadn't been rude. I hadn't done anything wrong. He had come onto me. If anyone should be apologising, it was him for making me feel uncomfortable.

By the time I got home, I had talked myself in circles and was more confused than ever. I told Matt what had happened.

'And he just went?' asked Matt, pouring red wine into the two glasses on the table.

'Yes. It was really awkward.'

'You didn't say sorry or anything?' Matt gulped back his wine in one go.

'No. I didn't,' I said, feeling defensive. I was surprised by Matt's lack of concern.

'Jesus, Laurel. Thanks for that.' Matt refilled his glass.

'Thanks for what?' I asked, trying to keep my voice down so I didn't wake Declan.

'You being off with him might blow my chances of getting his backing.'

I stood in disbelief for a moment, the anger bubbling up inside me. 'Anyone would think you were more worried about the business deal than about your wife.'

'What?' He took another slug of wine.

'He came to my shop and made me feel uncomfortable.'

Matt looked at me as if I was talking another language. 'Look, babe, I think you're getting this all out of proportion. Unless there's something else? I mean, what exactly did he do?'

'Well, nothing, but—'

'Exactly. He just stopped by when he saw you working and, to be fair, he has got a point. You shouldn't really be there alone at night.'

'I'm really busy with work. I didn't have any choice.'

'You might not have to worry about work if I get this backing from Sully,' said Matt, picking up his phone and beginning to scroll through it. 'That's if your acting all weird in front of him hasn't put him off.'

'I like working. Besides, we shouldn't put all our eggs in one basket. I've worked hard to get my business off the ground again. I don't want to give it up just because of one deal.' I stopped talking. Matt was clearly not listening. I was confused about my own reaction to Daniel Sully and niggled by my husband's. Maybe I was overreacting. I was tired and I didn't have the energy to wrestle with it anymore.

Matt and I ate our meal in silence. He was on his phone most of the time, checking his inbox and informing me there were no emails from Daniel Sully. He didn't voice his earlier criticism that I might have ruined his chances of getting the backing, and I didn't mention it either. If I saw Daniel again, I'd make sure I was more polite and friendly. He'd probably gone away thinking I was the weird one and he'd be best off steering clear of me. I hoped that wouldn't influence his decision about putting money into Matt's business.

When I woke the following morning, I was even more convinced I had overreacted. Matt seemed to have forgotten all about it and was in his usual cheerful mood, leaving early for the office with promises of a takeaway that evening. It was always a nice thought that I wouldn't have to cook on a Friday night. Amy turned up and when I left her and Declan, I was in a much better mood than I had arrived home in twelve hours earlier.

I'd only been in the shop for ten minutes when the bell rang. A delivery van was parked outside and a woman carrying a bunch of flowers was standing at the door.

'Hi. Laurel Jordan?' she asked when I opened up.

'Yes, that's me.'

She thrust the bunch of flowers at me. 'For you,' she said before jumping back in her delivery van and zooming off.

The bouquet was beautiful, made up of lilies, roses and forget-me-nots. There was a card tucked inside and, once I'd arranged them in a vase, standing it on the counter, I opened the envelope. It was unusual to get flowers from Matt, but despite his occasional abruptness, he could be romantic when he wanted to. Maybe he'd realised he'd been a bit too dismissive last night and should have at least reassured me if nothing else.

I was surprised then to see the card wasn't from my husband but from Daniel Sully.

Sorry for dropping by unannounced last night.

Didn't mean to make you feel awkward.

Best wishes

Daniel

I read the card again. It sounded sincere enough. I felt embarrassed that he'd noticed my reaction. So much so that he'd felt the need to apologise. I looked at the sign-off: *Best wishes*. That was rather formal. God, what an idiot I'd made of myself. I wouldn't be able to look at him again without cringing. Ugh.

I turned the card over and saw that Daniel had written his mobile number down.

Did he want me to call him? Was I supposed to thank him or tell him it was all right, I wasn't freaked out over last night? I wasn't sure.

I gave Matt a call instead. 'Hi,' I said as he picked up.

'Everything all right?' he asked.

I didn't often ring Matt during the day. I knew some couples spoke and texted each other throughout the day, but that had never been our style. 'Yeah, all OK.' I eyed the bunch of flowers and the card, and thought of the deal Matt was desperate to get. 'Just wondered if you'd heard from Daniel Sully yet?'

'No. Not yet.' Matt gave a sigh. 'Beginning to think he's not going to back the project.'

'No news is good news though, isn't it?'

'I guess so, but it's just a gut feeling. He didn't say anything to you last night when he called by, did he?'

'No... but he has sent me a bunch of flowers this morning.'

'What?'

'Daniel Sully has sent me a bunch of flowers with a card saying he's sorry if he made me feel awkward last night,' I replied. 'He didn't have to do that. I think he'd only be worried if he thought he was going to have to see me again. What I mean is, if he was going to be working with you and might see me at some point.'

There was a silence while Matt considered this, before speaking. 'So, what – you think it's like a sorry to me as much as you? He thinks if you're upset, then I'll be upset and that might mean I won't want to work with him.'

'Maybe.' Matt was coming at this from a slightly different angle than me, but I didn't want to split hairs.

'God, I dread to think what you said or did last night to make him send flowers as an apology,' said Matt. 'But I guess this could be good news.'

'He wrote his phone number on the back of the card. I thought I might text him to say thank you.'

'Good idea. You can also say something like, "oh, you didn't make me feel uncomfortable at all",' said Matt.

'Although he did,' I said.

'But you don't have to tell him that. Just butter him up a bit for me, will you?' When I didn't respond, he continued. 'I'm not asking you to fucking sleep with him. This isn't a rerun of *Indecent Proposal*. I'm asking you to put his mind at rest, that's all.'

'Glad to hear it,' I said, aware I sounded prickly. 'I'll message him, but only because I know this job is important to you. I don't care if I never see him again. In fact, if you do get his backing, you can make sure we don't have to socialise with him as a couple or anything like that.'

'Jesus, Laurel. Don't go getting it all out of proportion again. Just text him. Look, I've got to go. Love ya.' He cut the call.

I let out an irritated breath and once again reminded myself this was for the greater good, before I composed a brief reply to Daniel.

> Hi, it's Laurel Jordan, thank you for the flowers. They are lovely.

My finger hovered over the arrow icon to send the message as I considered whether to add Matt's suggestion. In the end I kept it simple, adding, *You didn't have to, but much appreciated.*

Best wishes, Laurel. I sent it and hoped Matt wouldn't want to see the text I'd sent. No doubt he'd say that wasn't enough of an apology on my part.

I'd barely put the phone down when it rang. I'd saved Daniel's number so could see straight away it was him calling me.

'Hello?' I said as I accepted the call. There wasn't any point pretending I was nowhere near my phone when I'd literally just sent a text message.

'Hi, Laurel, it's Daniel Sully.'

'Hi, Daniel. You OK? I messaged just now to say thank you for the flowers.'

'I know. That's why I'm phoning.' There was that softness in his voice that had crept in yesterday evening.

'I am sorry if I upset you last night and thank you for being so gracious in accepting my apology.' He cleared his throat. 'But there is another reason I'm calling. A business reason.'

I can't deny I was relieved to hear that but was confused. Shouldn't he be calling Matt? 'Yes, what's that?' I asked, trying to sound casual.

'I've got a property I need fitting out,' he said. 'I wondered if you would be interested in taking on the interior design side of things. I'm useless at that and the designer I usually work with has gone on maternity leave rather unexpectedly. Unexpectedly to me, that is.' He gave a small laugh. 'I'm pretty sure she knew about it beforehand.'

I couldn't help smiling. 'Women tend to know these things first,' I said.

There was a small silence, and I knew he was smiling down the phone; when he spoke, I heard it in his voice. 'So, would you be interested in the job?'

'Erm, I'd have to look at it first,' I said, stalling while the cogs whirled in my head. It was going to be a bit awkward working for Daniel if he turned Matt's proposal down. I wasn't sure how Matt would feel about that.

'Look, if you're worrying about Matt, then please don't,' he said, as if reading my mind. 'I shouldn't really be telling you this, but it's looking highly likely I'll be investing in Matt's business. I just have to run a few more checks.'

'Oh, wow, that's amazing. He'll be delighted.'

'So, from my point of view, if you're both happy working with me, then I don't have a problem with it at all. Wouldn't want to cause any division between you and your husband.'

I wasn't quite sure whether his decision to go into partnership with Matt depended on me saying yes. Was it a bit conceited of me to think that? I didn't want to be accused of standing in Matt's way and, of course, we needed the financial security of a backer. Plus, I was sure this refurb with Daniel would be bigger than any of my other clients so far. The kudos of having him listed as one of my clients would give me a boost. The more I thought about it, the more attractive the offer sounded. What could possibly go wrong?

'Yes then, thank you, I'd very much like to work with you,' I said.

'Great. I'll get my assistant to fix up a date we can get together and go through it all,' he said, sounding genuinely pleased.

'I'll look forward to that,' I replied.

'Me too.' And there was that soft caressing voice of his again. 'As I said, I'll be in touch with Matt soon, so don't say anything yet. It's our secret for now.'

'No, of course not.' I wasn't entirely comfortable with keeping secrets from Matt but I didn't want to jeopardise this opportunity for either of us.

'Promise?' Daniel's voice was soft and somehow persuasive, as if sensing my dilemma.

'Promise,' I repeated.

'Good.' There was a pause as if he was savouring my compliance.

I felt the need to fill the silence. 'I'll wait to hear from you, then.'

'See you again soon, Laurel,' he replied, lingering over my name.

'Yes. Sure. Bye.' I ended the call and I stared at my phone for several seconds, feeling like I'd just been ambushed and had entered into some sort of conspiratorial pact with Daniel Sully.

TEN

Hannah

Annabelle and I strolled back along the beach. It was mid-afternoon and I had stayed longer than I'd planned but being in Annabelle's company was easy and a glass of wine in the afternoon had certainly felt decadent. I would even go as far as saying I felt relaxed around her. Maybe the wine had something to do with that. Conversation came easily and, equally, the silences were comfortable.

As we neared the end of the beach where my house was, I spotted Bryan and Sandra Chamberton in their garden, talking to Elizabeth.

'Oh, God, hide me,' I said. 'I don't think I can face talking to Elizabeth right now. It will be about all the vandalism from earlier.'

'I'm glad you said that,' replied Annabelle, lowering her voice and slipping her arm through mine. 'If I'm honest, they all get on my nerves. So bloody nosy. They love a good gossip.'

We picked up our pace and purposefully looked out to sea.

'I think Elizabeth means well, but she clearly hasn't got

anything better to do with her time,' I said. 'She's probably talking neighbourhood watch and late-night patrol strategies with Bryan. I hope Jasper doesn't get roped into anything.'

'Late-night patrols?' asked Annabelle. 'I haven't had time to catch up on the Residents' Gossip Group— I mean, Facebook Group.'

'Some sort of vigilante idea Elizabeth's got,' I explained.

Annabelle gave an eye roll. 'She loves all that organising shit. I once put the wrong colour bin out. Within ten minutes she was banging on my door with the offending bin and a handout stating what day was recycling and what day was household.'

'You mean you hadn't checked in the residents' handbook?' I said, side-eyeing her. She grinned back at me and I had a genuine feeling of friendship.

As we walked by the trio, Bryan raised a hand in acknowledgement and Sandra smiled but carried on talking. Elizabeth, however, gave us both a rather frosty look. I smiled back but noticed Annabelle dipped her gaze, breaking eye contact. She was clearly not quite as indifferent to Elizabeth as I thought. It was amazing how Elizabeth could make someone feel guilty, just by looking at them, even if they hadn't done anything wrong.

'Thanks so much for today,' said Annabelle as we reached the steps to my garden.

'No, thank you. It was good to have company,' I replied. I hesitated a moment before adding, 'You do know you can talk to me any time you want to.'

'You're so kind.' Annabelle gave me a hug. 'And likewise, you can always talk to me.'

I felt like there was more to say, but we were both silent. 'I'd better shoot off,' I said, jogging up the concrete steps, then pausing at the top. 'Mind you don't get caught.'

Annabelle looked a little startled but then broke into a smile as I nodded towards the Chambertons and Elizabeth by way of explanation. 'Wish me luck!' she said, and then she was off, heading back along the beach towards her apartment.

I went inside and I could hear Jasper on his Zoom call to work. It didn't sound like they would be wrapping up any time soon, so after making sure Luna had some fresh water, I made myself a cup of tea and took it outside to drink on the terrace. It wasn't until I reached into my pocket for my phone that I realised I didn't have it on me.

A surge of panic welled up. I never left my phone anywhere. I was usually religious about making sure it was always with me. I must have been so distracted, chatting with Annabelle, I hadn't given it a second thought. It was so unlike me. I hated not having my phone. The thought that the school wouldn't be able to get hold of me in an emergency was my number one concern. Irrational, I know. The school would, of course, call Jasper if I didn't pick up, but it was that feeling of having no control over a possible situation.

I was trying to think whether I'd had it with me when I was walking back, but I honestly couldn't remember. Had I taken it out of my pocket at Annabelle's? I closed my eyes, trying to retrace my steps and actions in my head. Yes. I'd taken a picture of Luna sprawled flat out on Annabelle's cream rug and we'd laughed about the dog making herself at home. I must have left my phone on the sofa or something.

I made sure Luna was settled inside and after closing the door so she wouldn't follow me, I jogged along the grass at the top of the beach and then down the path that ran alongside Annabelle's apartment. Despite spending time with her earlier, it felt over-familiar to go in through the back garden.

From the road, Annabelle's apartment building looked like a pair of semi-detached Georgian-fronted houses with bow windows and two front doors, but those doors both led to the first-floor flats. Access to the ground-floor flats was via a door at the side.

As I reached the path, I saw Bryan Chamberton coming out of Annabelle's apartment. I realised I hadn't seen him or the others on my way back here. He was on his own and I assumed he'd been to talk to Annabelle about the neighbourhood watch initiative. There was something about his demeanour that felt off, though. He looked back at the door and smoothed down his hair with one hand, stuffing his phone into his pocket with the other. As I jogged down the footpath, he hurried along in my direction, his head down, looking at the ground. He hadn't seen me, and I slowed my pace to a walk, moving to one side so he could pass. He still didn't look up and I don't think he even realised I was there until his shoulder brushed mine.

'Ugh. Err. Hannah. Sorry, didn't see you there.'

'Don't worry,' I replied.

We stood there for a second and I thought he was going to say something. He looked up and down the pathway, swallowed hard and then offered a smile which missed the reassuring mark. 'I... err,' he stopped.

'Is everything all right?' I asked, watching his expression slip into a frown.

He rubbed his chin with his hand. 'I saw you with Annabelle earlier,' he said at last, gesturing with a nod of his head towards her apartment.

'Yeah. I'm on my way back there actually. Forgot my phone.'

'Look, just between us, be careful around her, won't you?'

It was my turn to frown. 'What do you mean?'

'I don't trust her. And given your... circumstances, maybe you should be wary. I went to see her—'

Before he could finish, we were interrupted. 'Bryan!'

We both looked up and saw Elizabeth at the other end of the footpath. She must have headed home along the road rather than the beach. 'I can't talk now,' said Bryan, raising a hand in acknowledgement to Elizabeth. 'But I do need to speak to you.' He patted my upper arm. 'Mind how you go.'

Elizabeth was upon us now. 'Hello, Hannah,' she said, and then to Bryan: 'I almost forgot to mention it, but Carol Bradley wanted you to have a look at her CCTV. She thinks someone was prowling around outside her house the other night.'

Elizabeth hooked Bryan's elbow and was walking him out onto the estate as she spoke.

It would normally have made me laugh, but I was preoccupied by his rather guarded message. As I approached Annabelle's door, I couldn't think why he'd warned me off her. To be honest, it made me feel a little disappointed. I thought I'd found a friend and yet Bryan seemed to think it was a bad idea. Did he just mean having a close friend was a bad idea or was it Annabelle in particular?

I pressed the intercom and waited for Annabelle to answer. I knew she'd be able to see me from the monitor's screen in the hallway. A few moments later she opened the door.

'Hannah? You OK?'

'I think I left my phone here. You haven't seen it have you?'

'No. Sorry.' She was looking downward, her gaze not meeting mine.

'Can I come in and look? I had it when I was sitting on the sofa.'

'Sure.' She opened the door wide and stepped aside, allowing me in.

I found it straight away. It had slipped down the side of the cushion. 'Got it.' A wave of relief washed over me.

'Good,' replied Annabelle.

'I didn't realise until I got home. We were too busy chatting,' I said. It was only as I looked up at her, I realised she was still not meeting my gaze. Over the years I had become good at reading body language and Annabelle might as well have held a neon sign over her head that something was up. I went over to her, and she moved her head away, shielding one side of her face. 'Annabelle,' I said gently. Very slowly she turned to look at me. I let out a small gasp as I saw her bloodied lip and a red mark to her cheekbone. 'Your face. What happened?'

'Oh, I'm so clumsy,' said Annabelle. 'I tripped on the rug and went flying. Caught my face on the coffee table as I went down.' She put a finger to her lip and winced. 'It looks worse than it is. Honest.'

I studied her for a moment, trying to weed the truth from the lies. Because I could tell something wasn't adding up here. I thought of Bryan and his demeanour as he'd left Annabelle's house, when he didn't know I was there. Then his word of warning. And now Annabelle's injuries.

'I saw Bryan Chamberton on my way here,' I said carefully. 'He said he'd been to see you.'

She looked flustered for a moment but covered it up with a smile. 'Oh, yes. We were right, he wanted to speak to me about the vandalism. I told him I hadn't seen or heard a thing. Not much help to his investigations, I'm afraid.' She gave a self-deprecating laugh.

I didn't buy it. 'Did you trip over before or after Bryan called by?' I asked.

'Just as you left,' she said. 'Look, please don't worry. I'm fine.'

'He looked flustered when he came out of yours.' I paused, letting the silence stretch out, hoping that Annabelle would open up.

She shrugged. 'Probably frustrated I couldn't help.'

'Are you sure?'

'Hannah, please.' Her tone held a note of irritation. 'I promise you, I'm fine. If there was anything sinister to tell you, then I would. I mean, we're friends, aren't we?'

'Sorry. I'm overreacting,' I said. I adjusted my mental

stance. Of course, Bryan wouldn't do anything violent to Annabelle. He wasn't that sort of man. I'd spent enough time in his company to know that.

'You didn't answer my question,' said Annabelle.

'What?'

'We're friends, aren't we?'

Annabelle looked almost shy as she posed the question. And I probably looked uncomfortable, but I pushed Bryan's warning from my mind. 'Yes, of course we are.'

She beamed back at me. 'Excellent.'

My phoned buzzed with a message. 'It's Jasper,' I said, reading the text. 'He's just checking I'm all right. Wondering where I've gone.' I tapped a quick reply that I'd be back in five minutes. 'I'd better get off.'

'He really loves you,' said Annabelle. 'You're lucky.'

'I know,' I said, not wishing to sound smug. 'And you'll be lucky too, now you're away from your ex.'

'I hope so.'

As I made my way home, I tried to make sense of what had gone on between Bryan and Annabelle. I was certain something had, but Annabelle wasn't going to tell me. For now, I'd have to wait until I was able to speak to Bryan and find out what he'd meant about being wary.

ELEVEN

Hannah

'Ah, there you are,' said Jasper as I returned to the house. 'I thought I heard you come back just now.'

'Yes, sorry. I suddenly remembered I'd left my phone at Annabelle's,' I said, waving it in the air. 'Had to run back to get it.'

'Is that where you've been? You've been gone a long time.'

Jasper didn't keep tabs on me, and I knew he was asking probably out of curiosity as much as anything else. Sitting around with someone, chatting and having a drink, was definitely out of character for me.

'Yes. I bumped into Annabelle and she invited me back to hers for a cheeky glass of wine,' I said, wondering how much I should confide in Jasper. What Annabelle had told me was private and personal; I wasn't sure she'd want me sharing it with anyone, even if it was Jasper.

'Is she OK after yesterday?' he asked.

'She said she was fine but she seemed a little down. We had a nice chat though and she was much happier when I left.'

'That's good.' Jasper came to stand in front of me. 'And what about you? Are you OK?'

I nodded. 'I'll be fine.'

'Sure?'

'Positive.'

Jasper put his arm around me and kissed the top of my head. 'You don't have to be brave all the time.'

'I know.' I looked up at him, feeling that overwhelming sense of love I had for this man. I made a point of looking at my watch. 'You know we have some time to kill before we have to pick Pia up from school.'

He raised his eyebrows. 'Do you have something in mind?'

'I do, as it happens.'

Making love with Jasper always made things right and today it was as if he had a sixth sense and knew I needed him. Having him hold me, caress me, kiss me, want me, made me feel treasured and reminded me that I had a life worth living. Someone who cared about me and would protect me all the time the sun rose, and the sun set. Every single day, he'd be there for me.

Afterwards, I lay in his arms, the sun shining in through the window, and all I could hear was the gentle hum of the radio from the kitchen against the backdrop of the waves, softly lapping at the beach and the faraway squawk of a seagull.

It sounded like paradise, and on the surface, it was. I let the after feeling of our lovemaking wash over me like the outgoing tide and allowed myself the luxury of wondering what the day would have been like in a *Sliding Doors* episode of my life, where I still had my son with me. Where I would bake a cake and proudly present it to him while everyone sang 'Happy Birthday'. He'd make out he was embarrassed by the fuss, but really, he'd love it and later, before he went to bed, he'd thank me for making his special day, well, special.

An errant tear unexpectedly pinged from my eye and trickled onto Jasper's chest. I felt his body tense and then he squeezed me a little tighter, holding me closer. 'You OK?' he asked.

I nodded. Swallowed the ball of emotion in my throat before managing to produce a fairly normal-sounding response. 'I'm fine.'

Jasper rolled over, moving me onto my back as he did so. He swept the hair from my face and studied me with his slate-blue eyes. His features were soft but there was a troubled look to him. 'I wish I knew what was going on in your head sometimes,' he said without reproach. He touched the tip of my nose with his finger. 'I might be able to fix whatever demon it is that won't leave you alone.'

I gulped and closed my eyes. Sometimes I longed to tell him the whole sorry truth, but I couldn't. If I did, then things would never be the same. I had come too far with my lie to backtrack now. How would he understand? He'd be horrified. And rightly so.

I opened my eyes and smiled at him, holding the palm of my hand against his face. 'It's nothing to worry about. Annabelle told me some stuff about her ex-husband. She had it bad.'

I wasn't sure if Jasper believed me, but he didn't challenge my explanation.

Over the years, every so often, he would probe into what was on my mind and I always managed to deflect the question or explain my mood away as something else. I hated not being able to tell him the truth, but I couldn't risk it. I couldn't risk losing him. I'd lost my life once before. I wasn't going to let it happen again.

'OK, just take your time getting to know her,' he said. 'I mean, I'm glad you've made a friend as I know it's not always easy for you, but take it steady, won't you.'

I gave a laugh. 'You make me sound like a basket case.'

'Never.' Jasper looked at me for a long moment, before rolling back off me and getting up. 'We should get going. Don't want to be late picking up Pia.' He winked as he gathered his discarded clothes.

Pia was delighted to see us and spent the whole journey back home telling us about what a great time she'd had and how many new friends she'd made.

'I played with Lucy and Olivia,' said Pia. 'Lucy is going to ask her mum if I can go to tea.' She carried on telling us about the rest of her day and what she'd had to eat.

I exchanged a smile with Jasper. Pia was a friendly child and, much like her father, made friends easily. I would have to try to be one of those mums in the playground who also made friends easily. Laurel would have. Hannah not so much.

We got back home and as I prepared the evening meal, Jasper logged on to Facebook. 'I had a call from Elizabeth today, to tell me about the Silverbanks Facebook Group. She noted I hadn't joined it yet.'

'Make sure you do; you'll never hear the end of it otherwise.'

'I sent a request to join earlier and ticked all the boxes about abiding by the group rules.'

'I bet there were a few of those,' I said, taking the pizzas from the freezer. It was Pia's favourite food and a nice treat for her at the end of the week.

'Right, I've been accepted,' said Jasper, looking at his phone. 'I'm in the inner sanctum of the Residents' Association Facebook Group.'

'Pia, why don't you go and get changed out of your school uniform?' I said before she got too settled in front of the TV. 'You can bring your school reading book down as well. I'd like to see what you've got.'

'OK,' replied Pia, giving Luna a hug on the way as she headed upstairs to her bedroom.

'Thought it would be best if she didn't hear anything about vandalism around the estate,' I said. 'I don't want to worry her.'

'Sure. So, it seems several men on the estate have volunteered to do a few patrols in the evenings over the next few weeks.'

'Vigilantes.' I rolled my eyes.

'Silverbanks Guardians, apparently,' said Jasper.

'You're joking? Is that what they are calling themselves?'

'Not all heroes wear capes, according to Jill Highland.' Jasper looked at me in amusement.

'I didn't think real people actually said that. I thought it was a quote.'

'Apparently not,' said Jasper. 'One of the good guys. One for all and all for one. I'm quoting, just so you know. Hero at home.'

'Please stop. I think I'm going to be sick.'

'I'll spare you the rest. Someone has suggested a WhatsApp group, but Derek Tompkins doesn't have WhatsApp. He wants in-person briefings and debriefings for confidentiality purposes.'

'No. I'm not listening to any more,' I said, waving the spatula in my hand towards Jasper.

'I'll be staying well out of it,' said Jasper, closing the app and leaving his phone on the side. 'Detective Chamberton will have to look elsewhere for new recruits to fight the OCG operating in the area.'

We both laughed at the organised crime gang reference but only one of us was being genuine.

Later that evening as I was settling Pia for bed, I glanced out of her bedroom window which overlooked the front of the property. It was eight thirty, and the sun was setting.

I was about to draw the curtains when I saw a figure coming out of the house across the road. A male who we hadn't met yet but who I thought Elizabeth said was Derek Tompkins. He gave a wave to someone on the other side of the road. I looked down to see Bryan coming out of his driveway. They must be the Silverbanks Guardians for the night. They exchanged a few words and then both set off in different directions, Bryan with his hand-held flashlight and Derek with a head torch on.

I drew the curtains and pulled the duvet up over Pia's shoulders. She was already asleep, bless her. It had been a busy week for her, adjusting to her new home and new school. She did seem to have settled in really well, for which I was grateful.

I closed the door gently behind me and went down to the kitchen where Jasper was waiting. He handed me a glass of wine.

'I think you deserve this,' he said. 'It's been a full-on week. Well done.'

'You deserve it too,' I said, giving him a kiss.

My phone pinged through a text alert which had us both looking in surprise at the device. I didn't get text messages often because I didn't really have many friends. Even in London, where we'd lived for eleven years, I had very few friends, which was mostly by design rather than desire.

I picked up the phone and read the text message.

> Meet me at the lifeguard tower at nine o'clock.
> It's important. Bryan.

TWELVE

Hannah

I reread the message to make sure I hadn't been mistaken. Why on earth did Bryan want to meet me at that time of night? I'd just seen him go out on patrol. In my mind, I air-quoted the word patrol.

'Who's that?' asked Jasper, putting on some music. It was 'Brown Eyed Girl' by Van Morrison. He turned and smiled at me, holding out his hand. It had been playing the day we had met and had instantly become our song.

I took his hand, and he pulled me into his arms, swaying from side to side. I smiled and moved from one foot to the other, hoping he'd be distracted from asking me about the text message again. He put his lips to my ear. 'Who messaged you?'

Jasper had never been a jealous man, so I was a little startled by the doubling down on the question. 'It was Annabelle,' I said. 'Saying thank you for listening to her today.' I hated myself for lying. I had only lied about my life before I met Jasper. I'd never lied to him about anything else.

The song came to an end, and we sat out on the terrace on two of the chairs that had been spared the slashing.

The music played in the background and Jasper looked happy. I wished I could have said the same about myself. I was on edge after that text message. I couldn't think what Bryan needed to tell me so urgently that couldn't wait for the morning. Had I been compromised?

Nerves rattled around inside me like a tin of nails being shaken. I checked my watch. It was five minutes to nine. There was no way I could meet Bryan. Whatever it was would have to wait until the morning.

Jasper's phone rang. He looked at the screen and frowned. Then swore. 'I'm so sorry, sweetheart. It's my client in New York. I told him to ring me. I totally forgot.'

'You should take it then,' I said.

Jasper looked apologetic. 'I'm sorry.'

'Honestly, don't worry.' I could barely contain my enthusiasm. If he didn't answer it, then I would. 'I'll take Luna for a quick run on the beach.'

'It's late.'

'I'll only be five minutes. It's not properly dark yet.' I nodded at the still ringing phone. 'Answer it.' Then I got to my feet and, as he accepted the call, I dropped a kiss on his forehead. Jasper squeezed my hand and then got up to take the call indoors.

'Don't be long,' he mouthed to me.

I gave a mock salute and then called Luna, who must have thought it was her lucky day, going out at this time of an evening. I grabbed my hoodie from the back of the chair and headed down the garden and over the wall, onto the beach.

I could see the outline of the lifeguard tower a little way ahead and beyond that in the distance Silverbanks lighthouse. It was black against the backdrop of a pale orange sky as the last rays of sun glowed dimly from the horizon.

As I approached the tower, I couldn't see Bryan. There was no one about. It was nine o'clock exactly. I peered into the now murky light to try to see if Bryan was making his way along the beach. I had a real sense of being alone, despite the reassuring lights of the properties that ran along the top of the beach. The way the beach dipped down, I doubted I could be seen by anyone up there.

When I'd seen Bryan out of the window thirty minutes ago, he was heading down First Avenue. If he wanted to meet on the beach, I assumed he'd either come from his garden or the footpath near Annabelle's apartment. Luna was sniffing all about and trotting back to me every so often. When I next looked around, she was further down the beach, heading towards the water. A wet dog was the last thing I needed.

'Luna! Here! Come here!' If she heard me, she had decided to ignore me. I really needed to get one of those long leads for her so she couldn't run off. Recall was not her strong point. 'Luna!' Nope, she was definitely ignoring me. I jogged after her. She was at the water's edge now.

She gave a bark. Followed by another one and then several more together. Her head dipping as she sniffed at something she'd found on the beach.

As I neared I could make out a dark shape at the water's edge, alongside the heavy wooden breakwater. A big bulky shape. A dolphin? Did they get dolphins around here?

I put the torch light on my phone and shone it over the dark bulk on the sand.

It took a moment to register exactly what I was seeing.

When I did, I let out a scream and leapt away, almost dropping my phone in the process.

'Fuck!'

My heart was pounding, and my breathing was heavy and rapid as if I'd completed the 100 metre Olympic final.

I took a deep breath. Collected myself and then cautiously stepped closer to what was without a shadow of a doubt a body.

A man, lying face down in the water. The back of his head was blood-soaked.

I angled my torch light on the face, which was partially submerged. Despite not being able to see clearly, I was certain it was Bryan Chamberton, and he was undoubtedly dead.

I had seen a dead person before. This wasn't a new scenario for me, unfortunately, and I had to push thoughts of that incident to the back of my mind. I could feel the panic rising.

Adrenaline was shooting through my veins, sending a rush of tingles to my fingertips.

What should I do now?

Run?

Phone the police?

Get help?

'Shit,' I said out loud as I thought of Sandra. Someone was going to have to tell her Bryan was dead. What if she came out here looking for him because he hadn't got back from his stupid vigilante patrol? Thoughts crashed around in my head, conflicting, confusing, and overwhelming.

I turned and looked up at the beach. There was no one there.

I seriously considered going back home and pretending I'd never seen Bryan. Who would know I had been out here? Then I remembered the text message. I swore again, out loud. Luna had at some point stopped barking and was now off on another scent. All interest in the body lost.

'Stop and think,' I said out loud to myself. 'The text message.' I took deep steadying breaths. The police would find his phone and look at the text message. They'd be able to trace it to me. I'd be the prime suspect. My past would all come out. I had visions of being questioned in front of Jasper and the police officers saying I was Laurel and telling Jasper what I'd done.

I shook my head. No. I couldn't let that happen. No. No. No.

I rubbed my face with my hands. His phone. I should take his phone.

I dropped to my knees. 'I'm sorry, Bryan,' I said as I patted his jacket pockets. I could feel a phone in the zip pocket of his blue waterproof. Pulling the cuff of my cardigan over my hand, I reached into the pocket and was surprised to find not one, but two phones. Wait, this didn't make sense.

And then it dawned on me. He must have some sort of burner phone. Which one had he called me on? I called up his message on my phone and then pressed call back. I watched the smaller black phone light up. The word Camelot appeared on the screen.

Camelot. Operation Camelot. It was the name of the police operation I had been involved in.

I pushed the phone, along with my own, back into my pocket, before replacing the iPhone and zipping the pocket back up.

I was conscious of how much time I was spending unaccounted for. When he was found, the police would ask who had been where. Jasper would say I was out walking the dog. I had no alibi. I needed to get home. I hated the thought of leaving Bryan there, all alone in the water but I couldn't risk staying.

I went to walk back and then realised my footprints and those of Luna's were clearly marked in the sand. The tide was on the way out, so they wouldn't be washed away.

But if mine were there, where were Bryan's? It didn't make sense. Unless he had walked along paddling in the water. He must have come onto the beach at some point. There would be footprints, surely?

Before I had time to think, my phone began to ring. It was Jasper. And then at the top of the sand, a dark figure appeared.

They had a flashlight, and the beam was sweeping back and forth along the beach.

For a moment I wondered if it was the person who had caused all the vandalism the night before. But then they called out.

'Bryan!'

Before I had time to decide what I was going to do, Luna was barking and shot off up the beach towards the voice.

My phone was ringing still. And then the beam of the flashlight landed on me, lighting me up like I was on the stage.

'Help!' I shouted. 'Help me, please?' I shielded my eyes from the light and started running up the beach towards the man, who, as I got closer, I was sure was Derek from across the road.

I jabbed at the phone. 'Hannah? You OK?' Jasper sounded worried. 'I was just debating whether to leave Pia to come and look for you.'

'Something's happened,' I said. 'Not to me. I'm fine. I...' I was at the top of the beach now, panting, trying to get my breath with Derek standing in front of me. 'I've found Bryan on the beach. I think he's dead.'

Both Jasper and Derek gasped in unison.

'I'm coming down to you. Where are you?' said Jasper.

'No. Don't leave Pia. Please don't leave her,' I begged. 'I'm with...' I looked at the man.

'Derek. Number eight.'

'I'm with Derek. He's going down the beach now to where Bryan is.'

'I don't care. I'm coming down,' said Jasper.

'NO!' I shouted. 'Do not come down. Do not leave Pia.'

'OK. Shit. I'll ring the police. I want you back here though, Hannah. I don't want you down there on your own.'

Less than a minute later Derek came running back up the beach. 'I think he's dead.'

'Jasper's called the police,' I said. 'I don't know what to do.'

'You'll have to wait for them to come. You're the one who found him.'

'What about his wife, Sandra?'

'We can't tell her yet. We need to wait for the police.'

I wasn't sure Derek would let me leave, even if I had tried. I had a sudden and overwhelming feeling of tiredness as shock took over me.

I slumped to the ground, pulling my legs up and wrapping my arms around my knees. I was shaking uncontrollably. Not from fear of what had happened but fear of what was about to happen. My carefully constructed world was about to be blown apart and there was nothing I could do about it.

THIRTEEN

Laurel

'YES!' Matt shouted, jumping up from the sofa and punching the air in delight. 'YES! Yes! Yes!'

I nearly spilt my tea and Declan gave a cry of alarm at his father's sudden excitement. 'It's OK, Declan,' I said, lifting him up onto my lap. 'Shhh. Don't cry.'

'I've got it!' cried Matt, oblivious to Declan's tears.

'Don't shout,' I said. 'You're scaring him.'

'Oh. Shit.' He came over and bent down. 'Sorry, mate. Didn't mean to scare you. Your old dad's had some good news.' He looked at me, grinning from ear to ear.

I didn't need to ask. I could guess. It could only be one thing. 'Daniel Sully said yes?' I said, already smiling at the good news.

'Abso-bloody-lutely, he said yes.' Matt cupped my face in his hands and kissed me. 'It's all happening, babe. Can't wait to see the look on the bank manager's face when he sees my account balance next week.'

'Congratulations. That's brilliant. Well done.' I was

delighted for Matt and relieved for us. We were pinning every-thing on Daniel's financial backing, or at least that's how it felt, especially as I'd all but agreed to undertake some work for him. His assistant had phoned me the next day and a meeting was fixed for tomorrow. 'So do you have to formally accept it now or do you have a meeting with him?'

Matt looked at the email again. 'I formally accept now, and we set up a meeting in the next week to sign contracts.'

'Are you going to get anyone to look it over first?' I asked, picking up a teddy and dancing it on Declan's knee. His tears had subsided, and he was smiling now.

'I guess,' Matt said, although he didn't sound very convinced.

'You should. Just to be on the safe side.'

'Yeah. Sully's not dodgy or anything,' said Matt, putting his phone away and taking Declan from my lap. 'Daddy's not that stupid, is he?'

I hated when adults spoke to kids to relay a message to another adult. 'I know, but...'

'Yeah. But you can't be too careful. Don't be worrying now, Laurel. We should be celebrating. How about we open a bottle of fizz tonight?'

'Why don't we wait until tomorrow night after I've had my meeting with Daniel and then hopefully we can have a double celebration?'

'Oh yeah, I forgot you were seeing him.' He put Declan down, who toddled off to the toy box under the window. 'Look, if Sully doesn't want you to do the refurb, don't take it to heart. Once I've said yes, he might not feel he has to be so charitable.'

It took a moment for me to realise what Matt was implying. 'I'm not a charity case,' I said. 'He actually wants me to do some work for him, regardless of what your arrangement with him is. We're separate things.'

'Yeah, I know. I was only saying, the refurb might have been a sweetener for me to accept his offer.' He headed for the door. 'Anyway, don't feel you have to take it. We're going to be all right for money now.'

His phone rang and he answered it before I had time to say anything. I spent the rest of the day trying not to let Matt's dismissal of my work get to me. I also didn't want to spoil the day for Matt by getting into an argument. He was thrilled about the backing, and I didn't want my anger at how little he valued my abilities to sound like sour grapes. Despite that, it somewhat tarnished my excitement which then made me feel guilty for not being happy for him. When I went to bed that night, a little heady after drinking two glasses of champagne which Matt hadn't been able to resist opening after getting off the phone with Daniel.

The next morning I was grateful for the large glass of water I had remembered to drink before going to sleep. My meeting with Daniel was at eleven thirty, so I had time to make myself presentable and shake off any aftereffects from the late night and alcohol.

Years of rugby and the social life that went along with that meant Matt could handle his drink far better than I could. I was always surprised by how chirpy he was in the mornings after drinking, although that hadn't been for a while, since our finances had come under pressure. Maybe that's why after two glasses of fizz I was ready for my bed.

I arrived at the property Daniel wanted refurbished a few minutes before eleven o'clock, armed with my iPad. At this stage, actual sample fabrics, colours and accessories weren't necessary. It was more of a meeting to discuss themes and get an idea of space, use of space, the lighting, the outlook and the general vibe the client was looking for.

I hadn't seen Daniel since he'd turned up at my office that night so hoped there wouldn't be any awkwardness. Although there was a part of me that was disappointed. I tried to ignore that sensation, not wanting to examine it too closely. We'd spoken on the phone and emailed though, so I tried to convince myself that seeing him in person would be no big deal.

There were several steps up to the front door of the Georgian property and as I reached the top step, the door opened. Daniel smiled at me.

Despite my efforts to think in purely business terms, I couldn't deny how attractive he was. Every time I saw him, he seemed better looking than the last. I couldn't quite put my finger on what it was, but he had this aura of confidence that didn't come across as big-headed or conceited just... well, attractive. Everything about him was pretty damn sexy.

'Hi,' I said, breathlessly, when I absolutely shouldn't have been out of breath. I'd only climbed five steps for God's sake.

'Hey,' he said, giving the kind of smile you give to someone you know well, not someone you work with. 'Come on in.' He stepped back, opening the door wide.

It was an impressive entrance hall with many of the original features still in place. 'Wow. This looks good,' I said, eyeing the cornices, coving and ceiling rose.

'Most of it is original,' said Daniel following my gaze. 'Some of it has been restored but some parts I had to have reproduced.'

'You can't tell,' I said.

'No. I was really pleased with the result. Come on through to the lounge.'

I followed him across the black-and-white tiled hallway to the double doors on the left which opened into the reception room at the front of the property with the large bay window. Internal doors, which were open, led through to the dining room in the middle of the house.

'Love the light coming in through both windows,' I said. 'Quite often in older houses the back room can be a bit dark, but not here.'

'The light is great,' agreed Daniel. 'Can I get you a drink or anything?'

'No. I'm fine,' I said. I opened the case of my iPad, flicking it into life. 'What I like to do,' I began, 'is to take some pictures for my own reference and so I have a before and after to compare. Is that all right with you?'

'Of course,' he said.

'Before that, though, we can sit down and go through what it is you're looking for,' I said. 'What sort of thing do you like, or have in mind?' I looked up at him and I'm sure there was a twinkle in his eye. God, how on earth was I going to get through this meeting if everything I said could be taken as a double-entendre?

'Please, have a seat.' He indicated to one of the cream-coloured sofas. He took the one opposite me. 'I'm looking for understated elegance,' he said. 'Something classically beautiful that catches your breath and makes you look again and again.'

I was a little taken aback by his vision. It wasn't the usual sort of answer I got from clients, but then again, Daniel Sully wasn't my usual client. I called up some inspirational pictures on Pinterest and turned the iPad to show him. 'If we can look through some of these, it will help me get a clear idea of what you're looking for.'

Instead of taking the iPad, he came and sat next to me, leaning in a fraction as we scrolled through the different pictures. Daniel seemed oblivious to our close proximity, and I found myself once again wondering if it was all in my head. I was getting this all out of proportion and if Daniel had any idea what was going through my mind, he'd probably think I was quite mad.

I was pleased when Pinterest was no longer needed in terms of reference photos, and we were able to move from the sofa so I could take some photographs and measurements.

The alcoves on either side of the chimney breast were

shelved and held a vast selection of what looked like special editions and collector copies. One shelf was dedicated to Shakespeare. Their red leather-bound spines with gold embossing and lettering, lined up perfectly.

'I didn't have you down as a Shakespeare man,' I commented, noting another shelf of Shakespeare books but clearly different editions. 'I'm impressed.'

He stepped closer, so his mouth was just behind my ear. 'Good to know I can impress you,' he said softly.

'Do you have a favourite?' I asked, more for something to say than any real desire to know.

'*Romeo and Juliet*, of course,' he said.

'Ah, a tragedy,' I replied, lifting my iPad to take some photos.

'A love story,' he corrected.

'A tragic love story.' I looked at the images I'd captured, wishing he'd move away and yet not wanting him to.

Then he was all business again. 'I'll be in the kitchen making some calls,' he said, walking towards the door. 'Come through when you're done.'

I let out a small breath in relief as he went. There I was totally imagining things. He was being the perfect gentleman and I was allowing my imagination to run away with me. I did acknowledge that a little part of me was, well, I couldn't say disappointed – that was the wrong word – but maybe a little deflated. I was getting carried away thinking someone as good-looking and charming as Daniel Sully would be interested in me. For a start, he was older than me by a good few years, if my memory served me correctly from my Google search. He was forty-two years old – I was fifteen years his junior, married with a two-year-old. He no doubt had a string of sophisticated women on speed-dial. I was most definitely in a lower league. I caught sight of my reflection in the bay window. I still made an effort with my appearance, my hair, my make-up, and my clothes, but that was all on the outside. On the inside, I was shattered.

It was another hour before I'd finished making notes on the two rooms and went down the hallway to find Daniel.

I was amazed when I stepped into the kitchen area. It was huge. Daniel was standing at the glass doors which ran the width of the property, his back to me. He'd taken off his jacket and rolled up his sleeves. He had his phone to his ear, and I couldn't help hearing what he was saying.

'That's bullshit, Leo, and you know it.' There was a cutting hardness to his voice that I hadn't heard before. 'I didn't plough my money into that fucking twat's business to have him waste it on hospitality with what is essentially a couple of prostitutes... No. I'm not having him take the piss out of me... You need to deal with it. If I have to go around and speak to him myself, he'll be lucky to walk out of there afterwards.'

I came to a halt and went to turn around, hoping I could sneak out of the room before I was noticed.

My shoe betrayed me as it squeaked on the highly polished floor tile.

Daniel spun around.

'Sorry,' I said quietly.

He shook his head, moved the phone away from his mouth. 'It's OK, Laurel. Don't go.' He turned back to his phone. 'I'll speak to you later, Leo.'

'Sorry,' I said again as he pocketed his phone. 'I didn't realise you were taking a call.'

'No. Don't apologise. All sorted now.' He looked at his watch. 'Shit. Is that the time? It's nearly one. You must be starving. You've not eaten since you've been here.'

'Oh, I'm fine. Honest. I'm kind of done now. I was only coming to let you know. I should get off, really.'

'Really?' He looked at me with mock suspicion.

'Yes. I don't want to take up any more of your time.'

'You're not running away from me again, are you?' He began a slow walk towards me.

'Technically, I didn't run away last time,' I said, trying to make a joke, but my nerves were hammering away in my stomach. 'You left.'

He came to a stop at the end of the island counter. 'It was the gentlemanly thing to do,' he said. 'I didn't want to scare you then and I don't want to now. It could get expensive in flowers if I have to apologise every time we meet up.' He smiled and I felt myself relax.

I couldn't deal with his intense stare and that low sexy voice of his. Much as I hated to admit, it did things to my body that no man other than my husband should. 'Well, rest assured, you don't need to send me flowers tomorrow,' I said. 'You didn't need to the other day either, but they were lovely.'

He ran his finger and thumb along his lip as if in thought. 'I liked buying you flowers,' he said. 'I'd like to buy you some more, but under the current arrangements, that would mean I'd have to do something bad first.' He took several more slow and deliberate steps towards me. He was borderline in my personal space, but I didn't move away.

My breathing was deepening, and if he tried to kiss me, I didn't know if I would resist.

It was a sobering thought and one that snapped me out of the trancelike state I was in. 'We'd better make sure you don't do anything bad in that case,' I said. My nervous laugh rang out in the sterile kitchen.

'Define bad,' said Daniel.

I was rooted to the spot. My legs were totally blanking any message from my brain to move away from Daniel Sully. 'This,' I said.

His phone rang out. He didn't take his gaze from me as we stood there staring at each other, the intensity of the moment palpable. He took his phone from his pocket, his eyes still on me. 'Yes,' he said as he answered it. He listened for a few seconds before speaking again. 'I'll be there in twenty minutes.' He put his phone back in his pocket and let out a controlled breath. 'Sorry. Business. Got to go.'

'Sure,' I said, my voice coming out a croak. I tried again. 'I need to get back too.'

'Can I leave you with the key to lock up?' he said. 'Maybe we can meet up in a couple of days to go through your ideas?'

'Sure,' I said again.

He smiled. A warm and somehow intimate smile that left me feeling like we had experienced something personal together. And then he was striding out of the kitchen and down the hall.

I leaned back against the counter wondering what the hell had just happened between us. Daniel Sully was dangerous – in every way.

FOURTEEN

Hannah

'So, Mrs Gunderson,' began Detective Sergeant Owens.

'Ms Towers,' I corrected.

'Yes, sorry.'

'But Hannah will be fine.'

'Thank you.' Owens made a note in his pocketbook. 'As you stated last night to my colleague, you were taking your dog for a walk, and you came across Mr Chamberton in the water?'

It was the morning after I'd found Bryan and the two detectives from the local CID, having taken an initial statement from me last night, were back to ask some more questions. Jasper had already arranged for his parents to take Pia out for the morning so she wouldn't be about while the police were here.

'That's right. Luna, my dog, she found him. I was up on the top bank and Luna was down at the water's edge. She was barking. I went down to see what she was barking at and' – I gulped – 'that's when I saw Bryan.'

'And he was lying face down in the water?'

'Yes.'

'Did you check for a pulse?'

'Err, no. It wasn't necessary.' I closed my eyes as I pictured his blood-soaked head.

'Do you often go for a walk on your own on the beach at that time of night?' asked Owens' sidekick, who I think introduced herself as Barnes, or something like that.

'We've only just moved here,' said Jasper. 'I took a work call. My client is in New York. Hannah took the dog out.'

'Thank you, if you'd let Hannah answer,' said Barnes.

I knew Jasper would want to roll his eyes at the pedantic officer, but he was good at keeping his feelings to himself. I realised Barnes was looking at me to answer and I can't pretend it didn't annoy me. 'Exactly what Jasper told you,' I said, trying not to let my irritation show.

I hadn't wanted to volunteer any information to the police that might have them poking around in my old life. Or perhaps they already knew and were waiting to see if I was honest enough to admit to it. Had I told my partner? Did that mark me as someone who would murder another human being? I wasn't sure there was much basis for that, but still I was anxious and on edge. Any minute now, Barnes or Owens would pull out the trump card and ask me about Laurel.

'Is everything all right, Hannah?' asked Barnes. She looked pointedly at my hands. I followed her gaze. I was gripping onto the hem of my hoodie so hard that my knuckles were turning white.

I released the fabric. 'I'm fine. Just, well, you know, I found a dead body. Bryan – my neighbour. It's very upsetting.' I needed to stop talking. I was gabbling with nerves. This wasn't like me. Usually, I was able to keep it all together and had become an expert at shutting away my past. But this was all too close. One life was encroaching on the other and I had no control over it.

'Hannah's very upset by it all,' said Jasper. 'She's been over this several times now. Is there anything else you need to ask her?'

While I appreciated Jasper's concern and his innate urge to protect me, I didn't want him to go head-to-head with the police.

'Just a few more questions,' said Owens. 'I know this must be very stressful for you but, prior to you finding Mr Chamberton on the beach, when was the last time you saw him?'

'Err... I'm not sure.' I frowned as if trying to recall the last encounter with Bryan. It was, of course, yesterday afternoon when I'd gone back to Annabelle's for my phone, but she had been adamant she was all right. I don't think she'd appreciate me saying anything; after all, she had assured me she was fine, even though I didn't believe her, and she knew that. I needed to speak to her first.

'Ms Towers?' prompted Barnes. 'When was the last time you saw Mr Chamberton?'

This earned Barnes a reproachful look from Owens, but he didn't say anything, remaining professional.

'The last time I saw Bryan was yesterday. I saw him leaving to go out on patrol with Derek,' I said.

Owens scribbled a note in his pocketbook.

'Did you touch Bryan's body at all?' asked Barnes. 'We need to rule your DNA out, or in, depending on what we find.'

I wasn't sure I liked what she was implying but she looked at me with a practised innocence. I suspected she was trying to get under my skin to see if I would slip up, to monitor my body language, my responses both verbal and non-verbal. It made me wonder whether she really did know my background.

'I leaned over him,' I replied, thinking how I'd gone through his pockets and touched his phone. I'd used my cardigan to avoid fingerprints and hoped I'd been careful enough. 'I think I patted him.'

'Patted him?' queried Barnes.

'Yes, you know, to see if I could get a response from him,' I explained, using my hands to show what I mean. 'I shook him. Called his name. I... I touched his face to see if he was breathing.'

'And your dog?' asked Owens.

'I'm not sure. I can't be certain. I didn't see her, but she was down at the water's edge before me.'

'Do you know the cause of death?' asked Jasper.

'Does that matter to you?' asked Barnes. She certainly was trying to earn her stripes as she played bad cop.

'Naturally, we're concerned there might be a murderer about,' said Jasper with patience. 'If Bryan slipped and banged his head, then it's an accident. But as you may or may not know, there was a spate of vandalism on the estate the night before – which is why Bryan was out – and if he was murdered, then that has consequences for us residents.'

'We can't comment until we have the results of the autopsy,' said Barnes, pressing her lips together to underline the fact she wasn't going to give us any information.

Owens, however, had other ideas. 'At this stage,' he began, 'we are treating it as a suspicious death where a third party is likely to have been involved. We don't know the exact cause of death, as my colleague rightly said. But it's either the blow to the head or maybe drowning. I think it's safe to assume the blow came first.'

'Poor Bryan,' I said. 'He didn't deserve that.' I caught myself before I said any more. To all intents and purposes, Bryan was a stranger to me, Hannah. To Laurel, however, he was a good man who had looked after her. Helped her. And was still helping her even though he had no duty to.

'What makes you say that?' It was Barnes again.

'Because no one does,' I said. 'He seemed a nice man, from what little we knew of him.' I realised I was gripping the edge of my hoodie again. I made a conscious effort to relax. I was sure at any minute now Barnes was going to say something about my past, but it never came.

Owens cleared his throat and got to his feet. 'I think that's all we need for today,' he said. 'Maybe you could come down to the station to give an official statement in the next day or two. Here's my card. Give me a call and we'll sort out a convenient time.'

Jasper and I got to our feet and finally, with obvious reluctance, so did Barnes.

'Thank you, detective,' said Jasper, holding out his hand. 'I have to travel to London tomorrow and stay over a couple of days – for my work. I assume that's OK.'

'Of course,' said Owens, shaking hands with us both. Barnes gave a polite nod as she sidestepped us. 'If you think of anything else, no matter how irrelevant you deem it, please let us know.'

'Is there anything else, Ms Towers?' asked Barnes.

'Not that I can think of.' I smiled to cover my lie as I thought of seeing Bryan leave Annabelle's apartment.

Jasper showed them out and chatted for a few minutes longer with Owens on the doorstep. I waited in the kitchen but listened to what they were saying. I knew I was being a little paranoid, but I had visions of Owens whispering to Jasper that he knew who I was. However, Jasper was asking about Sandra next door and how she was.

'Thank God for that,' I said when the police finally left, and Jasper came into the kitchen where I was waiting.

'They're only doing their job,' said Jasper with a sigh. 'Owens said Sandra's daughter is with her. She's in shock, naturally.'

'The poor woman,' I said. 'I should go around and see her. I assume that's allowed, or will Barnes think that's suspicious?'

'Ignore Barnes. She's rather officious. I'll come with you.'

A young woman around our age answered the door to us. I could see straight away she was Bryan's daughter; she looked very much like him, despite her eyes being red and swollen from crying.

'Yes?' she said.

'Hi, we're Hannah and Jasper from next door,' I said. 'You must be Bryan and Sandra's daughter. The police said you were here.'

'Who is it?' came Sandra's voice from down the hallway.

'Your next-door neighbours,' called back the daughter.

Sandra appeared in the doorway. 'Oh, Hannah,' she said, stifling a sob. 'You poor thing. You found Bryan, didn't you? Come in. Come in, both of you.'

I gave Sandra a hug and she clung onto me tightly. 'I'm so sorry, Sandra,' I said, rubbing the older woman's back. 'So very sorry.'

'It's terrible, isn't it?' she said, before embracing Jasper. 'Please come and sit down. This is my daughter, Beverley.'

'You're the one who found my dad,' said Beverley.

'Yes. I did. I'm so sorry,' I replied, taking a seat next to Jasper on the sofa where Sandra had indicated.

Beverley looked at me with accusing eyes and I wished now we hadn't come around. 'Did you try to help him?'

'Sorry?' I looked from daughter to mother and back again.

'Did you try to help my dad?' Beverley spoke a little slower, as if she was trying to explain to a child or someone whose first language wasn't English.

I felt Jasper's hand on my leg. Reassuring. Supportive. He spoke before I did. 'There was nothing anyone could do for your father,' he said gently. 'We are very sorry for your loss.'

Beverley hadn't taken her eyes off me. 'But you're not a medical expert, are you?'

'No, I'm not.'

'So, you didn't know for certain that he was beyond help.' Beverley's voice was hard.

'Beverley,' said Sandra. 'Not now.'

It was obvious that they had spoken about my actions or lack thereof, and at least one of them thought I bore some responsibility for Bryan's death.

I tried a sympathetic smile. 'Your father had already passed away,' I said. 'His injuries were apparent.' I glanced at Sandra and could see she physically flinched at what I was saying.

'They think someone killed him,' said Beverley. 'Maybe someone with a grudge.'

'Beverley,' reprimanded Sandra again. 'They don't know that for certain.'

'It's pretty obvious. You don't need to be CID to work that one out,' snapped the younger woman.

'Have they any ideas who it might be?' I asked, trying to stop myself from bunching up my hands like I'd done when the police were interviewing me.

'The list is long,' said Beverley. 'He's been responsible for putting away organised crime gangs, murderers, drug dealers, rapists.'

'It's all speculation,' said Sandra, looking at Jasper and me. 'Sorry.'

Beverley let out a huff of impatience and got to her feet. 'I need some fresh air.' With that, she left the room, and I heard the rear door slide open and then close again.

'I'm sorry for my daughter,' said Sandra. 'She's in shock. We both are.'

'No need to apologise,' said Jasper. 'It's understandable.'

'She's convinced it's someone from Bryan's past. You know, a criminal he arrested or something fanciful like that,' said Sandra, taking a tissue from her sleeve and dabbing at her eyes.

'Do you think it could be?' I asked, as my stomach performed nervous somersaults.

'I don't know what to think. They've asked me to look through Bryan's things, his laptop, in case there's something there that can help them. They want the notebooks too, but I'm not sure where they are at the moment.'

'He kept a diary?' I asked. Sweat broke out under my arms at the thought he had documented our conversation and who I was. Surely, he wouldn't put that down in black and white.

'He kept records in his notebooks,' replied Sandra. 'Don't tell Elizabeth, but Bryan liked to monitor the estate. I told him it was silly, but he would always say not only did it relieve the boredom of being retired – he missed his life as a detective – but it might come in handy one day.' Sandra gave a sob. 'I don't think for one minute he thought it would be useful for his death.'

'And have the police got the notebooks?' I asked.

'Not yet. They took his laptop though,' said Sandra. 'They did ask me to have a look for the notebooks, although they sounded a bit sceptical. I think they were just humouring me. Anyway, Beverley and I haven't had time to look yet.'

There was a small silence as the conversation came to a natural end. I exchanged a look with Jasper, and he gave a slight nod.

'Look, I know people say it all the time, but if there's anything at all that Hannah and I can do to help, please let us know,' said Jasper.

'Yes, you must,' I said, as we got to our feet.

'Thank you both,' said Sandra. 'Beverley is here for a few days, but she has work and her family. She lives in London. She'll be back down again next week.'

'That's good, you're not on your own,' said Jasper.

We didn't see Beverley as we left, for which I was grateful. Even once we were indoors, I made sure the doors and windows were closed so she couldn't overhear us from her garden. 'Gosh, the daughter's a bit scary,' I said.

'I guess she's just trying to deal with an awful situation,' said Jasper.

'Yes. I can hardly believe it myself, so it must be even worse for Bryan's family.' I went over to Jasper and hugged him. 'I'll miss you when you go to London.'

He kissed the top of my head. 'I can cancel or try to rearrange it for a Zoom call.'

'No, don't do that. You need to be there. You said the other day, you needed a site visit.'

'I don't like the idea of leaving you and Pia alone with all this going on. Why don't you go and stay with my parents?'

It was a tempting idea but not practical. 'I don't want to take Pia out of school when she's only just started,' I said. 'I'll be fine.'

We spent the rest of the morning casually observing the comings and goings of the police and the forensic experts. Although I wasn't sure what they'd be able to find as evidence, since the tide was in now, completely covering the part of the beach where Bryan had died.

We went over to Jasper's parents in the evening and stayed the night and for most of Sunday. By the time we got home late afternoon, all evidence of police activity had gone. We gave Pia a very sanitised version of what had happened, just in case it was mentioned at school. I wasn't sure she really took it in, but I didn't want to frighten her.

Jasper had decided to delay leaving for London until first thing in the morning. 'I'd sooner not be away any more than I have to,' he explained. 'I'll drive up. That way I can go early and make the site visit.'

As ever, I appreciated his consideration. I knew after the site visit he had several meetings and then a presentation to give in the evening, followed by dinner at a restaurant. At least this way, he would only be gone for one night.

While Jasper rearranged his travel plans, I decided to take Luna for a walk before it got dark. I couldn't face walking past the spot where I'd found Bryan. Instead, I walked around

Silverbanks, tracking my way up and down the avenues until I was on the other side of the bank and heading down towards The Loop where I could walk back around to my house.

As I got to The Loop, I looked towards Annabelle's apartment. It was as if I had summoned her. She appeared at the window and waved at me, beckoning me over.

She came to the door. 'I was going to call you later,' she said. 'All that business with Bryan.'

Despite the nature of the conversation, I couldn't help a small feeling of warmth sweep over me at Annabelle's casual remark about calling me. It was the sort of conversation friends had with each other. I really felt like we were friends, and I hadn't felt like that in a long time. 'Did you hear that it was me who found him?'

'Elizabeth told me,' said Annabelle. 'Look, I need to talk to you but not here on the doorstep. Come in.'

Annabelle had an odd look on her face, as if it was something serious she needed to say.

FIFTEEN

Hannah

I followed on behind with Luna and sat on the sofa. There was a diary open on the cushion next to me and Annabelle swiftly picked it up, snapping it shut. 'Sorry, that's my work diary. Client details and appointments.' She put it on the sideboard and went through to the kitchen to make us a drink, reappearing a few minutes later. 'Where's Jasper today?' she asked, handing me one of the cups.

'He was supposed to go to London tonight, but he's postponed it until the morning,' I said. 'He did offer not to go at all, but I said he should.'

'That's very good of you.'

'He's got an important meeting. He'll be back Tuesday.' I blew on the hot tea before taking a small sip. 'Don't you mind being on your own?'

Annabelle sat on the opposite sofa. 'It's better than the alternative,' she said.

'Oh shit. Sorry. I wasn't thinking.' I wanted to bite my tongue off for such an insensitive comment.

'Don't worry. I'm not offended. Besides, I'd sooner you didn't feel you had to be careful about everything you said to me. We're friends, we're supposed to be able to relax in each other's company.'

'Thanks, but still.'

'Forget it,' Annabelle replied, not unkindly. 'I keep thinking of Sandra and how she must be feeling.'

'I saw her earlier,' I said, pleased the conversation had moved on. 'Her daughter's staying with her for a few days.'

'That's good. Poor woman. You saw her, you say?'

'Yes, Jasper and I popped in,' I continued.

'What was the cause of death, do we know?'

I closed my eyes momentarily as the image of Bryan's bloodied head came to me. 'He had a significant head injury,' I said. 'Sorry, makes me feel a bit sick just thinking about it. He could have slipped and hit it on a breakwater, but equally someone could have inflicted it.'

'Murder?'

'I guess so.'

'Gosh,' said Annabelle. 'That's worrying. Did they say whether it was random or was Bryan a target?'

'They don't know. Apparently, Bryan kept some sort of diary about the comings and goings of everyone on the estate.'

Annabelle gave a derisory snort. 'That doesn't surprise me. He was an ex-policeman. Personally, I think he couldn't cope with being retired. Hated it, even. Doing something like spying on people probably gave him a bit of a power trip, especially as he and Elizabeth were always in direct competition about what happened on the estate.'

I was a little surprised by her attack on Bryan.

I chose my next words carefully. 'The police asked me when I'd seen Bryan, prior to finding him on the beach.' I looked pointedly at her.

Annabelle shrugged. 'OK.'

'I didn't mention that I'd seen him leaving your apartment.'

'Ah. Right. Well, thank you,' said Annabelle, looking down at her hands. 'I appreciate that.'

'I'm sorry, but I need to ask,' I began.

Annabelle held up her hand. 'No, you don't. I should tell you. I know I can trust you.'

Luna gave a whine and settled herself down on the rug by my feet. 'What happened?' I asked.

'He'd been drinking. I could smell it on his breath,' said Annabelle. 'It was all a bit silly really. He made a fool of himself. Silly old man thought I was interested in him because I'd laughed when he'd made some sexist comment about my arse in my shorts at the barbecue. I pushed him away. He pushed me back and I caught myself on the table. It was nothing.'

'Annabelle! That's not nothing,' I said, although the thought that Bryan would behave like that shocked me. It sounded so out of character for the man I knew, but of course I couldn't voice that to Annabelle. I took a moment to soothe my initial knee-jerk reaction. Just because it shocked me, it didn't mean it hadn't happened. 'That's assault at the very least,' I said, adopting a more even tone.

She shook her head. 'When you've lived my life, a little push and a ridiculously sexist comment is not assault. It's just men being pricks. Or letting their prick rule their head.' She took a sip of her tea. There was no emotion on her face, nothing to say she was upset or outraged. To her, it was all quite normal. 'But thank you for not saying anything to the police about him being here. It would muddy the waters.' She put her cup down.

'I didn't think it was my place,' I said. 'I assumed you would. Have they questioned you?'

'Briefly. I told them I hadn't seen him since the other day when I saw him with Sandra and Elizabeth on the beach as I walked back to yours.'

'And you don't think you should say anything about what happened?'

'No.' She frowned at me. 'What's the point? They won't do anything. It's not like they can interview Bryan for his version of events. Telling them would put me well and truly in the frame, giving me a motive to attack him.'

I could see her point of view, and who was I to pass judgement on being economical with the truth?

'I'm glad I didn't say anything in that case,' I replied, not wanting to fall out with her about it. Like she said, what would be the point saying anything now?

'There was something else I didn't tell them...' She had that serious look on her face again.

'What was that?' My fingers automatically went to the hem of my top.

'I didn't tell them that I saw you and Bryan arguing on the beach the night of the barbecue.'

My stomach jolted. Bryan and I had been seen. I remembered feeling I was being watched. I should have trusted my gut instinct.

'We weren't arguing, though,' I said, thinking back to that night. There definitely hadn't been any confrontation between us. Intense talking, yes, but heated exchange of words, no.

'That's what it looked like to me.'

'We were only talking,' I said with a frown. 'Why didn't you say hello or something?'

Annabelle shrugged. 'I was getting some fresh air. I like to have a walk before bed when there's no one about. It kind of makes me feel safe. But, yes, I saw you both. I didn't want to intrude, so I stayed out of the way until you went in.'

'We weren't arguing,' I repeated, trying not to sound too bothered, when in fact, my heart was racing.

'Then I saw you again on the beach, right before you found Bryan,' said Annabelle.

'I was walking Luna,' I said. 'Why didn't you call out to me?'

'If I'm honest, I wasn't in the best frame of mind after what had happened with Bryan at my apartment. I just turned and walked back here. I didn't mention that to the police, either.'

I looked at Annabelle, unsure what to make of this exchange. Did she think she was doing me a favour by not mentioning it? Was it the same as me not telling the police about Bryan being at her apartment and what happened? I felt wrong-footed and confused, like I'd walked into some kind of trap, but just didn't know it yet.

'I haven't done anything wrong,' I said.

Annabelle gave a laugh. 'Neither have I.'

There was an undeniable tension in the room. I was immediately questioning whether I'd been right to think of Annabelle as a friend. The fear that was never far away, constantly tapping in the back of my mind, rocked up like a heavy metal band. I got to my feet. 'I should go. Jasper will worry where I am.'

Annabelle gave a laugh and jumped up too. 'Oh, listen to us,' she exclaimed with a broad smile. 'We're getting paranoid. Come here.' She was hugging me before I had time to protest. 'We're both a bit jumpy about it all. Hardly surprising, two women on their own when someone was murdered yards from our doorsteps. I'm sorry if I upset you.'

She looked genuinely sorry, and I returned the smile. Maybe she was right, and I was overreacting. 'It's fine,' I said. 'Neither of us have done anything wrong. It's not like we killed Bryan.'

'Exactly. And if we tell the police, then it might make them poke around and ask questions where it's not necessary and nothing to do with it at all. Also, if we say anything now, it will look bad on us for not mentioning it in the first place. Again, more suspicion on us. Have you told Jasper?'

'No. I haven't told anyone.'

'Good. Let's keep it that way.'

After agreeing on our vow of silence about when we last saw Bryan, I headed back home. I hadn't wanted to fall out with Annabelle over it, but I couldn't shake the uneasy feeling that had pitched up in my stomach. I felt vulnerable. It was different to the usual feelings of wariness and caution. This time it was stronger, more potent, and I didn't like it.

SIXTEEN

Hannah

Before Jasper had left at five o'clock on Monday morning, he'd asked me if I wanted him to come home that evening.

'I can cancel the meal,' he said.

'Not at all. I'll be fine. I promise.'

'If you're worried, call me and I'll come home,' he replied. 'Even if it's the middle of the night.' He kissed me, telling me to go back to sleep.

It was all well and good feeling brave while I was snuggled up in bed, but as the day wore on and I had to face the prospect of being alone in the house that night, my bravado was rather dented.

By the time I picked Pia up from school, I was sorely regretting my insistence on Jasper going ahead with his London trip, and having declined the offer of an overnight stay at his parents' place.

'Can we play on the beach?' asked Pia as we arrived indoors.

'Maybe not tonight,' I said. 'Let's stay in the garden.' I still hadn't been able to face going back on the beach and I knew I should, but I wanted to wait for Jasper. It sounded silly even to my own mind, but today, I wanted to stay close to the house.

'Aw, I want to paddle in the sea,' she protested.

It wasn't fair of me to keep her from enjoying the beach. It was after all one of the reasons we moved here. 'OK,' I relented. 'But just in front of the house. I don't want to walk anywhere.' What I meant was, I didn't want to go anywhere near the lifeguard tower.

We changed into shorts and T-shirts, grabbed our towels and Luna, and set off down the beach. It was the best decision we could have made. The water was a beautiful silvery blue-green and the May sun had been beaming down all day, warming it up. The sand tickled our toes, and we laid our towels out.

'Race you to the water,' I said, already running.

'Hey, that's cheating!' called back Pia as she came tearing down the beach after me.

I slowed up and we splashed into the water together, both squealing and laughing. It was just what I needed.

Jasper FaceTimed us at around seven o'clock and chatted with Pia about her day. They spoke in English and then a little in Danish. It filled me with immense pride to listen to them talking, despite not really knowing what they were saying.

'Be good for Mummy,' Jasper said in English.

'I will,' replied Pia.

'Godnat, skat. Jeg elsker dig.' Goodnight, darling. I love you, Jasper said in Danish. I couldn't speak the language, but I understood that from when Jasper sometimes said it to me. Although he had been born in England, his parents had made a point of speaking Danish to him from birth so he'd have the benefit of being bilingual.

'Jeg elsker dig,' replied Pia.

'Go and brush your teeth now,' I told Pia, taking the phone

from her and smiling at Jasper. 'How did the meal go this evening? Are you all set for the presentation tomorrow?'

We chatted for a while about his meeting with the clients and how he imagined it was going to go the next day, but really neither of us could concentrate fully. The elephant in the room was Bryan's death.

'Are you going to be OK tonight?' Jasper asked.

'I promise, I'll be fine,' I said. I didn't want him to worry about me. 'I'll probably have an early night anyway. I feel quite exhausted by everything.' That wasn't a lie. The past few days had drained me. Thoughts of Declan and his birthday, then Bryan's death –and to top it all my conversation with Annabelle – kept preying on my mind.

I went up to bed later than I normally would, feeling unsettled and confused as question after question rattled around in my head. I wasn't sure I'd be able to switch off and wondered whether I should take something to help me sleep. I had been prescribed sleeping tablets years ago and although I had barely used them since I'd been with Jasper, I did now and again take them. Sometimes when the mental load of how my life had changed got too heavy to bear, I'd take one.

I sat on the edge of the bed with the packet in my hand, my fingernail hovering over the foil backing, ready to pop a pill out. Whenever I'd taken these in the past, Jasper had always been home. When he'd first asked me about the sleeping tablets, I'd blamed it on my hormones and passed it off as something that was quite normal to take now and again. Tonight, though, I hesitated. I had Pia in the house. What if she woke in the night or there was some sort of emergency? I might not wake up or, if I did, I might not be able to think straight.

I dropped the pack back into the bedside drawer. My decision made. I wasn't going to put Pia in danger. If I stayed awake all night, then so be it.

I'd brought Luna up to sleep on the bed with me. Not something I would usually do. We always had a no pets in the bedroom rule, but I was throwing the rule book out tonight. Luna must have thought she'd won the dog lottery. After twirling around in a circle several times, she nestled herself on the bedspread I'd laid over the top of the duvet for her. Curled up, she was soon asleep, oblivious to anything around her. Oh, for it to be that easy for me.

I got into bed, put the TV on and found some garden rescue programme to passively watch in the hope it might bore me to sleep if nothing else.

The mundane show must have worked, as the next thing I knew a loud bang brought me right out of my sleep. My whole body jolted, and I lay motionless as I tried to work out what I'd heard, whether it was an actual noise or whether I had been dreaming.

I listened intently for a noise within the house. Luna hadn't even stirred. She was still snuggled up in a ball on the bed. The distant sound of the sea at low tide could be heard, as could the gentle tingle of next-door's wind chimes.

As I listened, I realised the sea sounded different to how it usually did at night. It wasn't so much the sound but the noise level. It was different. Louder.

I nudged Luna with my foot. 'Come on, Luna,' I said, getting out of bed and pulling on my dressing gown.

Luna reluctantly followed me out onto the landing, and I made my way down the steps. The house was in darkness, apart from the moonlight shining through from the kitchen, the silvery fingertips reaching the foot of the stairs.

The first thing I noticed was the draught around my ankles. Then I heard the dulled thud of the single back door against the doorframe.

My heart was thudding far louder I was sure. I had my mobile in my hand and I tapped in 999 ready to press call.

I flicked on the lights as I made my way down the hall, illuminating the whole of the ground floor. The kitchen was empty, and the door was indeed open, swinging to and fro in the wind. The motion had triggered the sensor outside and the garden was bathed in light. I yanked the door closed and locked it.

Then a thought struck me. Someone could be inside the house. I stood stock-still, listening intently for any sound of an intruder. Was it possible to sense someone was in the house? My leg shook involuntarily as I thought of Bryan being murdered. Had the killer come for me now?

I thought of Pia asleep in her bed and without another thought, ran through the kitchen and upstairs, bundling into her room and breathing a sigh of relief to see her soundly asleep.

Stepping out onto the landing, I listened again for any movement in the house. I was sure no one was there but I wasn't taking any chances. I hit the call button and got through to emergency services.

Ten minutes later the blue flashing light of the police car signalled their arrival. There were two officers who quickly checked out the rest of the house, garden and beach, before coming in and talking to me.

By now I felt rather stupid, as if I'd overreacted at the whole situation. Despite their assurances that it was best to call them, I convinced myself that I couldn't have closed the door properly.

Amazingly, Pia slept through it all, which is more than I could say for Sandra and Beverley, the latter coming out in her dressing gown to find out what was going on. Thankfully, one of the police officers spoke to her and reassured her it was a false alarm.

They left the estate an hour later with reassurances that they would increase their patrols in the area and I mustn't hesitate to call them again if I needed to, especially in light of recent events.

I considered going back to bed but didn't feel sleepy. I was too awake now, so opted for a warm milky drink.

It wasn't until I went over to the cupboard and put a cup down on the island counter that I noticed something I was sure hadn't been there earlier. It was a business card. I assumed it belonged to Jasper; he was always exchanging the things with his clients.

I picked it up and was about to put it to one side when I caught sight of the name on it. I stopped in my tracks.

My hand was shaking as I reread the card, just to make sure I hadn't made a mistake.

I hadn't.

The Enclave, London, SW1

I dropped the card as if it had burned my fingers and backed away from it, almost tripping over Luna in the process, who had decided to follow me around like a second shadow. She gave a yelp and jumped out of the way.

'Sorry! Good girl,' I half-whispered, trying to placate her. Really it was me who needed soothing.

I eyed the business card. How the hell had that got there? I tried to think logically. Daniel's group of hotels and the nightclub were under the name of the Enclave Group. Had Jasper stayed in one of the hotels or gone to the club at some point and just by chance left it in the middle of the island counter where I hadn't seen it until now? No, that was a ridiculous scenario. I certainly hadn't put it there. That left only one other answer. Someone else had. My eyes shot towards the door. It had been open. Someone had been in the house and put the card there for me to find. Someone was messing with me, and I didn't know who or why.

SEVENTEEN

Laurel

'I don't know about this working for Daniel Sully,' I said to Matt as we sat down for dinner at the weekend. It had been a few days since I'd met Daniel at his house, and I had wrestled with my conscience ever since. Although nothing had happened between us, I felt that we were on the brink of something. My belief that Daniel was dangerous hadn't abated and I needed to protect myself from him, and the only way I could see doing that, would be to avoid him at all costs. Even if it meant giving him up as a prestigious customer.

Matt nearly choked on his mouthful of chicken Balti. 'What? Are you crazy?'

'I have other jobs,' I said. 'I don't necessarily need this one.'

Matt swallowed his food. 'Honestly, Laurel, I thought we'd been through this before. You can't drop Daniel Sully. He's my business partner, or is about to be once we sign on the dotted line next week. You can't sack him – because that's essentially what you'll be doing. It will look like you strung him along until I got the deal.'

'Only the other day, you were saying I could quit the job if I wanted to,' I argued. 'You even said I was a charity case.'

'Yeah, well, I've changed my mind. Daniel mentioned you when I last spoke to him. He sounded really keen to have you working for him, so I don't want to upset him now.'

'I could say I'm too busy and recommend someone else.'

'No. No. You can't do that.' Matt waved his fork around like a wand. 'You've got to do this job for him. It will make me look a complete prick if you don't.'

'Can't have that,' I muttered into my dinner.

'What is it you don't like about him?'

I shrugged. 'I don't know. He's quite intimidating in a way.'

Matt let out a laugh. 'When have you ever let anyone intimidate you?' He put his cutlery down and wiped his mouth with his napkin. 'Look, Daniel Sully has a bit of a reputation as a shrewd, astute businessman who doesn't tolerate fools gladly. I get that. It's how it should be, but it also means I don't want to piss him off. He won't mince his words if he thinks we've stitched him up.'

I wasn't sure we could ever be accused of stitching him up, but I could hear the conviction in Matt's voice and, to be honest, I didn't want to embarrass him or make him feel he was in a difficult position, especially not at the start of the partnership. And he was also right about me not being intimidated easily – it wasn't my style. Why I was letting Daniel Sully get under my skin, I didn't know. I'd just have to keep a tight check on myself whenever I was around him. I'd get the job done and then I wouldn't have to have anything to do with him again. And if I did have to meet him, it would be in a social environment where I'd have Matt with me.

I smiled at my husband. 'Ignore me. I don't know why I'm getting in a tizzy over it.'

But Matt was looking at his phone again. Checking emails, probably. I guessed this was a sign of things to come.

. . .

The following week passed in a blur. I was busy juggling two clients as well as Daniel's commission. By the end of the week, I had completed the first 3D digital design of the two reception rooms at Daniel's property, Beaumont House, and Matt had signed the contract with Daniel. I still had the door key for the property, Daniel's assistant having passed on his boss's instructions that I should keep the key until the project was complete so I could pop in and out as I needed.

'You are now looking at the new business partner of Daniel Sully,' announced Matt as he came through the door that night. He held his arms out wide and then flexed both arms like a body building champion. 'Just call me sir from now on.'

'Yay! Congratulations,' I said, clapping my hands together and looking excitedly at Declan. 'Isn't Daddy clever. That's it, clap!' Our almost two-year-old joined in with gusto. I got up from the rug where I had been sitting playing with Declan and gave Matt a hug and kiss. 'Well done. You deserve this.'

'Thanks, babe.'

'Shall I order a takeaway to celebrate?' I said, going over to the bureau and rummaging around for a menu for the local Chinese takeaway.

'Oh, no. Don't bother with that,' said Matt. 'We're going out tonight. Daniel's request.'

'We are? But what about Declan?'

'I texted Amy. She's going to babysit.'

'The poor girl only went home an hour or so ago. I hope you didn't pressure her to come back.'

'Of course I didn't,' said Matt with a frown. 'Don't spoil the evening. She's quite happy to babysit. I offered her double rates, seeing as it was short notice.'

My eyes widened. 'Double rates? That's not cheap.'

'No. And we don't have to worry about that now. Not now Daniel has invested.'

'We should still be careful,' I warned.

'For fuck's sake, Laurel. You really know how to spoil the evening,' snapped Matt. 'Just relax and enjoy it for a change. Tomorrow you can get all anal about money, but not tonight, eh? Tonight is all about celebrating.'

'Yeah. Sure.' What else could I say? Matt was right, tonight wasn't a night I should put a damper on things by talking about being careful with money. 'Sorry. Old habits die hard and all that.'

'Go and get ready, then,' he said. 'I'll watch Declan. Put something sexy on.'

I went upstairs, irritated by the instruction to wear something sexy. I wasn't a trophy to be paraded about. But after sifting through my clothes, I ended up picking out a blouse and short skirt that played to my strengths of slim legs, small waist. After I showered and dressed, I was aware that I wasn't just dressing for my husband. I pretended I was unaware of this fact though.

Matt was impressed with my choice of outfit and threatened to drag me back into the shower with him. 'Shame we haven't got time for that,' he said, drawing me into a kiss. 'I guess I'll just have to wait until we get home.'

'Yes and hopefully that won't be too late when I'm knackered,' I said. It was awful to bribe your husband with the promise of sex for an early night, but I had a feeling staying late with Daniel Sully was not a good idea.

Amy arrived back at the house just before we were due to leave and assured me it wasn't a problem and that she had nothing planned for the night anyway.

'Cheers, Amy,' said Matt as he shepherded me out the door.

'Declan's already fast asleep,' I said over my shoulder. I was glad I'd been able to bathe Declan, read him a story and have a snuggle with him before he went to sleep. Precious moments I cherished, knowing they would pass all too soon – or at least that's what my mum always said. She lived in Cambridgeshire, and I hadn't been to see her for a while. I made a mental note to check my diary and take Declan up there for a weekend in the near future. She had lived alone for the past three years after my dad had died. I had toyed with the idea of moving her in with us, but she was fiercely independent and said she didn't want to leave her home. I liked going to visit her anyway, it was nice to get out of London regularly.

'Have a lovely time,' Amy called from the door as we got into the taxi.

The restaurant was next door to a club called The Enclave, which according to Matt, Daniel owned, along with the restaurant we were dining in.

'I'd love to get into something like this one day,' said Matt, gazing up at the premises. 'You never know, one day I might be the next Daniel Sully.'

I laughed for Matt's sake, but mentally rolled my eyes at my husband's adulation of his new business partner.

Daniel was already waiting at the bar for us. I had half-expected him to have some stunning blonde or brunette draped over his arm as his Plus One, but he was alone. He shook hands warmly with Matt, the two men all smiles at each other. Definitely in the honeymoon period of their partnership. Daniel turned to me and, although his glance was quick, it wasn't quick enough for me to miss him look me up and down. I could tell from the look in his eyes that he liked what he saw. He leaned in and kissed my cheek.

'I guess it's OK to greet you like that now,' he said. 'Seeing as Matt and I are partners.'

'Fill your boots, man,' said Matt.

I internally winced at the disparaging comment from Matt.

Daniel kissed the other side of my face. 'Very generous of

your husband,' he whispered in my ear. His hand lingered on my shoulder for a moment and I laughed in that awkward way women do when they don't want to offend a man. I hated myself for doing that, but Matt would have a fit if I told Daniel to fuck off.

Soon we were sitting at a circular table, tucked away in a more private area of the restaurant. It was clear Daniel came here often, the waiting staff called him by name and treated him like a king. I could see Matt lapping up the attention by proxy. And when the waiter afforded Matt the same sort of flattery, I thought he was going to burst out of his shirt the way his chest swelled up with macho pride. It was a little cringe, I thought guiltily. I couldn't even look at Daniel, as I was sure he would be finding it highly amusing that Matt was literally inflating with every passing compliment.

The conversation was pleasant enough and the two men mostly talked business. Daniel did apologise at one point, but Matt waved his apology away, saying I was used to it and not to worry. It was rather dismissive, and it hurt me more than I cared to admit. I knew it was Matt's night, but I had also secured a contract with Daniel. Although in Matt's eyes it was only significant in that it kept Daniel happy, which irked me. As if sensing my resentment, Daniel brought me into the conversation.

'I have to say, Laurel,' he began. 'I can't wait to see what designs you've come up with for Beaumont House. How's it coming along?'

'Really well, thanks,' I said. 'I hope you won't be disappointed.'

'I doubt it.' He gave me that intimate smile of his. I'm sure I blushed red and made an excuse to use the bathroom. I hoped Matt hadn't noticed my reaction.

If he had, he didn't let on.

When I returned to the table, he was deep in discussion with Daniel about their project. I sat back in my seat and picked up my glass, which had been topped up while I was gone. I was going to pay for this in the morning with a bit of a hangover, but it seemed worth it if I had to listen to Matt drone on about the project again. It was uncharitable of me, I knew, but I'd been hearing about the conversion of the barn in Surrey for the past two years. I knew every detail about developing it into a luxury hotel and converting the old stables into a spa.

We'd just ordered our desserts when the restaurant manager came over to the table. 'Mr Sully, apologies for the intrusion,' he said. 'But I need to speak with your guest, Mr Jordan.'

'Of course, Alberto,' said Daniel.

Alberto turned to Matt. 'Mr Jordan, I have a police officer on the phone wishing to speak to you. He says it's very important.'

'A police officer?' Matt looked bewildered. 'Wants to speak to me?'

'Yes, that's right. You can take the call in private in my office.'

Matt got to his feet and followed Alberto through the restaurant.

'I don't understand,' I said. 'How did they know he was here and why didn't they ring on his mobile?'

Daniel shrugged. 'Sorry, I can't help you there.'

'Maybe it's his mother,' I said. 'She lives in Perth, Australia. Maybe something's happened. God, I hope it's not that.' I fiddled with the heart pendant around my neck and as I glanced down to adjust it, I realised the button on my blouse had come undone and rather more of my cleavage was on show than I intended. Nothing indecent, but enough to make me scrabble with the button and fabric to refasten it. 'Shit. Sorry,' I said.

'No need to apologise.' His voice was doing that soft low thing again. The thing that ignited all the wrong sorts of feelings within me and my eyes were drawn to his. There was no denying the desire emanating from him and I knew my own feelings were on more display than my bra had been. He leaned forward and topped up my glass. I was certain I was having some sort of out of body experience as I picked up the glass and took a sip, all the time looking right back at him.

The arrival of Matt at the table broke the deadlock. He looked flustered and I was certain he hadn't even noticed Daniel and me staring at each other. 'The barn in Surrey's been broken into,' he said. 'I need to go down there and secure it.'

'What, tonight?' I asked in alarm.

'Yeah. Nightmare. The police said they've already tried to get a locksmith out to another incident but there's been a spate of break-ins and he can't get there until tomorrow.' He looked at Daniel. 'I'm really sorry.'

'No. Don't be,' said Daniel. 'No need to apologise. These things happen. Thieving bastards, eh?'

'Yeah. I'm going to have to get a taxi home and get the car,' said Matt. 'Don't know if I should be driving really.' He looked accusingly at his wine glass.

'I can't offer to drive you myself, for much the same reason,' said Daniel. 'But I'll get on the phone to Alex. He works for me. He'll drive you down there.'

'No. I couldn't do that,' said Matt.

'Of course you could,' said Daniel. 'We can put it through the expenses.'

'But Laurel?' Matt looked over at me. 'Can you get a taxi back?'

'Sure. Not a problem,' I said.

Daniel was already on the phone and I half-listened as Daniel instructed rather than requested Alex to drive Matt to Surrey. 'He'll be here in a minute. He's parked around the corner.'

Matt looked suitably impressed that Daniel had a driver on call whenever he needed it. It would no doubt be something

Matt aspired to – a sign that he had made it in the business world.

Within a couple of minutes, Matt had left.

'So, if you've sent your driver away,' I said, as I finished my glass of wine. 'How are you getting home?'

Daniel patted his jacket pocket. 'I'm driving. I've barely had anything to drink. I tend not to. I like to keep my wits about me.'

I eyed the half-filled glass and realised Daniel had been drinking mostly water, despite him implying to Matt he couldn't drive because he'd be over the limit. 'Why was Alex here, then?'

'In case I changed my mind,' said Daniel. 'It also means I can drive you home.' He paused. 'If that's where you want to go.'

My mouth dried at the loaded question, and I swallowed hard. 'Is there a better offer?' I asked.

'There's always a better offer,' said Daniel.

'Is that right?' I knew I was a bit tipsy, and I would like to have blamed my flirting on the alcohol, but in all honesty, I wasn't so drunk that I didn't know what I was saying.

'Want to skip dessert?' he asked.

'For a better offer?'

'A much better offer.'

Daniel was leading me out of the restaurant in no time, having settled the bill. Out in the fresh air, he put his arm around my waist and guided me to his car. He unlocked the Jaguar and opened the door for me. As I went to get in he put his hand in front of me. 'Just so you know, Laurel,' he said. 'You're in control. What happens now is entirely up to you. We go at your speed. If you want to put the brakes on at any time, then that's OK with me.'

I nodded. 'OK.' He moved his hand away and I got into the car, fastening my seat belt. All the time this voice at the back of

my head was asking me what the hell I was doing. I chose to
ignore it.

A short time later, we practically bundled through the door
of his house in Chelsea. We couldn't keep our hands off each
other. As the door slammed shut, I found myself up against the
wall with Daniel kissing me. I didn't try to stop him. In fact, I
clasped his head in my hands and kissed him back hard and fast.

'God, you're beautiful,' he muttered between kisses. His
hands roamed across my body, over my breasts, down my back
and over my backside, before hooking me up under the thighs. I
wrapped my legs around him and he carried me through to the
living room.

I heard myself moan as he trailed his kisses around my neck
from one ear to another, while his hand slid up the inside of my
thigh under my skirt. I gasped as he deftly slipped his fingers
into the front of my underwear.

I don't know what it was but something, a noise maybe, the
clock chiming in the hallway, a car door banging in the street,
I've no idea, but it snapped me back into reality. What the hell
was I doing? I pulled away. 'No,' I said. 'No. I can't. I'm sorry.'

'Hey, it's OK, Laurel,' said Daniel as I took another step
back. He didn't try to move closer to me.

'I can't do this,' I repeated, as if to convince myself as much
as I wanted to convince Daniel. 'This isn't right. Not here. Not
yet.' I put my hands over my face as if I could hide my true
feelings. I wanted Daniel, but I suddenly felt on edge. I was
also a married woman. Morally, this was wrong. Married or
not, I shouldn't even be entertaining the idea of a relationship
with him. I didn't want to be another conquest but, at the same
time, I couldn't help feeling whatever was happening was
different for both of us. I don't think I had ever been so
conflicted in my life. I dropped my hands and looked up at
him. 'I'm sorry.'

'You don't have to be sorry. You're in control, remember?'

'I'm not sure I was just then.' I tried for humour but missed. 'Sorry. It's not that I don't want to, but...'

'You don't have to explain.' He gave a soft smile. 'Not the best time or place.'

He looked so sincere and understanding, it threw me a little. It wasn't the sort of reaction I expected, not from someone powerful like Daniel Sully.

'I should go,' I said, looking around for my bag, which I had discarded somewhere. 'I'll phone a taxi.'

'No, you won't,' he said. 'I'll drive you home.' He smiled. 'I promise you're safe. I'm not going to kidnap you.'

I gave a small laugh. 'Shame,' I said, trying again to lighten the mood.

'You can trust me, Laurel,' he said. 'I promise.'

Of course I trusted him and allowed myself to be driven home. He even suggested I call Matt to see if everything was all right. There was no way I could speak to my husband while I was in the car with Daniel, knowing that he had no idea what had just gone on between his wife and his new business partner. I couldn't help wondering if Daniel would get some sort of kick out of that too.

He pulled up outside my house and walked me up to the door. 'Don't be worrying now,' he said.

'I am sorry, I...' I didn't know what to say. I felt embarrassed at my behaviour.

He put his finger to my lips. 'It will happen. At some point.' He leaned in and kissed me briefly on the mouth. 'You want me as much as I want you. It will just make it all the sweeter when it does.'

I pulled away and pressed the doorbell, wishing I'd brought my keys out with me, or I'd thought to get Matt's from him before he'd left. 'It can't happen,' I said. I knocked on the door again. Where the hell was Amy?

'Don't be scared,' said Daniel, as he ran his finger down my cheek. 'Goodnight, Laurel.' He stepped back off the step as Amy opened the door.

'Sorry,' she said. 'I must have nodded off.' Then she saw Daniel there.

'I'll explain inside,' I said, almost rugby-tackling her into the hallway and closing the door behind me.

My phoned pinged through with a text message. I looked down, expecting it to be Matt. It was from Daniel.

> I guess I owe you another bunch of flowers.

I tapped back a reply.

> If that's the case, then I owe you some too.
> Let's just forget about it.

> If you really want to. If you think you can. I know I'm going to find that difficult.

> I have to. We have to. I'm sorry.

> Did my heart love till now? Forswear it, sight!
> For I ne'er saw true beauty till this night.

I looked at the text message, deciding I needed to Google which Shakespeare play it was, but before I could, Daniel sent another message.

> Romeo and Juliet in case you're wondering. We can talk about this when I next see you.

> There's nothing to talk about.

> Goodnight, Laurel. I'll be thinking of you.

I didn't reply but I knew I'd be thinking of him too.

EIGHTEEN

Hannah

'Bye, bye, darling,' I said, giving Pia a kiss. 'Daddy will be back tonight. Have a good day at school. Love you lots.'

I watched Pia skip off happily in line with the rest of her class. I was shattered. I hadn't been able to sleep after finding that business card on the countertop. I'd stayed sitting in the chair for the rest of the night, waiting for dawn to break and the darkness of the night to disappear. Now Pia was safely deposited at school, I felt my whole body almost sigh in relief. I could go home now and try to get some sleep.

Thank goodness Jasper was coming home later. I wouldn't have made it another night on my own. He'd messaged this morning to check in with me. I hadn't mentioned calling the police last night as I didn't want to worry him while he was away. He'd insist on coming home even though he had more meetings today.

On the drive home, I stopped at a small grocery shop to purchase some fruit. As I left the shop, I paused outside and taking a tissue from my pocket, I dabbed at my nose, before dropping it into the bin. Inside the tissue was part of the SIM card from Bryan's phone I had cut up that morning.

After that, I went into a nearby café and ordered a coffee, using their toilet to dispose of the other half of the SIM card.

Another stop to have a stroll around a park, had me depositing several smashed-up pieces of Bryan's phone across three different bins.

Satisfied I'd got rid of any evidence I'd had Bryan's phone, I went back to my car and headed home.

As I swung the car through the gates of Silverbanks estate, a black VW Golf pulled over to allow me through. I put my hand up in acknowledgement and realised it was Beverley, with Sandra in the passenger seat. Beverley gave a nod and Sandra managed something of a smile. The poor woman looked absolutely broken.

Any thoughts of having a nap as soon as I got in were squashed. Luna was pawing at the bifold and whining.

'Just a quick walk this morning, Luna,' I said, picking up the dog lead.

It was another gorgeous day and I headed away from the lifeguard tower. I still wasn't ready to go that way. When Jasper got home, I'd take him with me, but I didn't want to face it for the first time on my own.

I walked for about five minutes before turning for home. As I climbed the three steps over the wall at the back of my garden, something made me look over the fence towards Bryan's house. I caught sight of someone opening the back door and slipping inside. I ducked down out of sight, waiting to hear the door close before I moved.

I knew exactly who that was going into the Chambertons' house and it wasn't Sandra or Beverley.

I took Luna indoors and nipped through to the living room where I could see the Chambertons' driveway. It was empty.

No sign of the black VW. The house should, by rights, be empty too, but it wasn't.

Annabelle was in there.

I tried to come up with some plausible reason why she would be letting herself in the back door. She must know the alarm code as it certainly hadn't gone off. I didn't think she knew Sandra that well to be doing anything for her. Besides, what would she need to do, especially as Beverley was there?

I liked Annabelle, I genuinely did. I felt she was a friend. Someone who I wanted to spend time with but, at the same time, after what she'd said about Bryan, I didn't feel quite so sure about her. My paranoid instincts were telling me to steer clear of her, but my desire to have a good friend had blinded me somewhat.

No, I was overthinking, I decided. She was probably helping Sandra in some way.

To prove the point to myself, I went back out and around to Sandra's garden, letting myself in through the gate, which was unlocked, and was how I assumed Annabelle had got in.

I opened the back door.

'Hello!' I called out, one foot over the threshold and the other on the doorstep. 'Sandra!' It felt right to call her name just in case she had come back on her own. When I got no response, I tried again. Surely, Annabelle would have heard me. 'Annabelle!' I called this time, stepping fully into the kitchen.

A door banged within the house, making me jump, and then Annabelle appeared in the doorway.

'Hannah,' she said. 'What are you doing here?'

She was doing a good job of trying not to look flustered, but I was an expert in masking my true emotions, which also made me an expert in spotting others when they were trying to cover up something. Annabelle was good, but not that good.

'I saw you come in,' I said, noting the pair of gloves she was wearing. 'Sandra's not here though.'

I waited expectantly for her to say something, to come up with a random excuse, so I was surprised when she didn't. 'I was looking for something,' she said.

'Looking for what?'

'Do you want to come in so we can have this conversation in private?' said Annabelle. 'Close the door behind you.'

It felt rather surreal standing in the kitchen of a house neither of us had any right to be in. 'OK. Why are you here?' I asked again.

'I'm looking for Bryan's notebook or whatever it is Sandra told you he wrote things down in about everyone on the estate.'

I was surprised by her honesty but more concerned why she was looking for it. 'What do you want the book for?' I asked.

'I wanted to see what he'd written about me,' said Annabelle. 'You know, after the attack.'

'Does it matter?'

'It does actually. I don't want the police to know he attacked me. That will make me look like I had a motive to kill him.'

'And have you found the book?' I asked cautiously. If she'd found the book, and Bryan had written about me in it, then she'd know my secret. I couldn't have that. I couldn't have anyone knowing about me – about Laurel.

'Not yet. Do you want to help me look for it?' said Annabelle breezily. 'It might be in your interest to find it and see what he's written about you.'

There was a little glint in her eye that sent a slither of fear through me. Did she know something? Or was she just fishing? 'There won't be anything of interest in there about me,' I said, trying to laugh it off. 'How did you get in here?'

'The door was left unlocked.' She gave a shrug. 'Look, I haven't got that much time. Are you going to help me find the book or not?'

I wasn't quite so sure about the door being unlocked. I couldn't ever imagine Bryan doing that but, then again, maybe

Sandra wasn't thinking properly at the moment. 'We shouldn't be in here.'

'Absolutely we shouldn't but I want to know what that creep has written about me and I'm sure you do too, so come and help me.'

I hesitated. Annabelle was of course right. I did want to know what he'd written about me, but how this was going to play out, I had no idea. I needed the book as much as she did. What were we going to do, wrestle for it?

Annabelle was already walking out of the kitchen and, against all my instincts to get out of there right that minute and forget about the book, I found myself following her.

I went through into the study where Annabelle was going through the desk drawers, taking care to disturb the contents as little as possible. 'Did Sandra say what sort of notes he kept?' she asked without looking up.

'She said a book, so I think it must be handwritten,' I replied, going over to the bookshelves. I scanned the spines, looking for something resembling a notebook.

'I've already looked over there,' said Annabelle. 'Try in that cupboard.'

I found myself obediently doing as I was told and then cursing as I realised I didn't have any gloves on. I pulled the sleeve down on my shirt and rubbed the top of the door where I thought I had touched. I scanned the contents of the cupboard. It was mostly full of camera equipment, CDs, and several photo albums. 'Nothing here,' I said, closing the door with my elbow. I was feeling decidedly nervous about being in the house. Book or no book, I wanted to get out. 'We should go.'

'Not yet,' said Annabelle. 'Aha! Bingo!' She pulled out a book from the bottom drawer and placed it on top of the desk. 'There are several in here,' she said. 'All dated. This one looks like the most recent.' She opened the book and flicked through several pages. 'This is it.'

I needed that book. I needed it before she did. 'Can I look at it first?' I asked.

'Why?' There was a small smile on her mouth.

'Because I know what he's said about you, but you don't know what he might have said about me. I think it's fair I look at it first.' I moved towards the desk but before I reached it, Annabelle snatched the book up, holding it to her body.

'Finder's keepers,' she said, followed by a small laugh.

'Please, Annabelle, it's not fair.'

'But what if he's written things about me that you don't know?' she said. 'One of us has to read it first.'

The sound of a car pulling up on the drive brought an abrupt halt to the debate. We looked at each other for a second and I'm sure the look of surprise and panic on Annabelle's face reflected my own expression.

The study was located between the kitchen at the rear and a reception room at the front. I edged towards the door to sneak a look down the hallway to the front door, which was made of heavy oak with four square glass windows running down the centre. Two full-length glazed panels of opaque glass ran either side. I could just make out the shape of a blue-coloured car. The engine was cut, followed by the sound of two doors opening and closing.

'We need to get out of here,' hissed Annabelle in my ear.

I shook my head. 'No. They'll see us, or at least see movement through the glass. It's not Sandra. It's the wrong colour car.'

'Shit,' muttered Annabelle. 'Stay back out of the way.'

I wanted to say I wasn't stupid but decided now wasn't the time to discuss my escape and evasion skills.

The doorbell chimed and we both instinctively took a step back into the room. Several seconds elapsed before the bell rang again, followed by a knock.

'The police,' I whispered to Annabelle.

She nodded her agreement. 'They'll go in a minute, with any luck.'

As we stood there, I pondered my predicament, unable to quite believe I was in this situation while simultaneously trying to come up with a plausible excuse why we were here should the police come into the house. And then I remembered the back door. I caught my breath.

'What?' whispered Annabelle.

'I didn't lock the back door,' I replied in a hushed voice.

She rolled her eyes and whispered, 'Fuck.'

I edged towards the study door and very slowly peeked back into the hallway. I could see the outline of someone and, judging by the build and height, guessed it was Barnes. I could hear indistinct talking and then Barnes moved out of sight. In the hallway, opposite the door to the study was a mirror and, probably by design, I could see into the front reception room and the bay window. I silently thanked Bryan for this crafty way of seeing who was at the front of the house without having to leave his desk.

I motioned for Annabelle to duck down in case Barnes could see us in the mirror. I suspected that in a sitting position this wasn't possible, and Bryan would have made sure he had the upper hand. I knew there was a doorbell on the front of the house, together with the alarm system, but the Chambertons hadn't invested in any sort of CCTV, fortunately. There was side access to the rear of the property via a gate, which I hoped was locked but couldn't be certain.

I watched Barnes put her face up to the glass and peer through the window. I remained stock-still, and so did Annabelle. For one gut-churning second, I thought Barnes had seen me. It was as if her eyes had locked with mine. I didn't dare move, but after a second or two, she looked away. Owens joined her and after another brief discussion, he seemed to be walking back towards the car.

Barnes, however, had other ideas and started heading around the side of the house.

'Quick,' I hissed, grabbing Annabelle's arm. 'She's coming around the side.'

We almost fell over each other in our haste to get out of the study and into the kitchen which, fortunately, had no side windows and was within the boundaries of the back garden. Annabelle hastily locked the rear door and we both crouched down behind the breakfast bar, safely out of sight from anyone coming around the back.

Eventually, the sound of car doors closing and the engine starting up broke the silence. I listened intently as the car reversed out of the drive and then pulled away. I wanted to be certain though and, feeling slightly ridiculous, I crawled on my hands and knees out of the kitchen and down the hall to the reception room, where I slowly put my head above the precipice and looked out of the window. The drive was empty.

I let out a long sigh of relief, got to my feet and hurried back to the kitchen. 'They've gone,' I said. 'And we should too.'

Annabelle let out a laugh. 'That was fun,' she declared, standing up.

'Fun?' I shook my head.

'Oh, don't be such a stick in the mud,' she reprimanded me. 'You've got to admit that got the heart rate going, didn't it? Wasn't it Eleanor Roosevelt who said to do one thing every day that scares you?'

I wasn't sure I agreed with that sentiment, but I wasn't going to stand around in the Chambertons' house and discuss the merits of it either. I was already at the back door. 'Do you need to reset that thing?' I asked, pointing at the alarm system.

'Don't fret. It's all under control.'

Only after the alarm was set, the door locked and we were on the other side of the gate to the beach, did I finally relax a little. 'How did you know the gate would be open?' I asked.

'I left through the back gate yesterday, on my own. I was hoping neither Sandra nor Beverley would think to check it. If they had, I'd have had to climb over by using your wall. A little risky, but sometimes you have to take a risk. Can't play it safe all the time.'

Annabelle had a gleeful look on her face. She'd actually enjoyed all the excitement and drama. She was clutching the book in her hand. I momentarily thought about snatching it from her but decided against it. She'd probably fight me for it, and I was beyond rolling around on the beach in a tussle.

'What do we do about that?' I asked.

'The book?' She turned it over in her hand. 'I guess you'll just have to trust me,' she said. 'I'll let you know when I've finished with it.'

With that she turned and headed off down the beach towards her apartment. Trust her? For a while I thought I could but today, I'd done a complete one-eighty on that thought.

I watched her go. All I could do was hope Bryan had been discreet enough with his diary entries not to blow my world apart.

NINETEEN

Hannah

The next couple of days passed agonisingly slow. Jasper had come back from his trip and was in a good mood. It had gone very well, and he thought he'd be able to close the deal by the end of the following week.

He was, of course, concerned to hear that I'd had to call the police Sunday night, and in a bid to reassure us both, had immediately ordered CCTV for the house. Jasper had also phoned Owens and discussed it with him. Owens added to the reassurance that it was nothing to worry about. He certainly didn't seem to think it was connected to Bryan's murder. In fact, he gave the distinct notion, he didn't think it was anything at all, other than me forgetting to lock the door.

I gave the impression that I agreed with this hypothesis. I couldn't very well disagree unless I wanted to tell both Jasper and Owens about the business card. Of course, I didn't want to do that because that would mean revealing my past.

I hadn't heard from Annabelle at all and had resisted the urge to text her or to call around to see her. I was desperate to know what was in the book but didn't want it to look like I was worried or that I had something to hide. I was certain if there was anything in there about me, or indeed about Laurel, then Annabelle would have been in touch. I just needed to play it cool and stay as calm as possible until there was something to get stressed about. It was a tactic I had employed over the past eleven years and had worked very well up until now.

'Any news on Bryan's death?' asked Jasper.

'I saw Elizabeth this morning when I was out with Luna,' I said. 'Apparently, the police are treating it as suspicious.'

'Which means murder,' said Jasper.

'I guess so.'

'Do they think it's to do with the vandalism?'

'No. They told Sandra it was a bit of a leap going from pulling up tulips to killing someone.'

'I'm going to have to be in the office a bit more next week while we get the deal finalised,' said Jasper. 'Are you OK with that? I can stick around here if you need me.'

'No. I'll be fine,' I said. I didn't want to prevent Jasper from doing his job.

The weekend came and went, and I still hadn't heard from Annabelle. It seemed odd, even Jasper had asked me if I'd heard from her. I think he was more worried about me losing a newfound friend than anything else.

When Monday came around, I waved Jasper off to work and took Pia to school. It was such a nice day, I decided to stop and have a coffee at the little café in Seabury. I sat at the window, watching the gentle rhythm of the town. People going about their business, to work, the school-run parents on their way home, the older generation out to get their daily newspaper, chatting in the shops or on the pavement, tradesmen stopping by for a takeaway coffee and a bacon sandwich, people out with their dogs and toddlers. The little seaside town had it all going on.

I was gazing out of the window, not paying any particular attention to the traffic, when a car pulled up outside the florist's shop across the road. I absently watched the driver get out. It took a moment for my brain to compute and then relay that it was Annabelle who had hopped out of the car. She went into the florists.

I was paying full attention now to the shop and a few minutes later, she reappeared on the street, carrying a small bouquet of flowers, lilies, forget-me-knots and greenery, tied in brown paper with a green ribbon. It was the ribbon that made me question what she was doing. You didn't usually gift-wrap flowers for yourself. If they were for someone else, I couldn't help wondering who that might be.

I thought back to our conversations. Annabelle hadn't mentioned knowing anyone in the area or having any family. But then she was a dark horse, and I was beginning to feel certain there was more to her than she was letting on. I felt a disappointment. I had briefly enjoyed the idea of a friendship with Annabelle, especially so after we nearly drowned in that riptide, but I wasn't sure if that was possible. I thought back to that day and a cold shiver ran down my spine, not from the memory but from the possibility it could have been engineered. I shook my head. That was ridiculous, wasn't it?

My mind went to thoughts of the notebook she'd taken from Bryan's and the way she refused to let me look at it and the way she had laughed in delight at what she'd done.

Had I really got it so wrong about our friendship?

I left my unfinished coffee and, having already paid for the drink, I exited the café, slipping into my car which was parked a few metres down the road. I waited for Annabelle to pull out into the traffic and then did the same myself, only, instead of heading back to Silverbanks, I followed her. I wasn't even sure why I was doing that, but I wanted to know where she was going.

I felt like I was in some sort of stakeout movie as I followed, a few cars behind, in the traffic. My silver Honda melted into the sea of vehicles, just as I had intended it would when I'd bought it. Jasper had offered to buy me a Mercedes or a Range Rover, but I had declined. Although it could be said, neither of those cars really stood out, especially on Silverbanks. Maybe my unassuming car was too average, in fact.

I kept a good distance between us, with one car still separating us even when we turned into Grand Avenue, a tree-lined road with large double-fronted detached houses on either side, dating back to probably around the 1920s. Annabelle's indicator came on and I saw her turn into the driveway of one of the houses. I slowed but didn't stop and glanced over as I passed. The house was discreet in that it looked like any other of the houses in the road, except for the board at the entrance to the property. Elm Tree Private Clinic & Hospice. I went a little further down the road, before performing a U-turn and parking up on the other side of the avenue. The property had a low hedge, which gave me a view of the entrance. There was room for several cars on the driveway, which once would have been a beautiful lawn, I guessed. Large hydrangea bushes formed a boundary hedge down one side and a well-established wisteria sprawled along the front of the cream-coloured building.

I could see the tip of Annabelle's car and then Annabelle appeared, walking up the steps of the clinic, flowers in hand, ringing the bell before being let in by a woman in a white nurse's uniform.

Now I really was intrigued. Who on earth was she going to see? She'd never mentioned visiting anyone who was in the local private clinic.

I don't know why, but I felt I needed to know.

I settled myself in for a long wait.

I took out my phone and googled Elm Tree Private Clinic & Hospice. The information was sparse but enough for me to

establish it was a medical facility which offered care for the
terminally ill, both respite and end of life. They also ran an invi-
tation-only support group for friends and families of their
patients.

While I waited, I ran through all the possible scenarios that
might enable me to gain access to the clinic to find out who
Annabelle was visiting. I was uncomfortably aware that I was
prying into her private life. One that she hadn't yet shared with
me. Again, the irony of my own situation and withholding
private details about my life was not wasted on me. I really
shouldn't be here spying on her, and yet I felt an overwhelming
compulsion to know more. Maybe it was the deep-seated need
to protect myself that was at the root of this... this... I wasn't
even sure what to call it, but I needed to know more about her
before I could let her know more about me. Only then would I
be able to weigh up whether it was safe to nurture our friendship. I really hoped I was overreacting, but I couldn't afford a
misstep.

Less than an hour later, Annabelle emerged. I sank a little
lower in my seat as she pulled out of the driveway. She didn't
appear to notice me and turned right, heading back towards the
town and Silverbanks.

Once I was sure she was gone, I got out of the car and
crossed the road to the clinic still without much of a clue what I
was going to say.

The door was opened by a nurse, probably the same one
who had answered it to Annabelle.

'Can I help you?'

'Hi. Erm. I wondered if it's possible to have a chat with
someone about the clinic,' I began. The nerves in my voice were
real but lent themselves to my purpose. The nurse gave me a
quizzical look and I continued. 'It's a bit delicate. It's for my
sister who needs respite care.'

'We usually operate an appointment system,' said the nurse. 'Dr Rahman doesn't take walk-in appointments, as it were.'

'Oh, that's a shame. Is there anyone who could answer a few questions? Just so I can be sure this is the right sort of place for my sister. If it is, I could make an appointment.' She still didn't look convinced, and I tried again. 'Please, I don't want to waste anyone's time.' I looked down at my hands and then back up at her. 'I... we need help. You know, to make things easier for everyone.'

I wondered if I'd overplayed it, but after a moment of indecision, the nurse appeared to take pity on me and opened the door wider for me to step through.

I entered the hallway and was shown into a room on the right which would have once been a sitting room and was now the reception area. Another woman, not in uniform, smiled from behind the desk.

The nurse spoke to her. 'Hilary, I'm just going to fetch Eve to have a word with...' She looked at me.

'Miss Clarins,' I said, using my mother's maiden name. 'Fiona Clarins.'

'If I leave you with Hilary, she'll take a few details and Eve, our matron will be along shortly,' said the nurse.

I thanked the nurse and smiled at Hilary, who handed over an iPad. 'If you could sign in there, please,' she said.

I took the iPad, cursing modern technology as I had been hoping there was a traditional visitor's book I'd be able to look at to see who Annabelle had been to visit.

I entered the false name I'd given, together with a false phone number. I was about to hit enter when I noticed the three menu bars in the top right-hand corner. Hilary had just answered the phone and I quickly tapped the drop-down menu. Three options came up.

DELETE

NEW VISITOR

VISITOR LIST

I tapped the last option. The screen blinked and then a list of names appeared, with the most recent visitor at the top. But it wasn't Annabelle Burton that was first, it was Jessica Beaumont. I checked the other details. The time was an hour earlier, and it was definitely today's date. It had to be Annabelle. I scanned across to who she was visiting. Daniel Sully.

'Miss Clarins? Excuse me, Miss Clarins?'

My head was spinning and I thought for a moment I was going to throw up. I staggered, almost dropping the iPad but somehow managed to stay upright.

'Is everything all right? Do you need any help?' Hilary looked concerned.

'Oh, what? Sorry.' Sweat pricked my upper lip and my body was clammy. I hit the back button, thankful the screen returned to my details. 'I wasn't sure what button to press.' I went over to the reception desk, returned the device to Hilary, hoping she didn't notice my hand shaking.

'That's fine. I can do that for you. Thank you.'

I sat back down, trying to plot my next move while googling Daniel's name, desperately trying to find out anything I could. It had to be my Daniel; it was too much of a coincidence to be someone else. And Jessica Beaumont. Where did I know that name from? It sounded familiar, and yet I could not place it. I let out a sigh as my phone failed to respond.

'You have to stand in the hallway if you want decent internet,' said Hilary. She gave an eye roll. 'You'd think in this day and age there wouldn't be any dead spots. It's only luck the iPad worked properly while you were sat down. Sometimes you have to be over here behind the desk to get it work properly.'

I didn't trust myself to stand anywhere, fearing I might pass out. So I sat back and tried to look outwardly casual while internally I was slipping into deep panic mode. Utter confusion whooshed around in my brain, making it impossible to think clearly.

A few minutes passed before a member of staff in a dark-blue uniform came into the reception room. 'Miss Clarins?'

I got to my feet; grateful my legs didn't give way on me. 'Hello.'

'I'm Eve, the Matron of Elm Trees. I understand you'd like a chat.' She was an older woman, maybe in her early sixties with a kind expression on her face. 'Come this way.' She paused and turned to Hilary. 'Did the notes about the new patient in room ten come through?'

'Not yet,' replied Hilary. 'I've chased them this morning and they said to expect them the day after tomorrow.'

'Can you let me know when they arrive?'

'I'm not in for the rest of the week, but I'll leave a note for Kelly.'

'Perfect, thank you, Hilary.' The matron turned to me. 'Sorry about that. This way.'

'Actually, I'm not feeling that well,' I said to the matron. 'Maybe I could come back another day. Sorry to waste your time.'

'Can I get you anything? A glass of water?' asked the matron.

'You do look pale,' chimed in Hilary. 'I thought you were going to faint just now.'

'I'll be fine. I'll phone and make an appointment, so sorry to have taken your time,' I said, smiling at both the matron and Hilary, before making my way out of the building. Outside, I stood for a moment and took in several slow breaths, to steady myself.

As I stood there, I had this strong sense of being watched. I turned around to face the building, my gaze scanning the exterior. Something drew me to look up at the first floor. There was movement in one of the windows. So fleeting, I wasn't even sure what I'd seen.

I gave an involuntary shiver and hurried over to my car, desperate for the safety and sanctuary of my own home.

TWENTY

Laurel

When Matt had got back in the early hours of the morning from the break-in at the barn, I was still wide awake. Racked with guilt over what I'd done with Daniel. I couldn't let anything like that happen again. I'd never once in all our married life even looked at another man in the way I'd looked at Daniel. No other man had never ignited such a physical and emotional response from me. I wasn't trying to make excuses for myself, I was the one wholly responsible for my own actions, but it was as if Daniel had the power to bend me to his will.

'Sorry, didn't mean to wake you,' said Matt as he stripped off and went into the en suite for a wash. He emerged a few minutes later after a splash of water and quick brush of his teeth. He flopped down into bed.

'Was everything all right?'

'Yeah. Waste of effort though,' said Matt. 'I got there, and the police hadn't even bothered to stick around. I had to secure the door myself. Managed to book a locksmith for the morning.'

'Did you speak to the police again?'

Matt was already lying back with his eyes closed. 'That's the weirdest thing. They didn't have any record of phoning me. Honestly, this country is unbelievable. It's times like this I wish I was back in Australia.'

'Like there's no crime in Australia,' I said.

'We should move there.' His words were heavy, and I wasn't sure whether he was just thinking out loud. But then he propped himself up on one elbow and looked at me. 'I'm being serious, babe. Maybe once this project is complete, we should think about moving home. We'd have enough money, and our standard of living would be better. Think of all the opportunities for Declan.'

'Wow. That's a sudden about-turn. I thought you and Daniel Sully were embarking on a business venture together.'

'We are. It's a one-off though. Anyway, I was thinking in the car on the way home that he might be interested in investing in some overseas ventures.'

'Matt,' I said, interrupting him before he got carried away. 'You know how I feel about emigrating. I couldn't leave Mum. I don't know how much time I have left with her; I'm not moving to the other side of the world where it could be a year before I see her again. She's not getting any younger.'

'Hasn't it occurred to you that I feel the same about my mum?'

That was a curveball. Matt had never given the slightest indication he missed his own mother. 'I didn't know that,' I said. 'I'm sorry.'

'Yeah, well, it's not all about you. Don't forget I have feelings too.'

'I know. It's just you've never in all the time I've known you said you felt homesick or anything,' I replied. 'And, not being funny, but you chose to move to the UK. Moving to Australia has never been on my wish list.'

He flopped back down. 'Didn't think you'd understand.'

'That's unfair.'

'Probably the wrong time to talk about this.' He rolled over, turning his back on me and pulling the duvet up over his shoulder.

When we awoke the following morning, there was still a frostiness between us, even though we were both pretending we were fine. It was a Saturday, and instead of coming to the park with me and Declan, Matt said he needed to go back down to Surrey to meet the locksmith. He'd said the night before that it wouldn't be necessary, so I could only guess he was trying to avoid me. I tried not to let it bother me and to enjoy my precious weekend time with Declan. Yet my thoughts kept finding their way to Daniel and reminding me I had turned him down and for what? A husband who didn't seem to care about me.

The frostiness continued for the rest of the weekend, with Matt arranging an afternoon of golf on Sunday, although he did grace us with his presence on Sunday morning when we went swimming.

'He's a proper water baby,' enthused Matt as Declan was already able to swim unaided. 'He'd love it on the beaches back home.'

I noticed he was starting to refer to Australia as home and, yes, it was his home, but he'd never called it that before. It was always Oz or Perth. Home had always been our home together as a family in London. I didn't comment though, preferring to let it slide as I thought it was for my benefit more than anything else. The same way I ignored Matt talking to Declan about how he was going to take him home and all the fun things they'd do together, living the stereotypical outdoor life Down Under.

By the time Monday morning rolled around and Matt had headed off to work and Amy had come to look after Declan, I was glad of the breathing space from my husband. Guilt had been hanging around all weekend, despite the undercurrent of disharmony between Matt and me. At one point, I wondered whether I was being selfish in not considering moving to Australia. But I knew I couldn't leave Mum. Maybe one day it would be on the cards, but not right now.

I'd been working in the shop for about an hour when there was a ring of the doorbell and standing outside was a delivery of flowers again. It had to be Daniel. I didn't think for one minute it would be Matt. I opened the door and got a shock when from behind the flowers Daniel stepped out.

'This doesn't mean you have to buy me some in return,' he said. He looked almost apologetic – not an expression I associated with Daniel. I got the feeling he wasn't ever really sorry for anything he did.

'You shouldn't have,' I said.

'I know, but I wanted to.' He smiled. 'Look, can I come in? Just for a moment. I'd sooner not discuss this on the doorstep.'

I opened the door and locked it behind him. He handed me the flowers, which I laid on the countertop. 'I'm not sure there's much to discuss,' I said, deciding to take the lead. 'We both got carried away on Friday night. I should have gone home when Matt was called away.'

'I take it you haven't told him.'

'God no,' I said. 'I assume you're not going to mention it either.'

'Don't look so alarmed. I'm not that bad. I won't be saying anything to Matt,' replied Daniel. 'I like him, and we've got a working relationship.' He paused. 'I like you too, which I think is obvious, but I'm not one for coercing women into sleeping with me, so I respect your decision.'

I nodded. 'Thank you. I'm glad we've got that sorted.' I wanted Daniel to leave. The longer he was anywhere near me, the more difficult I found it not to throw myself at him. I didn't know what was attracting me to him; maybe it was the flattery or the possibility of danger. Had I subconsciously started thinking of myself as unattractive, settled and maybe even a little boring? I must be pretty pathetic if I'd throw myself into bed with the first man I'd had anything to do with since being back at work. I seriously needed to get a grip on myself.

'I just wanted to say one thing before I go,' said Daniel, moving closer to me. 'We both know that, whatever this thing is that's going on between us, it's probably not going to go away in a hurry.'

I gulped. 'I know, but we have to ignore it.'

'Yeah.' He was standing right in front of me now. He grazed his knuckles gently down my face. 'For now, we do. I'm a patient man.' He kissed the top of my head, pausing as he inhaled. 'So, for now, it's strictly professional. But remember, you're in control.'

I didn't reply. I could only stand rooted to the spot as he left the shop. Then I let out something between a laugh and a cry. In control? Who was he kidding? He knew as well as I did that he had the control. Just look at the jabbering wreck he'd reduced me to.

Despite that encounter, my every interaction and meeting with Daniel from thereon, whether we were alone or at his offices or at the house I was working on, was totally professional. He conducted himself with the utmost courtesy, respect, and professionalism. It got to the point where I wondered if I'd imagined the whole thing and had blown it out of all proportion. Daniel was a complex character and in the couple of months I'd known him, I had seen several of his personas. The businessman, all smiles, charm, and oozing professionalism. The seducer, although I had to admit, I hadn't been much of a challenge for him. And I'd seen a little of the ruthless side of him. I still remembered the way he'd spoken to his assistant on the phone the first time I'd met him at the property. I wondered what had happened to the chap he'd been pissed off with that day. I was sure there were other sides to

Daniel that I hadn't been privy to – and maybe that was a good thing.

I was now at Beaumont House, walking around, carrying out a final inspection of the refurbished rooms. I felt like a proud mother at the blue-and-green palette colour Daniel had settled on. Highlighting the heritage of the property yet in a modern way, giving it a masculine feel but one that wouldn't intimidate women or make it feel as if they'd just walked into a Soho gentleman's club. We had laughed when I'd referenced that in the planning stages, and it made me smile again remembering it.

I went out through the utility room which led to the garage via an internal door where the leftover materials and old furniture had been stored. I took some photographs to show to some contacts who liked to up-cycle furniture. I knew someone at a TV production company who bought furniture which would then miraculously appear in a skip only for their show host to find. Smoke and mirrors, as with everything.

My phone rang. Matt. 'Hey, babe,' he said. 'You OK? You home yet?'

'All good. Still at work. I'm about to hand over Beaumont House to Daniel. What's up?' He hadn't mentioned moving back to Australia again since that weekend months ago and I hadn't brought it up either. It was something we did need to address, but not right now.

'I've left my bank card at home, and I need to pay the builder's merchant. I was wondering if you could give me your card details for the joint account.'

'The joint account? Shouldn't you be using your business account?'

'Yeah, but I don't want to pester Daniel. I'll look a right mug, asking him to pay for it.'

I knew the importance Matt put on projecting the right

image to Daniel. 'OK. I'm assuming we have enough in the joint account?'

'Yeah. Yeah. I'm going to transfer it to you now. I did ask them if I could send it direct by bank transfer, but they want card details. Bloody archaic, but there you go.'

I took my card out and placed it on the counter in the utility room. 'I'll send you a photo of both sides,' I said.

'Thanks, babe. Catch you later.'

I'd just sent the photo through when I heard the front door opening. It was Daniel.

The handover and walk-through didn't take long – less than twenty minutes. Daniel was thoroughly impressed. 'It's amazing,' he said. 'I absolutely love what you've done, Laurel. You have such an eye for this type of thing.'

I knew I was beaming with pleasure at the compliments.

'I've really enjoyed working on it,' I said. 'Do you mind if I put some of those pictures on my social media? I won't reveal the address, it's purely to build up my portfolio.'

'Of course. No problem.'

'Right, well, if there's nothing else, then I'll send my invoice over.' I held out my hand.

Daniel hesitated but then shook it, his thumb strobed my skin and my heart threw in an extra beat. He looked me directly in the eye. 'I'll be in touch again soon,' he said. 'I've got another proposal I'd like you to consider.'

'Brilliant.' An automatic response; I wasn't sure I dared have anything more to do with him. Quite frankly, every interaction with Daniel was a test of my resolve. It was exhausting, fighting the urge to embark on an affair with him. 'I'll get off now. Bye, Daniel. Thanks again.'

I trotted down the steps of the property and out through the gate onto the path, feeling relieved I was away from him and yet disappointed for the very same reason. I glanced up at the bay window. Daniel was standing there with his hands casually in his trouser pockets. He smiled and gave a nod of his head. As I walked down the road, I could sense his gaze on me all the way.

I put thoughts of Daniel out of my mind, and tried to convince myself I'd had a lucky escape, while simultaneously hoping he really would contact me again about his new proposal. I tried not to acknowledge the fact that I was well and truly under his spell.

It was a Monday, but I felt like celebrating the completion of the project. I'd get a takeaway and a bottle of fizz for tonight. Matt had been working hard under the guidance of Daniel, and the break-in at the barn had thankfully seemed a one-off setback. It was still a bit of a mystery how it was reported to Matt, but what with all the work and plans ahead of him, he had left it, citing it as a paperwork trail not filled in correctly. I had my own suspicions. It was a rather outlandish conspiracy theory, but it had crossed my mind more than once that Daniel had been behind it. I wasn't sure how, but maybe he'd got someone to call the restaurant and pretend to be the police, just so he could get Matt off the scene. It was kind of crazy and far-fetched, yet at the same time, I could imagine Daniel doing that. He was, after all, a man who got what he wanted, as he reminded me.

And there I was, thinking about him again. Ugh. I had to stop this.

I pulled up at a mini-supermarket a few miles down the road from Beaumont House and nipped into the shop, grabbing a few bits and a bottle of champagne. It wasn't until I came to pay that I realised I didn't have my bank card. 'I'm so sorry,' I said to the cashier. 'I've left my card at work. I'll have to nip back and get it.'

I still had a set of keys for the house. I was hanging on to them so I could organise the removal of the things from the garage. I found a parking space in the road behind Beaumont House which gave residents access to their back gardens. I casually glanced towards the rear of Daniel's house, and saw a man, dressed in a suit, entering the garden through the gate. It seemed a bit odd, and I couldn't quite think why he'd be doing that unless he was viewing the property or something, or maybe he was an estate agent. Daniel had said he wanted to sell the place.

It wasn't my business anyway, so I hurried down the road and around the corner towards the front of the property, where I saw another man enter Beaumont House from the front. Not wanting to disturb them, I decided I'd use the key to the garage. That way I could slip in without being noticed and grab my card, which I'd left in the utility room.

The shutters were closed now, and I assumed Daniel must have done that, which seemed a strange thing to do. Surely the estate agents would want to see the living room in daylight?

The garage opened easily, and I slipped in without making a sound. I tried the handle of the internal door from the garage to the utility room, but it was locked. I felt like an intruder as I slid the key into the lock and very slowly turned it, all the time listening out for any sound of someone being on the other side. The door opened and I could hear voices coming from within the property. They sounded like they were at the back of the house, in the kitchen – the hard surfaces amplifying the deep male voices coming from inside.

The monitor flickered from the corner of the utility room, and I looked at the screen. It was black and white, and I could clearly see the man who'd come through the front door sitting on a barstool in the middle of the open-plan area that looked out over the garden. The blinds were all drawn on the glass at the back, but enough light was coming in through the feature roof lantern, almost spotlighting the scene. Daniel was standing facing the man with his arms folded and the third man, standing off to the left, I assumed must be the guy I saw going in through the back gate.

I could pick out Daniel's voice and it sent a shudder down my spine. He was using that same tone I'd heard him use on the phone to his assistant that time. The cold steeliness of his words penetrated through the walls and, although I couldn't make out exactly what he was saying, I knew it wasn't an amicable conversation.

I was transfixed as I looked at the screen. It felt like I was watching a Channel 4 documentary where they were replaying CCTV footage of a crime.

The desire to leave was overwhelming. I had a bad feeling about what was going on in there. I backed away and barely managed to stop myself from banging into the mop and bucket behind me.

The sound of Daniel's controlled but dangerous voice, raised by a few decibels, had me looking at the screen again. I looked on in ever increasing horror at what happened next.

Daniel stepped towards the man and punched him right on the jaw, sending him crashing to the floor, the stool clattering to the ground, echoing around the room. I let out a gasp and immediately clasped my hand over my mouth. None of the men appeared to have heard me. The man who'd come in through the gate stepped forward, hoisted the other man up from the floor and, holding him by the lapel with one hand, delivered a punch to his stomach. The victim dropped to the ground, clearly wheezing for breath.

Then he staggered to his feet. The other man went to attack him again, but Daniel put an arm out to stop him.

I breathed a sigh of relief. At least Daniel had the sense to put a stop to the beating.

What happened next was the single most traumatising thing I had ever witnessed.

The younger man was standing straight now and clearly mouthing off to Daniel. Again, I could hear his voice but only catch the odd word here and there.

Daniel stood facing the man, appearing not to respond to anything the man was saying. Then, with what I could only later describe as a calm, calculated action, totally devoid of emotion, he turned and picked something up from the countertop.

I couldn't see what it was, but he strode back over to the man and at first I thought Daniel had punched him in the stomach. The younger man appeared to clutch Daniel's hand. He staggered but stayed on his feet. Then Daniel pulled his hand away and I could clearly see he was holding a knife.

Fuck!

Daniel had stabbed him. I had witnessed it with my own eyes. I grabbed onto the worktop in the utility room to stop myself from collapsing. I couldn't breathe. I thought I was going to suffocate. I gasped for air, forcing myself to stay in control. The only thing I was certain of was that I couldn't let them know I was there. My legs were shaking violently as I looked back at the screen. The man was on the floor and Daniel and the other guy were standing over him. The knife was clearly in Daniel's hand.

They were standing there, watching the man die in front of their eyes. The younger man's leg twitched, and he tried to drag himself across the floor. Neither Daniel nor the other guy made a move to help.

I don't know what part of my brain took over, but I knew I had to get out of there. I had witnessed, at best, attempted murder, at worst first-degree murder. There was no way I would be afforded the luxury of walking out of there if they knew I had seen all that.

My heart was racing as I exited the utility room, not bothering to lock the door, just closing it gently behind me. I slipped out of the garage door, which was on a latch and locked itself as I pulled it closed behind me.

I stepped out onto the path and hurried down the road away

from Beaumont House. As I rounded the corner, my stomach heaved, and I vomited into the gutter. My car was in sight. I was scared Daniel's accomplice was going to come out of the back gate and see me. I ran to my car, my legs almost buckling as I reached it. Frantically, I inserted the key into the ignition and with several jerky starts, I sped away from the crime scene with no idea what I was going to do or where I was going.

TWENTY-ONE

Hannah

I wasn't quite sure how I managed to drive home. My hands were shaking violently, sending tremors up my arms and into my shoulders. My stomach churned and more than once I thought I was going to have to pull over and throw up. Somehow I made it home without crashing the car or having some kind of mental breakdown.

When I got in, I was relieved the house was empty. I sagged down behind the closed front door, my head lolling back against the oak.

It was a minute or two before I felt calmer. I was home. I was safe. I was not anywhere near Daniel Sully.

I dragged myself to my feet and went through to the kitchen. I was planning on getting a glass of water, but the wine bottle in the fridge was my friend. I gulped down the first glass I poured but managed to restrain myself from doing the same with the second. I still had the school run to do, so tipped it down the sink instead.

I sat down on the sofa with my laptop and tried to think

logically and rationally as I sifted through the questions, not trying to answer them yet.

Why had Annabelle used a different name?

Why had she gone to see Daniel Sully? What was her connection to him?

Was it actually Daniel Sully in the clinic?

If it was Daniel, my Daniel, then was he behind all the things that had been happening to me?

This begged the question, if Annabelle knew him, was she involved somehow?

Both notions were unthinkable. Or at least I would have liked not to have to consider them, but I was in no position to dismiss them. Complacency was my enemy.

I berated myself for letting my guard down and even thinking things would be different here on Silverbanks. That I could somehow live a life without the deep-set anxiety always wriggling in my stomach and plaguing the dark corners of my mind.

Think.

I had to think clearly.

I needed to take a mental step back and work out what was going on and if I was safe. If my family was safe. I couldn't think beyond that. I needed some facts first.

I googled the hell out of Daniel Sully and surprisingly, there wasn't much I didn't already know about him. The internet was a hotbed of information about the murder and the ensuing court case and finally his sentencing, but after that, it pretty much went cold. Just reading about the case brought so many unwanted memories back to me. Emotions and memories I had suppressed for all these years. It was like a crack in a dam wall, at first slowly trickling out, but with each detail I recalled the crack got bigger until the wall broke, and I felt like it was only yesterday I had walked into that courtroom to give evidence.

I cried for Laurel. The woman who at that point was in no

man's land of life. How naive she'd been to think she could just walk back into her old life, and everything would be all right again. She had no idea. I cried for Hannah too. Without Laurel, she wouldn't be here and that would mean no Jasper and no Pia. How could I possibly want to go back to my old life and yet, how could I possibly not want to?

Once I'd pulled myself together, I searched for Annabelle Burton. I wasn't surprised when nothing significant was revealed. Next I tried Jessica Beaumont.

I found plenty of people with that name, but none of the pictures matched Annabelle.

With no luck on the internet, I felt I was at a standstill before I'd even got going. I needed to know more about Annabelle, but I couldn't ask her directly without raising suspicion. What exactly she was hiding, I still didn't know, but it was dawning on me that the secret I thought she had wasn't to do with her ex-husband, it was to do with Daniel Sully.

There was, of course, only one person here on Silverbanks who would be able to help. If she couldn't, then nobody could.

I picked up my phone and dialled the number on the Residents' Association handbook.

'Hi, Elizabeth, it's Hannah Towers.'

'Hannah. Hello, dear. So nice to hear from you. How can I help you?'

I smiled at the receptionist-like greeting. 'It's about the Summer Swimathon, actually,' I began. 'I'm keen to get involved and wondered whether you could pop over for a chat.'

'Oh, I say, that's fabulous to hear,' gushed Elizabeth. 'I'd be delighted to talk to you. When would you like me to come? I'm free this morning, although that might be too short notice. I could rearrange my afternoon appointment. When's best for you?'

I smiled at her eagerness and felt slightly guilty at the deception but then, it was nothing compared to the deception

I'd been living for the past eleven years. 'This morning would be perfect,' I said. 'Half an hour?'

'Wonderful. I'll see you soon.'

'I'll get the kettle on.'

I hung up and went over to the kitchen, getting out my best teacups and teapot. I knew Elizabeth would love to feel special and I needed to get her on side so I could quiz her. I was relying on her vanity at being the font of all knowledge for all things Silverbanks; she wouldn't be able to resist sharing her inside information with me. I wondered how many lies I'd have to tell her to find out what I needed.

'Right, Luna, you need to be on your best behaviour,' I warned the dog. 'No jumping up at Elizabeth, no whining, and no barking. Understood?' I ruffled her fluffy head, and she licked my hand. 'No licking either.'

Exactly thirty minutes after getting off the phone with Elizabeth, she was ringing the bell at the door. She had her diary and an A4 notebook in one hand and a packet of biscuits in the other.

'That's very kind, thank you, Elizabeth.'

We settled in the living room overlooking the front of the property and I could see I'd scored a few Brownie points already by bringing the tea set out on a tray and pouring Elizabeth's for her.

'I do love a cup of tea from the pot,' she said. 'So much nicer than being made in the cup.'

'I think so too,' I said. Lie number one. I really couldn't care less how the tea was made; it all tasted the same to me.

'So, you're thinking about the Summer Swimathon, are you?' asked Elizabeth, before biting into a biscuit.

'Yes. I had a lovely dip in the sea with Annabelle the other day and she mentioned it.' Lie number two. The dip in the sea was anything other than nice. 'I'd love to get involved. If you need help with organising it, then I'm all yours.' I gave a laugh and Elizabeth beamed back at me.

'That would be wonderful,' she declared. 'I usually do it myself, but all help gratefully received, as they say.' She leaned towards me. 'And it will help you get to know the residents more. I can sense you're a little shy.' She patted my knee, rather like I imagined she would have done to one of the children when she was a governess.

'Everyone has been very welcoming,' I said, sensing this was a good way to take the conversation in the direction I needed. 'Annabelle has been looking after me.'

'Annabelle, yes, she's relatively new too. She doesn't know the residents as well as I do, of course, and she doesn't mix as much. She could mix more, if I'm honest.' Elizabeth frowned. 'Maybe you could get her involved too. That would help her as well as you.'

I could sense Elizabeth getting distracted. 'It's funny you should say Annabelle doesn't mix much,' I began. 'I'd noticed that too. I didn't like to pry, but... How can I put this? No. Sorry. Ignore me. I shouldn't gossip.' I sat back in my seat and took a sip of tea, eyeing Elizabeth over the rim of the cup.

She put her own cup down on the coffee table. 'No. No. What was it you were wondering?'

I schooled my face into what I hoped was an uncomfortable look. 'Honestly, I shouldn't ask. It's a delicate matter.'

'You can ask me anything and it won't go any further than this room,' said Elizabeth. 'It will be just between you and I.'

I put my cup down and sat forward, clasping my hands together. 'I was wondering how Annabelle could afford to live on Silverbanks,' I began. 'Gosh, that sounds so pompous, saying it out loud. I don't mean it to.'

Elizabeth was already waving my apologies away before I'd finished. 'No. It's a perfectly reasonable question.'

'You don't have to tell me if you don't want to.'

'This is strictly between us...' said Elizabeth. I nodded and waited for her to continue. 'She doesn't own the property. She's renting the apartment. It belongs to George Sanders, a former resident, who has gone off on a round-the-world cruise. I manage it for him. Well, the estate agent does, but it all goes through me so as not to bother George.'

'Oh, wow, I didn't realise,' I said. Lie number three. Annabelle had told me she had a short lease. 'That explains it. Although, I imagine the rent is very high – do counsellors earn that much?'

Elizabeth hesitated but the desire to show off her inside knowledge was too much for her to resist. 'The apartment is on a six-month lease. Annabelle paid for it in advance. The whole sum.' Elizabeth raised her eyebrows. 'But it didn't come from her.'

'No? Where was it from?'

'I really shouldn't say.'

'I promise you, I won't breathe a word,' I said. 'To be honest, as homeowners, it's always good to know a little more about tenants than we would about residents who own their property. It's... it's reassuring. Peace of mind.'

Elizabeth gave me a knowing look. 'Exactly. I'm so glad you said that. I think that too. One can never be too careful, and tenants come and go. Personally, I'd like it if it was homeowners only on Silverbanks.'

'Definitely,' I said. Lie number four. I hated the pretentiousness of being a homeowner and the false superiority it gave them over those who rented. 'So, where did the payment for Annabelle's apartment come from?'

'It was from a company. Now, let me think, what were they called?' She brought her finger to her lip as she concentrated on recalling the name. 'Ah, yes, a strange name. The Enclave Group.'

If I hadn't already found that business card on my worktop,

I might have been shocked by this information, but coupled with what I'd found out when I'd followed Annabelle, my heart didn't miss a beat.

'I don't think I've heard of them,' I said with a frown.

'I know, such an odd name. She said it was her employer. They were relocating her. I must admit, it piqued my interest, so I tried to look them up on the internet but couldn't find them.'

'Her employer?' Now that did throw me. Counselling was definitely not on the list of services the Enclave Group offered.

'Is everything all right, dear?' asked Elizabeth giving me an odd look and I wondered if my poker face wasn't quite up to scratch.

'Oh, yes.' I forced a smile. 'Erm... has Annabelle ever mentioned any family or friends to you?'

Another quizzical look from Elizabeth. 'What makes you ask that?'

'Oh, nothing. Just that she's never mentioned anyone and, what with everything she's been through, I wondered.'

'Whether she has or not, it's nice you're being so supportive of her,' said Elizabeth. 'Now, the Swimathon.'

I sat through thirty minutes of Elizabeth talking about the charity event and it wasn't until my online shopping delivery turned up that she eventually thought about leaving.

'Thanks so much for popping by,' I said as we stood on the doorstep among the bags of groceries I'd asked the delivery driver to leave there.

'No problem. Thank you for inviting me.' She stepped over the bags. 'Are you sure you don't want me to help you carry all this in?'

'I'm fine, honestly.'

'Right-o. Well, lovely to chat to you, Hannah. I really feel you and I are going to get along famously.'

I had to admire her optimism. 'I'm sure we will,' I said. 'And thank you for all your help too.' I gave her a knowing look.

'Any time,' she said.

With that she scurried off down the drive and, with a final wave at the gateway, she was gone. I breathed a sigh of relief. I needed time to think everything through.

By the time I had packed away my shopping, I knew what I had to do. Instead of being the hunted, I had to become the hunter.

TWENTY-TWO

Hannah

I had spent most of Monday night trying to figure everything out. Was that my Daniel at Elm Tree Clinic? What was Annabelle visiting him for? Why the different name – I had no idea which name was false, maybe they both were? What was her connection to the Enclave? Her employer apparently, but I doubted they offered counselling services, so what did she do for them?

After a restless sleep, I was up early and watching the sun rise while I deliberated my next move. I had to be proactive and take control of the situation. I'd had enough of waiting around for her to bring Bryan's notebook to me. I needed to know what was in it and I wasn't taking no for an answer. As soon as I got back from the school run, I headed down First Avenue towards The Loop.

It was Tuesday morning and I remembered Annabelle saying that she didn't work Tuesdays, so with any luck, she wouldn't be on a counselling call. Her car was on the drive, and

I knocked on the door as well as rang the bell. She'd be able to see it was me from the intercom monitor. I knocked and rang again after Annabelle didn't appear at the door. Maybe she'd gone out on foot or was on the beach.

I walked around the side path and pushed open the gate, I remember Annabelle telling me there was no lock on it and, after the vandalism and Bryan's death, she had asked the estate agents if she could have a lock fitted. Fortunately, it hadn't been done yet.

I knocked on the glass of the back door, in case for some reason she'd been in the shower or something and hadn't heard me at the front. I half-expected her to be sitting in the garden having breakfast or sitting on the sofa but there was no sign of her.

I cupped my hands around my face and peered through the patio door glass. A cup of tea was sitting on the worktop, together with a cereal bowl. Annabelle didn't strike me as someone who left things lying around. The few times I'd been in her apartment, it had been spotlessly clean to the point of being minimalist. I guess that suited her narrative that she was escaping an abusive marriage, which I now doubted was the truth.

There was still no answer from Annabelle and as I took another look through the glass, I spotted Bryan's notebook sitting on the coffee table.

Without thinking too much about what I was about to do; I tried the handle on the patio door and to my surprise it moved. I pulled on the door, and it slid to the left.

I paused, half-expecting Annabelle to come rushing through from the bedroom or bathroom and demand to know what I was doing. I was at the point where I didn't care. I was going to get that book with or without her knowledge.

I stepped into the apartment; my trainers silent on the tiled flooring. Two strides and I was at the coffee table, picking up the book. I paused, listening for any tell-tale noise she was at home.

'Annabelle?' I called out softly. 'Hey. It's me, Hannah.'

Silence. I called her name again, but still no answer.

I was about to leave with the book when I stopped. That would mean taking it home and, if Jasper saw it, I'd have to explain it to him. Also, what if the police decided to search my house? I couldn't risk them finding the book. It was better here in Annabelle's apartment, where it had no connection to me. I put the book down and, using the cuff of my hoodie, I wiped my fingerprints from the cover. Then, using a pen that was on the coffee table, I flicked through the pages, coming to the last entry.

Bryan had made mention of the new neighbours – that would be Jasper and me. He'd also said about going to the barbecue the following day. That was the last entry. I scanned the pages for anything to do with Annabelle, but again there was nothing. How often Bryan wrote in the book was difficult to say. He used the same type of pen each time so no clues there.

I don't know what made me do it, but I found myself looking around the living room. What I was hoping to find, I didn't know. Maybe some clue that Annabelle had left lying around, telling me who she really was. I noticed her laptop on the breakfast bar and next to that her moleskin diary, the one she'd moved last week, mentioning it was her appointment diary.

Careful not to directly touch the book with my fingers, I leafed through the pages. Every page was blank. I got to the month of May, wondering whether this was when she'd started using it for appointments. I wasn't surprised to find those pages blank as well. Not a single appointment. No client names. Nothing.

I gave a half-laugh. This diary was nothing more than a prop for what I was now sure was a fake job.

'What other secrets have you got, Annabelle?' I said to myself as I closed the diary.

I looked towards the door to the hallway and where the bedroom was. Did I have the nerve to poke around in there? Would I ever get another chance like this? Probably not, in answer to the last question I posed myself.

With the sleeve of my top still over my hand, I pushed open the bedroom door. It was simply furnished in white and had the same sterile show-home feel the rest of the apartment had. There were no personal effects dotted around the place and it certainly didn't have a lived-in feel. On the dressing table was a make-up bag, which was zipped closed, and next to it a hairbrush.

Still making sure my hand was covered by my sleeve, I pulled open the drawer of the dressing table, but it was empty. I moved quietly around the room, looking in the chest of drawers where Annabelle's clothes were all neatly folded and set out with set-square precision. I daren't move anything as I was sure Annabelle would notice.

Built-in wardrobes ran the length of one wall and, on inspection, I wasn't surprised to find one half empty while the other half had clothes hanging up. Several blouses, a couple of skirts and mostly pairs of trousers, together with a coat.

I didn't know what I was looking for. Something that would prove Annabelle's identity one way or the other, or possibly something connecting her to Daniel.

I was suddenly aware of voices coming from outside. Female voices, talking, although I couldn't make out what they were saying.

I got to my feet and stole a look through the window. The Venetian blinds were tilted downwards, which meant I could see out without been seen. From my position on the other side the room, I was confident I was at an advantage.

My heart nearly somersaulted when I saw Annabelle say goodbye to the woman she must have been talking to, before heading up her path. I didn't recognise the woman, who headed off down the road.

I had just made it to the hallway when I heard the key in the front door. My breath hitched in my throat and my heart almost bashed through my ribcage. I spun around and ran out of the living room, sliding the door closed behind me. I didn't have time to run the length of the garden and clamber over the wall onto the beach. If I went back through the gate, I'd run the risk of bumping into her.

Shit.

Halfway down the garden, there was a small shed, painted like a beach hut, and I sprinted as fast as I could towards it, cornering hard around the side of it and throwing myself to the ground like a baseball player making a home run.

I got to my feet and stood with my back to the wooden building, trying to control my breathing, which I was sure could be heard a mile away. I heard the patio door slide open and the sound of heels stepping out onto the flagstones.

Please don't come up the garden. Please don't come up the garden.

How on earth was I going to explain myself if she caught me there, hiding like a fugitive behind her shed? I sidled along the wall. There was a hedge marking the border of the property and I eyed it speculatively. Yes, I could get over it if I had to. I listened again but Annabelle was either standing still or walking along the grass. I somehow managed to squeeze behind the water butt at the corner of the shed and crouched down as far as possible.

I waited for what seemed like an age but eventually my patience was rewarded as I heard the patio door close. I let out a long sigh of relief, hoping she'd gone back inside.

I needed to get the hell out of there before anyone spotted me and reported me to Annabelle. I hauled myself over the fence and out onto the path that ran between the apartments and the residence next door. The path led down to the beach and, a few minutes later, I was jogging back along the beach to the safety of my own home.

TWENTY-THREE

Laurel

'Thank you, Mrs Jordan, you've been very helpful,' said DCI Bryan Chamberton. 'If you want to check that over with your solicitor and sign each page where indicated. While you're doing that, I'll get you another cup of tea.'

'Thank you,' I replied, gathering the several sheets of paper with my account of what I had witnessed at Beaumont House several months ago. Chamberton left the room.

'Take your time reading through it,' advised my solicitor, Craig Mitchell of Mitchell & Hodder. We'd been recommended them by someone Matt knew. They were a reputable firm who operated outside of London from offices in Brighton and had no connection whatsoever with Daniel Sully.

I felt exhausted as I read through the pages of testimony. Evidence that was going to be used to bring Daniel Sully before the Crown Court on a murder charge. As the key prosecution witness, I would be instrumental in his downfall. And the weight of the role I would play was proving a heavy burden.

After seeing that young man murdered in cold blood, I had somehow driven home and collapsed in Matt's arms. I had barely been able to speak, let alone offer any sort of coherent explanation for the state I was in. Initially, Matt hadn't been able to believe what I was saying. He kept asking me to go over it. Was I certain that's what I saw? Was I certain it was Daniel?

'I need to call the police,' I said as I paced the room, unable to sit still for more than a few seconds at a time. I kept looking out of the window, expecting Daniel to pull up at any minute, demanding I let him in. My imagination was going to all sorts of dark places. What if he wanted to kill me? Kill Matt? Kill Declan? At one point I was almost hysterical, and Matt had grabbed my arms, yelling at me to calm down. Declan was in the room and my hysteria had set him off crying. For several minutes it was complete and utter chaos.

Then I'd somehow pulled myself together and phoned the police.

I'm not sure the precise order of events, but the police had arrived, while at the same time an armed response team was dispatched to Beaumont House. They'd arrived to find Daniel and the other man, who I later learned was Ivor Kowalski, hired muscle, on the premises. Daniel was apparently on the phone calling the emergency services, while Ivor was attempting to resuscitate the victim. Daniel had admitted to stabbing the man, but claimed it was in self-defence. Naturally, Ivor corroborated this version of events. Unsurprisingly, there was no video footage from the monitor in the utility room. I had to assume it had been wiped before the police had arrived.

Obviously, my account was very different and I knew very soon after entering that interview room that I was going to find myself under immense pressure to give evidence against them.

As it turned out, Daniel was already a person of interest to the police, thanks to suspected, but as yet unproved, links to organised crime.

Matt had taken it badly. He hadn't wanted me to give evidence, not because he was concerned about me but because of the impact it would have on his business, and on us as a family.

'I can't believe you're putting your bloody business before me,' I shouted at him during one of our stand-up arguments.

'It's not a case of putting the business before you,' he had retorted. 'With no business, how can I support us? Your interior design income isn't enough for our lifestyle.'

'But we're talking murder,' I insisted. I didn't want to testify against Daniel but my conscience wasn't allowing me to walk away. I still couldn't really believe what I'd seen. Didn't want to believe it. Didn't want to believe it of Daniel.

'I don't think you should get involved,' said Matt. 'I'd go as far as saying, I don't want you to give a statement. Who is that man to you anyway? He's just another lowlife scumbag.'

'That's not the point. And you didn't say that about Daniel when the police told you he was part of an organised crime gang and that his entrepreneurship was all a cover for what he was really getting up to. Why was he never lowlife, then?'

'Daniel's business, the money he sank into my company, was nothing to do with organised crime. It was legit. I'm not saying he wasn't involved in some illegal stuff, but that's separate.'

'You can't separate the two. You don't know that for sure.' I was trying to convince myself as much as Matt. My feelings for Daniel both confused me and shamed me. How could I still have some kind of desire for him after what he'd done?

'That's beside the point. The fact of the matter is, you're about to become a key witness in a trial that could put Daniel Sully behind bars for the rest of his life. Don't you see how dangerous that is? And you're doing it because it's "the right thing to do", even though the bloke who died—'

'The bloke who was *killed*. Murdered. He didn't just die,' I had corrected him.

'Whatever, he's still a fucking criminal, and you're risking everything for him.'

'I'm stopping Daniel Sully from ever doing that again to someone else,' I said, realising I sounded pious.

'You're going to have to live with the consequences of what you're doing,' snapped Matt. 'And those consequences affect me and Declan. Have a think about it, Laurel, before you do something stupid.'

The pressure had been on from the moment I spoke to the police, and we were informed of the true nature of Daniel Sully's business activities. The pressure wasn't just from Matt; I was being pulled in the other direction by the police. And to top it all, then came the pressure from Daniel's associates.

It was low level at first, like dropped phone calls, a brick through my shop window, my car tyres slashed. They, whoever they were, soon stepped up their campaign of intimidation. Notes left on my car, pushed through my letter box, withheld numbers telling me to keep quiet. The threats began referring to my family and how I was putting them at risk. That's when it got serious. By this time, I had signed the statement and agreed to give evidence. It had been presented to the CPS and the green light was given to prosecute Daniel, who was being held on remand.

The threats obviously weren't coming from Daniel himself. The phone calls came at random times throughout the day and night, when he wouldn't have had access to a telephone.

Although we hadn't had any sort of relationship, there had been a connection from the first time we'd seen each other; even when I'd rebuffed him, he'd been the perfect gentleman, and deep down I'd known that the thing between us wasn't over. Since the murder, I couldn't count the number of times I'd thanked my lucky stars that nothing more had happened. My gut instinct that Daniel was dangerous had been right, but I also knew that he, personally, wouldn't hurt me. However, I couldn't say the same about his associates, and that was where the threats were coming from.

I had even considered going to visit him in prison, but soon dismissed that idea. Not only was it reckless but it would put me in a very difficult position when it came to giving evidence. A date for the court case had been set and I was dreading it. With every passing day, I became more and more nervous, constantly looking over my shoulder. I had stopped going out. My interior design business had folded, and I'd let Amy go as I was a prisoner in my own home.

Several times I had voiced my concerns to DCI Chamberton, telling him I was afraid of what would happen to me if I testified. And each time he had convinced me that everything would be OK. That once the court case was over, I could go back to my normal life without a care in the world. Because it wasn't just Daniel who was being brought down, it was his whole gang. The murder trial was all tied in to a bigger operation the Met had been running for the past three years. Withdrawing my statement could put three years' worth of work in jeopardy.

As the court case drew nearer, my paranoia increased, and so did another wave of intimidation. I was home alone with Declan when there was a knock at the door. I had taken to not opening the door, and that day was no exception. I thought whoever it was had gone away when I didn't answer, but suddenly there was the sound of smashing glass at the back of the house and two masked men burst into the kitchen, charging at me. Declan was upstairs in his cot, and I raced towards the staircase but one of the men grabbed my ankle and pulled me down the stairs, my jaw thumping against each step. I kicked and screamed but a backhand across the face sent me flying and I landed in a heap against the front door. Too stunned to resist, I was yanked to my feet and pushed up against the wall. The man had his hands around my throat, and I could barely touch the ground, only my tiptoes were in contact with the carpet.

'You know why I'm here, don't you?' hissed my attacker through the mask covering his face.

I made some sort of grunt. Tears were streaming down my face. In that moment, I didn't care what he did to me, I just didn't want them to hurt Declan.

'I can't hear you,' snarled the man.

'Yes,' my voice was a rasp as his hands squeezed my windpipe.

'Give evidence and see what happens to you then.' He moved one hand down my body and shoved it roughly between my legs. I whimpered. He gave a snort. 'That will be the least of your worries. I hear you've got a two-year-old kid. Declan, isn't it?'

'Please,' I wheezed the word out.

'You want to stop anything bad happening, you know what you have to do. Make sure you do it.' He let go and I slid down the wall, cowering from him.

The two men then left calmly out of the back door. As soon as they were gone, I rushed upstairs to Declan's room, grabbing him from his cot where he was napping and holding him tightly as I sobbed in fear. He woke up startled. 'I'm sorry, darling,' I said. 'Mummy's sorry.' I wiped my eyes and took him downstairs, where I phoned the police.

By the time Matt arrived home after the police had contacted him, I had made up my mind.

'I want to withdraw my statement,' I said. I looked at Matt and I could see the relief wash over him.

'Are you sure about this?' asked Chamberton later that day when I'd asked the detective to come over and I had relayed my change of heart to him. 'That's a big decision and you know there will be repercussions. Withdrawing won't make all this go away.'

We debated the decision for a good hour. Matt got increasingly frustrated and at one point I had to ask him to leave the room. 'I need to speak to Bryan on my own,' I said to him.

Reluctantly, Matt had acquiesced and gone into the kitchen with one of the other officers. I could hear him preparing something to eat for Declan.

'I can't put my family through this,' I said to Chamberton. 'If anything happens to Declan, I will never forgive myself.'

'I understand all that,' said Chamberton. 'Look, I'll go back to my boss and see what he says.'

'He can't force me.'

Bryan sighed. 'Technically, we can. We could charge you with withholding evidence, conspiring to cover up a crime, maybe even charge you in connection with the murder.'

'What? No. You wouldn't do that.'

Bryan shrugged. 'I might not, but that's not to say my boss wouldn't.'

'That sounds a lot like blackmail to me.'

'I'm sorry, Laurel,' he said. We sat in silence as I contemplated my future. I was a condemned woman whichever way I looked at it. All thoughts of the morality of giving evidence had been suffocated by the need to protect my family. To protect my son. But if I refused to give evidence, the Metropolitan Police would bring charges against me that could result in a prison sentence. I was damned if I did and damned if I didn't.

How had I got myself into this position? If only I hadn't gone back for my bank card. If only I hadn't stayed and watched the CCTV. If only I'd never met Daniel Sully. If only Matt had never won that contract with him. I could trace the If Only scenarios all the way back to if only I'd never met Matt, but then of course I wouldn't have Declan. I dropped my head into my hands, feeling utterly and completely broken.

'There is one other option,' said Bryan.

I looked up. Was he about to throw me a lifeline? 'And that is?'

'UK Protected Persons Service,' he said. And when I gave him a blank look, he explained. 'Witness protection. We can do it for you and your family. I think there's a very strong case for you, Matt and Declan all to go into the PPS programme.'

TWENTY-FOUR

Hannah

At least I now knew that Bryan hadn't written anything in his notebook that revealed my past. I silently thanked him. He had kept my secret, even in death. That probably explained why I hadn't heard from Annabelle. Her lack of contact was troubling me, purely because I didn't trust her, but, at the same time, it was a relief. There was something I had to do, something I needed to find out, before I saw her again.

Jasper had FaceTimed every evening and on Tuesday afternoon his parents had been over to see me. I suspected this was at Jasper's request even though they didn't say so. Although it was lovely to see them, it did mean I'd had to put off what I needed to do until today – Wednesday.

I pulled my car up in the road outside Elm Tree Clinic. I had been on edge from the moment I'd woken up and had tried my hardest not to be distracted or impatient with Pia, but my nerves were practically shredded. I hadn't been able to face any food and the one cup of tea I'd had was now gurgling in my stomach and making me feel queasy.

There was no getting away from the fact that I had to do this. I had to face Daniel Sully if I wanted to get my life back once more. His actions had taken everything away from me once before and I was fucked if I was going to let him do that a second time.

A feeling of determination swept over me, and I drove the car into the car park, reversing into a space.

I was relieved when a different member of staff from the last time I was there opened the door and invited me into the reception room. There was no sign of Hilary, which meant I didn't have to lie about my name.

'I've come to see Daniel Sully,' I said, smiling and trying to sound natural.

'I'll phone through and let him know he has a visitor,' replied the woman. 'Who shall I say is here?'

'Laurel,' I replied.

'Laurel... Your surname?' she asked, the telephone receiver at her ear and her finger poised over the buttons.

'Laurel Jordan.' It felt strange saying my name again after all these years and yet familiar, like I was going back to visit a childhood home or school. I waited while the receptionist rang through to Daniel.

'Hello, Daniel. Maggie here. There's a young lady here to see you. Laurel Jordan.' She looked up at me with keen eyes as she listened to Daniel's response. 'Yes, that's right. Laurel Jordan.' More silence. 'Yes. OK. Are you sure?... Yes... OK. Bye.'

'If you can just sign in here on the iPad first,' said the receptionist, handing me the device. I quickly completed the digital form, remembering to use the name Laurel Jordan, and passed it back to her. 'Lovely. Room ten. Up the stairs. Turn right and it's halfway down on your right.'

'Thank you.' I wanted to ask how Daniel had sounded. Was he surprised? Shocked? Angry? But I didn't dare.

The stairway swept up to the first floor and I imagined it was very impressive when it was a private home. There was a fresh clean smell to the building. It was hard to imagine this was a place where patients had respite care, and some even saw their last days here. I wondered which applied to Daniel.

I was about to find out, as I stood outside room ten. There was still time to turn and walk away. But, of course, I wasn't going to do that. I was here to put an end to everything once and for all.

I knocked on the door and waited. My heart was thudding against my breastbone and as I clasped my hands together, I could feel the sweat gathering in my palms.

The door opened and I was surprised when a nurse stepped out of the room, pulling the door behind her. 'Hello, you must be Laurel,' she said.

'That's right.'

'Daniel tells me you haven't seen each other for a long time,' she said in a low voice. 'Try not to be shocked by his appearance. You do know he's very ill, don't you?'

I nodded. 'Yes. Thank you.'

'I'll leave you to it,' said the nurse. She moved away from the door and headed off down the hallway.

I hesitated. Took one more steadying breath and then, tapping on the door more gently this time, I entered the room.

It was a spacious room, decorated in neutral shades of cream and white, with two large Georgian windows, each draped with a white muslin curtain. If it wasn't for the hospital-style bed, I would have thought I was walking into an expensive hotel room. The bunch of flowers Annabelle had brought with her were in a vase on a side table. There were two chairs and a small coffee table at the window. There was a bookcase in the corner and I recognised the red leather-bound Shakespeare collection that I'd first seen at Beaumont House.

My breath hitched in my throat at the man sitting in one of the chairs. I knew before his eyes met mine that he was looking at me. After all these years, I could still sense when his gaze was on me.

Neither of us spoke. I hadn't been sure how I would react to seeing him again. I thought maybe I'd loathe him. Shy away from him. Even recoil at being in the same room. But none of that happened.

Daniel was thinner, his pale skin almost translucent, and he had clearly lost a lot of weight. And yet, his presence filled the room. The charge in the air between us was still there and those beautiful blue eyes of his hadn't faded. They still shone brightly and were as mesmerising as ever. He was wearing a pair of chinos and a white Ralph Lauren polo shirt. He looked immaculate – just like he always did.

'Laurel.' His voice was soft, almost a whisper, as if he couldn't quite believe what he was seeing.

'Hello, Daniel,' I said, my own voice equally soft. Now I was here in front of him, everything I had carefully planned to say deserted me.

'Please, come and sit down,' he said, gesturing towards the chair opposite him. 'Forgive me for not getting up,' he continued. 'Stage four, secondary bone cancer, courtesy of prostate cancer, is making standing something of a challenge.'

'Oh, Daniel. I'm so sorry,' I said. My sorrow was genuine, and I hated to look at this once beautiful, graceful and athletic man, now confined to a chair.

Daniel let out a sigh. 'I guess it just goes to prove I was always rotten to the core.'

'Don't say that,' I replied, crossing the room. I had such a deep urge to go to him, to hold him and comfort him, but I reminded myself what he was and why I was here. Daniel Sully was a killer. And I was here to save my family. I sat down in the visitor's chair.

As always, our eyes locked, unable to resist the pull.

'For a moment there it sounded like you cared,' he said.

I hesitated as I examined my feelings – my confusing feelings which, in all honesty, frightened me because there was a part of me that did care. 'It's an awful disease,' I replied eventually.

He gave a small smile of amusement at my attempt to avoid confessing to my feelings. He could still see straight through any pretence of mine. 'You're looking well,' he said. He held up his hand. 'And don't feel bad that you can't return the compliment.'

'Is there anything they can do for you?' I asked, my emotions threatening to spiral out of control. I was finding it hard to reconcile the man in front of me with the man I'd last seen in the dock of the Crown Court, and before that on a CCTV monitor, killing someone in cold blood.

Daniel shook his head. 'Alas, that ship sailed a long time ago. I'm serving a whole life sentence.'

A ball of sadness lodged in my throat, and I had to swallow hard to speak. 'How long have you been out of prison?'

'Six weeks. Early parole, a good lawyer and the right sort of friends made it possible.' He winced as he shifted position. 'They don't have the facilities to care for me. My health needs are too complicated.'

'Can I get you anything?' I asked.

He shook his head. 'I'm due some pain relief in a while.' He settled into a more comfortable position. 'So, to what do I owe this pleasure?' he asked after a while. 'And I promise, it is a pleasure. For me, anyway.'

I hesitated. This was harder than I imagined it would be. I thought of Declan and Pia, and why I was here. 'I thought you'd know,' I said eventually. He cocked his head and shrugged. The gesture irritated me. 'I need you to call a halt to all this.'

'All what?' Now he really did look bemused.

He was either genuinely confused or a very good actor. I

couldn't decide. 'To all this harassment. Trying to mess things up for me. Trying to destroy my life because I destroyed yours.' The words came out in a rush, and I had to remind myself to breathe.

'Laurel, I have no idea what you're talking about.'

The irritation levelled up to anger. 'Stop playing games, Daniel,' I said. Still he looked blankly at me. I was so angry, it was all I could do to force myself to continue in a controlled manner. 'Why are you here?' I asked.

Daniel gave a laugh. 'What sort of question is that?'

'I mean, why are you here at Elm Tree Clinic? Why not London, being cared for in your own home?'

'I considered it, but I'd rather be here where I'm looked after by a good team of health professionals and not be a burden to my daughter. She's living locally so she can come and see me easily enough.'

'Your daughter,' I said, as my suspicions morphed into something more tangible. Suddenly, it all fell into place. How could I have been so stupid not to realise before? 'That would be Jessica,' I said, sounding far calmer than I felt.

I was rather pleased to see a fleeting look of surprise sweep his face. 'Yes, Jessica. How do you know that?'

'It almost caught me out,' I said. 'Jessica Beaumont meant nothing at first. And now I've remembered. I mean, how could I forget? Beaumont House. She's used that name to sign in here, but I guess her real name is Jessica Sully.'

Daniel nodded. 'She doesn't like to use her real name because of what happened. Didn't want to be connected with me. How do you know Jess?'

I paused. Was he making out he was unaware of the connection? 'She came to visit you a few days ago. I saw her.'

'Jess and I don't have a very good relationship,' he began. 'I barely saw her when she was younger. I put my work first. Always. I was there, but never present. And now I regret that.'

He closed his eyes briefly and I felt a strange wave of sympathy for him. He had missed out on precious time with his daughter. I could relate to that, even though our circumstances were so different. He let out a sigh. 'Jess and I were estranged for a while.'

'And now you're here, you've reconciled?' I asked.

'Yes. But, of course, it's too late for anything meaningful,' he confessed.

'Why is she looking after you now?' I asked, wondering if it was at Daniel's request so he could get her to do his bidding?

He shrugged. 'To ease her conscience, maybe.'

'Not to finally be the most important thing in your life?' I asked gently.

'There is that,' he acknowledged.

And there was that sadness again in his eyes. 'I'm sorry,' I said.

Daniel studied me for a moment before speaking. 'What's this all about, Laurel?'

'I live near here. In fact, I live on Silverbanks,' I said. 'The same estate your daughter lives on, only she doesn't go by the name of Jessica Beaumont. She calls herself Annabelle Burton.' I watched carefully for any flicker of knowledge on his face, any expression, however fleeting, that Daniel knew what I was talking about. When he didn't reply, I continued. 'Since I moved there, my life has been turned upside down. Someone knows me and wants to punish me. And I'm guessing that someone is your daughter. And I'm guessing too, that you're behind this. Your final act of revenge. To prove to me that you still control everything. That you never lose, because Daniel Sully always gets what he wants. Bryan Chamberton, the DCI from your case, he was killed. But you probably know that already. Someone wants to expose me. Wants me to be charged for his murder. And that someone is you.'

The silence was heavy and the air in the room compressed

as we eyed each other. I wished I could read him like he could me. Finally, Daniel spoke.

'Do you really think I'd do anything to hurt you, Laurel?' he asked. That gentleness was back in his voice, together with something that sounded like hurt.

'I didn't until recently,' I replied.

'You were the best thing that happened to me in a long time,' said Daniel. 'And I ruined everything. If I hadn't lost my temper that night, I would never have lost you.'

'You never had me in the first place,' I whispered, shocked by the candid reply.

'No. Not then, but you were no more than a hair's breadth away. It was only a matter of time. You know that as much as I do.' He paused to let the significance of his words sink in. 'I could have had something as beautiful as you, but I fucked up.'

'I lost everything because of you,' I said.

'Don't you think I lost everything too?' He dragged his hand across his chin.

'You chose that path. I didn't,' I replied. 'And I found something good out of it all. Jasper.'

Again, there was that look of hurt in his eyes. 'We would have been better,' he said.

'I don't believe that.'

'Don't believe it or don't want to believe it? There is a difference.'

'Stop!' I said, getting to my feet.

'I wish it could have been different,' continued Daniel, ignoring me. 'I don't have many regrets in life, but you are one of them. I didn't fight hard enough for you.'

'Daniel, please,' I said, feeling tears sting my eyes. I sat back down, suddenly exhausted.

'Listen, Laurel. I don't know what's happening to you,' he said. 'I may be many bad things, but I was never and would never be any of those to you. Never.'

I couldn't cope with this. I didn't want to hear what he was saying. I jumped to my feet again. 'I have to go. Just make this end.' I hurried across the room, yanking open the door.

'Laurel.'

I paused. Closed my eyes. I couldn't look at him. 'Goodbye, Daniel.'

TWENTY-FIVE

Laurel

'No way, Laurel. No fucking way.' Matt shook his head to underline his feelings. 'I am not going into witness protection.'

'You haven't even listened to what I was going to say,' I protested. I had expected this response from Matt. I can't say the idea appealed to me either, but with the threats escalating I was in fear of my life and most of all, fearing for the safety of Declan. 'It's not forever, only until the trial is over.'

'I don't care. I'm not putting my life on pause for six months, twelve months or however long it takes. You know how hard I've worked to get to this point. It's bad enough that Daniel has been charged with murder. Already other backers are pulling out because they don't want to be associated with him. His assets have all been frozen and Chamberton said last time he was here that the Inland Revenue are now looking into his tax returns. The bloke is a financial ruin. I don't see how he can come back from this. Even if he isn't charged with murder or found guilty, the tax man is going to take him to the cleaners.'

We were in the living room of our home, which now had a

police guard outside 24/7. It was stifling but comforting at the same time. Several months had gone by since Daniel was arrested but the intimidation hadn't stopped. Two weeks ago I'd arrived at my shop to find the place had been broken into overnight and vandalised. I had barely been out of the house since then.

Even though we'd been given police protection, I still felt incredibly vulnerable and I was having trouble sleeping at night. My imagination was running wild, thinking that it wouldn't take much to overpower one police officer and get into the house. This wasn't like me. I was a strong, resilient woman, or at least I used to be. I was even considering going to the GP and asking for Valium, but I was frightened it would be held against me and someone would deem me unfit to look after Declan. He was all I had.

In the last few weeks, I hadn't even been to see my mum. I had spoken to her on the phone, but I don't think she quite understood what I was telling her. I had suspected for a while that dementia was setting in, but it had definitely gotten worse the past few months. I would have liked to get her assessed, and wanted to be there to support her, but there was no way I could do that right now and I felt tremendously guilty about it.

'I'm stuck between a rock and a hard place,' I said. 'I can't retract my statement. If I refuse to give evidence, I'll be charged with conspiracy and God knows what else.'

'God, I wish you'd never gone back for your card that day,' muttered Matt.

'And I wish you'd never pitched to Daniel Sully in the first place,' I snapped at him.

'Fucking grow up.' Matt got up and stalked out to the kitchen where I heard him open the fridge and take out a beer.

I sighed. We were behaving like petulant teenagers and blaming each other for the situation we were in.

He came back into the room a few minutes later. 'What

about this then?' I said, perching on the edge of the sofa. 'What about if I go into PPS with Declan? Chamberton said that I would still be able to have contact with my family. They could arrange secret meetings. It wouldn't be like I had to change my name, have plastic surgery, and start a new life in South America. It's not that drastic.' I stopped talking as Matt stared at me.

He placed his bottle down on the coffee table. 'Do you really think I'm going to let you take Declan away from me for all that time? The poor kid will be as confused as hell. He's starting nursery soon. He needs stability, not to be stuck in some halfway home, never seeing the light of day.'

'Then we're back to where we started. It's all of us or none of us,' I said. 'Matt, I can't live like this anymore. You have no idea how scared I am living here, even with the police guarding the door. How long are they going to be allowed to protect us for?'

'Hold on, it's not *us* that need protecting. It's you,' said Matt. 'You're the one who's giving crucial eye-witness testimony. Damning testimony.'

'But it affects us all.'

He hunched forward, resting his forearms on his knees, his fingers laced together. I could see he was thinking about what he wanted to say. He let out a long breath. 'If you weren't here, then me and Declan wouldn't be in danger,' he said, without meeting my gaze. 'If you were in witness protection, PPS or whatever it's called, then you would be safe and, by default, so would we.'

I shook my head in disbelief at what he was suggesting. 'You can't be serious,' I said, finally finding my voice.

'I couldn't be more serious,' said Matt, this time looking up at me so I could see the defiant look on his face.

'I can't leave Declan,' I said firmly.

'You said yourself, it won't be forever. Just until the trial is over. And you could still see us, like you said. And the benefit of you going is that Declan's life won't be disrupted as much. Amy can keep coming to look after him while I'm at work, and when this trial is all over, you can come home again.'

'No. I can't leave Declan,' I said.

'But you expect me to be OK with you taking him away,' retorted Matt. 'A minute ago you were quite happy for me to only see him a few times. Why is that good enough for me but not for you? You're being so selfish, Laurel. Can't you see it?' He took a long swig of his beer. 'In fact, the more I think about it, the more it sounds like the best solution. The one that keeps Declan safe, and happy.'

We went around and around in circles the next hour, neither of us wanting to give way, but in the end, I knew I didn't have a good enough reason to keep Declan with me.

I cried myself to sleep that night, knowing I was cornered and there was no escaping from the decision I had to make. I had to leave to keep Declan safe. It really was as simple as that.

Once I told Bryan that I would go into witness protection, it all happened quite fast. He confided in me that CID had been under pressure to remove the round-the-clock protection due to the strain on resources and funding. 'You couldn't have come to this decision at a better time,' he told me.

Five days later I had packed my bag and was being whisked away in the back of a police car. I had sobbed my heart out. I honestly thought it was going to shatter into a million pieces.

When it came to say goodbye to Matt, that was difficult for a different reason. Our relationship was under a tremendous amount of strain and even though I knew it was unreasonable, I blamed him for us being in this position. I think he also blamed me. We hugged right before I left, but it was awkward with little warmth. Neither of us declared undying love for each other.

'Take care,' said Matt. 'Hopefully it won't be too long before we can meet up.'

I couldn't bring myself to say anything. I was an emotional

wasteland. All I could think about was Declan. Amy had taken him out for the afternoon, so he wasn't there when I left. I didn't want one of his last memories of me to be me walking out of the door with my bags.

The first night I was put up in an Airbnb that had been rented for a week; after that, I was moved to a one-bedroom apartment in Northampton.

Bryan sat down at the kitchen table with me and slid over a brown A4 envelope. 'From now on you're Hannah Towers,' he said. 'All your official documents are there: birth certificate, National Insurance number, NHS number, driving licence, school records, job history and family history. If you need a passport for any reason, let me know and I'll get it organised – once the trial's over, of course.'

I rested my hand on the envelope, not wanting to look inside. They had gone to a lot of trouble for someone who wasn't staying in PPS for ever. 'Only until the court case is over,' I said.

'If that's what you want.'

'I need to see Declan regularly,' I said. 'Every fortnight.'

'We may need to manage your expectations on that score,' said Bryan. 'Once a month, tops. And it can't be regular. No patterns, remember. Not with your old life anyway.'

'You never said that before.'

'I don't make the rules. Every case is judged on its own merits, and we're guided by the PPS team on this.' He reached over and patted my hand. 'It's not forever... Hannah. You'll be reunited with your family as soon as possible and your little lad won't even remember you've been away. He's far too young to recall any of this.'

A tear dropped from my eye, puddling on the table. 'I miss him already and it's only been a week,' I said.

'It will pass,' said Bryan. 'I promise you; it will be OK.'

I held on to that promise. I don't know why, but Bryan had

the ability to make me trust him, rather like I would have trusted my father. He had also assured me my mother was all right. She had been placed in a residential care home and, apparently, was none the wiser as her dementia had moved on fast. That hurt. I had always planned to be the one to sort out her care or have her come and live with me and Matt, but even that had been taken away from me. That was something that belonged in Laurel's life, not Hannah's. The only comfort I could find was that my mother was totally oblivious to it.

Over the next four months, I saw Matt and Declan only twice. I had begged Bryan to arrange more meetings, but he said he was doing his best. Everything was considered through the lens of funding, rather than feeling.

I had been secured a job in a local bookshop, tucked away down a side street. I had no idea what went on behind the scenes for that to happen, but I couldn't turn it down. Besides, it gave me something to think about, something to get up for five days a week. The PPS may have set me up with a new identity, but I still had to pay my way and support myself. I was grateful to have some kind of employment, and it did keep me mildly occupied, though nowhere near enough to stop me from grieving for the role of mummy I had given up.

I was counting off the days until the trial started. It was expected to last for several weeks but once that was over, I could go back to my life as Laurel. All I wanted to do was to hold my son in my arms and keep him safe. I knew I wouldn't take my eyes off him for a moment. I had time I needed to make up for.

I was gutted then when Bryan came to see me one day with bad news. The court case was being moved back by another four months. The defence had asked for an extension and, as the case was complicated and high profile, an extension had been given.

It meant another four months away from Declan. I was heartbroken. 'It's bad enough as it is,' I said, wiping my eyes with a tissue from where I had been crying. 'You need to ask the PPS to let me see Declan more often.'

'Hannah,' said Bryan softly. 'We have been offering more dates but it's down to Matt whether he accepts them or not.'

I looked at him for a long time as I decoded his words. 'You mean, Matt's declined visits?'

'I'm sorry,' said Bryan.

It was almost like he was offering his condolences. I thought he was going to round it off with 'If there's anything I can do to help, let me know.' The kind of platitudes you offer to the bereaved.

I went to bed that night even more devastated than when I'd first entered the programme. At least then I'd had hope and could draw comfort from the prospect of seeing my son regularly, but now I had nothing. Only the knowledge that Matt was purposely staying away from me, knowingly stopping me from seeing my son. And I had absolutely no control over that.

My only hope was that Bryan would make good on his promise to fix up a visit soon and apply a bit of pressure on Matt to come and talk to me.

I knew giving evidence was the right thing to do but, God, was I so very angry at the unfairness of the horrendous repercussions to my life.

TWENTY-SIX

Hannah

I was so glad to wake up to Thursday and the knowledge that Jasper would be home that night. I rubbed my forehead, trying to ease away the headache that was threatening.

Seeing Daniel yesterday had taken a lot out of me, and I was emotionally exhausted. I had hoped after I had seen him I'd feel reassured that I'd be left alone, but his denial that he had anything to do with it had plagued my thoughts.

I didn't believe Daniel would lie to me. And what he'd said about Annabelle bothered me too. He hadn't had much of a relationship with her. He was the stereotypical absent father. What was it he said? *There but never present.* It didn't follow that they would both be attempting to ruin my life.

As I sat debating whether to confront Annabelle outright, my phone rang. It was Jasper.

He'd phoned every morning and every evening this week, his calm, caring, and loving voice easing my turmoil. We spoke for a few minutes before Pia appeared, eager to speak to him. I knew she had missed him too this week.

'So, I'll be back this evening,' Jasper was saying. 'Have a fun day at school.'

Pia skipped off to put her shoes on while I said goodbye to him.

'I can't wait to see you this evening,' I said.

'Are you sure everything's OK?' he asked.

'Oh, yes. I'm fine. I've missed you, that's all.' This seemed to reassure him, and we ended the call.

I loved that man with all my heart, and I hated the thought he was distracted and worrying about me. I owed it to him to relieve those worries. He had been my lifeline in my darkest days, and I would eternally be grateful for that, even though I could never tell him.

I poured Pia a glass of milk and placed it on the countertop, before getting a paracetamol from the medical box for myself. Hopefully that would shift the headache before it set in for the evening. I suffered from migraines from time to time, usually when I was under pressure. I guess with everything that had been going on lately, together with worry and lack of sleep, it wasn't surprising my head was protesting.

After I had got back from dropping Pia at school, I sent Annabelle a message, asking if she wanted to pop over for a coffee. I wasn't entirely sure what I was going to say, but I wanted to probe a little more into her past and see if she would open up. To see if I could get some kind of feel whether she was a threat to me.

I pottered around the house, tidying up, even though it didn't need it, but tried to keep myself occupied while I waited for a reply. But my phone was silent all morning. I sent another message at midday and an hour later got a text message back.

> So sorry. Been with clients all day. I'll pop around this afternoon.

It wasn't until I'd picked Pia up from school that she finally arrived.

'There's Annabelle!' said Pia, looking out through the bifold doors. 'Annabelle!'

I took a deep breath and plastered on a smile as I went over to the doors and waved at her to come in.

Annabelle trotted down the garden and held up a brown paper bag. 'Cakes,' she said. 'Peace offering.' She gave me an unexpected hug. 'Sorry I've not been about much. Work has been really busy.' She then bent down and gave Pia a hug.

'I'll make us a drink,' I said. 'Coffee?'

'Yes please.'

If Daniel had spoken to Annabelle about my visit, she wasn't letting on. I decided not to mention it yet. I had to keep the advantage. Know as much as possible and say nothing.

As I made the drinks, Annabelle chatted with Pia about the cakes and after checking with me it was OK, gave one to Pia.

'You and Mummy have one too,' said Pia.

Annabelle looked at me. 'I made lemon ones for you. I remember you saying they were your favourite.'

'Thanks,' I said. I wanted to tell her not to bother, but I couldn't in front of Pia. 'You're right. Lemon is my favourite.' I put two side plates on the counter and Annabelle popped a cake on each plate.

I had to admit the cakes were delicious. Annabelle definitely had a knack for baking. 'You should go on that baking show,' I said, as I dabbed the last of the crumbs with my finger.

'For obvious reasons – i.e. my ex-husband seeing me – I would hate to be on TV,' said Annabelle. 'Although part of me would like to, so all those girls who were mean to me at school would be laughing on the other sides of their faces when I won.'

I smiled at her confidence that she would emerge the winner, but I was more struck by the throwaway comment about girls at school. Rarely did Annabelle talk about her childhood. 'Did you have a rough time at school?' I asked, wondering if her narrative would tally with what Daniel had told me. I guess I was testing her. For some reason, I believed Daniel more than Annabelle.

She shrugged. 'A bit.' She didn't say anything else, and I didn't either as I waited for her to continue. She seemed to be deliberating. Maybe this would give me an insight into who she really was. Was Jessica Sully bullied? Why though? She looked up at me and then back down at the now empty cake case. 'A lot, actually. You know how mean girls can be if you're slightly different or come from a different background or haven't got the exact brand of clothing or got too much money, or go on too nice a holiday, or live in too big a house. Spoilt rich kid. Sad poor kid. You just have to be different.'

'Which were you? Spoilt rich kid or sad poor kid?'

'I was both of those things,' she said. The room was heavy as if all the atmosphere had been sucked away on the outgoing tide.

'Did your parents spoil you?' I asked.

'Yes. Especially my dad,' she said. 'But that was because he wasn't there. He spoiled me with material things, so that made me the spoilt rich kid, but he was never there, so that made me the sad poor kid. Rich in things, poor in love.'

At least that tallied with what Daniel had told me. 'I'm sorry,' I said, pinching the bridge of my nose and screwing up my eyes. My headache seemed to be launching a counterattack to the painkillers.

'Don't be. I hate being pitied,' said Annabelle. 'It was fine. In the end I wore my parents down by begging to be taken out of school. By the time I was thirteen, I was being home-schooled with a private tutor.'

'Wow. How was that?'

'She was the best thing to happen to me,' she smiled warmly. 'She had been my nanny when I was younger but left when I started school. When my father arranged for her to come back, I was delighted.' She sat up as if shaking herself from the memory. 'Anyway, enough about me. Are you OK?'

'Yeah. Fine. Well, I have a headache coming.' I tried to focus on Annabelle but the brightness of the sun behind her was making it difficult, causing me to squint. 'I'll sit down over there out of the sun.' I made my way around the kitchen island and over to the sofa, where I slumped down.

'Can I get you anything?' asked Annabelle. 'Water? Paracetamol?'

'No. I've taken a couple of tablets. They should start working soon.'

'What time is Jasper home?'

'Not until later.' I closed my eyes as a wave of nausea overcame me. I swore to myself. This was going to be a migraine I could well do without. 'Could you grab my phone from over there, please?' I waved my hand in the direction of the kettle. The noise of the television was hurting my ears. 'Pia, could you turn it down a bit, please? Pia, the television. Turn it down.'

'Here, let me,' said Annabelle, coming over and picking up the remote control. 'There that's better.'

'Thank you.' It was difficult to even speak, and I couldn't keep my eyes open. Boy, this migraine was coming on fast. 'I need my phone. Need to ring Jasper's mum to come over.' I wasn't sure if I'd said the words out loud or not. They sounded muffled and far away.

'Why don't you go and have a lie-down?' Annabelle said. 'Here, let me help you.'

I wanted to say no, but my head was killing me, and I felt so sick, I allowed myself to be taken upstairs and put to bed like I was a child. 'Pia,' I mumbled.

'Don't worry about Pia, I'll look after her,' said Annabelle.

Something made me try to sit bolt upright, but my body wasn't responding. I didn't want Annabelle looking after Pia. I didn't want her in my house while I was upstairs. 'No.' My voice was a slurred croak.

'Stay there, Hannah. It's all right,' said Annabelle, her hand resting gently on my shoulder, yet it felt like a heavy weight preventing me from sitting upright. 'You don't have to worry about anything. I've got it all under control.' It was the last thing I remembered hearing before I was out cold.

The next thing I knew, I woke up feeling sick. My stomach churned heavily. I threw the bedcovers back and rushed to the en suite where I heaved up the remains of the cake and the tea I'd drunk earlier.

I splashed cold water on my face and took a moment to assess my condition. I certainly felt better for being sick. My migraine had subsided. I had a dull ache in my head, but not the usual piercing pain I got with migraines. In fact, as I thought about it, I hadn't experienced that pain. It had been more like a fog. A heaviness that stopped me from thinking straight. How odd?

Pia!

Shit. The thought of my daughter instantly banished all thoughts of headaches, migraines and sickness. Where was she? Had I called Jasper's parents? What even was the time?

I checked my watch. I'd been asleep nearly two hours. My throat was dry and sore, and my stomach ached from throwing up. I hurtled down the stairs and into the kitchen. 'Pia! Annabelle!' I knew instinctively the house was empty, but I had to double-check all the rooms downstairs as I went.

On entering the kitchen, I was greeted by Luna, who gave a bark and jumped up from her bed, clearly delighted to find out she wasn't alone in the house. The bifold doors were closed. The sun was dipping in the sky and clouds had moved across it. Everything looked grainy and grey.

I looked around for my phone, trying to remember where I last had it. I spotted in on the counter by the kettle.

There were no missed calls or text messages. Why hadn't Annabelle let me know what they were doing? My anger and fear were vying for pole position. I didn't know which emotion to go with. I found Annabelle's number, pressed dial, and held the phone to my ear while I grabbed my cardigan from the sofa.

'Pick up the phone,' I muttered, going out through the bifold doors, which were unlocked. As I ran down the garden towards the wall, I reasoned with myself that I would get to the top of the sand dunes and look down to see Annabelle and Pia paddling in the water, having just popped out for a few minutes.

Annabelle's phone rang out and went to voicemail. I attempted to keep my voice calm and collected as I left a message.

Annabelle, it's me, Hannah. Whereabouts are you? I take it Pia is with you. Call me as soon as you get this.

I really wanted to shout down the phone, *Where the fuck is my daughter?* I climbed over the wall and down the three steps onto the dunes, before jogging across to the ridge.

The beach was empty apart from someone walking their dog. I scanned left and right. Empty.

I rang Annabelle's number again as I began jogging towards the lifeguard tower. Again, it went to voicemail. I didn't bother leaving another message. My rage was hitting uncontrollable levels. I made it all the way to Annabelle's apartment without seeing either her or my daughter. Maybe they were inside the apartment for some reason.

I ran down the road, stumbling a couple of times as I found it difficult to coordinate my limbs. I banged on the front door and pressed the doorbell for several long seconds before repeatedly stabbing at it. No answer.

I went around to the back gate but today it was locked. I

wouldn't be able to get over the fence from the outside as there were no posts or crossbars to gain a footing, unlike the other side where I had climbed out of the garden.

'Annabelle!' I shouted over the side gate. 'Pia!'

Panic was now setting in. My daughter had disappeared with Daniel Sully's daughter and now both were nowhere to be found. I was going to have to call Jasper. Where was he? Had he even left for home yet?

I jogged back along the beach. My head was throbbing, and a queasy feeling was welling in my stomach. I didn't know if it was nerves or something else that had caused me to throw up earlier. My vision was blurring every now and then, but I made it back to the house. Maybe I had some sort of bug, and it wasn't a migraine at all.

I burst my way into the kitchen, coming to an abrupt halt. There was Pia, sitting at the island counter, and Annabelle pouring her a glass of squash.

'Oh, Hannah, are you OK? I thought you were still sleeping,' said Annabelle. 'How are you feeling?'

'I've been looking for you,' I said, going over to Pia and kissing the top of her head and placing a protective arm around her shoulder. I wanted to hug her and drag her away from Annabelle. Never had I been so relieved to see my daughter. I could feel the emotion well up inside me and I had to blink back the tears.

'You're squashing me,' said Pia.

'Sorry, darling,' I said. 'I didn't know where you were.'

'We went for a walk,' said Pia.

'That's nice.' I looked over at Annabelle and I couldn't make out her expression. I expected her to look embarrassed, confused, remorseful even, but it wasn't that. It was almost pleasure.

'Do you want a cup of tea?' she asked.

I couldn't believe she had the audacity to stand there, so

comfortable in my kitchen, serving my daughter squash and offering me a drink, as if I was the visitor and Pia was her child. That small act riled me more than anything.

'No. I don't,' I said, and then more gently to Pia, 'Go and watch telly in the sitting room, please.'

'In the other room? Not here?' she queried.

'Yes. The other room, please, Pia.'

'I don't know how to put it on.'

'I'll do it for you.' I turned to Annabelle. 'I won't be a minute.'

Less than a minute later, I was back in the kitchen, where Annabelle was casually sitting at the island, flicking through her phone. She looked up as I came in. 'Is everything all right, Hannah?'

I closed the kitchen door behind me. 'No, as a matter of fact, it isn't,' I snapped. I hated the way Annabelle didn't even flinch at my words. She looked blankly at me.

'What's wrong?'

'You taking Pia out and not telling me where you were going. Not answering your phone. Not leaving me a message. I woke up and had no clue where my daughter was.' I stalked around to the other side of the island, not trusting myself to have a clear line of attack to her. I really wanted to throttle her and yet she didn't seem to understand the severity of her actions, nor sympathise with my anxiety.

'Hannah,' she began, sounding surprised. 'I'm so sorry. I never meant to worry you, but I did tell you what we were doing.'

'No, you didn't.'

Annabelle frowned, looking concerned. 'I did. You were complaining of a headache and sat down on the sofa. I suggested you have a lie-down and that I would take Pia out.'

'You did not,' I contradicted.

'I absolutely did.' She got to her feet. 'Why would I lie to you about that?'

'I don't know. You tell me.'

'Hannah, please, don't get so angry. Like I said, I honestly didn't mean to upset you.'

'Why didn't you answer your phone?' I demanded.

'Because it was on silent. I'm literally looking at it now and seeing that I have a voicemail from you.'

'You had no right to take my daughter out without my permission,' I said, trying to keep my voice under control, but failing.

The kitchen door opened, and I expected to see Pia walk in so was taken by surprise when it was Jasper.

'Hello, ladies,' he said with a smile. He stopped, the smile dropping from his face as he took in the scene in front of him. The tension in the room was sky high. He looked from me to Annabelle and back to me. 'Is everything all right?'

'No, everything is not all right,' I snapped.

'Hannah...' began Annabelle, almost pleading.

'Don't Hannah me.' I glared at her for a moment before turning to Jasper. 'Annabelle thought it was a good idea to take Pia out without telling me. I had no idea where she was. She didn't even leave me a note or answer my calls when I tried phoning.'

Jasper looked confused as he computed the information.

Annabelle stepped towards Jasper. 'I was looking after Pia because Hannah was sleeping. She didn't feel well. She left Pia with me. I'm so sorry, I have apologised, but Hannah, well, I guess she's still not herself.'

'That's not what happened!' I found myself yelling in frustration and slamming my hand down on the countertop. Jasper raised his eyebrows in my direction in surprise. 'Don't look at me like that either,' I snapped.

'There's obviously been a misunderstanding,' said

Annabelle. She wiped at an imaginary tear under her eye. 'I helped Hannah to bed. Her headache was really bad. She was a bit disorientated. I did say I could take Pia for a walk and, Hannah, you thanked me and told us to have a nice time.'

'Don't get upset now,' said Jasper. 'It really does sound like a misunderstanding.'

'You never said any of that,' I insisted.

Annabelle looked down and gave a little sniff, before dabbing her face again. 'I should go,' she said. 'Hannah, I am truly sorry for upsetting you. I was only trying to help.'

They both looked at me expectantly, like I was going to accept her apology. Well, they could go fuck themselves. 'Yes, you should go,' I said tersely.

I knew Jasper was throwing me a look that said he couldn't quite believe I was acting like this. And he'd be right. This was out of character for me, but Annabelle had frightened me and then infuriated me. I was not in the mood for accepting her insincere apologies. As for the crocodile tears in front of Jasper, he might fall for it, but I wouldn't.

'I'm sorry,' I heard Jasper saying as he followed Annabelle out of the kitchen and into the garden. 'She's not usually like this.'

'It's fine. Honestly,' replied Annabelle. Whatever she said next was lost as they made their way down the garden.

I watched from the kitchen window as they talked for a few moments at the wall before Annabelle left.

Jasper came back indoors.

'And before you say anything, I am not overreacting,' I said.

'I wasn't about to suggest you were.'

'She,' I pointed towards the garden, 'did not tell me she was taking Pia out.'

Jasper came over to me and gently took my hands in his, sliding his hands the length of my arms, coming to rest on my shoulders. 'I believe you,' he said. 'But that doesn't mean it wasn't just some misunderstanding between the two of you. I thought you two were friends.'

'We are. Were. I don't know,' I confessed. 'I don't know what to think. I woke up alone in the house and I didn't know where Pia was. I couldn't get hold of Annabelle. I was scared. I even ran down to her apartment, but they weren't there.' I could feel the tears welling in my eyes. 'I thought something had happened, but I didn't know what.'

Jasper gave a sympathetic smile. 'I can imagine how upset and frightened you must have been – it's only natural. And maybe when you got back and they were here, maybe that adrenaline, that fear, came out in an angry release.'

What he was saying sounded perfectly logical, but I remained adamant. 'I know what you mean, but I promise you, she did not tell me she was taking Pia out.'

'How are you feeling now?' asked Jasper, sidestepping what I'd said. 'You were all groggy and headachy, apparently.'

I couldn't argue with that. 'It was weird,' I said. 'It wasn't like one of the migraines I usually get. I was tired. Exhausted. I could barely keep my eyes open, and my head felt... I don't know, thick. That's all I can explain it as. Everything was muffled.' I realised I was condemning myself as I spoke. I was convinced Annabelle hadn't said anything about taking Pia out, but now my anger had subsided, maybe I was wrong? Could I be wrong? I looked up at Jasper. 'Oh, God. I don't know what came over me. I was certain she didn't say anything, but now I'm doubting myself. And I flew at her like something possessed.'

I buried my face in his chest, taking comfort from his strong arms around me. I felt sick again. Maybe I was ill, and it wasn't just a headache. To be honest, at that point, I didn't know what to think about anything.

TWENTY-SEVEN

Hannah

The following morning, after breakfast, Jasper took Luna for a walk while I went upstairs to shower and dress. I had just finished drying my hair when I happened to glance out of the window – a habit I'd acquired, unable to resist the beautiful view.

It was then I spotted Jasper down on the beach talking to Annabelle. I still hadn't messaged Annabelle as Jasper had suggested. I knew in the normal run of things I would want to apologise, but I couldn't quite bring myself to do it.

My feelings about Annabelle had continually shifted since I found out she was Daniel's daughter. I was wary of her and yet I needed to keep her close so I could work out if she was involved in any way with the campaign against me.

Going by her version of events yesterday, that was looking increasingly more likely.

When Jasper got back from walking Luna, I could tell straight away his mood had changed. He seemed distracted and slightly distant from me. It was odd.

'Is everything all right?' I asked.

'Yeah. Sure. Just a lot on my mind with work right now.' He smiled but the underlying warmth that was usually there was missing.

'Do you want me to pick Pia up from school this afternoon?' I asked, wondering if that would take a bit of pressure from him. It was Friday and he had already booked the afternoon off so he could pick Pia up from school. It was something he had always done when we were in London.

'No. It's OK. I still want to get her.'

I liked the way he still put our daughter first, even though he was under a lot of pressure. I went over to him and wrapped my arms around him.

'I am really sorry about yesterday with Annabelle. I'm going to apologise to her today.'

He smiled at me. 'I think that's a good idea.' He studied me and there was that odd expression on his face again.

'What?' I asked, leaning back to look at him properly.

'You know I love you, don't you?' he said.

'Of course.'

'And that I'm always here for you.'

'Yeah. What's this all about?' I asked, confused, and concerned. He seemed less confident, as if worried about our relationship. This was not the Jasper Gunderson I was used to.

'This is difficult as I know you don't like talking about it,' he said. 'But...'

His hesitancy worried me, and I pulled away. 'What?'

'You've never really spoken about your past. I know you don't like talking about it. That much you've said, but I know there's something big you're not telling me.'

'Jasper, please, not now,' I whispered.

'It's always not now, though, isn't it?' he said. 'Sooner or later, it's got to be now.'

I could see the pain in his eyes. This man was a saint to love me for so long despite knowing I had secrets. I had thought it was too good to be true and for a long time I was just waiting for Jasper to end our relationship over it. But he hadn't and, after a while, I'd begun to hope he never would. I relaxed at some point, believing he was content not knowing. I had misjudged it so badly.

'Just not today. Please?'

He let out a long sigh and ran his hands through his hair. 'Has your past caught up with you?'

'What... what do you mean?'

'Are you seeing someone else? Another man? An ex-boyfriend maybe? I don't know. Help me out here, Hannah. Something has been up for a couple of weeks now. I don't need Annabelle telling me. I need to hear it from you.'

'Annabelle! What's she got to do with this?' I demanded, stepping out of his embrace. Why was Jasper suddenly paying attention to what she was saying?

'I need to know. Is that why you've been on edge lately? Have you been taking anything?'

'Taking anything? What are you on about?' I had no idea where any of this was coming from. 'For your information. No, I'm not seeing anyone and quite frankly, I'm insulted that you would even think that, let alone ask. And as for taking something – I really have no idea what you're talking about.'

Jasper stepped around me and strode over to the cupboard where we kept all the medication and first aid kit. It was on a high shelf beside the cooker hood. He pulled out the box and several bottles of cough mixture, dumping them on the worktop. Then he reached into the back of the cupboard and retrieved a small rectangular pill box.

'What are these?' he asked, chucking them onto the island counter.

'I've never seen them before in my life. How would I know?'

I picked up the box and examined it. 'Temazepam. What's that doing up there?'

'You tell me,' replied Jasper. And then more softly, 'Hannah, what's going on?'

'It's not mine,' I said. 'I've never seen this before. I didn't even know it was up there. Wait, how did you know it was there?'

A guilty look swept across his face before he answered. 'It doesn't matter.'

I knew the answer instantly. 'Annabelle,' I said. 'She told you.'

'You're not denying it.'

'Because I don't have to!' I grabbed the box. 'These are prescription only. There's no sticker on here with my name and dosage like you usually get from a pharmacy. They are not mine.'

'There are other ways of getting these drugs,' said Jasper.

We looked at each other for a long second. 'You think I've managed to get drugs on the black market and that I took one yesterday. That's why I went to bed, because I had drugged myself? Is that what you really think? Oh, and not forgetting that you think I might be having an affair.'

Jasper looked so hurt and bewildered. I had never seen him look at me in that way before and it sliced my heart. He felt he had been betrayed. God, if only he knew the truth. If it was just about a sedative and an affair, then life would be so much easier. I would have told him. But how could I, when even that was enough to break him?

'Hannah,' his voice was nearly a whisper. 'Please tell me the truth. About everything.'

I slowly shook my head. I wanted to tell him, I really did, but I couldn't. I would lose him completely if I did. Maybe I was already losing him. I didn't know what to think. 'There's nothing to tell,' I lied.

'You're wrong, Hannah. You're so very wrong.' He walked past me, picking up his jacket and grabbing his car keys from the console table in the hall, before leaving the house.

I watched Jasper leave and didn't do anything to stop him. I should have run after him, pleaded with him to stay. I should have told him the truth. But I couldn't. I was too scared. Telling him would mean losing him and, selfishly, I couldn't face the thought of losing him and Pia. I'd already lost too much.

Maybe I'd be able to talk him around. Make him realise we could carry on as we'd always done. I loved him with all my heart, as I did our daughter. Wasn't that enough? It had always been enough, but something had changed.

Pia came down the stairs, her hair all mussed up from her sleep. Immediately, my heart swelled with love for her.

'Morning, beautiful,' I said. 'Did you have a nice sleep?'

'I'm hungry.' She came over and hugged me as she did every morning. 'Where's Daddy?'

'He had to leave early for work,' I said. 'But he's left you a kiss and a cuddle.' I kissed her head and hugged her again. 'There, go sit down and I'll make you some breakfast.'

Jasper always told her he left a kiss and cuddle for her if he had to leave without saying goodbye. I watched our daughter munch her way through the toast, oblivious to the drama going on around her. That was at least something to be grateful for. Just watching her innocent face gave me a sense of calm.

Whatever was going on between Jasper, me, and Annabelle, I would put to one side while I got Pia ready for school. I didn't want her going off with any sense that things might not be well at home.

As I drove home after the school run, I realised that I had to do something. I couldn't sit back and let my whole life fall apart around me. I kept thinking back to Daniel and him claiming he had no idea what was going on. The more I thought about it, the more I was beginning to believe him. However, I was also wary of the way he could convince anybody of anything. Maybe he was just playing me.

I needed to be proactive. I couldn't rely on anyone, only myself.

A plan began to formulate in my head as I drove out through the gates of Silverbanks.

I thought of Jasper. I didn't want him to know what I was planning. If I was able to pull this off, then he'd never have to know. Another lie, but I didn't care. It was still a better alternative than risking the truth.

Everything needed to happen today, before I picked Pia up from school. So I drove back to the house and, once inside, I sat down and reworked my plan in my head before sending Annabelle a text message.

> Hi Annabelle, I'm sorry about yesterday. Could we talk, please? Can you come over to mine this morning?

I waited for the reply, which came five minutes later.

> Hi Hannah, yeah sure. I'm out this morning but could pop over this afternoon if that works for you.

I texted back that was fine. Ideally, I would have liked her there that morning, but the afternoon would suffice.

I spent the rest of the morning barely able to settle. I prowled around the house, absent-mindedly tidying up. Not that the three of us made much mess, but I needed to keep myself busy. I could feel the nervous energy and anticipation building up inside me.

Things were starting to make a lot more sense now. The Temazepam in the cupboard must have been put there by Annabelle when I was out cold yesterday. I certainly didn't take any, but I did eat a cake she'd baked. A specific cake that she had put on a plate for me. It must have been laced with some kind of sedative. I googled Temazepam. It took about thirty minutes to work and lasted seven to eight hours, so I doubted she'd given me a full dose of it. She must have put enough in the cake for it to have a milder effect on me than a regular dose. Enough that I would comply and go to sleep, but not enough to knock me out for hours.

Taking Pia out and frightening me had all been part of her plan. She knew I'd freak out over Pia not being there. I had played right into her hands. But now it was payback time. If she thought she'd won, or very nearly won, then she was mistaken. I hadn't survived for this long without fighting.

TWENTY-EIGHT

Laurel

Another three weeks went by before a meeting with Matt was arranged. As usual, I was picked up in an unmarked police car and driven to a safe house. It was all very clandestine and hard to believe it was real. I couldn't help feeling it was like an episode from a TV drama but no, it was my reality. This was really happening to me.

Though we never met in the same place twice, the drive took longer than usual. I wanted to tell the driver to put his foot down. I was desperate to see Declan. I had missed him so much.

The car pulled up outside an innocuous mid-terrace house on the outskirts of a small town called St Neots. I didn't know exactly where we were, but I didn't care either.

The door opened and I was ushered into the living room.

Matt was standing at the window and turned to face me as I entered. My eyes scanned the room, looking for my son.

'Where's Declan?' I asked, turning to go to look in the other room.

'Laurel...' called Matt. To him I was still Laurel. For security reasons, even Matt didn't know what name I was going by now. I ignored him. It was Declan I wanted.

In the room at the back sat Bryan Chamberton. He didn't say anything as I poked my head around the door, looking for my son. I hurried down the hallway to the kitchen. Again, no sign of the little boy I was yearning to hold.

'Declan!' I called out as I went back through the house again. 'Declan! Where are you?'

I was about to take the stairs when Matt stepped out of the living room in front of me. 'He's not here.'

I stopped. 'What do you mean?'

'I didn't bring Declan with me,' said Matt flatly.

'Why the hell not?' I couldn't believe what I was hearing. 'Why didn't you bring him?' Tears stung my eyes, but anger burned in my heart. 'Why didn't you bring him?' I repeated.

Matt went back into the living room, and I followed him. He resumed his position in front of the window. I wanted to pummel the answer out of him.

'I need to tell you something,' said Matt.

My heart plummeted. I could tell from the look on his face this was serious. I could barely form the question. 'Is he ill? Is that why you haven't brought him?' He had to be ill. It couldn't be anything worse, could it? 'Matt, for God's sake, tell me.'

My mind was racing. If Declan was too ill to travel, did that mean he was in hospital?

'He's not ill,' said Matt. 'Declan is fine. There's nothing wrong with him at all. He's at home and Amy is looking after him.'

I didn't understand. 'Then why haven't you brought him?'

'There's no easy way to say this,' began Matt.

'Spit it out.' I couldn't bear the suspense any longer. 'What the fuck is going on?'

'I'm going back home,' said Matt. 'Back to Perth. Australia.'

He didn't need to clarify the country. I didn't for one

minute think he meant Perth, Scotland. 'Right,' I said. 'When are you going and how long for? What's going to happen about Declan?'

Matt held up his hands. 'Stop firing questions at me, Laurel, and listen,' he said. 'I'm going back to Australia and I'm staying there. I'm moving back home.'

I swallowed. 'What about us?'

'Come on, babe,' said Matt. 'You know we're done for. There is no us. Even after this court case, I think we both know, our marriage is over.'

I was stunned. I hadn't expected Matt to be so blunt, but he was probably right. As I thought about it, I realised I wasn't that upset. It was more a sad acceptance. An acknowledgement that we'd gone as far as we could as a married couple. 'I'm sorry,' I said. 'I mean it. I am sorry, but I know you're right.'

'I didn't want it to end like this,' said Matt. 'But it's for the best. There are far more opportunities out there, and Declan loves the ocean. He'll fit right in.'

'Wait. What? Declan.' My brain caught up with what Matt was saying. 'You're taking Declan with you? No. No. You can't do that. We haven't even discussed this. You can't take our son to the other side of the world.' Panic raced through me. 'I won't let you. You're not taking Declan. End of.'

'You can't stop me,' said Matt. 'You're not his mother anymore. I don't even know who you are, but I'm a single parent with sole custody of Declan. You gave up those rights when you signed up for this shit.'

'No. That's not true. I only did that because I had to. I didn't really give up those rights. He's still my son.'

'He'll always be your son, Laurel,' said Matt. 'Like I'll always be his father. And I'm taking him to Australia with me.'

'I'll fight you through every court on this earth to get him back!' I somehow managed to force the words out.

'Do what you like, but I'm not breaking any law.'

'You can't do this to me,' I cried. 'You can't take my son away from me.'

'You left us,' said Matt.

'I had no choice. It was your idea. I did it to protect you both, not to lose you. To lose Declan.'

'It's for the best. I'm doing it so Declan can start afresh. He won't have all this crap about Daniel Sully hanging over him,' said Matt. 'I'm done here in the UK. My business is collapsing because of this shit. I can't carry on here. The house is on the market, I'm going home and I'm taking my son with me.'

I grabbed hold of Matt. 'Please, Matt, don't do this. I'm begging you. Don't take Declan away from me.' I was sobbing. I didn't care. All my dignity was gone. It didn't matter. I just wanted my son.

Matt was peeling my fingers from his arm. 'Come on, Laurel. Let go now. When this is all over, you can come and visit us.'

'Matt, please don't do this,' I sobbed, grabbing hold of him again.

Two arms came around me and were holding me as Matt extracted himself from my grip. 'Let him go,' said Bryan. 'Come here.' He sat me down on the sofa and held me like my father had held me when our dog had died. Except this wasn't just the family pet passing away, this was my son. I was losing my only child and there was nothing I could do about it. Never in my life had I felt so powerless and so distraught.

TWENTY-NINE

Hannah

The day dragged so much. It got to two o'clock and there was still no sign of Annabelle. I had texted her an hour earlier to make sure she was still coming, which she assured me she was but was running a little late. It frustrated me as I didn't want her here when Jasper got back from picking Pia up from school. I wanted the house to ourselves so we could really talk. I had a lot of things to say to her that I didn't want anyone else over-hearing.

I was about to message her again to say I'd come down to her when I saw her standing on the low wall at the end of the garden. I waved her to come on down and opened the door for her.

She greeted me with an air kiss and a bunch of flowers.

'Peace offering,' she said.

'Thanks. They're beautiful.' I placed the bunch of bright yellow sunflowers in some water and set the vase on the windowsill.

'Sorry I couldn't get over earlier. Got held up with some

work,' said Annabelle, taking a seat at the centre island. 'You home alone?'

I turned to face her. 'Yes. Jasper is at work. He's collecting Pia today.' I glanced at the clock on the wall. 'That gives us just enough time for a chat. Or rather, for me to talk to you.'

'O-K,' said Annabelle slowly. 'Is everything all right, Hannah?'

'Not really. Don't pretend you don't know why either.' I folded my arms across my body. 'For a start, I don't appreciate you talking about me to Jasper.'

'What do you mean?'

'This morning on the beach you told him a complete pack of lies. You said I took something.' I picked the box of Temazepam from beside the kettle and in much the same way Jasper had chucked it at me this morning, I did the same to Annabelle. The box landed right in front of her.

She picked it up and read it, before placing it back down. 'Is this what you took?'

'You know damn well I didn't. You laced that cake you gave me with something.'

Annabelle let out a laugh. 'What? Are you serious?'

'Deadly.'

'How on earth could I do that? We all had cakes. Pia chose hers. Why would I lace a cake if she might eat it?'

'Because you knew perfectly well that she would choose a chocolate cake and that lemon was my preference. You made sure you put the cake on my plate. You knew which one you had laced, and you made sure I ate it.'

Annabelle sat back in her chair, folding her arms, mirroring my stance. 'Well, this is all rather unexpected. I came here thinking you wanted to apologise for your outlandish accusations yesterday, but here we are with your theory becoming even more far-fetched. I wouldn't even know where to begin lacing a cake with this' – she picked up the box and dropped it again – 'or anything else, for that matter. I'm a counsellor, not a scientist.'

'It's easy enough to look things up on the internet,' I said. 'Anyway, you're not a counsellor. That diary with all your so-called clients in, your busy schedule, your calls, is empty. A fake. Like you. Like Annabelle Burton.'

She raised her eyebrows. 'You seem to know a lot about me. Tell me, Hannah, what else do you know?' She emphasised my name.

'More than you would like me to,' I said.

'Knowledge is power, I suppose,' replied Annabelle, getting up from the barstool. She wandered around the island, so we were opposite each other now. 'I know things about you too.'

'No surprise there.' I wasn't going to allow myself to be intimidated by this bitch. I was fighting for survival. For the survival of my life. Of my family. Of everything I loved. She was not going to take this away from me. I'd come too far.

'Let's cut to the chase,' said Annabelle. 'You clearly think you have something on me. Let's hear it and then I'll tell you what I have on you.'

I hesitated. I didn't like the way she was getting control of the situation. I needed to regain the upper hand. 'I know who you are,' I said.

'And who might that be?' Her smile was so patronising it was making me doubt whether this information held any weight at all.

'You're Jessica Beaumont. Or rather Jessica Sully. Daniel Sully's daughter.'

Annabelle looked momentarily startled. She raised her eyebrows. 'I'm impressed. I didn't expect you to work that out. How did you find out?'

'I saw you go into Elm Tree Clinic. It was quite easy to find out who you'd been to visit. I guess your father hasn't mentioned that I also paid him a visit.'

This was clearly a trigger for Annabelle. The colour drained from her face and her whole body tensed. 'You went to see my father?' Her words came out in a venomous hiss. 'How dare you? After what you did to him and my family, you had no right to see him.'

'Now we're getting to the point of all this,' I said, feeling more confident. 'For some bizarre reason, possibly out of misplaced loyalty to your father, you think I'm to blame for what happened to you after he went to prison.'

'If it wasn't for you, my father wouldn't have spent his last years in prison, only to be released so he can die. I wouldn't have suffered the humiliation of everyone at school knowing my father was a criminal and having to leave there and go to a local school. You made my life at school horrendous. I was bullied. The physical stuff I could cope with, but the mental and emotional trauma I suffered was down to you.'

'So now we're getting to the point,' I retorted. 'It's not about your father going to prison, it's about how it affected you.' I shook my head as I began to understand. 'All that talk about him not loving you was bullshit. You didn't want his love, you just wanted what he could give you. Privilege. Money. Gifts. It was never him you wanted. It was what you could get. And that's why you came here. You wanted to get some sort of revenge on me.'

'It's not revenge. It's justice,' she snarled.

'Call it what you like, but you want to see me suffer for something that you think I did to you. It doesn't work like that. I saw your father kill someone. Murder a man in cold blood. The blame lies with him. Not me. I was a victim of that too. I had to give evidence. I lost *my* family because of him.'

'You didn't have to lose your family. You chose to.'

'Don't you dare comment on something you know nothing about. I had no choice.' I emphasised every word of that last sentence. 'I did it to protect my family. To keep my son safe.'

'You didn't have to. You could have kept them safe by not saying anything.' Annabelle was seething as she spoke, barely able to control her anger. I could see her face reddening now as her blood pressure rose with the effort to stay in control.

'Don't you think I've thought about that? Every day of my life since then, I have regretted speaking up, but I also know it was the right thing to do.' I could feel my own outrage mounting. My hands were by my sides, clenching and unclenching. I wanted to fly across that room and shake her, slap her, make her understand what I was saying. Knock that twisted sense of what was right and what was wrong out of her. 'I had to leave my old life behind. My husband. My son. I let them walk away and start a new life because I loved them so much, I had to keep them safe.' The tears were coming now, I couldn't hold them back any more than I could quell the anger that coursed through my veins. 'Everything I lost was because of your father. And by default, everything you lost was also because of him. We are both victims.'

'That's not true!' She slammed her fist down on the worktop. 'You caused this. You. You. YOU!'

It was the first time I'd seen Annabelle completely lose control and I think it shocked her as much as it did me. She stopped dead still, her breathing hard and fast. She glared at me.

We were at a stand-off. An impasse.

I waited for the anger and tension to subside a little before I spoke. 'You need to leave Silverbanks,' I said. 'You need to leave me and my family alone. If you don't, then I'll go to the police.'

It was amazing how quickly she regained her self-control. When she spoke, all the anger had disappeared, replaced by what I could only describe as condescension. 'Are you really trying to threaten me? Intimidate me?' Annabelle gave an incredulous laugh. 'What exactly are you planning to tell the police?' She didn't wait for an answer. 'What we really need to consider is who has the most to lose here, before you go rushing off to tell tales.'

'I think a minimum jail sentence of twenty-five years for premeditated murder is quite a lot to lose.'

'For you.' Annabelle ran her finger along the edge of the worktop. 'I'm assuming we're talking about Bryan's death?'

'You were the last person to see him alive. You had reason to kill him.'

'Technically,' said Annabelle. '*You* were the last person to see him alive, as far as the police are concerned. You practically bumped into him when you were on the way back to my apartment that night. You know, when you left your phone there.'

'Your word against mine.' I wasn't entirely sure if that was true. Annabelle had a security camera on her front door, and I couldn't be certain if that had caught any footage of Bryan and me.

'Well, it's not really, though,' said Annabelle. 'I saw you and Bryan on the beach, the night of the barbecue, having an argument. And then again, the night of his death. Of course, I was too scared to say anything because you had threatened me.' She looked very smug. 'And that's just for starters.'

'What are you talking about?'

She didn't reply, simply carried on as if I'd not said anything. 'It would be quite poetic if you could no longer see Jasper and Pia whenever you wanted. Rather like you can't see Declan.'

She'd hit my trigger point. 'You keep away from my family. My daughter. My son. Stay away.' My hands were clenched in fists, ready to pummel her, but a little voice of reason at the back of my head was telling me not to. That's what she wanted. She wanted me to attack her.

I glanced up at the clock. Jasper and Pia would be home soon. I had to get this over with by then.

'If you bring me down, then I'll take you with me. And that is a fucking promise.' It was my turn to snarl the threat.

'You have more to lose, though,' said Annabelle. 'I could of course make sure that you're charged with attempted murder.'

'What?'

Before she had time to answer, the front door opened, and I heard Jasper calling out hello. Pia skipped into the kitchen, not noticing Annabelle at first and gave me a hug.

'Hello, darling,' I said. 'How was your day?'

'Good. I had macaroni cheese for lunch.' She turned around and saw Annabelle. 'I didn't know you were here.'

Annabelle put her arms out. 'Do I get a hug?'

I wanted to yank Pia back, but she was already scurrying across the kitchen to embrace Annabelle, who looked over the head of my daughter and smirked at me.

'Hello, ladies,' said Jasper. His eyes flicked between the both of us. 'Everything OK?'

'Hi, Jasper,' said Annabelle, releasing her hold on Pia. She grimaced at him before looking at me.

Oh, I could see what she was up to. Trying to play the innocent. We were far from done here. 'Hi,' I said, as Jasper came over and kissed me. He gave me a look which needed no words. 'Erm, do you fancy taking Luna out for a walk with Pia? Annabelle and I are just sorting a few things out.'

'Sure,' he said. He gave me another questioning look.

'Great,' I replied and backed it up with a smile and a gentle squeeze of his forearm.

'Pia,' said Jasper. 'Keep your shoes on, we're going to take Luna out for a walk on the beach.'

'But I'm in my uniform.' Bless her, I always made her change out of her school clothes when she got home.

'Doesn't matter today,' I said. 'It's Friday. Go on now.'

'OK.'

'See you later!' called Annabelle blowing Pia a kiss as she went out the door with Jasper and the dog. I was sure she was doing it on purpose to annoy me.

I watched through the window, making sure they had gone, before turning back to Annabelle.

She smiled at me. 'Lovely family. Such a beautiful child. So innocent.'

'Shut the fuck up talking about her,' I snapped.

'Sure. Now, where were we? Oh yes. Attempted murder.' She spun around and pulled a kitchen knife from the block. The silver blade glinted in the sunshine. They were top quality chef's knives that Jasper had bought. Barely used and super sharp. 'It could be that you attack me with the knife, thinking you could kill me and make it look like self-defence,' continued Annabelle. She had a crazy yet delighted look in her eye.

'Annabelle, put the knife down,' I heard myself saying.

But she wasn't listening and carried on talking. 'The attack could be quite nasty and only I would survive. I mean, you killed Bryan, so it wouldn't be hard to believe you thought you could kill me too. Oh, by the way' – she looked up at me – 'you killed Bryan because he knew who you were. You didn't want him to expose you. He was blackmailing you. Just thought I'd let you know that bit, in case you're not around to hear it at a later date.'

I watched her rest the blade of the knife on her forearm. She looked up at me and smiled again. Then, without looking away, she drew the blade across her flesh. 'Oopsie,' she said.

I watched in horror as blood oozed from the precision cut.

'What the hell are you doing?' I cried out. Annabelle held her arm downwards and the blood trickled down her arm, over her wrist, weaving a path down her forefinger and dripping onto the white tiled flooring. I couldn't believe what she was doing. 'You're crazy.'

'Possibly.' She held the blade up, tilting it one way and then the other, inspecting the bloodstained edge. 'I could actually kill myself, but I'm thinking that would be a waste.'

'Be my guest,' I said.

'Ah, I do love your humour,' said Annabelle. 'What a shame, because I think in a different lifetime we could have been friends. You could have been like my big sister. I've always hated being an only child.'

I didn't know what to do. Should I rush her and try to wrestle the knife from her? Was she going to try to stab me? Stab herself? She was still talking as I contemplated the limited options open to me.

'I know my dad liked you,' she said. 'But you didn't like him. Not in the way he wanted you to.'

I was shocked. How on earth did she know that? 'I was married.' I didn't know what to say. Annabelle was clearly unstable. I suddenly felt the need to placate her. To keep her calm. I was kind of regretting sending Jasper away now. This was not how I'd imagined things would go.

'I was there that night in the house when you came back with him,' said Annabelle. 'He thought I was asleep, but I always stayed awake when he was out. I couldn't sleep unless I knew he was home. I had this awful feeling if I went to sleep, he wouldn't come back.'

'How old were you?' I asked. I didn't know why, but keeping her talking seemed like a good option now. I needed time to decide what to do.

'I was sixteen,' she replied. 'I went to go downstairs to see him. I saw you two together. You let him kiss you. His hands were all over you and you let him. You led him on. He was... well, I don't need to tell you, you know what he was doing.'

I gulped as unexpected shame and guilt hit me. I remembered that night clearly. I had been so close to having sex with Daniel Sully. I'd let his hands roam all over me and for a moment his fingers had settled between my legs. I felt myself blush. Annabelle, a sixteen-year-old, had seen her father do that.

'I had no idea anyone else was in the house,' I said.

'I wasn't supposed to be there,' said Annabelle. 'I'd had an argument with my mum and stormed out. You know, the usual teenage thing. I figured I'd stay the night at Beaumont House. Didn't expect you to turn up though.'

I thought back to that night and the sound that had brought me to my senses. I hadn't known what it was at the time. I thought it was a car door or a creak of the house, but it must have been Annabelle on the stairs.

'You will know what happened next then,' I said.

'Yes. You pushed him away. You said something about being a married woman. Such a cliché.'

I nodded. 'And that was all that ever happened. Nothing like that ever happened again.'

'But my father was obsessed with you,' said Annabelle. He always got what he wanted, and he wanted you. But he was prepared to wait and play the long game.'

'I would never have had an affair with him,' I said.

'That's not true. You should have let him have what he wanted then,' she said. 'It would have saved you all the trouble that followed. If you'd let him, then you would have still been able to see your son. He would have made sure your husband didn't have custody of your boy. You wouldn't have had to lose him like you did.'

Tears gathered in my eyes. What I would have done to have Declan. If only I'd known what was to come. But then I wouldn't have Pia or Jasper. How could I want one and not the other? Even in my mind, I couldn't trade one child for another.

It was an impossible scenario. One I couldn't entertain, for that was the path to madness. Literally.

'Annabelle... Jess,' I said, remembering Daniel had called her that. 'It was just adult stuff. Two adults who liked each other but knew it wouldn't work.'

She had a glazed look in her eyes, and I wasn't sure if she was listening to me. Then she looked at me and there was that sardonic smile of hers. 'I could actually kill myself. I don't have anything to live for.'

'Your mother? What about her?'

She sighed. 'My mother is probably going to spend most of her life in and out of some sort of psychiatric clinic. She's bipolar. That's why my parents split up. I wanted to live with Dad, but he said it was best if I stayed with Mum. In other words, he didn't want me cramping his style. So I had to make do with a part-time dad. As if my life wasn't already hard enough, you ruined everything for us.'

'I'm sorry. I didn't know that.'

'No. Why would you? And my dad won't be alive for much longer. So, that's going to be it. All these years, I've been thinking about this moment when I could ruin your life once again, but now I've got to that moment, I think things could pan out differently. It might be better for us in the long run.'

'How's that?' I asked gently, hoping she was having a change of heart.

'If I killed myself, you'd have to explain my death. You might get away with manslaughter or self-defence.' She drew the knife across the palm of her hand this time. Blood gushed from the new cut. 'Oh dear. Look at that. A self-defence wound.'

'Stop it!'

She didn't listen. Just carried on talking. 'Or I could kill you, on the same principle, that it was kill or be killed, and then I would console Jasper in his grief. I would comfort Pia and slowly but surely take your place. How does that sound to you?'

Rage flared up in me like a burning inferno. I had never experienced such an utter feeling of anger. She was not taking my place. She was not taking my child. I'd sooner be locked up for murder than let that happen.

Before I could stop myself, I flew across the kitchen and grabbed her arm. I was strong, but although she was petite and smaller than me, she had an unexpected strength. I was aware of the blade dangerously close to my heart. I grabbed her wrist with both hands. Blood from her palm was dripping and spreading everywhere. I felt a sharp pain to my own arm and realised the knife had sliced through the skin.

I used my height to gain an advantage, pushing her hand backwards as we arm-wrestled for several seconds. Finally, with one Herculean effort, I managed to slam her arm down against the countertop and the knife dropped from her hand, clattering onto the floor.

She was too quick and scooped the knife away with her foot, before throwing herself down to the ground and grabbing it. I was on top of her, trying to pull her away.

Somehow she managed to flip me over. The knife was in her hand. I'm not sure what happened but I was grabbing at her wrists again. We rolled across the floor, bashing into the island counter.

Without warning she let out a groan of pain and stopped struggling. I looked down at Annabelle. Her eyes locked with mine. She was making a gurgling sound. I looked down between us and let out a cry. The knife was embedded up to the hilt just above her ribcage.

I leapt backwards. Then I realised she was trying to pull the knife out.

'Don't!' I yelled. I knew how dangerous that was. I needed my phone. I needed to dial 999.

She made a gurgling noise. Blood seeped from the corner of her mouth. She looked at me and I was sure she smiled. She said something but it was a rasp. I crawled closer to her. She tried to speak. 'Laurel,' she whispered. 'I win.'

Her body flopped and her eyes stared lifelessly up to the ceiling.

THIRTY

Hannah

I stared at Annabelle's motionless body. The knife halfway out of her ribcage, her hand limp around the handle where she had tried to remove it.

I sat there slumped, breathless beside her for several seconds as my brain processed what my eyes were seeing. It was only the sound of Pia's voice in the garden that snapped me from my trance.

I jumped to my feet, grabbing my phone, rushing over to the door, just as she stepped onto the terrace.

She stopped as she neared the entrance. Her face full of confusion and fear as I snatched the door, slamming it shut and locking it. 'Mummy?' she said.

Beyond her, Jasper was walking down the garden with Luna following him. He smiled at me, but then his expression changed. Like Pia, first there was confusion, then fear, but then on Jasper's face there was disbelief and something akin to realisation. He began running down the path, calling Pia. She turned and ran towards him. Jasper scooped her up in his arms, holding the back of head to his shoulder, so she couldn't see me.

He put her down, still facing away from me and crouching so he was eye level, he spoke to her. Then, taking her hand, he sat her down on her swing, so she was facing the beach. He hooked Luna onto her lead, and got Pia to hold it. I imagined he was telling her to stay there and not to move.

Jasper sprinted back to the house, trying the door handle to get in. 'Hannah. Let me in,' his voice only just carried through the double-glazing. 'What's happened?' He was staring at my top. I looked down and realised I was covered in blood. Annabelle's blood.

'You can't come in,' I called out, as tears began to freefall down my face. 'Stay there.'

I will never forget that look in Jasper's eyes. Terror. Panic. I'm sure they were an exact reflection of my emotions. I dialled 999, all the while our eyes locked on each other. As calmly as I could, I explained to the call handler what had happened.

'Is the patient breathing?'

'No.'

'Are you sure? Can you check?'

'I'm certain. I've checked.'

My eyes never once left Jasper's. I knew that I could be losing him and Pia. In my peripheral vision, I saw Pia move. I refocused on her. My darling girl. My daughter. My world. Everything I'd ever done, I'd done to protect my family, but even though Annabelle was dead, her last words were already haunting me.

'I win.'

And she had won. I would have to tell Jasper everything. My house of cards was about to collapse.

.   .   .

After the police and medics arrived, I was examined by a paramedic. The few wounds on my arm and hand, classed as superficial, were cleaned and dressed, with a recommendation I attend hospital. I had insisted they examine me in the living room without Jasper present. I wasn't ready to talk to him yet. I certainly didn't want Pia to see me. She was traumatised enough as it was after seeing all the blood on my shirt.

At one point, Jasper had to be stopped from barging his way into the living room. It was Owens who prevented him. Owens and Barnes had both happened to be on duty when the call came in about a stabbing on Silverbanks. Owens was patient as before and Barnes continued her bad-cop approach.

After a quick assessment of what had happened, the kitchen was secured as a crime scene, I was cautioned.

I felt numb. Scared. And weirdly calm. For the past eleven years, I had at the back of my mind been preparing for this day. Not killing someone, but the day that Jasper knew the truth about me. And now it was here, I was aware I was mentally removing myself from the whole situation. It was the only way I could cope by shutting myself down. I'd done it before, I'd have to do it again. There was only so much pain and grief a person could take, and I didn't know if I was strong enough to go through it a second time. I had to close my emotions and feelings off from reality.

'Jasper is asking if he can see you,' said Owens.

'Am I under arrest?' I asked.

'No, but you are under caution,' said Owens.

'Can you question me about what happened at the police station, please?'

I saw Owens and Barnes exchange a look. 'We don't have to do that yet,' replied Owens.

'I don't want to talk here,' I said. 'I don't want Jasper to hear what I have to say now.'

Another confused look, or was it intrigue, passed between the detectives.

'So, you don't want to see Mr Gunderson?' said Barnes.

'No.'

'What do you want me to tell him?' It was Barnes again.

'I'll speak to him,' said Owens, crossing the room and stepping into the hallway, closing the door behind him.

I heard the muted tones of Owens speaking to Jasper. A minute or so later, Owens came back into the room. 'Jasper isn't happy, obviously,' he said. 'But I've told him it's our decision to take you in for questioning, given the serious nature of the incident. He's going to get you a solicitor.'

I nodded. 'Can we go now?'

'Yes. Come this way, Hannah.'

'I don't want Pia to see me,' I said.

'She's upstairs in her bedroom with one of our female officers,' said Barnes.

I followed Owens out, with Barnes behind me. Jasper was standing in the hallway. 'Hannah,' he said, his voice almost a whisper. He stepped towards me, but Owens put out a hand to stop him.

'You'll be able to talk to her later,' he said.

'I've phoned Carl,' said Jasper as I walked past him. Carl Jeffers was a long-term friend of Jasper's and happened to be a barrister in criminal law. 'Don't say anything until you've spoken to him.'

There were numerous police cars, two ambulances and several unmarked cars outside the house. I couldn't help thinking that Annabelle would have been impressed. She would have liked all this fuss she had caused. The havoc she had wreaked, not just in life but in death.

As Owens drove us off the Silverbanks estate, I wondered if I'd ever be back again. Would they believe my version of events? And how far back into the past would I have to go?

I did as Jasper had instructed and waited for Carl to turn up. I knew I'd have to tell him everything before I told the police and before I told Jasper. There was no room for surprises.

Carl, ever the professional, took the revelations in his stride, but even he couldn't hide his surprise when I told him about Laurel.

'Wow. I was not expecting you to say that,' he said, taking a deep breath. 'Does Jasper know?'

'No.'

'Double wow.' He took another deep breath. 'Well, Hannah – it is Hannah, isn't it? Or I can call you Laurel, if you prefer.'

'Hannah is fine. I'm Hannah. I haven't been Laurel for a long time.'

He nodded and there was pity in his eyes. 'Well, Hannah, this is all something of a clusterfuck but I'm an expert at un-fucking the cluster.'

I smiled at his reach for humour. I'd always liked Carl and I was grateful he was here. 'Thank you. There is a lot to un-fuck.'

'Right, let's get started.' He opened his leather-bound notepad and took out a fountain pen, which I had no doubt was a Smythson or a Montblanc. Whatever, it was a symbol of his success, and I needed Carl to pull out all the stops here if I was ever to see my family again from anywhere other than behind bars. 'I need to know everything, Hannah. Absolutely everything. No keeping anything back.'

I returned his steady gaze. 'I know.'

'If it helps, Jasper said that whatever it is, whatever you've not told him, he will always stand by you. He's not turning his back on you.'

Tears sprang to my eyes. 'He said that?'

'Indeed. And you know Jasper, he wouldn't say it if he didn't mean it.'

'He might need to revisit that promise once he knows,' I said, picking at the thread on the cuff of my jumper.

'That's something for another day,' said Carl. 'First of all, we need to get you out of here. Whatever you say, I promise you, it won't be the first time I've heard it. And you have my word that whatever you say is strictly between us and the police. I won't say a word to Jasper. You can do that once you're home.'

I curled the thread of my cuff around my finger and snapped it in half. 'There's so much to tell.'

'Let's get on with it, then.'

I liked Carl's no-nonsense approach and, true to his word, as I told him about my life before Jasper, he didn't bat an eyelid. There was no intake of breath, no raising of the eyebrows, no sucking through teeth. Nothing, he just nodded, asked questions to clarify points, wrote in his notebook and offered me tissues as I cried. I'd never told anyone my story as Laurel. A small handful of people knew and two of them had died because of that knowledge.

He got me to go over the events in the kitchen with Annabelle several times, in detail. 'I just need to make sure you haven't forgotten anything that the police may bring up at a later date and ask why you didn't say anything.'

I was exhausted by this point. All the emotions of the last couple of weeks, the tension, the strain, and the knowledge that Bryan had died because of me and Annabelle, or Jess as she was really called, had died because of a distorted loyalty to her father even though he was a murderer.

'You've done really well so far,' said Carl. 'I know that wasn't easy for you. We can have a rest now. I expect the police will be back in soon, wanting to question you, but we'll take a few minutes while we can.'

'Thank you,' I said in almost a whisper. I just wanted to sleep but I knew I had to go through the whole story again before I would be allowed to either leave or be put back in a cell.

'You've been through some really difficult times,' said Carl. 'You should be proud of yourself for making it this far. I'm not sure a lot of women could have survived what you've endured.'

I didn't feel brave or proud of what I had gone through or endured as Carl put it. I felt exhausted. That was the only way I could describe myself. On the edge, teetering with no safety net. I had exposed my deepest secrets to one of Jasper's best friends, soon the police would know and eventually, it would be in the press. But all I could think of were Jasper and Pia.

A knock on the door heralded the arrival of Owens and Barnes.

I always knew Carl was excellent at his job, he hadn't earned his reputation as being top of his game for nothing, but even so it was several long hours later before I was finally released from custody, thus far without charge, pending further investigation. I had hated going through my past with them. Owens seemed fairly sympathetic, and Barnes was more surprised than anything. I guess my story was going to make a good talking point in the staff room. They of course had to double-check what they could, but it was well into the night and Owens said that they'd complete their enquiries the following day when they could speak to the right people. By that, I assumed he meant the witness protection team.

'Is there anything you'd like to ask us before we close the interview?' asked Owens.

I looked at Carl. We'd discussed this and he gave me a nod to go ahead. 'Can you tell me how I can get in touch with my son, Declan, please? He'll be fourteen years old now.'

THIRTY-ONE

Laurel

The court case came around. By that time I was on medication to help me battle with the depression that was setting in. Matt had moved back to Australia three weeks after he'd come to see me. I hadn't seen Declan again and I had no idea if I ever would. My life as Laurel Jordan no longer existed.

The court case was gruelling. As the day got closer to when I needed to give evidence, the more nervous I became. I was going to come face to face with Daniel Sully for the first time in nearly a year. I'd started having dreams about the killing. It replayed over and over in my mind when I went to sleep, mixed up with images of Declan running down the hall of Beaumont House. I was always running after him, trying to catch him, but he was too fast.

The dream didn't need an expert to decode it. Every time I dreamed that I woke up crying. My heart had never been so broken. When I'd gone to see my GP for antidepressants, I couldn't even tell her what was at the root of my problems. I had to blame the break-up of my marriage. I couldn't give anything

away about Declan being in Australia in case it put him in
danger. I knew I was being paranoid, but I had visions of one of
Daniel's men paying the GP a visit to find out information they
could use to get to me.

Bryan had called by regularly to see me. I think he was
worried about my mental health and what sort of witness I was
going to be. He needed me to be strong, certain, and confident
when I went to give evidence. The CPS barrister had coached
me on how to answer questions and what to expect when I was
cross-examined.

I didn't really care. I cared about nothing. My only reason to
live had been taken from me.

When I did see Daniel, I was surprised at his appearance.
He had lost weight, and his hair was flecked with silver. The
months in prison had not been kind to him. I was scared to look
at him at first, in case that connection between us was still there.
I knew he was looking at me. I could sense his gaze. I was
compelled to look up and, yes, I felt that connection immediately. It zinged across the courtroom like a static charge, it was a
wonder no one else noticed it. I had to force myself to look
away. I couldn't let him get to me.

Just get through this, I kept telling myself. *Tell the truth and
then it will all be over.*

My testimony and subsequent cross-examination went on
for two days. The defence grilled me, asking me the same questions but in different ways, waiting for me to slip up, but I
remained steadfast in my account of what I saw.

I couldn't look at Daniel as I described the actual stabbing
of the victim, who I now knew was called Jez Bateman. The
argument had been over money Jez owed Daniel. Apparently,
Daniel had been operating an upmarket money-lending service,
which, needless to say, breached just about every section of the
Financial Services Act. No matter what way it was dressed up,
Daniel was a loan shark.

I wondered if Matt would have been caught out in some way had the partnership between them continued, or whether it was a vehicle for Daniel to launder money. But the charges relating to Daniel's loan shark operation seemed insignificant when he was facing life in prison for murder, with my testimony the key evidence against him. The only evidence, as it happened. No wonder he hadn't wanted me to stand up in court and tell the jury what I'd seen.

After I had given my testimony, I was not required to appear in court again. I thought that maybe I'd be allowed to go home. To resume my life as Laurel Jordan and somehow convince Matt not to stay in Australia for ever. Or, if he insisted on living there, that I could go there too.

I shouldn't have given myself such false hope. Matt and Declan may have been safe on the other side of the world, but Bryan advised me that the police had evidence I was still in danger.

'You're not out of the woods yet,' he'd said. 'If you come out of PPS, then we can't protect you. And if you go to Australia, you might lead them straight to your family.'

'Are you serious?' I couldn't believe what I was hearing. I'd been under the impression this new life wouldn't be forever. I thought once the trial was over and Daniel sentenced, then I would be free.

'I don't want to scare you, Hannah, but the threat to your life is very real right now.'

'As Laurel, how high is the risk level?' I asked.

'Very,' said Bryan. 'I'm not saying it will always be like that, but right now and for the foreseeable future it will remain high. Daniel Sully isn't a man who forgives easily.'

'If I spoke to him,' I began, but Bryan was shaking his head before I'd even finished the sentence.

'No. You can't. Not now. That's a very bad idea. He'll get inside your head. He'll enjoy scaring you.'

'God, you're making him sound like Hannibal Lecter.'

'I'm just being honest with you.'

I held my head in my hands as Bryan's words sank in. I was trapped. There was no way out for Hannah Towers. No going back to Laurel Jordan. 'But my mother,' I said after a while. 'I won't be able to see her again, will I?'

'In time, we can arrange something.'

'But I don't have time.' I howled like a baby at that point as the realisation I was losing my son and my mother hit me. It didn't matter that Mum had dementia and didn't know who I was, I still knew who she was, and I wanted to care for her. I wanted to show her I still loved her. I wanted her to feel that love, even if she was unaware I was her daughter.

'I'm so sorry, Laurel,' said Bryan, using my real name for the first time in many months. He was apologising to me, the real me, not Hannah, some woman we created between us and the PPS. It made me feel human again, rather than just a commodity to the Met. It made his words feel sincere. He was the only person who cared about me right then. I had no one else left. My old life was dead, along with everything and everyone in it.

I grieved long and hard for my old self, for Laurel and everything she had. I didn't want to be Hannah who had nothing and at twenty-nine years old had to start all over again.

Daniel was sentenced to life imprisonment, with a recommendation that he served at least twenty years before he was considered for parole. His organised crime empire had crumbled, and no doubt new blood had filled the vacuum caused by his departure.

After that, life went on for everyone, except for me. I was stuck in a new life I didn't want.

On the face of it, I was carving out a way forward for Hannah Towers, but underneath the surface I was in deep mourning. I wasn't sure what the purpose of it all was. I tried so hard to be OK, to look to the future, but the horizon was black and bleak. I went through the motions of existing rather than living. It was a struggle. Every day was difficult. When I went to bed at night, I marked another twenty-four hours off in my head. I often laid awake at night, contemplating the future and what worth was it. The only thing that kept me going was my mum.

Six months after the trial, Bryan arranged for me to see her. It was the first thing I had looked forward to in a long time. When I walked into her room at the care home, I burst into tears and threw my arms around her. Finally, I could have that human contact with someone who I loved. It wasn't Declan but it was my mother. And for a minute, I really felt she knew me. Her hand rubbed my back, and her other hand cupped the back of my head.

'There, there,' she said soothingly in that voice that had comforted me so many times in my life. 'There, there, ducks. It's all right.'

The moment was fleeting but I clung to that with all my heart, and I was so thankful that Bryan had been able to arrange the visit. He was such a good man. He made it possible for me to see my mother several more times over the next few years. She was the only thing that I had to live for, and I swear if it wasn't for her, then I don't think I would have been around to meet Jasper.

It was a bittersweet meeting, because Mum had passed away the month before and I was devastated. Losing her had been a hard blow to my fragile heart and mind.

As I'd looked over into the river that night, I had seriously and, somewhat matter-of-factly, considered how easy it would be to drown. Once I was in the water, how fast would it happen? Who would even notice I was gone? Bryan, maybe? But he was on the brink of retirement, would he even think of me? Especially now he didn't have to make arrangements for me to see Mum.

As I stood there, looking out at the water that night, Jasper had come to stand beside me.

'The River Thames, two hundred and fifteen miles long. Home to approximately one hundred and twenty-five species of fish. Crossed by two hundred bridges. Has the second largest flood barrier in the world, second only to Oosterscheldekering Barrier in the Netherlands.' He'd smiled but his eyes held concern. 'Not my greatest chat-up line,' he'd continued. 'Do you want to come inside for a drink? It's pretty cold out here. And I promise I'll come up with some better conversation than that.'

I don't know what made me accept the offer of a drink from Jasper, but I found myself agreeing and we walked back into the bar together. I can't even remember what we talked about but when I got home that evening, in a cab Jasper had arranged for me, for the first time since becoming Hannah I felt seen as a person. I felt the warmth of humanity. Jasper saved my life that day. He gave me hope that night. Eventually, even though I had no idea back then, he would also give me a life to live for.

THIRTY-TWO

Hannah

Carl drove me back to Silverbanks and walked me to the door, where Jasper was already waiting, his figure silhouetted by the early-morning dawn filtering through the back of the house to the front.

'Thank you, Carl,' I said, as he cut the engine. I looked at Jasper, through the windscreen, trying to read his expression without success.

'You'll be OK,' said Carl. 'He might need a little time to adjust and take it all in, but he loves you like no other.'

'I hope you're right,' I replied.

We both got out of the car, and I held back while Carl approached Jasper first. They shook hands and Jasper thanked Carl for everything he'd done.

'No problem,' said Carl. 'I'm confident it will all work out. I'll be in touch in the next couple of days.'

'Thanks, mate.'

Carl turned and gave me a kiss on each side of the face.

'Audentes fortuna iuvat. Fortune favours the brave – or the bold, if we're being pedantic.'

I watched him go and waved as he reversed out of the drive, steeling myself before facing Jasper. My stomach was churning, and I felt queasy. I didn't know if that was lack of sleep, hunger, or nerves. Probably the latter.

I turned and looked at Jasper, searching his face for any indication of what he was thinking. Carl said he hadn't told Jasper the details of my previous life. As he rightly said, that was for me to tell, and I know Jasper wouldn't want to hear it from anyone else. I owed him to tell him myself.

Jasper and I stood there for a moment, just looking at each other. I wanted to rush into his arms. For him to hold me tight like he always did when I was worried, but I daren't make the first move. I was wearing a T-shirt he'd brought down to the police station the previous night, the police having taken my blood-stained shirt away for forensics and maybe evidence at a later date.

It was Jasper who made the first move. He reached out a hand. 'Don't stand out there like a stranger waiting to be invited into your own home,' he said. 'I've cleaned the kitchen. The police said that forensics had everything they needed.'

A slither of apprehension slipped away at his words. I took his hand, and we went inside. Jasper didn't let go as he closed the door behind us and then stood in front of me, taking my other hand so we were facing each other. 'Are you OK? I mean specifically, and also, generally.'

I nodded. 'I think so, generally. But specifically, I'm a wreck and I'm so scared.' I gulped down a ball of emotion trying to wedge itself in my throat. I had no right to ask for pity or compassion. I was about to tell Jasper something that would shake the very foundations our life had been built on. The guilt was almost as heavy.

He stroked my face gently, resting the palm of his hand

against my cheek. 'You don't have to be scared, Hannah. Whatever this is, whatever has happened, we'll get through this. I promised you I would never leave you. I don't intend to break that promise.'

My heart was threatening to break at his words. I didn't deserve this and no matter what he imagined, he could never imagine the truth. 'I'm sorry we've got to this point,' I said, looking up at him. 'I wish it could have been different.'

He nodded. 'I know.' Then he leaned forward and kissed my forehead. 'Go and have a shower. Get some fresh clothes on and I'll make us some breakfast, then we can talk.'

'Pia? Where's Pia?'

'She's at my parents. She's going to stay the weekend with them, and they'll take her to school on Monday. I said we'd FaceTime her later.'

'She saw me, last night – my clothes. What did you tell her?' More emotion balled in my throat. I could just about cope with Jasper seeing me but knowing my daughter had seen me with blood on my clothes and hands was something almost unbearable.

'It's OK. She was worried you'd hurt yourself. I told her there'd been an accident and you were going to get checked out by a doctor and then let the police know what happened.'

I appreciated his dumbing-down of the whole affair. Of Annabelle's death. 'Thank you,' I said. 'I'll get cleaned up now.' I moved away and stopped at the foot of the stairs, turning to look at him. 'I love you.'

Another nod. He didn't say it back, but I hoped the look in his eyes was saying more than words ever could – that he still loved me. Whether he'd be able to continue loving me, I didn't know.

Upstairs, I showered, washed my hair, and changed into fresh clothes. As I put my dirty clothes in the laundry bin, I wondered if I'd ever be able to wear them again without thinking of Annabelle and the night in police custody. I dried my hair off, before tying it up in a ponytail.

I stared at my reflection for a long time, trying to work out who I was. A mother to two children. A wife to one man and a partner to another. I was a witness to a murder and had just been involved in another. And I was a liar. I thought of Annabelle and when I'd first met her a couple of weeks ago. I thought I'd found a friend, finally allowed myself to get close to someone and for them to get close to me but I had been deceived. I wanted to feel offended, wronged by Annabelle, but I couldn't. That would be the pot calling the kettle black. How could I be outraged at being lied to when I was a liar myself and I had been lying for so many years. The only consolation I could find was that I was lying for a good reason. Annabelle had been lying for different reasons. She wanted to take me down. To ruin my life the way, in her eyes, I had ruined hers.

I needed to speak to Jasper and get this over with. The longer I was putting it off, the worse it was getting.

When I went downstairs, he was serving up poached eggs on toast. I wasn't sure I had an appetite, but he'd gone to the trouble, so I sat down at the bistro table and ate breakfast. Images of Annabelle lying on the floor bleeding came to the fore of my mind. I forced myself to look down at the floor where she had died. I didn't want the memory of yesterday to haunt me, to intrude into my home. She'd done enough of that when she was alive.

'You OK?' asked Jasper.

I gave a shake of my head to dispel the images. 'Yeah. I'm fine.'

He gave me a look which said he didn't believe me, but he didn't say anything and placed the plate down in front of me.

It seemed farcical really. Here we were, a picture of domestic bliss, when in fact, we were both going through the motions. I wondered if Jasper was delaying hearing the truth. Was it a conscious decision or was he scared like I was?

'Thank you,' I said, pushing my plate away, unable to eat it all.

'I don't have much of a mind for food either,' he said with a sad smile. He picked up the plates and took them over to the sink. 'I suppose we'd better have this talk.'

He looked so sad and my heart broke just looking at him.

We sat down on the sofa, and he took my hands in his. 'Whatever you're going to tell me,' he said, 'please know that I can cope with it. I may need a bit of time, but I have no intention of leaving you.'

'Don't,' I said, interrupting him. 'Don't say anything. You've no idea what I'm going to tell you.'

'I'm listening.'

'You remember when we first met? On the South Bank. I was looking into the Thames?'

He nodded. 'Yeah. It was dark. Something drew me to you. We've spoken about this before.'

'Well, that night, I was seriously considering ending my life,' I said carefully. I'd never vocalised this before, not to anyone, and certainly not to Jasper. I'd always assumed it was an unspoken knowledge that neither of us wanted to visit and dissect. It was too dark a hole for the happiness we'd found in each other to fall into. We didn't even want to be near the edge.

'I know you've never said, but I knew that,' replied Jasper. 'I thought about it several times in our early years together and I had some inherent awareness that you were contemplating jumping in.'

I dipped my head, shame rolling over me. 'The reason I didn't was because of you.'

'I know that too.' He offered a weak smile. 'I know the reason you didn't, but I need to know the reason why you wanted to.'

I fiddled with the ring on my right hand that Jasper had bought for me when Pia was born. He'd bought it in lieu of an engagement ring as we'd already discussed marriage and I had steadfastly stuck to my guns that I didn't want to be married. I didn't need a slip of paper to show my commitment to another person, blah, blah, blah. All the typical and clichéd reasons why I wanted to remain single when really it was to hide my past. I looked up at him. 'You know, I always wished we could have married,' I said. 'I would have loved nothing more than to be your wife and I could have done, in theory.'

His eyes were bright with suspicion when he met my gaze. 'In theory?'

'I was Hannah Towers, but I haven't always been Hannah Towers. I've also been Laurel Jordan, I was married to an Australian man called Matthew Jordan, Matt.' I paused, letting the words sink in. I could see from the changing expressions on Jasper's face at what point of understanding he was at with my confessions.

'You were married?' he asked. I nodded. He let out a breath. 'Divorced?'

'Not exactly.'

'What the hell does "not exactly" mean? You were either divorced or not. There's no in-between.'

I winced at the sharpness to his words. 'We split up.' Before I could carry on, Jasper was asking more questions.

'Laurel Jordan? What's that, your middle name or something?'

'It was my name before it was changed by Deed Poll.'

Jasper frowned and pinched the bridge of his nose. 'You're not making much sense, Hannah. Help me out here. I want to understand.' He blew out a breath. 'Kids? Did you have children with this Matt? Please tell me you didn't.'

'I had a son. Declan. He was four years old when I last saw him. Nearly six when I met you.'

'What?! You had a son? And in the eleven years I've known you, you've never thought to tell me?' He got to his feet, unable to hide his disbelief and agitation. Jasper paced the room and came to sit back down beside me. 'Tell me straight, what happened. Just tell me. I don't need this drawn out like some sort of torture. Please, Hannah, I need to understand. God, I want to understand it, but you've got some ground to make up now.'

And so, I told Jasper my story and how I came to be Hannah Towers. And how Annabelle was connected in all this and had set out for revenge, justice, whatever she thought she was looking for.

To his credit, Jasper sat there through the whole sorry story of my life before him. How I'd met and married Matt, about my son, my beautiful boy Declan, the business agreement with Daniel Sully, the murder and how I ended up in the witness protection programme alone without my husband or child. I told him all about Annabelle and how really she was Daniel Sully's daughter, though having never met her before, I had no idea. Jasper sat in silence through it all.

During my revelation, Jasper had gone through the whole gamut of emotions, each one clearly etched on his face, reflected in his body language, and most damaging of all, shown in his eyes. His blue eyes staring incredulously at me as if I'd torn his heart in two. I tried not to cry. I didn't want him to pity me or think these were self-pitying tears, a ploy for sympathy. All I wanted was forgiveness.

'I really thought I could go back to my husband and son after the trial,' I said, the tears falling from my eyes. 'I never in a million years realised that giving evidence would mean giving them up.'

'Fuck,' he whispered. This time he was holding his head in both hands. Then he got to his feet. Strode across the room. Agitated. Angry. Sad. Confused. Betrayed. I could see all those emotions coursing through him, showing on his face, his stance, his body language. He didn't know which emotion to deal with first, which one was the strongest and which one to push aside for now. He swore again. Several more times.

He gripped the mantelpiece as if he needed it for support. I could see him breathing slow and heavy to regain his composure. He had his back to me. He sniffed then wiped his face with his hand. He was crying. Oh, God, what had I done? I had broken this man. The man who loved me without condition. The man who had saved my life eleven years ago and had saved my life every day since then.

I got to my feet and went over to him, placing my hand gently on his shoulder. 'I'm so sorry, Jasper. Sorrier than you'll ever know.'

'Is that everything?' he asked without moving.

'Yes.'

'I mean everything. Absolutely everything?'

'Absolutely everything.'

He turned to face me. 'Is that a promise?'

'I promise. On everything and everyone I love. I promise that is everything.'

'And this... this Daniel. Do I need to worry about him?'

'No.'

'But you went to see him?'

'Only to try to get him to stop what he was doing,' I said.

'I don't want you going to see him again.'

'I have no intention of doing that.'

He contemplated my answer before speaking. 'I need some fresh air.'

I watched him leave the room, stepping out onto the terrace. He dropped to a crouching position, his head in his hands. His shoulders heaved. Then he stood up and let out a cry of anguish. The pain was so raw, it ripped right through me. I swear I felt the physical force of that outpouring of misery. He walked to the end of the garden and looked out at the English Channel before him.

I wanted to go to him, to comfort him, to take away that wound I had inflicted on him, but I sensed he needed this time for his own thoughts. I couldn't force him to stay with me. Our future was totally in his hands.

It seemed an eternity before Jasper came back into the house. I got to my feet, like the condemned waiting their sentencing from the judge. I could almost see the black cloth on Jasper's head as he prepared to deliver his verdict.

He walked over to me, stopping a metre away. More running of his hand over his face. His eyes shone with tears. 'I... I'm so full of anger,' he said. 'No, anger isn't the right word. Devastation. Pain. I'm not even sure I know what I'm feeling or what the word for it is.' He rested his hands on his hips. 'I feel I've been run over by a tank.'

'I'm so sorry,' I said, knowing how inadequate my words were. If there was some way I could show my regret visually, some sort of physical mass I could produce to represent it, then he might understand. If only it were that simple.

Jasper put his hands together, resting his fingertips against his mouth and took a long breath in through his nose, blowing it out slowly through his mouth. 'I need time to think. To try to take this all in,' he said.

I grabbed his arm. 'Don't leave me, please, Jasper.' I couldn't bear the thought of him walking away from me.

He looked down at my hand clasped around his wrist. 'Who said anything about me leaving?'

Tears sprang to my eyes. 'I'll make it up to you. I promise.' I sounded desperate even to my own ears. I wanted Jasper to wrap me in his arms and tell me it was going to be OK, but I was acutely aware he hadn't made a move towards me. I took my hand away feeling helpless.

'It's a lot to take in,' he said, as if reading my thoughts. 'Give me some time.'

I nodded. 'OK.' I had no right to demand anything from him. Not after the bombshell I had dropped into his lap. I had to be patient and give him the time he needed.

'I need some fresh air,' he said. 'I need to think.'

He didn't have to say he needed to be alone. 'OK,' was all I could say as he headed out of the kitchen.

'Hannah,' he said, pausing in the doorway and turning back to look at me.

'Yeah?'

'Just now, when you said about us first meeting on the South Bank, and you thought... you thought...'

'About ending my own life,' I finished the sentence for him.

'Yeah. That time,' he said. 'Don't do anything stupid.'

I shook my head. 'I won't.'

He took another deep breath. 'I'll be back later. Promise.'

I sank down into the sofa, hugging the cushion to my body, and rocked myself as some sort of self-comfort as I cried my heart out, unable to believe all that had happened.

THIRTY-THREE

Hannah

Jasper was true to his word, not that I should ever have doubted him, but when I heard his key in the door, I could have cried from the relief. He'd said he still wasn't able to talk about it yet but was going to do his best. When we'd gone to bed that night, he had curled up against my back like he always did, wrapping his arm around me. The small act of kindness nearly sent me over the edge again. I was wavering on the edge of sanity, I was sure. I felt like I was reliving all the desperate, heart-breaking, and physically painful emotions I'd experienced when Matt had walked away with Declan. Where everything was out of my control and all I had was hope.

When I woke up on Sunday morning, for a split second everything felt right and then the events of the last few days crashed into my consciousness, and I couldn't help crying. I think it must have been some sort of delayed reaction.

Jasper held me in his arms and eventually I had cried all the tears possible.

'I want everything to go back to normal,' I said, my head resting on his chest.

'We've got to get used to a new normal, Hannah. We can't go back to how it was.'

My world had shifted once again, and I had to get used to the new axis it spun upon. Jasper was right. Things were different now. I had to try not to panic about it.

We had breakfast at home and then took Luna for a walk, opting to walk along the beach towards Seabury and not on Silverbanks. Neither of us were ready to face any of the residents and I was grateful of the time together.

It did us both good and I could sense the warmth gradually thawing Jasper's resolve. When I slipped my hand into the crook of his arm, he reached across with his other hand and held mine. A small but not insignificant gesture that gave me hope we could weather the storm we were in.

'If you need help, I mean like a therapist or something,' said Jasper, 'we'll pay for you to go privately.'

'Thank you. I'm not crazy or anything like that.'

'I wasn't saying you are,' replied Jasper. 'But you've been through quite an ordeal, not just yesterday, but before that. If you need to talk it through with a professional, then don't be scared to say.'

'I'll keep it in mind, but right now I don't want to even think about it. Not today.' I'd never been one for talking about things. Being in the PPS meant keeping secrets became second nature. My whole mindset had been conditioned to internally processing and coping.

It was nice to have some normality later that day when we collected Pia from school. She was delighted to see me, and it was a balm to my heart when she ran across the playground and threw herself into my arms. I hugged her tightly, never wanting to let go. Her unwavering and unconditional love made me feel whole again. Made me feel human.

When we arrived home and went through to the kitchen, my mind, once again, assaulted me with an image of Annabelle lying on the floor, blood pooling around her and me standing over her. It was like watching a film reel or CCTV footage where I couldn't quite feel a connection between the person who was me and yet wasn't me.

'Mummy.'

I felt Pia tug at my hand. She had an expectant look on her face as if she was waiting for an answer. 'Did you say something?'

'She asked if she could have a glass of milk and a cookie,' replied Jasper. He was already opening the fridge door and taking out the milk.

'Sorry,' I said. I blinked away images of Annabelle and forced a smile. 'Of course you can. Daddy's getting it for you.'

While Jasper was seeing to Pia, I opened her schoolbook bag to see what reading she had that day. Along with the book was a piece of folded paper that looked like it had been torn from a spiral bound reporter's notebook. Letters home from school were unusual these days now that everything was done via the school app.

I unfolded it and read the handwritten message.

Vengeance is in my heart, death in my hand
Blood and revenge are hammering in my head.

I frowned as I reread the words.

'What's that?' asked Jasper.

I handed him the piece of paper. He looked equally bemused and shrugged. 'From her teacher? That's not a child's handwriting. Look at the way they've written the capital B. Very fancy.'

'Pia,' I said, going over to where she was sitting at the table. 'Is this something your teacher gave you? Is it for assembly?'

Pia looked at the paper. 'I don't know.'

'Your teacher didn't give it to you?' I pressed.

'No,' replied Pia, looking concerned.

'It's OK, nothing to worry about,' said Jasper.

'It probably got put in there by mistake,' I added, smiling reassuringly at my daughter. And then in a low voice to Jasper. 'I'll check with her teacher tomorrow.'

'I don't think you need to make a big deal out of it.' He took out his phone and tapped on the screen.

'I'm not making a big deal, I'm merely going to check with the teacher,' I replied.

Jasper looked up at held the screen of his phone towards me. 'It's a Shakespeare quote.'

I gave it a cursory glance before looking at Pia, who had taken her drink and cookie over to the sitting area. I picked up the remote control and flicked the TV on for her, before going back to Jasper. 'They're a bit young to be doing Shakespeare. Besides, even if they were, it's a weird thing to put in her bag,' I said in a low voice. 'I want to know if it came from the school.'

'Where else is it going to come from?' asked Jasper.

He was unusually argumentative, and I wasn't used to this side of him. 'Someone might have put it in there.'

'Hannah, you're not making any sense. Why would someone do that? And what harm is there?'

'You're not looking at it from my point of view,' I persisted. 'What if some put it in there to get at me?'

Jasper closed the fridge door and rested his hands on the counter. Dipping his head a fraction as if he was trying to keep his patience or working out what he was going to say next. Finally, he spoke. 'How is that getting at you?'

'It's talking about blood and revenge. It could be revenge for

Annabelle or something that happened before. Can't you see that?' My voice rose in volume and pitch.'

'Please, Hannah,' said Jasper with a sigh. 'Don't start getting all paranoid.'

'I'm not getting paranoid,' I snapped back, trying to keep my voice to a whisper.

'Look, Annabelle is dead.' He puffed out a frustrated breath and then his face softened. 'Sorry, I don't mean to sound harsh. But she was waging a campaign against you because of what happened to her father. She was twisted. Mentally ill. She tried to kill you, for God's sake. But she's no longer a threat. She can't hurt you or us.'

I buried my face in my hands. Jasper was right. Annabelle was dead and couldn't hurt me again and yet, I couldn't relax. I was still in a state of high alert. 'I'm sorry,' I said eventually. 'I'm finding it all very difficult.'

He came over to me and pulled me into his arms. It felt so good to be held. 'It's hard for everyone,' he said. 'Don't take this the wrong way, but please think about seeing a therapist or a counsellor.'

I stiffened at the suggestion, but I didn't want to get into an argument about it. 'I'll think about it,' I said, trying not to sound half-hearted.

'Thank you.' He kissed the top of my head and withdrew from the embrace. 'I'll feed Luna and take her out for a walk.'

I got the feeling it was a walk he wanted to take alone. I hated that idea. Jasper and I had always been so tight, always wanting to spend time together, and now he needed time away from me. Perhaps I should seriously consider therapy of some sort. Maybe I did need counselling. If it was going to save my marriage, then I'd do it.

I caught sight of the piece of paper that Jasper had left on the worktop and was going to pick it up, when Jasper got there before me. 'We'll throw this away,' he said, dropping it into the pedal bin.

A few minutes later, after Luna had gobbled up all her food, Jasper headed out for a walk. As soon as he disappeared over the wall at the end of the garden, I was straight back to the bin, fishing out the note. I looked at it again, wondering who had written it. If it was a teacher, surely they would have printed it out on the computer. I couldn't make up my mind whether it had been written by someone young or old. The capital letters took away a lot of the distinguishing features. However, the letter 'V' was distinctive in that there was a long flick leading into the letter and a loop at the top – a flourish, I guess was the right way to describe it. The same for the letter 'B'. It still didn't help though, it could be some sort of calligraphy or an older person's writing, although if the latter, I would have expected to see more distinctive letters.

I sighed. I really had no idea. Despite Jasper's attempts to dismiss it, I couldn't. I folded the piece of paper in half and slipped it into the inside zip pocket of my handbag. I didn't know why or what I was going to do with it, but I wasn't going to throw it away.

Everything Jasper had said made sense. I was overreacting. Even paranoid. Logically, Annabelle could not harm me. But no matter how hard I tried to reason with myself, I couldn't shake the feeling that this thing, whatever it was, wasn't over.

THIRTY-FOUR

Hannah

I hadn't heard from the police at all that day, and I didn't know if it was a good or a bad thing. Jasper had spoken to Carl who'd said to sit tight and try not to worry. Try not to worry? Easier said than done when you weren't the one who was being investigated.

I'd just put Pia to bed, and Jasper and I had settled down in front of the television, when I heard a car pull up on the driveway.

I stood up and looked out through the shutters.

My heart missed a beat.

'Who is it?' asked Jasper.

'Owens. And Barnes.' I turned and looked at Jasper as panic began to well up inside me. 'Something's happened. They wouldn't be here at this time of night if it was good news.'

I momentarily thought about running through the house and escaping out onto the beach. Running as fast as I could, without stopping. Fleeing. On the run.

'Don't jump to conclusions,' said Jasper, switching off the TV and getting to his feet. 'Wait there.'

He opened the door before they had a chance to ring the bell. I listened to the exchange between the men.

'Ah, Jasper.' It was Owens. 'Sorry to disturb you at this time of the evening.'

He didn't elaborate further, and this added to my anxiety. I wiped my sweaty palms on my jeans.

'It is rather late,' said Jasper.

'Is Miss Towers there, please?' This time it was Barnes. Starchy as ever.

'What's this all about?' asked Jasper.

'We really need to speak to Hannah,' said Owens.

'Can't it wait until the morning?' God, I didn't deserve such loyalty from Jasper, and I loved that man for still trying to protect me despite everything that had happened.

'No. I'm afraid it can't,' said Barnes. 'We'd like to come in and speak to her, if you don't mind?'

There was a pause and even from my refuge in the sitting room, I could feel the tension. Jasper cleared his throat. 'I do mind, actually. My daughter is asleep upstairs, and I would rather this visit was rescheduled. I'd like Hannah's lawyer to be present.'

'Look,' said Owens. 'I don't want to make this any more difficult than it is already, but it would be in everyone's best interest if you could let us in to speak to Hannah.'

It was no good. I didn't want Jasper getting arrested for obstructing the police or something ridiculous like aiding and abetting a criminal. I went out into the hall.

'It's OK, Jasper,' I said, walking down the hallway to the front door.

I looked from Barnes to Owens. The former looked smug while the latter looked almost apologetic. Nevertheless, I smiled at the officers. 'How can I help you?'

Barnes stepped forward. 'May we come in?'

After a few seconds of stand-off, Jasper moved to one side to let the officers in, showing them to the sitting room. 'Right, what's this all about?' he asked.

Owens spoke. 'Some new evidence has come to light.' He paused before continuing. 'Hannah Towers, you are under arrest for the murder of Bryan Chamberton. You do not have to say anything. But...'

'Bryan?' I gasped.

'What the hell?' It was Jasper.

Barnes whipped out her handcuffs as Owens continued to read me my rights. '...when questioned something which you later rely on in court.'

'Is that necessary?' Jasper asked incredulously as Barnes took hold of my wrist. 'She's not resisting or trying to escape.'

'... may be given in evidence,' concluded Owens. He put a hand out and stopped his colleague. 'I don't think we need to use those.'

To say Barnes looked disappointed was an understatement, but reluctantly she put her handcuffs away and let go of my arm.

'This is ridiculous,' said Jasper.

'Come this way, please, Hannah,' instructed Owens.

I looked back at Jasper. 'I'm sorry.'

'Don't say anything until Carl gets there. Understood?' Jasper was already scrolling through his phone. 'Not a word.' He looked at Owens. 'She has a right to legal representation. Don't try to bully her or persuade her to talk without her lawyer being there.'

'We do know how this works,' said Barnes.

But Jasper was talking into the phone. 'Carl. It's Jasper. The fucking police have turned up and arrested Hannah... Yeah, arrested her for murder... Bryan Chamberton... No, I don't know either.' He followed us out to the door. 'What station are you taking her to?'

'Same as before,' said Barnes.

Jasper relayed the information to Carl and hung up. 'He'll be there to meet you,' he called out to me as Owens opened the rear door to the car and ushered me in.

Carl was indeed waiting at the police station when we arrived. After I was booked in by the duty officer, I was taken to an interview room where Carl was allowed to talk to me.

'Well, I wasn't expecting this,' he said, opening his notebook again. 'We really need to start meeting up in much more civilised surroundings.' He smiled and I appreciated the small gesture of comfort.

'I didn't kill Bryan. I'm innocent,' I said, and almost laughed at myself for sounding so clichéd.

Another warm smile from Carl, who must have thought the exact same thing. 'Yes, that was a rather surprising plot twist,' he said. 'So, first of all, don't panic. Did you say anything to the police when they brought you in? Did they ask you any questions?'

'No. Nothing. Just that they had new evidence. I didn't say anything nor did they.'

'Good. So, what we need to do first, is listen to their evidence,' said Carl. 'See what they have to say. Just answer their questions – you don't want to start acting like you have anything to hide. If I think it's a leading question, I'll interrupt and advise you not to answer. You will then say "no comment". Once they're done, we can have some time to discuss it further.'

I nodded. I had been blindsided by the accusation. How on earth had I gone from being investigated for one death to being charged with murder for another? 'I don't know what's going on,' I confessed, feeling I wanted to cry but desperately trying to hold it together.

'Before we go ahead with the interview,' said Carl. 'Is there anything you need to tell me? Anything at all?'

'You mean, did I kill Bryan?' I replied, noting the irritated tone in my voice.

'I'm sorry, but I have to ask.'

It wasn't Carl's fault, and I knew I shouldn't be bad-tempered with him. 'Sorry. No. They didn't even ask me about Bryan last time.'

'OK. Well, let's see what they have to say.'

Carl left the room and returned a few minutes later with Owens and Barnes. The tape recorder was set up and Owens advised me they would be recording the interview.

'So, Hannah,' he began. 'I want to go back to the day of Bryan Chamberton's death. Can you talk me through what you did that day?'

'Erm, so that day, Jasper and I took Pia to school and after-wards we stopped in town for a coffee,' I said, as I cast my mind back. 'We came back and saw Bryan and his wife, Sandra. They were outside. There had been some vandalism on the estate, and we talked about it.'

'Bryan was your next-door neighbour, wasn't he?' asked Barnes.

'Yes.'

'How did you get on with him?' Barnes didn't give anything away in her questioning.

'OK,' I said. 'As you know, Bryan and I knew each other before...' I stopped as Carl held up his hand.

'We don't need to expand any further.' He looked to the officers. 'Next question.'

Owens took up the baton. 'After you spoke with the Cham-bertons, what did you do next?'

'I took Luna, my dog, for a walk along the beach.'

'On your own?' asked Barnes.

'Yes. And I bumped into Annabelle.' I swallowed as her name lodged in my throat.

'Annabelle Burton?' It was Barnes again. I got the feeling she was only clarifying because she enjoyed watching me finding this very difficult.

I nodded.

'For the tape, Hannah is nodding,' said Owens. 'Now, Hannah, you saw Annabelle, then what?'

'My client has already told you this in a previous statement,' cut in Carl. 'When you questioned her two days ago.'

'We're just establishing facts for this interview,' said Owens. He looked back at me. 'So, you saw Annabelle and then what?'

'I went back to hers for a drink. Stayed for a couple of hours and then went home.'

'And what did you do for the rest of the evening?'

'Actually, I had to go back to Annabelle's because I left my phone there,' I said.

Owens consulted the notes in front of him and I guessed that he was double-checking my previous statement. 'And you didn't see Bryan Chamberton?'

'No.'

'You didn't see him on the beach?'

'No.'

'He never asked you to meet him at the beach?'

'No.'

'I think my client has made it clear she didn't see Bryan Chamberton,' interjected Carl.

Owens and Barnes exchanged a look. The atmosphere in the room shifted a little and I had the distinct sensation they were about to reveal whatever evidence it was they had which they were going to use against me.

Barnes opened the manila file in front of her and took out

several coloured photographs, taking her time to lay each one out on the desk between us.

I couldn't help letting out a small gasp as I looked at the images.

'Miss Towers,' she began. 'Do you recognise the item of clothing in these pictures?'

I went to answer but stopped myself, looking at Carl for guidance. He had no idea that the item of clothing was in fact the blouse I'd bought from the boutique in town, the one with the distinctive bow and the one I hadn't been able to find last week. My missing blouse. Except there was one difference. The blouse in the pictures was covered in blood.

'Miss Towers,' pressed Barnes. 'Is that your blouse?'

Carl leaned towards me and whispered in my ear. 'No comment.'

I looked from the pictures to Barnes and then to Owens. 'No comment.'

Barnes remained undeterred. 'Can you explain how the blood got on the blouse?'

'No comment,' I replied. The fact was, I couldn't. I had no idea. I started to panic.

'We've run tests on the bloodstains,' said Barnes. 'And it's a match for Bryan Chamberton's blood.'

'I believe Bryan Chamberton died from drowning,' said Carl.

Barnes's gaze never left mine as she replied. 'He did, but he also sustained a significant head injury. Blunt force trauma. Probably attacked from behind. We believe the blow was to incapacitate him so he could be held down in the water. The attacker may well have sprawled across him, using their body weight to keep his face in the water.'

'There's a lot of supposition going on there,' said Carl. 'We need to deal in hard facts and proof.'

'Why don't you tell us what happened, Miss Towers?' asked Barnes, ignoring Carl.

'No comment,' I replied.

'Did you get into an argument with Bryan? Did you hit him over the head with a piece of wood? And then hold him down in the water?' Barnes's shoulders were tense, and I could tell she was trying hard to remain professional. She probably wanted to shake a confession out of me.

Despite being terrified and wanting to answer their questions to convince them I hadn't killed Bryan, I stuck to Carl's advice and offered another no comment reply.

Owens stepped in to give his colleague a break. 'Hannah, it's best if you tell us now. We will find out the truth and if you cooperate with us, then it's easier for everyone in the long run.'

'My client has no comment to make,' said Carl.

Owens tried again. 'We are running further tests on the blouse. We're looking for your DNA now.'

'That doesn't prove my client was wearing the blouse at the time of the murder,' said Carl. 'If you find her DNA, then it's purely circumstantial. It will only prove it's my client's blouse, not that she was wearing it at the time of the attack.' Carl closed his notebook dismissively. 'Now, if there are no further questions, perhaps you can release my client? We've been here long enough and it's the middle of the night. She has a young daughter at home.'

'I think we'll take a break now,' said Owens. He noted it on the tape and switched the machine off. 'We'll be back in half an hour.'

As the door closed behind them, I turned to Carl. 'The blouse. It looks like mine,' I said. 'But I couldn't find it the other day when I wanted to wear it. Someone must have taken it from my house. Someone's trying to set me up.'

Carl placed a hand on my arm. 'Don't get all worked up

now,' he said. 'We can talk about this properly once you're out of here. For now, we stick to no comment. They need to prove it's your blouse. They need to prove you were wearing it at the time of the offence. I don't want you to answer now but think carefully about how your blouse could have been taken from your house. Who would have done that? Why? What's their motive?'

'How did they even get the blouse?'

'That's something else they will need to explain,' said Carl. 'Especially if they need to prove it's yours. As I said, strictly no comment to any of their questions, no matter how innocent they may seem.'

It was in fact another hour before the two detectives reappeared. A tactic to try to unnerve me, Carl said. 'We'll just sit and wait patiently,' he replied. 'This tells me they don't actually have any real evidence.'

Owens and Barnes tried for another forty minutes to get me to confess, but I steadfastly remained tight-lipped, replying no comment to every question they posed.

Once again, I found myself released from police custody. This time, still under arrest but no charges at present.

'Let's get you home,' said Carl, opening the door to his car for me. 'This is getting like déjà vu.' He smiled and closed the door behind me before going around to his side of the car.

Jasper was, of course, waiting for me when I got home and insisted I go straight up to bed while he spoke to Carl.

I heard Carl's car leave about half an hour later and then Jasper came upstairs. He perched on my side of the bed, and just looked at me.

The light of the bedside table cast a shadow across his face, but I could still read his expression. My heart wanted to break. For the first time, I could see the doubt in his eyes.

'I didn't do it,' I whispered, silently begging him to believe me. To tell me, he knew that. To reassure me, he believed me.

Two days ago I could have counted on his support. His

unfaltering trust in me. But I had broken that trust and now it was gone.

Jasper gently pushed a strand of hair from my face. He tried for a smile, but it barely tipped the corners of his mouth before his expression dropped to one of desolation.

'Get some sleep,' he said, before getting up and leaving the room, closing the door softly behind him.

I buried my face in my pillow to deaden the sound of my sobs.

THIRTY-FIVE

Hannah

It was a lonely night in the bed without Jasper. I thought he might come up to bed at some point and I drifted in and out of a light somewhat disturbed sleep. Each time, I rolled over, looking to see him next to me, but the bed was empty.

Finally, I got up at five thirty and, wrapping my dressing gown around me, I went out onto the landing, standing outside the closed door of the spare room. Eventually, I tapped on the door and opened it. The duvet cover was pulled back to the end of the bed to air it. Something Jasper had always done, a habit passed down by his mother.

I went downstairs and Jasper was standing at the bifold doors looking out towards the beach. He turned as he heard me enter the kitchen.

'Hi,' I said.

'Hey.' He turned back to the beach.

I froze. He wasn't even going to offer to make me a cup of tea. It was something he always did in the morning. Such a small insignificant gesture any other day and yet today, hugely significant in its absence. I could sense the tension coming off Jasper in waves, stronger than the tide outside. I went over to the kitchen area and made myself a drink. Not that I wanted one now, but I needed something to do while I worked out what was going on. I was in unchartered waters which I didn't know how to navigate.

Finally, Jasper turned to face me. I looked expectantly, knowing he was about to say something I wasn't going to like. 'Hannah,' he began.

I shook my head. 'Don't do this, Jasper. Please.' My voice wasn't much more than a whisper. He was going to leave me. He didn't have to tell me. I knew.

'I think it would be a good idea if Pia stayed with my parents for a few days,' he said. 'While all this is going on.'

'What?'

'And I'm going to go with her,' he said evenly.

I closed my eyes. Surely, I'd heard wrong. 'What did you say?' I asked, opening my eyes again.

'Pia and I are going to stay with my parents for a few days.'

'No!' I shouted and then lowered my voice. 'You can't do that? I mean, why do you even want to?' Panic was coating my every word. 'You said you wouldn't leave me. You can't take Pia away.'

'Listen,' said Jasper, firmly. He went over and closed the door to the hallway before coming back to stand on the other side of the kitchen island. 'I never said I was leaving you, just having a few days away, that's all.'

'You might as well be leaving me. You're taking my daughter away from me.' I held my head in my hands as I began to pace the kitchen. This couldn't be happening. Not again. I wouldn't let it. 'You go, but Pia stays with me.'

Jasper shook his head. 'No can do. She needs somewhere calm. Where there's no tension or drama. No police coming and going. Her mother not being whisked off in the middle of the night. That way, she might not even have any idea what's going on.'

'No. No. I won't let you take her.' I strode over to him, my hands in front of me, shaking as I clenched and unclenched my fingers. 'You can't do this.'

'Listen to me,' said Jasper. 'Hannah. Listen to me.'

My breathing was fast and shallow. I could feel a desperation taking hold but somewhere in the back of my mind I also knew I couldn't lose it. That would play straight into Jasper's reasoning for taking Pia away. 'What?' I managed to say, while trying to catch my breath.

'I'm only thinking about Pia and what is best for her. You should too. She's better off with my parents while all this is going on.'

'You're trying to make me feel guilty,' I snapped back. 'This is emotional blackmail.'

'I'm being realistic.'

'If that's the case, then why are you going?' I retorted. 'Why aren't you staying?'

He didn't answer and I saw the abject sadness in his eyes. 'Don't do this,' he said.

'No! You don't do this!' I shouted. I began pacing again. Everything was spiralling out of control. Everything I loved was being taken away from me. How could this be happening a second time? 'Jasper, please. I'm begging you. Please don't go, and please don't take Pia.'

'I've made up my mind,' he replied.

I stopped pacing and looked at him as a cold and cruel realisation wound itself around me. I shook my head slowly from side to side. 'Oh, God,' I said. 'Oh, please say it's not true.'

'Hannah…'

'You think I killed Bryan, don't you?' I was on the brink of hyperventilating. I gulped for air. 'Admit it. That's what you think.'

'It's not that,' said Jasper.

'Then what is it?' I demanded.

He couldn't answer me.

For the first time, that level-headed, calm, and under-standing man I had known for the past eleven years wasn't present. In front of me stood another version of Jasper Gunderson. A stranger to me. Was that how he felt about me? Was he seeing me now through different eyes?

'I'm sorry,' said Jasper. 'It's for the best. But, just so we're clear, I am not leaving you. I'm simply taking Pia to my parents until all this mess is resolved.'

A fog was descending over my brain. I couldn't think straight. I flew at him, my arms flailing like a windmill as I let out a roar unlike anything I'd ever heard before. A primeval, gut-wrenching cry from the bottom of my stomach, tearing my heart out along the way. 'No! No! No!' I sobbed.

'Hannah. For God's sake.' Jasper caught my wrists to stop the blows landing. Somehow, he managed to wrap his arms around me. I was thrashing and writhing, trying to break free, but he held me tightly to his body until I had no more energy to fight, and my body sagged, limp in defeat.

Jasper led me over to the sofa, sitting me down. I was exhausted. I couldn't fight him anymore.

When he came down with Pia an hour later, she was dressed ready for school. Where I managed to summon the energy from to appear happy and normal, I have no idea.

I forced a smile, injected false cheer into my voice. There was no way I was going to cause a scene in front of her.

'Daddy says we're going to stay at Granny's,' she said, skipping over to me.

I pulled her into a hug. 'That's right.'

'It's only for a few days,' said Jasper.

'Are you coming, Mummy?' asked Pia.

'No, I'm going to stay here.' The words felt like knives in my throat.

'Why?' asked Pia.

'To look after Luna,' I said.

Pia seemed satisfied with the answer.

'Right, we need to get you to school,' said Jasper, smiling at his daughter. He had the decency to look sympathetically in my direction.

I wrapped my arms around Pia. Hugging her tightly. 'Have a good day at school, sweetie,' I said. 'Love you lots.'

'Love you too,' she replied.

I got to my feet and walked out to the front door, like I would any other day that Jasper was taking Pia out. Except this time, neither of them were coming back. I could feel myself withdrawing. Emotionally removing myself from what was happening. It was the only way I knew how to cope.

'I'll phone you later,' said Jasper, coming back to the door after fastening Pia's seat belt for her.

There was an awkward pause where neither of us knew how to say goodbye to one another. In the end, Jasper just turned away and got in the car.

I watched them drive away before retreating into the house, closing the door behind me.

Never in my life had I felt so alone. Somehow this was even worse than before. How could history be repeating itself?

THIRTY-SIX

Hannah

When I had walked away from Daniel a few days earlier, I truly had thought I would never see him again. It had been a weird sensation, one where I was grieving for the man he could have been and the knowledge that our... I didn't even know what to call it, but our connection would finally be severed and the nightmare I was living would be over.

How wrong had I been?

I should never have trusted him.

Today, I didn't sit in my car summoning up courage to meet him. Today, I swung into the car park, almost performing a handbrake turn. I was angry. I was desperate. Jasper leaving with Pia was going to break me. They were all I had left, and I couldn't let them go. I was going into battle to save the two people who I loved most on this earth. I had promised Jasper I wouldn't see Daniel again, but that was then, when the stakes weren't so high. Daniel, the man whose actions had forced me to lose one family, was now the man whose actions would ensure I didn't lose another.

I rang the bell and moved from foot to foot as I waited for the door to be answered. Inside, Hilary was on the reception desk. I saw a flicker of recognition in her eyes, but I wasn't even going to pretend I was whoever I'd said I was the last time I saw her.

'Hi,' I said as I approached the desk, forcing myself to loosen the hard expression I knew my face had settled into. 'I've come to see Daniel Sully.'

'Good morning. Yes, if you can sign in, I'll let him know you're here. It's...'

'Laurel Jordan,' I said cutting her off and ignoring the frown she gave.

'Oh. OK.' She picked up the phone and tapped in a number. 'Hello, Kelly,' she said. 'I have a Laurel Jordan to see Daniel... Yes... OK...' She cupped the mouthpiece with her hand. 'The nurse is just speaking to Daniel.'

A few moments passed before Hilary announced I could go up to room ten. I was already at the foot of the stairs before she'd finished giving me directions.

As before, a nurse answered my knock on the door and stepped outside to speak to me. 'Daniel is very weak,' she said. 'Don't be alarmed if he nods off mid-conversation.'

I thanked her and went into the room.

All the bluster and anger were knocked out of me as, instead of sitting in the chair like before, Daniel was in bed, hooked up to some sort of monitor which pulsed silently at the side of the bed.

'Laurel,' he said, his voice soft and lacking in strength. He raised his hand a fraction. 'You're the last person... I thought I'd see.'

I approached the bed but remained standing as I grappled with my emotions. I knew he wouldn't want pity, but I did pity him. It was clear he didn't have much time left and I wondered, if I was just a little more patient and let nature take its course, perhaps I wouldn't have to worry about Daniel persecuting me any longer.

He looked at me with questioning eyes and gestured towards the chair again.

It was a bizarre scenario. Here I was, sitting with the father of the woman I had killed only a few days ago. 'I'm sorry about Jessica, it was an accident,' I said, scrutinising his face for a reaction. All I could see was pain in his eyes. Those beautiful blue eyes that drew mine to his with some sort of invisible force that I had no ability to resist.

'Sorry?' he said, his voice rasping. 'You killed my daughter.' He gave a sharp intake of breath.

'It was an accident,' I repeated. 'She had a knife. I tried to stop her from...' I stopped as he held up his hand.

'I know what happened. The police told me.' His breathing was steady again. 'I'm glad she didn't harm you.' He turned his head to look out of the window for a moment before looking back at me. 'I may not have had much of a relationship with Jess, but she was her father's daughter, as they say.'

'In some ways, maybe,' I said. 'I'm still sorry I've caused you pain.'

'Now I know how you feel, huh?'

I shook my head. 'No, Daniel, that was never my intention. Never.'

His gaze fixed on mine for a long moment, before his face softened and he gave a small nod. 'Good,' he said, letting out a shaky breath. 'Why are you here? I didn't think I'd see you again.'

'It's still going on,' I said. 'Someone is still trying to ruin my life and if it's not Jess, then it stands to reason it's you. I've come to tell you, again, to stop.'

'You're asking me to help after everything?'

I nodded.

Daniel reached out and I felt compelled to take his hand. It was bony and withered but the zing of electricity ran through us. I realised this was the first physical contact we'd had in eleven years.

He squeezed my hand. 'You know, Laurel. This makes you just like me,' he said.

I recoiled, snatching my hand away. 'I am not like you,' I said.

He let out a sigh. 'Laurel. My Laurel.'

'Don't. I was never yours.' This had been a waste of time. He was messing with me, even on his death bed. 'Just leave me alone,' I said. 'You win. OK? You've proved that you still have control over the narrative. You still have the power, OK, Daniel? You win, my family will leave me again. But you can stop now. Game's over.'

'Sit down, Laurel,' he said, his voice surprisingly strong and I found myself doing as I was told and sitting down in the bedside chair. Again, he reached for my hand. 'I don't want to fight with you,' he said. 'This is probably the last time we will see each other. I don't want it to end like this.'

I took his hand. 'Daniel,' I said. 'If you have any thought for me, either then or now, then please make all this stop.'

'When I said I wouldn't do anything to hurt you, I meant it,' he replied. 'You were always special to me. Even when you stood up in the court and testified against me. I admired you for doing that. I knew you wouldn't back down. It's not in you to do that and that is why you're here now. You don't back down.' He paused, his breathing coming fast and shallow. It was a few moments before he spoke again. 'That's what made you special, Laurel. You didn't bow down to me like everyone else. You didn't throw yourself at me like all the other women.'

'I was married,' I said.

'He was a dick,' said Daniel, with a smile.

I gave a small laugh. Even now, he found humour and could make me laugh. 'I'm not going to argue with you on that,' I said.

Daniel's face grew serious again. 'I didn't know Jess was doing all that to you,' he said. 'If I'd known, I would have put a stop to it. I could have stopped it before it was too late. I blame myself for that.'

He sounded so sincere, and I felt myself believing him. 'If you weren't involved, then why is it still happening? Who hates me so much?'

He studied my face intently before speaking. 'I missed a lot of Jess's life, didn't know her all that well really. Truth be told, her nanny more or less raised her.' He was out of breath again and paused for several seconds. I could see the effort to speak was tiring for him. He took a deep breath. 'Jess was the pupil, not the teacher,' he said in nothing more than a whisper.

His eyes closed, fluttered, and closed again. For a moment I thought he had died, but I could make out the faint rise and fall of his chest and the sound of his breathing, albeit weak. Our meeting had exhausted him. I sat there for a moment, not wanting to leave him and yet at the same time, wanting to be as far away from him as possible.

I don't know what made me do it, but I rested my cheek against his hand, closing my eyes and remembering the man I could so easily have fallen in love with. But it was another place and another time. Another lifetime, in fact. A tear escaped from the corner of my eye, tracking its way down my cheek to where it met his hand.

Then I felt his other hand brush my head, his fingertips graze into my hair. 'Don't cry, Laurel,' he said.

I lifted my head and looked at him, his blue eyes a hazy grey. 'I'm sorry,' I said.

His mouth curved at the corners. 'So am I.' His gaze held mine. 'Not long now,' he whispered. 'I'm glad I got to see you one last time. Oh, for another lifetime.' He let out a sigh. His eyes were bright again for a moment. 'Laurel.' My name faded into a sigh. He smiled and despite the bizarre sadness in my heart, I smiled back at him. He closed his eyes, seemingly content.

I stayed with Daniel for the rest of the morning, in which time the nurse came in several times to check on him. 'It won't be long,' she said. And she was right. Shortly after midday, Daniel passed away. I swear I felt his hand squeeze mine just before, but maybe that was wishful thinking.

While the nurse went off to make the necessary calls, I said goodbye to the man who had both taken my life and given me a new life. And amongst all that, could have been my life.

THIRTY-SEVEN

Hannah

I left Elm Tree Clinic and headed straight home. In the absence of any kind of clinical smell from the place, I could smell Daniel's aftershave lingering around me and in my hair. It must have been the cologne he always wore as it took me right back to those strange heady days I'd spent with him.

As soon as I was home, I showered, washing my hair and every part of my body to remove the last traces of Daniel from me. As I stood under the jets of water, I shed a few more tears for Daniel, but ultimately I emerged with a sense of relief and hope for the future where I could envisage my life as Hannah being put back together.

By the time I had dressed, I was in the most positive frame of mind that I had been for a long time. I was safe. Much as I was sad Daniel had died, it meant that I could have my life back. He couldn't hurt me now. He couldn't taunt me or play games with me or ruin my life as some sort of justice for me ruining his.

Despite his protestations that it wasn't him, I didn't believe it.

I ran the hairdryer through my hair.

Of course, it had to be Daniel behind it and even on his deathbed he still wanted that control. He still wanted me to doubt myself. But he had underestimated me. He forgot I knew him.

It all tied in with him coming out of prison. That was when the trouble started. I knew what Daniel was like, he would have planned this to the nth degree. He would have made it happen and roping his daughter in to throw me off was the kind of move he'd make. It had his signature all over it. He would have got some immense perverted enjoyment in knowing his daughter had befriended me and I had fallen for it.

Ultimately though, he didn't win. I did.

I smiled at my reflection.

Now all I had to do was convince Jasper everything was all right. I'd tell him about Daniel's death and that now we were safe. Pia was safe and we could rebuild our relationship. We'd always been good together. Jasper was my true love, and I wasn't about to let him go without a fight.

I picked up my phone and sent Jasper a text message.

> Hey, how are you both? There's something I need to talk to you about. Can you come over tonight? I'll cook some food.

I got a reply by the time I'd made it to the bottom of the stairs.

> We're good. Is everything all right?

> Yes. But I need to talk to you.

> I'll call you. Can you talk now?

> No. Come over. Please.

The pause was longer as I waited for a reply but eventually it came.

OK. What time?

7.30. I'll fix us something to eat.

See you then.

It wasn't the warmest of exchanges, but I was glad he was coming over. I had the rest of the afternoon now to get something in and prepare a meal for us.

I was full of nervous energy and found it hard to settle. I so wanted to make things right with Jasper. I didn't want to mess up my chances and yet my mind kept wandering back to Daniel and those final moments.

They had felt personal, intimate almost, as if he had been waiting for me. It sounded ludicrous, but at the same time it felt true. If I hadn't gone to see him today, if I'd put it off until tomorrow, would he still have been alive? It was a fanciful idea, but I couldn't help feeling he had somehow engineered it so that his final breath was in my presence.

I couldn't help feeling sad that he had died. A life had gone from this world. But then, by stark contrast, I felt a relief that I was free and hoped that I could rebuild my life with Jasper.

In the end, I gave up trying to reconcile all my thoughts into some sort of order that made sense. Maybe they would in time, but for now, I would tuck them away in one of the dark corners of my mind, in the hope that with the passing of time I might make sense of the confusion.

I needed to get out of the house and decided a brisk walk around the estate and back along the beach would do me good. I changed into my trainers and, with Luna on her lead, headed out.

It was good to breathe in the fresh salty sea air, brought in on the gentle breeze. Today everything on Silverbanks looked bright and summery as spring slipped away with each day.

A few minutes later, I found myself on The Loop and approaching Annabelle's apartment. I paused, thinking back to the beginning of our friendship when I had no clue as to who she was. It could have been so different. We could have been friends, because I did like Annabelle. Then I reminded myself that I hadn't known her really. I knew the persona she wanted me to see. It was fake. Annabelle wasn't a real person. Everything about her had been generated to fool me. And boy it certainly had. The real person, Jessica, I had barely known had existed. I'd never got that far with Daniel in finding out about his family. He'd only ever referred to her as his daughter and I'd never met her.

She would have known all about me, courtesy of Daniel. He would have told her everything she needed to know to become my friend and win my trust. It was a calculated move, so very typical of Daniel. He would have made sure nothing was left to chance.

That thought hurt me. He had orchestrated everything and yet when I went to see him had claimed it was nothing to do with him. But then that would have been the final act of his warped game – to leave me in doubt. To die, knowing he had still tricked me.

God, I was such an idiot. Why hadn't I seen this? Tears welled in my eyes at my own stupidity and a sense of humiliation washed over me, mixed with hurt. I was so gullible. Even in death, he'd had the last laugh.

'Come on, Luna,' I said, heading for the footpath down to the sea. As I passed the side door to Annabelle's apartment, it opened and out stepped Elizabeth with a black bin bag.

'Oh, hello, Hannah,' she said, puffing at the effort of carrying the bulging rubbish sack.

'Here, let me help you,' I said, going over and taking it from her. 'Where do you want it?'

'In the bin, please.' She gestured to the wheelie bin tucked away behind a trellis. 'I take it you're clearing out Annabelle's apartment?' I lifted the lid and dumped the bag into the container.

'Yes. She doesn't have any family locally. Her solicitor got in touch with me about the tenancy and her belongings. Apparently, everything is to be thrown away. Such a waste. I offered to take the clothes to the charity shop.'

I nodded. It felt strange talking about Annabelle when it was me who had ended her life. In a way, I didn't even want to touch her belongings.

'I would offer to help...' I began.

'Oh, don't worry. I understand,' said Elizabeth. She offered me a sympathetic smile. 'How are you?'

I was touched by her concern and unexpectedly, tears sprang to my eyes. 'Sorry,' I said, wiping them away and wishing I'd brought a handkerchief with me.

'Come in a moment,' said Elizabeth. 'I'll find you a tissue.' Before I could protest, she was shepherding me into the apartment. 'Now, sit down for a moment. I saw a box of tissues in the bedroom.'

I shuddered as I perched on the edge of the sofa. Luna was having a good sniff around and I wondered if she remembered when she was last here and Annabelle made a fuss of her. I gave an involuntary shudder at the memory. I did not want to be here. It felt intrusive and somehow macabre considering the circumstances.

Elizabeth bustled back with a box of tissues. 'Thank you,' I said taking one and blowing my nose. 'I'm fine. I should go, really.' I got to my feet and hooked up Luna's lead; she was now taking a keen interest in a cardboard box with books and papers inside. 'Is that for recycling?'

'Oh, that. Yes. I've overloaded it. I'll have to take them out a few at a time,' said Elizabeth. She flicked open a black bin liner and went through to kitchen.

'I can take the recycling out for you,' I called out, picking up the box, glad of the excuse to get out of the apartment. Elizabeth had been right about the box being overloaded as the bottom gave way and everything fell out onto the carpet. It was mostly books, but there were also some papers and what looked like a couple of photographs. I looked around and spotted an empty carrier bag on the table which I could use to put the recycling into and began stacking the books in there, together with a couple of pieces of paper which looked like they'd fallen out of the residents' handbook.

I picked up the first photograph, which was of a little girl who looked about ten years old. I could tell almost straight away it was Annabelle. She was sitting on a swing in what looked to be a back. It seemed sad to be throwing the photograph out and I wondered if Elizabeth had realised it was there. Maybe it had been between the pages of one of the books. I put it to one side so I could check with her. The other photograph was face down. As I went to pick it up, my phone rang in my pocket. As I fumbled to get the phone out, I simultaneously picked up the other photograph and flicked it over, before glancing at the screen of my phone. It was Jasper. I swiped at the screen with my thumb to accept the call.

'Hi,' I said.

Then I saw the image on the photograph and my body froze. All I could do was stare at the photograph. Somewhere in the background I was vaguely aware of Jasper's voice saying my name.

I drew the image closer to me. I couldn't quite believe my eyes. But there was no doubt about it.

It was of Annabelle, around the same age as in the other photograph, probably taken on the same day, judging by her hair in two braids and the pink checked dress she was wearing. But she wasn't alone. Standing next to her was Elizabeth Rooke. She looked identical to how she did now, even down to the same short, bobbed hairstyle, grey in colour even then.

Elizabeth had lied. She had been Annabelle's governess. It was the only explanation. Was that how Annabelle had really got this apartment, because she knew Elizabeth? I closed my eyes for a second as I tried to figure it all out. If Elizabeth knew Annabelle from childhood, then she would know Annabelle's real identity. Where did she fit into all this?

Then I remembered what Daniel had whispered this morning. Annabelle was just the pupil, not the teacher.

Jasper's voice penetrated my thoughts. I realised he was still on the phone. I raised the device to my ear. 'Jasper?'

'Hannah,' his voice was full of fear. 'Hannah. Where are you?'

'At Annabelle's,' I replied, only half concentrating as I continued to stare at the photograph.

'Are you alone?'

'No. Elizabeth is here. She's clearing out the apartment.'

'Fuck. You need to get out of there,' he said.

'What?'

'Listen. That note in Pia's bag. The one with the fancy letter B. You know I said I'd seen it before.'

'Yes.'

'It's on the handwritten note in the Welcome to Silverbanks residents' pack. The one that Elizabeth gave us. She must have written that note.'

It took a moment for the information to sink in. 'Are you sure?'

'Positive. Look, I'm just turning into the estate. Get out of there now. I'll drive down to you. Hurry!'

I didn't know what made me turn, call it sixth sense, but I had an overwhelming feeling of someone behind me. I turned and looked up from my crouched position on the floor. Elizabeth was towering over me, her arm raised in the air, then it was hurtling down towards me. I caught a glimpse of something in her hand, but it was all happening too fast.

'NO!' I cried out, throwing myself across the carpet, but not before there was a thud to my shoulder blade. I screamed out as a searing pain shot through me. Luna's lead slipped from my fingers and I was aware of her scurrying away.

I rolled over onto my back, just as Elizabeth delivered another blow. I put my hand up to break the force, managing to grab her by the wrist.

For an older woman, she was stronger than I expected. She was using her weight to her advantage as she pushed back.

I could see then she had a paperweight in her hand.

Somehow I managed to push her off me, buying myself a few seconds to try to scramble away on my hands and knees.

But she was determined.

She came at me again. A roar of anger erupted from her as she charged at me. I looked around and this time couldn't avoid the blow as the paperweight caught the side of my head.

The sound was sickening, and the pain was unlike anything I had ever experienced in my life.

I couldn't see properly.

I thought I was going to pass out.

Luna was whining and running around the room in a heightened state of excitement.

I covered my head with my hands, totally disorientated and blinded by the pain.

Another blow landed. This time on my hands. My knuckles crunched and again I heard myself cry out in pain.

I tried to get to my feet, desperate to escape, but the next blow landed between my shoulder blades, knocking the air from my lungs. I gasped for breath, while still trying to get to my feet.

I stumbled and managed to avoid being hit again as the paper-weight crashed down onto the glass side table, shattering it.

Amongst all of it, I thought of Luna running in that broken glass.

And then the dog was barking.

I braced myself for another blow.

THIRTY-EIGHT

Hannah

The blow never came.

I heard Elizabeth scream. And then a voice I had never been so glad to hear in all my life.

Jasper.

He was yelling at Elizabeth to stop.

I rolled over and watched as he was now pushing her down onto the carpet, one hand wrapped around both her wrists, which were pinned behind her back. The other hand throwing the paperweight out of reach.

He looked over at me. 'You OK?'

I nodded. Tears of relief rendering me unable to speak.

'Bitch!' Elizabeth shouted at me. 'You don't deserve to live. You ruined everything!'

The next thing I knew, uniformed police were charging into the apartment, swiftly followed by Owens and Barnes. The police officers quickly took control of the situation, leading Elizabeth out to a waiting patrol car.

Jasper was at my side, helping me up onto the sofa, his arm around me, as my body began to shake with the shock of it all.

The next hour was all a bit of a blur as Jasper brought the detectives up to speed and I relayed the events that had taken place in the apartment.

An ambulance arrived and, although Jasper was keen for me to go with them to hospital, I refused. I was OK. Shaken. Had a bit of a sore head, but I didn't want to go.

'So,' said Owens, blowing out a long breath. 'This is not how I expected things to turn out. We were going to talk to you again tomorrow, as it happens.'

Jasper tensed. 'Why?'

'The results from the lab came back on the bloodstains on the blouse,' said Owens. 'It was just Bryan's blood on there. And what with Jasper bringing in your blouse, we can't conclusively say the blood-soaked one was yours.'

'My blouse?' I said, looking at Jasper. 'You found it?'

'Yes,' said Jasper. 'It was muddled up with some of Pia's clothing. Not sure how it happened, but I found it when I unpacked her bag at Mum's.'

'But...' I began, confused as to when it would have been put in Pia's bag.

'Don't worry about it now,' said Jasper. He squeezed my hand and turned to Owens. 'Can I just ask, the blouse with the blood on, where did you get that from?'

'Well, here's the thing,' said Owens. 'It was Elizabeth Rooke who phoned it in. She said she was clearing out Annabelle's apartment and found it in the wardrobe. She implied that it hadn't been there before and that someone must have put it there to try to implicate Annabelle in Bryan's murder. She said she'd seen Hannah buying it in town a week ago.'

Elizabeth had found it in Annabelle's wardrobe? That didn't make sense. Surely, I would have seen it when I was sneaking around in her apartment. I was having trouble understanding everything and then I suddenly remembered the photograph. Where was it? I'd had it in my hand just before my fight with Elizabeth. I scanned the floor and spotted it near the bag of books. 'Here, look at this!' I jumped up and scooped up the photographs. 'This is Elizabeth and Annabelle.'

Jasper looked at the images. 'So, Elizabeth was Annabelle's governess or nanny?'

'Yes. Annabelle said she had to leave school and had a private teacher who lived in with them. Her old nanny. That must have been Elizabeth. She must have been the one behind all this. She was the bitter and twisted one who still held some sort of influence over Annabelle,' I said, feeling I was beginning to make some sense out of it all.

'Wait, let me get this straight,' said Owens. 'Elizabeth was Annabelle's nanny and private tutor. So, when Daniel Sully went to prison and everything around him went to pieces, his daughter ended up with nothing. Her life as she knew it was destroyed. Which meant Elizabeth lost everything too.'

'Yes. That's right,' I said. 'Elizabeth sorted out this apartment for Annabelle. When we first came to view the house, Elizabeth must have recognised me from the trial. I don't remember her being there, but let's assume she was. She must have held me responsible for everything that happened. And so she and Annabelle put together their plan.'

Owens pinched the bridge of his nose. 'So, it was a coincidence that you bought a house where Elizabeth was living?'

'Must have been,' I said. 'She probably couldn't believe her luck, and decided she was going to make me pay for all the hardship she and Annabelle had endured in the last eleven years.'

'Christ, what a mess,' sighed Owens. 'Go home. Get some rest and we'll be in touch in the morning to take some formal statements.'

'We still need to interview Elizabeth and corroborate everything we've just spoken about,' huffed Barnes. 'No one is officially off the hook yet.'

'We understand,' said Jasper, helping me to my feet.

I couldn't help thinking that Barnes was rather disappointed I wasn't the one being arrested that afternoon, but she gave a begrudging nod of her head as we left.

'I really think you should go to hospital and get checked out,' said Jasper as he drove us back up the avenue to our house.

'I don't want to. All I want is to be at home,' I said.

We went inside and Jasper made us both a strong cup of tea each. I sipped my drink in silence, wishing it didn't have to be like this between us. I so wanted Jasper to stay. Finally, I couldn't stay silent any longer.

'Thank you for coming to my rescue,' I said. 'I don't know what would have happened if you hadn't showed up when you did.'

'Seems like I got the timing right,' he said. 'Not for the first time.'

I ran my finger around the rim of my cup. 'You've always been there for me. You're my hero, you know that?' He didn't say anything. 'I'm so sorry for everything I've put you through,' I continued. 'Whatever happens between us, I'll always be grateful for having you in my life, in whatever capacity that may be. I know things can't go back to how they were—'

He cut me off. 'Let me speak,' he said. 'My head is telling me this is ground zero for our relationship. It's telling me there is nothing to salvage, even our foundations have been obliterated. I should walk away and start afresh again.'

'I'm so sorry,' I whispered as my tears gathered momentum and slipped freely from my eyes.

'But I won't be listening to my head, because, no matter what you've done, we'll always have a connection – Pia. I could never stop you from seeing your daughter or deprive our daughter of her mother's love. A love like no other. I know how much you love her. I really do, and now I understand the power behind that love. It's exceptional. It's like no other.'

A sob escaped. One of relief. At least he was gracious enough not to want to take my daughter away from me. I truly wouldn't be able to cope with losing another child. 'Thank you,' I managed through hitching breath. I was sure I was going to hyperventilate sooner or later.

'You want to know how I know that about you and your love for Pia?' he asked. I nodded but couldn't look at him. I felt his hand take mine. 'Because it's the same love I feel for you.'

This time I did look up. 'What?' Was he playing games? Was he throwing me a lifeline just so he could snatch it away in his next breath?

'I've always known you had a secret,' he said. 'I've always hoped that one day you could tell me. I must admit, this was not what I thought it would be. And you know what they say about being careful what you wish for... well, I guess I'm living proof of those words of wisdom.'

'I've wanted to tell you so many times,' I confessed, swiping at the tears running down my face. 'But I've been too scared. So very scared.'

'You should have trusted me.'

'I know. I wish I had, but... I've been so stupid.'

He took a step closer. 'Not stupid. You've been scared. I still wish you could have trusted me more, but I get it. At least I think I do. I'm going to need to get my head around all this, but I love you more than life itself and, without you, it wouldn't be worth living, except for Pia. I love you like no other and I can't leave you now. I don't want to leave you. We just need to try to work through this.'

I couldn't believe what I was hearing. After everything, my wonderful man, the most loving and forgiving human on this planet, still wanted me. Still wanted us. Still wanted his family. I did not deserve this chance but, God, I wasn't going to pass it up. 'Really? You're not going to leave me?' My voice was so tiny, I wasn't even sure I'd said it out loud.

Jasper shook his head. 'I'm never leaving you, Hannah. We can work through this. Together as a family.'

He pulled me into him, wrapping those oh-so safe arms around me. I held him tight. I could not believe how lucky I was. 'I promise you, you won't regret this,' I said, my words muffled in his chest.

'There is one thing, though,' he said, pulling back a little to look down at me.

'What's that?'

'We need to find your son,' he said. 'Declan, right?'

I couldn't speak. Huge blobs of tears streamed down my face. I managed some sort of garbled yes.

'I don't know how it's going to work,' said Jasper. 'But our daughter has a brother out there. You have a son. I have potentially a stepson. He needs to know us.'

My legs went from under me and, as ever, since that day I'd met him, Jasper, caught me. My lifeline. My saviour. My true love.

'We do need to get some rest now,' said Jasper.

'I'm shattered. I must admit.'

'I'll go and run you a bath.' He kissed the top of my head and disappeared upstairs.

I made myself a fresh cup of tea while I waited for Jasper to run my bath. The relief and happiness I felt was immense. I couldn't believe how lucky I was that Jasper had come back to me.

I stirred the teabag around, then scooped it out of the cup and with my foot pressed the pedal bin lever. As I dropped the teabag in, something caught my eye.

It was a pink paper bag with the word Dizzy's in bold white letters.

I stared at it for a moment. What was that doing in there? It couldn't be the bag I'd brought my blouse home in. I would have put that in the recycling straight away. In fact, I remembered doing so.

I reached in the bin, took the bag out and looked inside. It was empty apart from a piece of paper in the bottom. A receipt.

1 x white bow blouse.
Size 12
£39.99

But that wasn't what stopped me in my tracks. It was the date. Not just any date. Not the date I'd bought the blouse when I was with Jasper after we'd had coffee. No. It was today's date.

'I knew I should have thrown that away.'

I spun around to see Jasper standing there. I was too stunned to say anything. He walked over to me and took the bag and receipt from my hands.

'What did you do?' I asked, my voice shaking.

He didn't answer but went through to the living room. I followed and watched him screw the bag and receipt into a ball, drop them into the fireplace and then set light to them.

I watched as the flames quickly licked their way around the edges of the paper, before engulfing it completely until all that was left was black and grey ashes.

EPILOGUE

Hannah

'Could all passengers please fasten their seat belts as we prepare to land,' came the cabin crew member announcement.

The overhead seat belt sign lit up and I reached over to Pia, on my left, to make sure her buckle was fastened. 'Hey, sleepy head,' I said gently. 'We're going to be landing in Australia soon.'

She murmured an acknowledgement but pulled her teddy closer to her and snuggled back under the blanket.

'She's OK until we touch down,' said Jasper. He was sitting the other side of me and reached out and took my hand. 'It will be OK. I promise you.'

I appreciated the gesture and words of comfort.

'I'm really nervous,' I said.

'You've got nothing to be nervous about. Declan is looking forward to seeing you.'

I nodded.

It was six months since Annabelle had died. In that time the police had conducted a full enquiry into her death and absolved me of all blame. They had believed I had been acting in self-defence and no charges were brought against me.

Elizabeth Rooke had been charged with attempted murder, which her solicitor had successfully reduced to aggravated assault. She had agreed to cooperate with the police for a lighter charge and thus the whole sorry story had come out.

She had been devastated when Daniel had gone to prison and had blamed me for everything that happened to her and Annabelle after that. In her twisted and warped mind, she was exacting justice on me. She had loved Annabelle as if she were her own child, so to lose her job had meant she'd lost daily access to Annabelle. And she could never forgive me for that.

In a strange way, I kind of understood how she must have felt. For a woman who unconditionally loved a child, to then have that child taken away was a pain almost too much to bear.

And while that part of my life was behind me, the part that came next scared me the most – getting in touch with Matt and ultimately my son, Declan.

Jasper had dealt with the initial contact, smoothed the path for me so when I did speak to Matt it was far easier than I ever could have imagined. Matt took some convincing about me having any kind of contact with Declan. And I understood that. It was never going to be easy to tell our son that his mother wanted to be part of his life now when the narrative had always been I had walked away from him and Matt. So typical of Matt to blame me, but I had let it slide.

Over the following weeks, contact between Declan and me began. Initially with email, then text messaging and finally FaceTiming. He had taken a while to adjust to it. He was now a teenager, not the toddler I remembered. My beautiful boy was so grown up. I could see him, talk to him in real time. His voice had broken, and he had an Aussie accent, of course. He looked and sounded so much like Matt. Our FaceTimes became a regular thing. There was some of the awkwardness that comes with being a teenager and I tried not to fire too many questions at him. I had so much catching up to do, but I knew I couldn't rush it.

I'd been given this chance to see my son again and I didn't want to mess it up.

Matt had gone on to have two more children – a boy and a girl who were a few years younger than Declan. I was happy for Matt. He deserved happiness and he'd found it. It was something I hadn't been able to give him in the end.

The drive out from the airport to the suburb in Perth where Matt lived took just under an hour. Jasper pulled onto the driveway and the front door opened, to reveal Matt and his wife, Demi, waving at us excitedly.

I was so nervous. I was finally going to see my son. I was going to be able to hold him. Something I had longed to do for longer than a mother should ever have to yearn for.

'You go ahead,' said Jasper, as Demi came across to sort out our bags while Matt waved me over. Jasper kissed me. 'We're right behind you. You've got this.'

I followed Matt into the house, my legs somehow carrying me forward. My stomach was doing somersaults, I was sure I was on the verge of throwing up.

And then I was in the family room, the cool breeze of the air conditioning tickling the back of my neck, the sun pouring in through the window. And there was my son. Taller than I'd imagined. He must be a good two inches taller than me. I took in his dark hair, his sun-kissed skin and his eyes the colour of golden honey. His straight nose and strong jawline. He was so much like his father. It was completely different, seeing him in person rather than on the small screen of my mobile. I wanted to rush to him and gather him in my arms, but I forced myself to take it slow.

'Hello, Declan,' I said gently.

'Hi.'

I took an uncertain step forward and then stopped. I had to wait for him. I smiled. 'I'm so glad to be here,' I said, my voice cracking at the end. I blinked hard to keep the tears at bay.

He nodded and I could see he was battling with his emotions too.

We looked at each other for what seemed like the longest moment ever.

I don't know who moved first, but the next thing we were hugging each other tightly. We clung to each other, and those years of separation just disappeared. I closed my eyes and the last memory I had of holding Declan, I replaced with the one I had now. My darling son was in my arms once more.

Eventually, we pulled away. 'Hello, Mum,' he said.

A LETTER FROM THE AUTHOR

Huge thanks for reading *Your Little Lies*, I hope you were hooked on Laurel/Hannah's story. If you want to join other readers in hearing all about my new releases and bonus content, you can sign up for my newsletter!

www.stormpublishing.co/sue-fortin

If you enjoyed this book and could spare a few moments to leave a review that would be hugely appreciated. Even a short review can make all the difference in encouraging a reader to discover my books for the first time. Thank you so much!

The little seed that inspired me to write this book was the question, 'Why would someone leave their child?' As a parent myself, it was hard to come up with a plausible reason and I guess the only answer I could think of was if it was to protect them. So I had to give Laurel/Hannah, a valid reason – a dilemma. I love delving into those types of questions and scenarios and it was immense fun to write. I hope you've enjoyed reading it as much as I enjoyed writing it.

Thanks again for being part of this amazing journey with me and I hope you'll stay in touch – I have so many more stories and ideas to entertain you with!

Sue x

KEEP IN TOUCH WITH THE AUTHOR

www.suefortin.com

facebook.com/suefortinauthor

x.com/suefortin1

instagram.com/sue_fortin_author

tiktok.com/@suefortin_author

ACKNOWLEDGMENTS

A massive thank you to my editor, Emily and her amazing feedback which I'd be lost without.

As ever, many thanks to my agent, Hattie Grunewald, who I'd be equally lost without.

Made in United States
North Haven, CT
04 April 2025